## KAYE WANTED ONLY
## THE SWEETNESS OF SURRENDER

Creighton kissed her with an almost frenzied
passion. The intensity, the eagerness of his
embrace swept her along until she herself knew a
passion that was wild and alien and sweet with
pleasure. It went on until there was no time, no
place, no existence outside the engulfing wave
that caught them both at the same endless
moment.

Creighton had said that he was leaving Montego
Bay for good. but Kaye knew now that
everything had changed. Their being apart had
no reality, no possibility.

So she was stunned when, instead of saying the
words she longed to hear, Creighton uttered the
unbelievable.

"It's too late. Go home, Kaye. Let's say goodbye
to each other now. This is nothing but torture
for us both...."

AND NOW...

# SUPERROMANCES

Worldwide Library is proud to present a
sensational new series of modern love stories—
SUPERROMANCES

Written by masters of the genre, these longer,
sensuous and dramatic novels are truly in keeping
with today's changing life-styles. Full of intriguing
conflicts, the heartaches and delights of true love,
SUPERROMANCES are absorbing stories—
satisfying and sophisticated reading that lovers
of romance fiction have long been waiting for.

# SUPERROMANCES
Contemporary love stories for the woman of today!

SERENA ROBBINS

# ISLE OF RAPTURE

A SUPERROMANCE FROM
WORLDWIDE

TORONTO · NEW YORK · LOS ANGELES · LONDON

Published October 1982

First printing August 1982

ISBN 0-373-70035-0

Printed in Canada

# CHAPTER ONE

AS THE PLANE ROSE over New York City, Kaye Belliston sat in the first-class lounge and looked down with a curious mixture of glumness and excitement. She was on an Air Jamaica jet on her way to Montego Bay, and she was eager to get there. But her reasons for leaving her duplex apartment on Park Avenue were not pleasant ones, and—for the moment, at least—her glumness was stronger than her eagerness.

It was she who had suggested the divorce. She had suggested it because, no matter how badly their marriage had deteriorated, Rod Cunningham would never have suggested it. That was essentially why she had divorced him. When she had met him during her senior year at Radcliffe, something had happened to her that she had perceived to be love. He was handsome—oh, there was no denying that—and he had seemed strong and virile. He was a senior at Princeton and on the rowing team and the swimming team and the wrestling team. His scholastic record was hardly dazzling, but it was respectable. He was the son of Courtney Cunningham, the senior partner in the brokerage firm of Cunningham, Hardy & Chase, and it was correctly presumed he would enter the family business. She had told herself at the time that none of these social aspects mattered. She had fallen in love with Rod, and none of the rest of it—his wealth, his family, his assured future—none of it was of any consequence. Now she realized it had had everything to do with it. She was the heiress to a substantial old family fortune, and she had been brought up in an atmosphere encrusted with obligation and tradition. It was expected of her that she marry a man exactly like Rod—rich, reputable and presentable. She was happy she had fallen in love with a man who was incidentally acceptable to her family. Now she wondered if she hadn't thought she was in love with him *because* he was acceptable to her family. From early childhood she had been her own person and had often willfully ignored the obligations and the traditions. She hadn't wanted to disappoint them again in this most important aspect of her life. She'd been glad she hadn't fallen in love with a bum or a wastrel. Instead she had married a well-placed weakling—and strength was the quality she most admired. She herself had it to spare. Nobody—family, friends, not even Rod himself— would have denied she had tried. She had bent over backward to make it work. In so doing, though, she had found herself making all the decisions: whether to have children, which apartment to buy, where to spend the summer, whom to entertain, what play to see. Rod had cheerfully left everything to her.

She had been battling her strength all her life, yet when she left things to others, they always seemed to turn out wrong. Finally all she had wanted was to be married to a man who would relieve her of those responsibilities, or at least share them with her. . . a man who would be dominant. She had thought Rod was that man.

Now, at twenty-six, the press referred to her as "the divorced heiress, Kaye Belliston Cunningham." She hated the appellation so much that she had dropped her married name two weeks earlier, when the divorce had become final. She was glad it was over, and she was sure that Rod was, too. Yet there was a sadness about it.

Two people cannot live together fairly genially for two years and not feel a sense of loss at parting. And, of course, there was the guilt—or at least the possibility of it. Was it her fault? Had she been intolerant? Again and again she told herself it simply hadn't worked. It was nobody's fault. Even Rod had said that. The questions remained, however. The only thing she was certain of was that she would not become involved with a man again until she was sure—not of him, but of herself. She knew it might take years, but she was determined not to repeat the terrible mistake she had made two years ago.

She could not face the New York winter season of charity balls and dinner parties and committee luncheons. She had told her mother this in her Southampton house the weekend she had returned from Reno. Her mother had suggested Europe, but Kaye had too many friends there, and that was exactly what she wanted to avoid. At last her mother had come up with the perfect solution: she should go to Montego Bay and stay with her Aunt Alice. The house was enormous; Aunt Alice liked having guests; she was dotingly fond of Kaye, and Kaye had never been there, so there would be no one she knew.

Kaye had gone straight to the telephone and called Aunt Alice, and it was settled. Now here she was, wondering if she'd done the right thing. The flight attendants in Jamaican costumes came by offering exotic rum drinks and Jamaican food. Her expectations began to overpower her apprehension.

The flight seemed shorter than the three and a half hours it actually took. When she looked down on the lushness of the island, she remembered the aerial view of New York's steel and glass and concrete, and she was glad she had come.

Aunt Alice's chauffeur met her at the airport in a

black-and-tan Rolls-Royce. The airport itself was an ugly temporary-looking place, but after they had driven for no more than ten minutes, Kaye felt as though they were traveling through a jungle. There was a paved road, and immediately on either side the forest began, so close to the road that the leaves of trees sometimes brushed against the car. There were cedar and mahoe and rosewood trees and trees Kaye had never seen previously, in such density that she rarely could see more than twenty feet into the growth. As they started up the steep winding road that climbed the hill, the bright faces of flowers peeked out from the verdancy of the forest: aloe, yucca, datura, mountain pride, wild orchids. They were no more than fleeting sparks of brilliant yellow and fuchsia, purple and red, orange and magenta. Here and there there was the pale yellow of huge stands of bamboo. It was breathtakingly beautiful. Suddenly, without warning, the car was on the semicircular gravel driveway that arced before Aunt Alice's white pillared house, which she had named for her husband's family estate in Surrey. The house seemed to have sprung up out of the jungle, and there, dwarfed by the two-story-high pillars, was Aunt Alice, tiny, stately and beautiful all at once.

As Henry, the chauffeur, opened the car door, Aunt Alice hurried down the few stairs from the veranda to meet her niece.

"Kaye!" she cried. "You're actually here! My dearest girl, how are you?"

"Oh, Aunt Alice, it's so good to see you. I'm well. And you must be, too, or you wouldn't look so beautiful."

Aunt Alice took her by the arm and said, "Come on in. Tea is ready."

Their arms still linked, Aunt Alice led Kaye through

the forty-foot-long drawing room to a small sitting room, where a tea tray with exquisite china and a plate of cucumber sandwiches awaited them. They sat opposite each other in antique English wing chairs.

As Aunt Alice poured, she said, "Was the trip all right, my dear?"

"It couldn't have been more comfortable," Kaye replied. "In fact, it was more than that. It was exciting, and I was so looking forward to seeing you and to being here."

"And to getting away from what you were leaving behind." She handed Kaye a cup of tea. "I'm so dreadfully sorry, my dear. I mean about you and Rod. I'm sure you've done the right thing, but there's always something sad about it."

"Yes, there is. But how do you know? It's never happened to you."

"Ah, don't presume. There are many things about my life you don't know. You're right, though. Nothing like that ever happened between Alex and me. We were in love the first moment we saw each other at a ball in London, and we were, if anything, more in love when he died thirty-five years later. Sir Alex—I always used his title when he became pompous—was the dearest man I've ever known. And now all I have is his money and his title. I'd give them both up and live in a garret with him if I could have him back. But death doesn't allow us such prerogatives.... Enough of that. Tell me about you. Are you all right?"

"Yes, I suppose so. There is a residue of sadness. It's kind of like an emotional hangover. But I'm sure it will pass."

"Hangovers are traditionally cured by a hair of the dog."

"Not for me. The last thing I want is another marriage. I don't even want an affair. As a matter of fact, I don't even want a flirtation." It was something she could never have said to her mother, but she had always been able to be free and honest with Aunt Alice. Beneath the almost Victorian facade of her personality was a bohemian quality. It was carefully controlled, but it was there, nonetheless.

"Oh? To the nunnery, is it?"

"For a while, at least."

"That could be a great mistake. You don't want to shut out what life offers you. Not ever. You must take what's there, *when* it's there. Regret is a paralyzing emotion, one I'm happy to note I've rarely felt. I remember Alex saying, 'The only things I regret are the things I *haven't* done.' He was wise."

"Is it unwise not to want to repeat an unfortunate experience?"

"Of course not. But it is foolish indeed to shun marriage as an institution because you've had one bad one."

"I just want to give it some time, auntie."

She paused and looked away for a moment. When she turned back to Aunt Alice, tears had begun to well in her eyes. "I want you more than anyone else to understand how I feel. May I tell you now, from the very beginning? I think it would make me feel much better."

"You must. I'd be hurt if you didn't confide in me."

"Then I will," Kaye said. "I haven't told this to anyone else. Not Rod, not mother, not anyone. Maybe it was pride that kept me from saying it—I don't know. But when I met Rod and accepted his proposal, I thought I had settled the rest of my life. I believed with all my heart that my dreams had come true, that Rod and I would love each other forever, that we'd have what everyone wants from life: a lasting marriage, a home, children—all of it for once and for all. It never occurred to me we could have made a mistake. It never occurred to me it could be anything but uninterrupted bliss. I didn't realize it could shatter like a fragile ornament dropped from a Christmas tree. Then suddenly it did just that. My whole life shattered. But you see, I believe it was more my fault than Rod's. I think he would have been willing to settle for what we had— which turned out to be more an agreement than a real marriage. I couldn't be satisfied with just that. I wanted lifelong love. I still want that, and I won't settle for less. But I've got to know myself completely before I try again. I'm not going to rush into a commitment again like a dewy-eyed schoolgirl. I will not let myself just fall in love without regard for the consequences. I won't let myself be hurt again. The recent past has been too painful, and I'm not going to repeat it. Not for anything."

"I'm all for that," Aunt Alice agreed. "And that's why you're here—to make a new start. I know you'll be chagrined to learn I'm giving you a dinner tonight, but I would never be forgiven for not presenting you immediately. Here in Montego—incidentally, to add 'Bay' is considered almost gauche, rather like referring to San Francisco as 'Frisco'—we live by a set of rules. They're elaborate and convoluted and sometimes even perverse, but they're ironclad. Whether you're here for a fortnight or an extended visit or forever, you cannot exist, are not welcome, if you don't live by the code. It has a nature, a rhythm of its own, just as Montego, just as the entire island, has. But you'll have no trouble. It's ultimately civilized. Occasionally I enjoy watching other people, young people mostly, try to run against it, but I'm comfortable with it. It suits me.... How is your mother?"

"She's perfectly fine. She sends her love."

"Dear Agatha. She was always such a mouse—a special one, but a mouse nonetheless. She's three years older than I, you know, but it was always I who protected her against any harm. I love her dearly."

"And she loves you."

"I know. I wish I saw her more often, but she won't come here, and I go to New York only on state occasions, so to speak. Now about dinner. We—the women, that is—wear dinner dresses, while for some reason I have never understood, the men are allowed to wear sport shirts and slacks. Oh, well. There will be about twenty people. I assure you I cut the guest list to the bone, but I couldn't get it down to fewer than twenty. It may all sound terribly pretentious to you, but that's the way we live, and no power on earth is likely to change it. They'll all be new faces to you, and that's just what you need: change."

"Oh, Aunt Alice, I do love you."

"And I'm very fond of you. When you live alone for a time, it becomes difficult to express affection. But I have always loved you dearly. I'm going to see to it that you have a marvelous stay. I hope it will be a very long one."

"I may never leave. It's all so beautiful, and you're so wonderful."

"Ah, good. There's one other thing for which I must prepare you—or for which you must prepare. Both I suppose. In your travels you must have heard of Lady Gladys Smith-Croydon."

"Indeed, I have."

"She is my dearest friend. We've known each other for nearly forty years. She is, among other things, the social arbiter of Montego. She arbitrates in consultation with me, but she doesn't like that to be generally known. I allow her her little conceits. Occasionally she does mad things. Next month she's giving a fancy-dress ball. It hasn't been done in Montego for decades, but Smitty, as everyone calls her, will not be dissuaded. Lord knows, I've tried. It's so tiresome. If you're here, and you certainly will be, you'll be absolutely required to attend. The theme of the ball is Shakespeare, God help us. It flies in the teeth of all the comfortable informality we've tried to establish in our society, but it's Smitty, after all. I'm going as Juliet's nurse, and you would make a lovely Juliet. We can design a beautiful diaphanous gown for you, and I have a smashing dressmaker from the town who'll come up and do the measurements and fittings.''

"It sounds like fun."

"Then it's settled." She got up and went to a bellpull. "I'll have Helen show you to your room. It's on the south side of the house, overlooking the garden. It's lovely and cool. You have time for a rest. Cocktails are at seven."

Helen, a short plump Jamaican woman of about forty-five, appeared in the sitting room. She smiled warmly but reservedly at her mistress and said, "Yes, Lady Armstrong?"

For the first time Kaye heard the lovely lilting Jamaican English at close range. She was soon to realize she was hearing only a diluted version of it, for Helen, in her years of service to Lady Alice, had modified her speech to make it a bit closer to British English. Heavily accented Jamaican speech spoken rapidly could be unintelligible to the unaccustomed ear.

"Helen, this is my niece, Mrs. Cunningham. She'll—"

"Aunt Alice, I may as well tell you straight out. I've dropped the Cunningham. I'm once again Kaye Belliston."

"Well," Aunt Alice said, "it *was* a difficult parting.

This is my niece, Miss Belliston. She'll be staying with us indefinitely. You must take very good care of her."

Helen smiled again and bowed her head at Kaye.

"I'm very pleased to meet you, Helen," Kaye said.

"Now do have a rest, darling," Aunt Alice counseled. "You must be tired after your trip."

"I will. I really am so happy to be here."

Helen opened the door of the sitting room and stood aside for Kaye to leave. She led her up the stairs from the entrance hall and along a gallery. She opened one of the doors along the passageway, and Kaye went inside. Helen followed.

Helen smiled again and said, "The bellcord, if you need something. I send Rosenda to help you unpack." Helen smiled a great deal.

"That won't be necessary, Helen. I'd really prefer to do it myself. Thank you."

Helen left and closed the door behind her.

The room was spacious and beautifully furnished with good English furniture. At the far end was a set of three French doors that led to a narrow balcony. Kaye went to the center doors and walked outside. The garden below was breathtaking. It was nothing like the English garden she would have imagined Aunt Alice to have. There was a certain vague order to it, but it was not the flower beds and borders and pathways of an English garden. It was a brazen profusion of flowering plants of startlingly brilliant colors. Many of them were the same plants that had peeked out at her from the recesses of the forest, but here they were plainly visible, and their bright beauty was extraordinary. The garden as a whole looked like a miniature cultivated jungle, and it filled the air with a mingled scent that seemed to her like jasmine. She stood for a moment, breathing in the luscious air, then turned and went back inside.

The room was even larger than she had perceived it to be at first glance. The bed and bath were at the end of the room nearest the windows, and beyond them was an area large enough to accommodate two chintz-covered settees and two armchairs. She knew she was going to be comfortable here.

She hadn't much luggage. She had expected—and she was right—that Jamaica would have its own fashion mode and that the kind of clothes she would need would be available in the local shops. She unpacked and decided to take a bath. She could rest and bathe at the same time. She undressed and started toward the bathroom.

On the far side of the bed, just beside the door, was a full-length mirror in a standing brass frame. She caught a glimpse of her naked self as she passed it. She stopped and took a step backward. She stood before the mirror and noted, without surprise, without conceit and without much interest, that she was very beautiful. She had always been beautiful. She had been a beautiful baby, a beautiful child and a beautiful adolescent, without any of the usual awkwardness. And now she was a beautiful woman. Her chestnut-colored hair hung several inches below her shoulders. Her skin was the color of ivory. Her entire body was in perfect proportion. Her breasts were firm and round, the nipples tilted slightly upward. Her waist was tiny, blossoming into hips that were properly broad. Her belly was no more than a gently rising mound. Her legs were long and beautifully shaped. She sighed and looked up again into the mirror at her jade-green eyes. There was an expression she had rarely seen previously, an expression of disinterest, of boredom, and she knew it was essentially boredom with herself. What good was beauty, after all? It could get a girl marriage, but it surely couldn't sustain it. And she was thinking of Rod again and of their failed union. She looked hard into her own eyes in the mirror and said to herself, *it's over, and it's good that it's over. All these feelings will pass. Just give yourself time.* She pulled herself away from the mirror.

She drew a tepid bath and lay in it for a long time. Her mind sank into a hazy half sleep, and she managed not to think about anything but the physical sensations the water created.

By six-forty-five she was dressed in a white silk blouse and a floral-print evening skirt. She did a last-minute check before the mirror. *Damn it,* she said to herself, *you are a good-looking woman. Go downstairs and see if you can't dazzle everybody. It would be good for your faltering ego.* She pulled back her shoulders, lifted her patrician head and left the room.

Aunt Alice was sitting in the drawing room in an armchair, with a martini on the table beside her. Her tiny figure was dwarfed by the huge room, but her presence was undeniable.

"Ah, there you are," she said. "I've been waiting for you. You look ravishing. I feel sorry for the few local eligible males."

"Why 'sorry'?"

"Because I sense that your frame of mind will make it a waste of time when they throw themselves at your feet."

"I'm afraid you're right—although I can't imagine anybody's throwing himself at my feet."

"Oh, yes, you can. You can't not know how desirable you are. Well, no matter. You're so enviably young. Now. I'm an inveterate martini drinker. I never have more than two, but I try to make it seem wicked. As Madame Arcati said in Noël's *Blithe Spirit* when asked if she wanted a cocktail, 'If it's a dry martini, yes. If it's a concoction, no.' Noël had a house here for years, you know. Not in Montego. At Round Hill. I knew him well and adored him. We all did. Ah, the memories. In any event, I do serve concoctions for anyone who wants them. Most of the men drink whiskey. It's become fashionable for the women to drink white wine before dinner. The bar is well stocked. Within reason, you may have anything you like.''

"I think I'd like to have a martini with you."

"Wonderful! Henry, would you make Miss Belliston one of your legendary martinis?"

Kaye hadn't noticed that Henry, the chauffeur-turned-butler, was standing at the far end of the room in attendance.

"Yes, Lady Armstrong," he said, and even in the three words Kaye could hear the mellifluous cadence of island speech.

When Henry had brought the drink to Kaye, Aunt Alice said, "Let's have our drinks out on the veranda. It's a lovely time of day to be out of doors."

The veranda, with its white wicker furniture was arranged in small seating groups, ran the entire length of the house. It overlooked a garden similar to the one beneath Kaye's window and was just as beautiful.

When they had sat down, Kaye said, "I've just realized what's been puzzling me about Montego—I almost said 'Bay.' I suppose it's true of all Jamaica. The quality of the light is different from that of anywhere else I've ever been. I don't know how to describe the difference; it's just different."

"I've been here so long I've forgotten what the quality of light is like anywhere else. But you're entirely right, of course. Everything about Montego is—"

Without warning, a man came through the doors from the drawing room to the veranda. He was very young and very good-looking.

"Lady Alice," he said.

"Ellis. You, five minutes early? How unlike you! Ah, I understand. Kaye, may I present Ellis Craig. Ellis, my niece, Kaye Belliston."

Ellis smiled a genuinely enthusiastic smile and took a few steps to Kaye's chair. He reached for her hand, and for a moment she thought he was going to kiss it. He didn't, but he held it longer than he should have.

"I'm delighted to meet you," he said.

"And I'm very pleased to meet you," Kaye replied.

As Ellis sat down, a young Jamaican man in a white jacket and black trousers appeared and asked Ellis what he wanted to drink. He started to answer, then hesitated, looking at Kaye's drink.

"I'll have a dry martini," he said. His speech was unmistakably British.

"Where are Netty and Harlan?" Aunt Alice asked.

"They'll be along. I was so eager to meet Miss Belliston I took the jeep and came ahead by myself." He smiled at Kaye.

She smiled back and said, "Please call me Kaye."

"Thank you, I will. How long will you be in Montego?"

"I don't really know."

"It would please me if it were forever," Aunt Alice declared.

"It wouldn't please me," Ellis replied. "I've got to get back to London *sometime*."

"I'm afraid you've become addicted to Montego, Ellis." Aunt Alice turned to Kaye. "Ellis came to Montego a year ago on holiday to visit Netty and Harlan Marlowe. Netty and he are. . .cousins, is it?"

"Yes."

"And he's been here ever since. Ah, I hear Sylvia Zimmerman's voice."

A middle-aged couple came out onto the veranda. She had a good figure and carefully colored blond hair. She wore a royal-blue organza evening dress, a diamond choker and two diamond bracelets. Her husband, Herman, looked older than she, though he was not, and had a band of white hair around his bald pate.

"Hello, Alice," Sylvia said as she went to Aunt Alice and kissed her cheek.

"Hello, Ellis," Herman replied. "Hello, Alice. How are you?"

"I'm well, Herman. I want you both to meet my niece, Kaye Belliston. Kaye, Sylvia and Herman Zimmerman."

Sylvia crossed to Kaye's chair and extended her hand.

"Do I love it when a fellow New Yorker comes here!" she said. "I love to hear somebody else speak English again. Later, when it won't bore the locals, we've got to sit down so you can tell me all the New York news."

"I'd love to," Kaye answered.

"Hello, Kaye," Herman said. "Welcome to the Bay."

Remembering what her aunt had told her about "Montego," she looked puzzled and said, "Thank you."

Aunt Alice chuckled. "Pay no attention to Herman, darling. He's one of those 'younger people' I told you about who enjoy flying in the face of custom. Since everyone else insists on calling it 'Montego,' refusing to add the 'Bay,' Herman insists on calling it 'the Bay.' He's very perverse."

Within the next twenty minutes several other dinner guests arrived. As the assembled company grew, arrivals became less prominent. They were all eventually introduced to the guest of honor. Kaye was engaged in conversation with Netty and Harlan when she was suddenly startled by a glance from a man who had just appeared.

She stumbled in what she was saying to Netty, and for a moment she wasn't able to remember what it was. She managed to go on, though, glancing back at the newcomer. His progress across the veranda toward Aunt Alice was hampered as every guest stopped him, not just to greet him but to chat with him. At last he reached Aunt Alice's chair. Kaye had been aware that each time he moved closer, he seemed more handsome. Now that he was only five feet from her, she realized he was the most attractive man she had ever seen. He was well over six feet tall, and from his conspicuously broad shoulders his body tapered to a lean trim waist. He was wearing a white linen shirt that, unlike the other men's, was tucked into the beltline of his dark slacks. The contours of his firmly muscled chest were clearly visible, but it was his face, Kaye thought, that was one of God's masterpieces. His hair was a dark lustrous brown. Beneath his broad straight forehead his eyes were large and wide set and a deep amber color. His nose was slightly hawklike, and the structure of his jaw made it look as if it had been chiseled out of granite. His lips were full and formed an almost square mouth. It was very hard to tell, but Kaye guessed he was in his late thirties. His greetings to everyone had been pleasant and controlled. There was no effusiveness about him; instead there was an impenetrable reserve. He had not yet seemed to look at Kaye, but somehow she was sure he had seen her, was aware of her.

Over the murmur of the guests' genial conversation Kaye heard the man say, "Alice, you look beautiful, as always."

Kaye noticed his speech was British but very slightly different from that of the other English people.

"Thank you, Creighton," Alice answered. "And you're tanned and healthy. . . and charming, as always.

Kaye, I want you to meet Creighton Jarvis. He's a neighbor and a very dear friend.''

Creighton turned to her and fixed her with a stare that Kaye felt was holding her like a vise. There was just a breath of a pause before he spoke. "Miss Belliston. I'm very happy to meet you.''

His greeting seemed as controlled as the others he'd offered, yet there was something in his eyes as direct and piercing as a laser, some spark that lit them briefly. The same warmth was not present in his faint smile or in the slight nod of his head, but his eyes would not release her. She felt called, invited by them. They caused a tinge of excitement at the center of her she couldn't remember ever having felt previously. She was so hypnotized by them she forgot the rest of his compellingly handsome face, the trim geometry of his body, so hypnotized she was unaware that she and Creighton Jarvis were locked in a gaze as intimate as an embrace. It was as if no one else were there, as if they were alone together.

She realized he had extended his hand to her. She was afraid to take it but found her hand drawn to his, as if by a magnet. His hand closed around hers, dwarfing it. His touch was at once astonishingly firm and gentle. His flesh was warm and resilient. She thought he could have crushed her hand as the paw of an animal might crush a bird, yet the pressure he exerted was only enough to make her know that he held her.

Kaye wasn't even aware she hadn't spoken until Creighton said, "I suppose it's a bit early to ask how you like our island.'' He seemed to have said it to reassure her.

"No,'' she replied, surprised at the sound of her own voice. "Not at all. I think it's absolutely beautiful.''

He released her hand, and she felt as if she'd been abandoned.

"Good. You may even learn to love it. And we already have something in common."

*We already have something in common,* Kaye told herself. She didn't know what it was. She knew only that it frightened her.

She regained her composure and said, "I'm sure it's just a matter of time."

There was a flurry across the veranda, and for a few seconds, as the others turned to look, Creighton continued to hold her with his eyes. Then he turned away.

A woman had swept onto the veranda with five people who followed her like a flock. She was certainly a contemporary of Aunt Alice, though of an indeterminate age. She had white marcelled hair and the face of a griffin. Although she was short—dumpy, actually—she was imperious both in manner and appearance. She was wearing the floor-length equivalent of an English garden dress, and around her neck on a jeweled chain hung a monocle in a tortoiseshell frame.

"Alice!" she cried, and her voice knifed through the crowd.

The voice, then her physical self, parted the crowd like the Red Sea. She made her way directly to Aunt Alice, with the five others following, as if they were somehow attached to her.

"Ah, my dear Gladys," Aunt Alice said. She stood up for the first time since she and Kaye had come out onto the veranda.

"Well, where is she? I didn't come here just to eat and drink."

Lady Alice smiled and said, "Just there, Smitty." The woman turned abruptly and stared at Kaye up and down, as though she were appraising her.

"Kaye, this is Lady Gladys Smith-Croydon," Alice said. "You mustn't be afraid of her, although she'll try to make you be. Gladys, this is Kaye Belliston, my niece.''

''Well, you're certainly a very presentable young woman,'' Lady Smith-Croydon said, placing the monocle to her right eye and peering at Kaye. ''Striking as a matter of fact. I think I'm going to like you very much. Introduce yourself to my friends while I conjure up a drink from Alice's lazy staff. Creighton, my love, I'm glad to see you here.''

''Hello, Smitty,'' Creighton replied. ''I thought you were leaving for Cannes.''

''I was. I stayed on to meet Alice's niece. Worth it, too, now that I've seen her. I think I'll give up the season in France and stay here to make sure she's taken care of. Alice, where *is* my drink?''

''Henry is standing just behind you with your brandy and soda,'' Lady Alice said.

Smitty turned and cried, ''Henry! Good to see you! Thank you.''

Among Lady Smith-Croydon's guests was Amanda Leyton. She was a beautiful blond fresh-looking girl of nineteen. She had the magnificent complexion often found in Englishwomen. Her eyes were bright and pale blue. She presented herself to Kaye and said, ''Welcome to Montego, Kaye. I hope you're going to love it.''

''I love it already. Am I wrong in thinking it's unique?''

''Not at all. The society is as insular as Jamaica itself, but the people are wonderful.''

''Do you live here permanently?''

''Oh, no. I come over from London for long stays with grandmother whenever I can. This one's been the longest ever. I've been here for four months, and I can't manage to tear myself away. So I hope we'll be seeing a lot of each other. I'm sure you've noticed that aside from Ellis and us, there aren't many young people."

"Yes, I've noticed. We'll be friends. I'm certain of it."

Lady Smith-Croydon turned to Kaye and said, "I'm giving a dinner in your honor on Wednesday. I do hope you can come. It would be troublesome to cancel the invitations to all the other guests."

"We can come," Lady Alice stated with a calm that was in deep contrast to Lady Smith-Croydon's acerbity.

"Oh, Alice, let the girl speak for herself. She may not want to come now that she's met me."

"I wouldn't miss it for the world," Kaye said.

"Good for you! We're going to be great friends! Alice, I'm so hungry I could eat an entire ox by myself."

"Dinner is at eight," Alice said.

"That's something we haven't done that we ought to. We should invite everyone in Montego and roast an ox. It would be very thrifty. We could make soup from the tail."

"You'd need more than one ox if you invited everyone in Montego," Creighton said.

There was a heavy pause as Lady Smith-Croydon fixed her eyes on Creighton. "If you're going to start *that* again, Creighton, I shall avoid you for the evening."

"I wasn't starting anything, Smitty. I was just reminding you that the population of Montego is—"

"Stop!" She raised her eyebrows and let the monocle fall from her eye. "You are impertinent. You know full well I meant everybody of our society."

"Full well," Creighton echoed.

"You also know full well that in every society in recorded history, even in tribal groups, there has been a social structure. There is a social structure. There will be a social structure. I did not create it myself. I simply live within it, and so do you. Stop behaving as if capitalism were my idea. Alice, it must be time for dinner.''

"Do sit down for a moment, Smitty."

"Very well," Lady Smith-Croydon said.

Creighton sat down, too—in a wicker armchair next to Kaye. She could almost feel the heat of his body.

"Do you ride, Miss Belliston?" he asked.

It had happened again, suddenly and without warning. It seemed he had only to turn his intense sultry gaze on her to lock her to him, apart from all the others. Kaye was a woman of consummate poise. She had been known in her own social set as the unflappable Kaye. Yet here she was, reduced almost to speechlessness by a man who could abandon her merely by turning his head, then recapture her entirely by turning it back again. Returning his stare—which she was determined to do—made her feel giddy.

"Yes, I do," she said, and again she was surprised she could speak.

"I don't mean to be impertinent, but I meant, do you ride well?"

"Extremely well," she answered, and felt some of her strength returning. "I've been riding since I was eight years old."

For the first time a flickering smile, a *genuine* smile, crossed his lips. "That couldn't be a very long time."

"What a nice compliment," she said, feeling utterly inadequate.

He went on without noticing. "I'm sure you've ridden in the National Horse Show in the States."

"Often."

"And won often."

"Yes." She felt herself blushing.

He turned his head again, and in the darkening twilight the candles in the wall sconces lighted his hair with auburn traces—a darker version of the color of his eyes. When he looked at her again, the smile was gone, and in its place was a stern authoritative expression.

"I'm quite serious about this. I think I'd better explain. You see, there's a stable down the hill where one can rent spiritless horses and ride them on neatly laid-out bridle paths. I have a stable of my own. My horses are trained just enough to accept a bit and bridle... reluctantly. I ride up here in the hills, where there are no bridle paths. There's barely even a flat surface. It's very....challenging. I don't as a rule invite relative strangers to ride with me, simply because the riding can be dangerous. I don't doubt for a minute that your own estimation of yourself as a horsewoman is entirely accurate, so I feel safe in asking you if you'd like to ride with me tomorrow morning."

Kaye was so flustered by such unaccustomed forthrightness that she misinterpreted it. She thought he might be doubting her and mocking her. He wasn't, and her response was misguided.

"I assure you, Mr. Jarvis, I'm entirely capable of riding your horses over your rough terrain."

Without changing his expression, he replied, "I just said I was quite sure of that."

She felt like a fool. This man, this hauntingly attractive man, was being gallant and courteous to her, and she was behaving like a spoiled child.

"I'm sorry," she said. "Of course you did. I'm... flattered, and I accept happily. What time do we start?"

"I'd like to say at your convenience, but I'm afraid it has to be at mine. I really do run my farm myself. It's a full-time career, and if I don't keep to a schedule, everything gets muddled. Would eleven be all right?"

"Perfect," she replied, smiling at him.

"I'll come and pick you up, and—"

"No, no. *That* couldn't possibly be in your schedule.

You see, I'm taking you seriously about your work. I'm sure Henry can drive me."

"That's very thoughtful of you." Something in his eyes flickered again; although Kaye saw it with vivid clarity, she didn't know what it meant.

Henry came out onto the veranda and announced dinner, and everyone went inside. Kaye and Creighton were seated on opposite sides, at opposite ends of the long mahogany table. Several times during dinner Kaye turned her eyes down the table to find Creighton looking at her. It happened the other way around, too. Creighton looked at Kaye to find her already looking at him. The looks were not lingering. Each turned away from the other immediately.

The dinner was not elaborate by island standards. It began with vichyssoise, followed by a saddle of lamb with oven-browned potatoes and fresh asparagus. The dessert was chocolate mousse served in crystal dessert dishes. Kaye was soon to learn that dinners in Montego were usually entirely English with occasional native Jamaican fruit—mangoes and guavas and melon—for dessert.

When dinner was finished, the company retired to the drawing room for coffee. Henry and the other servants circulated, carrying trays and offering the guests cognac and liqueurs.

Lady Smith-Croydon monopolized Kaye's time for the rest of the evening. It would have been considered rude for anyone else to do so, but Smitty was privileged. She could do no wrong. Her presence at any social gathering was *de rigueur* for every hostess, and her behavior was above criticism.

Amanda managed a brief moment of uninterrupted conversation with Kaye while Smitty was talking confidentially with Lady Alice.

"Kaye, I do hope my grandmother hasn't offended

you with her...well, her candor. She's really quite
lovable beneath the craggy surface."

"Not at all," Kaye answered, laughing. "I adore
her."

"Would you like to go to Doctor's Cave with me one
day? It's the best beach on the island. The water is supposed to contain all kinds of minerals and salts that are
good for—I don't know, anything that ails you, I guess.
The older people swear by it. I'm sure it sounds like an
odd invitation, but grandmother's house is always filled
with guests, and you rarely have an opportunity for a
one-to-one conversation. I love getting away now and
then."

"I think that would be lovely," Kaye said.

"I'll let you get settled first. I'll call you soon."

"That's perfect."

As Amanda crossed the room to return to a cluster of
Lady Smith-Croydon's guests, Kaye found herself suddenly, refreshingly, alone. Her inclination was to spring
to her feet and rush to some unoccupied room of the
house. Maintaining a degree of calm, she stood and
made her way casually toward the doors to the terrace.
She thought she had succeeded in attracting no attention
and found herself standing alone on the moonlit terrace,
her head filled with the sensuous fragrance of bougainvillea.

In the quiet her thoughts started with the immediate
present and worked backward. Why had she been so
eager to leave the drawing room just now? She had
always thought of herself as a gregarious person. Why
had she felt the need to escape? She was also an honest
person, and she answered herself instantly. It was
Creighton Jarvis. But why? He had been charming and
polite and generous to her. Why would she try to avoid
him now? Or was her casual departure from the drawing

room an unspoken invitation for him to follow? She remembered her near speechlessness at his first greeting,
her awkwardness at his invitation to ride with him. And
she remembered—no, relived—the helplessness she had
felt in his presence. She felt again the undeniable hot
flow of excitement her eyes had drunk in as they had
watched that sculptured face with its unfathomable mixture of remoteness and intimacy. *The need to escape,*
she said to herself again. Yes, it was the right word. She
needed to escape from the capture of Creighton's gaze.
How was he able to do this to her?

"I'm very much looking forward to tomorrow morning."

The voice seemed at once distant and near. She turned
toward it to see Creighton leaning against the balustrade, ten feet from her. He held a brandy snifter, its
fragile stem nestled between the vee of his first two
fingers, and she remembered how tiny her hand had felt
in his. A wing of the collar of his white linen shirt fluttered toward his jawline in a faint gust of warm breeze.
The bias-cut fabric of his slacks was pulled taut by the
muscles of his thighs. She felt the excitement again and
distracted herself with the thought that he had spoken
from so far away so as not to startle her.

In one supple movement he pushed his body against
the balustrade, was standing upright and walking toward her. She felt the warmth of him increasing as he
drew closer.

"So am I," Kaye said.

"I'm glad. I was afraid you were offended by my
frankness about the riding." He seemed able to read her
thoughts. "I'm intelligent enough to know the value of
compromise in many things," he went on, "but I will
not compromise my honesty or my common sense for
anything or anyone. My friends seem to consider it my

greatest fault. Not my only one, certainly, but the greatest."

"I consider it a virtue," Kaye said.

"Do you?"

"Yes. Maybe it's selfish of me. You see, my own notion of honesty has always got me into a great deal of trouble."

"I sensed that."

"Did you?"

"Yes. Immediately."

"I don't know how. The things I said when we talked before dinner couldn't have seemed very forthright."

"I said I sensed it. It has nothing to do with what you said. It has to do with what you are."

"And what am I?"

"Agonizingly beautiful, for one thing."

"Agonizingly?"

"One approaches your kind of beauty at his own risk."

"Don't tell me you're afraid."

"Yes, and so are you. I don't gamble for money because it would excite me only if I were gambling for more than I could afford to lose. I have too much money to make that practical, so I settle for the kind of gamble we'll take tomorrow when we ride half-wild horses over nearly impossible terrain...and the more exciting gamble of our doing it together—the gamble we're both afraid of."

She stared at him, feeling herself becoming breathless. "You don't think that's a bit...presumptuous? We've known each other for less than four hours."

He smiled again, a smile Kaye now felt was reserved for her, different from the sociable smiles he offered others. "Some people are together all their lives and never know each other. Some know each other before they've even met. Don't you believe that?"

She felt besieged by his unflagging truthfulness. "I don't know."

"I think you're deliberately trying to disappoint me. I'm sorry." He turned to go.

"Mr. Jarvis." When he turned back to her, his dark yellow tiger's eyes seemed to be looking into her rather than at her. "I *do* believe that. Do you want me to say I feel I've known you always?"

"Yes. Because it's true."

"All right, it's true. But I also feel that if I knew you forever, I'd never really know all of you."

"Would you want to?" he asked, but Kaye had turned away toward the garden. "Don't you prefer a horse who might shy when you least expect him to? Do you really want life to be planned and predictable, without any uncertainty—and therefore without any excitement?"

She was still looking out over the garden. "Sometimes I think I'd welcome it."

"I'm glad I don't believe you," he said. She turned to him, ready to say something angry. Before she could speak, though, he cupped her chin in his massive hand, and she felt as if electricity were shooting into her from his fingertips. "It doesn't make a hell of a great difference anyway. People like us haven't much choice in the matter."

He bent toward her and no more than brushed her lips with his, but she felt the firm full flesh of his mouth, and her body went rigid with excitement.

"We'd better go back in now," Creighton said. "Everyone will be leaving soon." He took her hand and led her toward the French doors. Before they reached them, he stopped and looked down at her. "Tomorrow," he said, and suddenly they were in the drawing room again.

It was shortly after midnight, and the guests began to depart. It wasn't a mass exodus. The Marlowes and Ellis

Craig left first. On his way out, Ellis took Kaye's hand again and again held it longer than he should have.

"I'm very glad you're here," he said, gazing into her eyes raptly. "You're very beautiful."

"I'm very glad to be here. And thank you."

As the Zimmermans approached to say their goodnights, Kaye looked toward them. She saw them for only a few fleeting seconds, for her eyes were drawn beyond them to Creighton farther down the hall. Her immediate impression was that he was chatting with Henry, Aunt Alice's butler. Then she realized they were not chatting; they were talking with great earnestness. And she saw yet another Creighton Jarvis. He seemed to have relaxed his iron self-control. He was animated and emphatic. This new Creighton filled her with the same excitement she had felt upon first sight of him—more excitement, if anything. He seemed a mystery distantly removed from her, and she wondered if she would ever penetrate the boundaries of that mystery. Moreover, she wondered if she wanted or dared to.

She turned her gaze away abruptly, asking herself what in the world she was thinking of. She had come here determined to be aloof, impervious, to any masculine charms, yet here she stood, imagining a psychological intimacy with a man she hadn't known for one entire evening. Never mind that he was the most attractive man she had ever seen. She had to get hold of herself. After all, even if she had wanted a man, he was everything she *didn't* want. She saw how easily his poise and charm could slip into arrogance. She had said *presumptuous* earlier, and that was it. Yes, once he thought he had won her over, he would be all self-satisfaction. Without thinking, she glanced at him, hoping to see all the unpleasantness she had imagined. He was smiling at Henry and shaking his hand, his left hand grasping

Henry's shoulder in a gesture of unmistakable camaraderie. Suddenly he turned his head and caught her eye. The smile changed to the one she had claimed for her own, and Henry and everyone else were excluded by it.

She heard Mrs. Zimmerman's voice. "Good night, dear. Now don't forget our date. You're going to fill me in on New York as soon as you're settled."

"I'm looking forward to it," Kaye said.

"Come over to the house," Herman added. "I'll pretend I'm not there because men aren't supposed to gossip, but I'll hover around so I don't miss anything. I have to tell you, you're a welcome addition to the Bay."

"I've never been anywhere that people have made me feel more welcome. Thank you."

"Good night, Alice," the Zimmermans said in unison.

"Good night, my darlings," Aunt Alice answered.

Kaye knew he was near. She was looking toward the front door, but she could feel his presence. She heard his voice.

"Thank you, Alice. I've had at least one unhappy night in every house in Montego, but never in yours."

"How kind you are, Creighton," Alice said.

"Me? Kind?"

"Oh, yes. You're nothing but an Australian sheep rancher in wolf's clothing."

He shook his head in mock dismay, and Kaye watched the light play on his dark brown hair. "I never intended anyone to know me as well as you do, Alice."

"Never mind. You can afford to be known by a woman of my age. That's the only reason you've let me inside your life."

Kaye was still watching him, and for the first time she saw a whisper of uncertainty cross his face. "Do you think there's such a thing as being too wise?" he asked Alice.

"No," she answered. "There's only *thinking* you're too wise."

He smiled faintly and shook his head. Suddenly his look shifted from Aunt Alice to Kaye. She thought for a moment she had imagined it—imagined he could change the color of the world merely by shifting the focus of his eyes. But it had happened again. She and Aunt Alice hadn't seemed to exist while he was talking to Henry. She and Henry hadn't seemed to exist while he was talking to Aunt Alice. Now no one, no place, nothing but Creighton and her seemed to exist as he gazed at her. His smile was gone again, and she didn't know if his look of longing was his own or merely a mirror image of what she was feeling. Then she heard his words, and they seemed abrupt.

"Good night. I'll see you tomorrow at eleven."

"Yes," Kaye said. "At eleven."

He took her hand for only a moment, and their touch was like the heat of a kiln. Then he was gone.

Lady Alice closed the door behind Creighton and turned to Kaye with an odd expression.

"Let's have a moment together in the little sitting room—unless you want to go straight to bed, darling."

"No," Kaye said. "I'd love to sit with you."

As they went through the drawing room, Aunt Alice said, "You'd think an old woman like me would be exhausted by an evening like this one, but I thrive on the excitement. You have to thrive on it if you're to live in Montego."

"First of all, you aren't an old woman. I don't think you'll ever be. You have more energy and vitality than I have. And auntie, you're so beautiful!"

"Thank you, my dear. It's no miracle. I've always tried to take care of myself, and I haven't had a difficult life. I've always had money, and I've loved and been loved by a wonderful man. It doesn't take much more than that and some luck to be well preserved. Ah, here we are. Do sit down. Would you like something? A brandy or—"

"Good Lord, no. I've had more than enough of everything."

"Well," Aunt Alice said, "I think it would be wiser if I gave you a brief rundown on the friends you've met—and, I hope, made—tonight. We're a close society, and you can't function in it without some knowledge of the backgrounds of its members. Where would you like to start?"

"Let's start at the bottom. Tell me about Ellis Craig. Oh, how dreadfully rude of me. I just meant that he seems to be the youngest."

Alice laughed and replied, "You're catching on. Seniority has a great deal to do with the pecking order. Ellis's family decided long ago that he was a genius, but they've never decided what he's a genius at. Neither has Ellis. His mother and father died two years ago in an auto accident and left him just enough money to live on for the rest of his life without his having to work. That is, if he doesn't squander it. He's a sweet callow young man. Next?"

"The Marlowes."

"Oh, dear Netty and Harlan. Harlan's father was a poverty-stricken Lancashireman—which it is better not to mention—who turned a thousand-pound loan into a manufacturing empire. I don't remember what he manufactured, and it hardly matters. Netty is a mystery. She seems well-bred, but nobody knows anything about her family or her background. That doesn't matter, either. She's a dear."

"And the Zimmermans?"

"The Zimmermans are American Jews of enormous

wealth. They came here somewhat later than the others and turned out to be so lovable that we couldn't do without them. I adore them."

"Tell me about Lady Smith-Croydon."

"There's nothing to tell that she won't eventually tell you herself. Her father was knighted by Queen Victoria and died without a son. He was a businessman who reportedly had a fortune of three hundred million dollars in the 1930s. I needn't tell you how it has appreciated since then. Why do I explain everybody in terms of finance? Right or wrong, it matters in Montego. Smitty is my dearest and closest friend. We have a tacit agreement that when one of us dies, the other will follow shortly."

"And Creighton Jarvis?"

Aunt Alice hesitated for a moment. "I'll tell you about Creighton after you've told me about this eleven-o'clock meeting tomorrow."

"We're going riding together. He invited me."

"Do be careful, my dear. Creighton's horses are almost wild. He has a few that are virtually unridable."

"I assure you I'm a very capable horsewoman, Aunt Alice. Anyway, that tells me very little—something, but very little—about Creighton Jarvis."

"All right. Creighton's family have been sheep ranchers in Australia for generations."

"Ah, that accounts for the accent."

"Yes. His great-grandfather—ha, money again—made a substantial fortune in the nineteenth century. Creighton goes back periodically. He's the sole surviving member of the family. He still has vast holdings there. He came here with his bride ten years ago and fell in love with Montego. They—"

"His bride?"

"Yes. They promptly built their house and settled

here. Victoria was a sweet young Australian girl. They tried for years to have a baby without success. Victoria died in childbirth eighteen months ago, and the baby died, too. Creighton was inconsolable. None of us even saw him for well over a year. It's only been the past few months that he's resumed even a vestige of a social life. I don't quite know why, but he and Victoria became a kind of central force in Montego life, in spite of their being newcomers. Perhaps it was because they represented new blood. Or perhaps it was because they were so obviously and dedicatedly in love. They were the envy of the island. They were inseparable. She was an enchanting creature, and Creighton doted on her. Their parties were frequent and lavish. They did everything with great taste and flair. Everyone adored them.

"Then, quite suddenly, it was all over. I've been to tea a few times since Victoria's death, but that's been the full extent of Creighton's entertaining. There've been no parties, no dinners. I think Smitty and I are the only two people in Montego who've been inside the house since the funeral. It's been a great loss to us all. Oh, I don't mean the parties. I mean Creighton. He was so gay and bright and witty. His laughter used to ring through every house in Montego. I still hear echoes of it now and then. After Victoria's death he became the somber withdrawn man you met tonight. Except for the echoes, I haven't heard him laugh in all that time. Nothing, no one, has been able to bring him out of it. I sometimes doubt that anything ever will."

"How terrible for him."

"I suppose I should be encouraged by his inviting you to Penrose, but—"

"Penrose?"

"That was Victoria's maiden name. He named the house for her. As I said, I suppose I should be encouraged, but. . . ." She stopped again, this time without being interrupted.

"But what?"

"I would be very fearful of anyone's becoming involved with Creighton just yet."

"Involved? Aunt Alice, I assure you there isn't the faintest chance of my becoming involved with him."

"You don't know him, my dear. He can be devastatingly attractive."

"Perhaps. But I've told you, the last thing in the world I want is any kind of involvement with a man."

"Nonetheless, I hope you'll be very circumspect with Creighton."

"Don't worry, auntie. I intend to be absolutely distant."

"You accepted his invitation?"

"I thought it would have been rude not to. And after all, I haven't become a recluse. Nor do I intend to become one. Trust me, darling. I can handle myself."

"I've heard other women say that in re____ to Creighton, both before and after Victoria's death, and they ended up throwing themselves at him—only to meet with total rejection and make fools of themselves."

Aunt Alice was interrupted by the look in Kaye's eyes. It lasted for only an instant, but fleeting as it was, it told her a great deal about what Kaye was thinking. It was a look almost of rapture.

"I don't doubt that for a moment," Kaye remarked. "Oh, don't worry, darling. I meant what I said. I don't want any kind of involvement. At this moment I think I'm incapable of falling in love. And I don't even regret it."

"Only the mentally aberrant are incapable of falling in love, and you're quite sane."

"Sane enough to resist Mr. Jarvis, charming though he

is. And I admit he is charming. More than that." She caught herself before she said more. "Please don't be troubled. Now would it be all right if Henry drove me into town tomorrow morning to buy some riding clothes?"

"Of course it would. Tell him to take you to Watson's. They'll have everything you need." She got up and said, "Well, it's time for us to retire. You'll sleep well. It's the reason people of Smitty's and my age survive: Jamaica is divine for sleeping. Come on."

But Kaye did not sleep well. She thought about Creighton for a long time before she drifted off, and she was awakened during the night by recurring dreams of him. They were warm sensuous dreams in which she saw Creighton's face close to hers. It always bore the same expression, which she had actually seen during the evening—an expression of possessiveness and desire. And in her dreams she was drawn to him just as she was in reality. The pull was so irresistible it frightened her into waking. Each time his arms were about to go around her, each time she was about to melt into them in blissful submission, the dream ended. And each time she woke up, it was more difficult for her to get back to sleep again. When she awoke at eight, she saw no reason to go back to bed. Helen served her a breakfast on the veranda: tea, fresh grapefruit juice, papaya and mangoes. Henry drove her into town before Aunt Alice had even come downstairs. She tried, without success, to quell her anticipation at seeing Creighton at eleven.

She came back to the house and changed into her new riding clothes. On her way out of the house she encountered Aunt Alice.

"Good morning, my dear," Alice said. "I see you've already been into town. You look very fetching."

"Thank you, auntie. Henry tells me the drive to Penrose will take ten minutes." She looked at her watch. "I suppose I should leave now."

"Yes. Do remember what I said last night?"

"And you remember what *I* said?"

"When you finish your ride, telephone, and Henry will fetch you. Unless, of course, Creighton brings you home, as he will undoubtedly offer to do."

"In which case I'll phone for Henry anyway."

"I hope you will. Have a good time."

The drive to Penrose was entirely on unpaved roads that snaked through the verdant hills. Creighton's house was slightly higher up than Aunt Alice's, and the forest and the flowers became even more lush as the elevation increased. Everything was incredibly beautiful. The car made a sudden turn onto another dirt road that, after a few seconds, opened onto a gravel drive. Then all at once Penrose was before her. It was a magnificent Georgian mansion that lay glistening in the morning sun.

As the Rolls navigated the semicircular drive and stopped in front of the house, Creighton emerged, wearing riding clothes topped by an Australian cavalry officer's wide-brimmed hat. His pale chamois shirt looked softly inviting in the sunlight, and the muscles of his arms and chest were highlighted as the fabric caressed them. He approached the car while Henry got out and opened the door for Kaye.

"Good morning," Creighton said to her. His eyes held her again. He turned away and added, "Good morning, Henry."

"Good morning, sir," Henry answered.

"You know I meant what I said last night, Henry," Creighton went on. "I'll do anything I can to help."

"You always have, sir."

"We'll talk more about it later." He turned back to

Kaye, smiling. "I see you're ready. We can walk to the stable. It isn't far."

"Fine," she replied.

As they started out, Henry got back into the car and drove away.

"It's a lovely morning," Kaye began.

"Mornings are always lovely in Montego," Creighton answered.

"That's very reassuring, Mr. Jarvis."

"Creighton, please."

"All right, *Creighton*."

"I trust you slept well."

"Like a log," Kaye lied. "Aunt Alice says Jamaica is divine for sleeping."

"Dear Alice is a romantic. We have a temperate climate, that's all."

They were walking on a lane that skirted the forest and wound toward the back of the house. Kaye soon saw the whitewashed boards of the stable. A groom was standing outside holding the reins of two stallions, one a huge chestnut, the other a roan.

As they approached, the Jamaican groom said, "Good morning, Mr. Jarvis."

"Good morning," Creighton answered. Then to Kaye he said, "The chestnut is yours. His name's Wellington."

"And what's the other's name?"

"Caligula."

"How fanciful!"

He looked at her askance. "Would you like me to help you mount?"

"Of course not, thank you."

She went to Wellington and rubbed his face vigorously. "Hello, Wellington."

The horse snorted and pulled his head away from her

touch. He had the wildest eyes Kaye had ever seen on a horse.

"He's not a kitten," Creighton commented.

Kaye attributed his near gruffness to the fact that he took riding very seriously. She glanced at him but didn't answer. She went to Wellington's left side and mounted. Creighton mounted, too, and led the way toward a narrow path that began at the edge of the wood. Kaye knew as soon as she wheeled Wellington around and started for the path that he was a difficult, possibly even dangerous, horse. He was champing at the bit furiously and prancing. She could feel his whole powerful body straining to break her control of him. She reined him in tightly and kept her knees firmly against his flanks. He whinnied and started to buck, but Kaye held him in with all the authority she could muster. As they reached the path, Creighton put Caligula into a trot. Kaye followed suit, and it took all her strength and skill to keep Wellington from breaking into a faster gait. She knew any riding horse could immediately recognize the slightest sign of fear in its rider. She wasn't afraid of Wellington, but she knew she had to treat him with respect.

By the time they had gone five hundred yards into the forest, the path had virtually disappeared. Kaye found herself having to duck the limbs of trees and control Wellington at the same time. Creighton allowed Caligula to canter, and Kaye had her first moment of real uncertainty as Wellington followed suit and broke into a canter without her leading him. She decided this was not the time to argue with him and gave him his head. Suddenly they came out of the forest into a vast meadow. She eased up on the reins and allowed her horse to catch up to Creighton's.

"This is quite an animal," she remarked when she was abreast of Creighton. "I've never known a horse so raring to go."

"Keep a firm hand with him. If you give him the slightest leeway, you'll lose control of him."

"Is this to be a pleasant morning ride or a riding lesson?"

"I'm sorry, Kaye. I didn't mean to insult you. It's just that we've had some nasty accidents with people riding up here in the hills. If I seem a bit somber about it all, it's only because it's so easy even for me—especially in your company—to forget one isn't cantering through a park. And Wellington does need a great deal of discipline. You mustn't let up for a moment."

He slowed his horse to a walk, and with some difficulty Kaye managed to rein Wellington in to the same gait.

"Is this still your property?"

"Yes. We're not likely to get off it. I have two hundred and fifty acres. I find all of it very beautiful. I'd hoped you would, too."

"It is beautiful—what I've seen of it. I wish I could see it all."

"There's no reason why you can't, given the time."

They rode in silence for a while. Kaye glanced at Creighton now and again. She could tell he was a magnificent horseman. He had undoubtedly grown up with horses and had had long experience with them. But she could tell, too, that he rode instinctively, that there was an affinity between him and his horse. She felt no such affinity with Wellington.

When they were two hundred yards from the far edge of the meadow, where the forest began again, Wellington bolted without warning. He was immediately in full gallop, and nothing Kaye could do brought him back under control. By the time Creighton had kneed Caligula into a gallop to follow her, she was far ahead of him and about to disappear into the trees. No sensible rider would gallop a horse through a forest, and Kaye knew she was in grave danger, but she simply couldn't rein Wellington in. She saw the trees looming before her and pulled so hard on the reins that she knew the bit must be digging into the soft flesh of the horse's mouth. Yet it had no effect on him. He galloped straight into the woods.

For a short distance Kaye managed to dodge and duck the low limbs of trees that came at her every few seconds as Wellington continued his mad race. She saw one big branch ahead of her and ducked so low her face was against the hot damp flesh of the horse's neck. She straightened up again just in time to hit a smaller branch that knocked her off Wellington's back. She was lying on the forest floor, dizzied by the blow to her head, when Creighton came galloping past in pursuit of Wellington.

In a few minutes Creighton and Caligula came back, leading Wellington behind them. Creighton dismounted and began tying the reins of both horses to a tree.

"Are you all right?" he asked.

"I think so," Kaye replied.

Creighton stopped and picked her up as if she were weightless. She could feel the muscles of his arm against her back, and his torso was like rock against her side. For a moment she thought there was a fleeting expression of tenderness and concern on his face, but she wasn't entirely sure. One thing she was sure of was that he was looking down at her breasts, which were quite clearly outlined beneath the pongee blouse she was wearing. This was the closest she had ever been to him, and he looked more handsome than ever. She wondered what it would be like to bridge that small distance between their faces, whether he would be even more attractive with their faces nearly touching as if he were about to kiss her. She pulled her mind away from such thoughts.

For the first time she recognized the emotion that seemed to be her only defense against her attraction to him. It was anger. She knew she had to remember his arrogance and his haughtiness, had to try to forget the amber eyes that sought her out and claimed her. She had to forget the raw strength of Creighton's magnificent body, which even now held her as if she were a toy. She had to remember that of all the things that could happen to her, the last one she wanted was to fall in love. The anger she felt was with herself, but she turned it on Creighton.

"It was a nasty spill," Creighton said.

"Yes," she answered, "you were so concerned you galloped right past me to retrieve Wellington."

He scowled at her and noted, "He's a very valuable horse."

"And I'm merely an inconsequential human being."

"You weren't likely to run away; Wellington was."

"That's very touching. Would you please put me down. I'm perfectly all right."

As he set her on her feet, he added, "I should never have let you ride him. I thought you'd be bored with a less spirited mount."

"I *can* handle him. I've been thrown previously, and if you tell me you haven't, I won't believe you."

"Of course I have."

"And I have every intention of riding him back to Penrose."

"I'm glad; it's a very long walk. Which is one of the reasons I went after him." She started to turn away. He took her by the arm and turned her back to him. "Kaye, if you had been hurt, Wellington would have been the fastest way to get you back to help. It was not neglect. It was a practical decision. Try not to be featherbrained."

His hand was still on her arm, strong and firm. She

stared into his deep golden eyes, and she had no idea what she saw there. She put her hand on his with the aim of removing it from her arm, but she didn't. She let her palm rest against the smooth tanned skin and found herself wondering what it would be like to touch him more intimately, what that hard muscled chest would feel like beneath her fingertips. She took her hand off of his but made no further attempt to end his touching her.

"You're right, of course. Thank you, Creighton."

With his hand still on her arm he said, "It might be better if you rode Caligula back to the house. He's at least somewhat gentler."

"I'd rather die."

"And you might."

"I'll take the risk," she replied.

He smiled at her and added, "I knew you would."

She felt her resolve melting away. In confusion she asked, "What do you mean?"

"Just as I like horses with spirit, I like women with spirit. You'd ride Wellington back to Penrose at any cost."

She felt herself blushing again and acknowledged, "I suppose I would."

"You *know* you would. And I know it, too. You have courage—and a great deal of pride."

She glanced into his eyes for a moment, then looked away. "I'm afraid I was brought up to believe pride is an admirable quality."

"So was I. We're alike."

The unwilling fondness was flooding through her again, and she kept her eyes averted.

"Why are you so afraid to look at me?" he asked.

With great determination she forced herself to gaze directly into his eyes. "I'm not afraid. Would you like the truth, Creighton?"

"From you, always."

"All right. You're a very seductive man, and you're very appealing. I'd be a fool to try to lie to you about that. You've certainly made it clear you find me attractive. All that can lead to only one thing... the one thing I will not have in my life just now. I'm simply not ready for any kind of attachment. You almost make me wish I were. If I'm afraid at all, that's what frightens me."

"You're too strong to be swept off your feet," he said, staring down at her with that look of intensity she had already come to know. It was as if he were holding her in his arms, physically touching her. Sparks seemed to be flying along her spine. "And I assure you I am not trying to do that."

"We'll be all right then, since we both feel that way."

"Yes. Except for one thing."

"One thing? What?"

"This."

His movement toward her seemed sudden to Kaye. In reality it was gentle and unhurried. She saw the big tanned hands rising toward her shoulders. She saw the carved face bearing a look of unmistakable tenderness as it bent toward her. The golden eyes smoldered now rather than flamed. The lips of his strong full mouth were slightly parted. Almost before she knew it, his arms were around her, and his lips were pressed against hers.

She made no attempt to escape him. She stood motionless in his embrace, feeling his slightly open mouth against her own, the lips moving almost imperceptibly. The sensation of his kiss was so intense it was a moment before she was fully aware that his taut muscular body was pressed against her in the embrace. She felt his rock-hard chest weighing on her breasts, his thighs touching her. His arms held her and drew her against

him with a gentle strength. She felt as if he had somehow made her part of him. Still, she didn't move away
or try to thwart him. She felt she couldn't if she had
wanted to—and she didn't want to.

She didn't know how long it was before he released
her. The moments had been magical and timeless. She
was looking up at his face hovering just above hers.

"What are we going to do about that, Kaye?" he
whispered.

She put her hands over her eyes and tried to turn
away, but his hands were still on her shoulders, and she
couldn't break their firm yet gentle grip.

"Do you have an answer?" he asked softly.

"I—I don't know, but I won't let it happen again. I
want to go back now."

He let his hands fall from her, and she moved away.
She unhitched Wellington's reins from the tree where
Creighton had tied them and mounted. She turned the
horse toward Penrose and started without waiting for
Creighton. The sun-tinted trees shimmered through her
tears.

Creighton and Caligula were soon beside her. They
rode back to the house in silence. They were surrounded
by the cool damp of the forest and the pungent scents of
the foliage and flowers. Whatever was between them remained unspoken. When they reached the stable, they
dismounted and started toward the house.

"Kaye, this morning was—"

"I don't want to talk about it," she interrupted him.

"We're going to have to."

"No, I'm going to forget it. . . simply forget it."

"Are you?"

"I'm going to try with all my heart."

"I suppose I should wish you luck."

They reached the driveway, and the only sound was

the crunch of the gravel beneath their feet. Then Creighton said, "I'll drive you back to Traymore."

"Thank you, Creighton, but I think it would be better if I called and had Henry come for me."

"Don't be ridiculous," he replied testily. "Are you pretending we're never going to see each other again?"

"I guess that would be impossible in Montego."

"It might be impossible anywhere."

He opened the passenger door of his Land Rover and waited for her to get in. She did so without further protest. He went around and got in beside her. The engine snarled as he revved it more powerfully than was necessary. Immediately they were on the open road, and without the cool moist protection of the forest, Kaye felt the heat becoming unbearable. It was actually the heavy silence weighing on her, and she made up her mind to break it with conversation that wouldn't invoke further involvement.

"I don't mean to intrude, Creighton, but I'm curious about something."

"Yes? What's that?" His tone was not quite cordial.

"Last night I saw you deep in conversation with Henry, and again this morning the few words you exchanged seemed . . . well, intense."

"Does that seem strange to you?"

Kaye bristled. "If you mean the landed gentry talking to the peasants, I'd be grateful if you didn't insult me."

"Sorry. I've got to stop underestimating you. Henry is two things I like: a Jamaican and a patriot. You're not likely to see him in the proper perspective. You see, Alice's servants live like royalty compared to ninety-eight percent of the native population, but that's not good enough for Henry. He won't be satisfied until *all* his people have decent lives. And neither will I."

"That doesn't make you unpopular among your peers?"

"My 'peers,' as you call them, would happily change the economic situation of the island—if somebody would just keep reminding them about it. That's my job and Henry's. Smitty and even your Aunt Alice—and the Marlowes and the Zimmermans—are all so accustomed to privilege they forget they have an obligation to share it. After all, this isn't their island—or mine."

"No, I suppose it's not."

"Never mind. I'm bringing them around gradually one by one. They're very good people." They were quiet again for a long while until Creighton asked, "Why so pensive?"

"I'm surprised, I guess, that you're so involved in the island's welfare."

"It's my home. I care about it."

"I take it back. I'm not surprised. I suppose it's like you to care deeply."

He smiled at her brazenly and said, "Finally. You admit that we're alike."

Before she could answer, they were on the drive of Traymore, and he stopped the Rover, got out and opened the door for her. Aunt Alice came out onto the veranda and greeted them as they came up the steps.

"How was the ride?" she inquired.

"Eventful," Kaye answered.

"Hello, Creighton."

"Hello, Alice. Did you know that your niece is a superb horsewoman?"

"I've heard so, but your opinion confirms it beyond all doubt. Will you stay for lunch?"

"No, thank you. I have a very busy afternoon. I have a tendency to neglect the house, and every now and then I find myself overwhelmed by chores I've put off. I'll see you Wednesday at Smitty's dinner."

"All right, dear."

"I'll see you, too," he said to Kaye. "Thank you for the 'eventful' morning." He went down the steps, got into the Rover and drove off.

Kaye was staring after him when she heard Aunt Alice's voice. "Come and sit down, darling. Lunch is almost ready. In the meantime you can tell me about your ride."

"There's nothing much to tell, except that I was thrown by a horse named Wellington. Well, not thrown really. He bolted, and—"

"Wellington?" Aunt Alice asked, her eyebrows arched in astonishment.

"Yes, Wellington. Why?"

"Nobody but Creighton has ever ridden that horse. He's the wildest, most unreliable horse Creighton owns. I'm shocked he let you take him."

"Maybe he was testing me. I did boast a little last night when he invited me."

"That's no excuse. The horse is dangerous. I'm going to speak to Creighton about it."

"I wish you wouldn't, auntie."

Aunt Alice studied her for a moment. "I think it would be wise if you didn't see too much of him."

"I'll try not to see any more of him than I have to in the normal course of things."

" 'The road to hell is paved with good intentions.' "

"I mean it, Aunt Alice. I don't want to see him any oftener than I have to."

"That's a dangerous sign."

"Dangerous?"

"I'd feel better if you were indifferent to him."

"So would I. Well, I soon will be. I guarantee it."

"We'll see. He'll undoubtedly be at dinner tonight at Netty's and Harlan's."

"Dinner?"

"I think my mind is finally slipping. I completely forgot to tell you we're going to the Marlowes' for dinner. I hope you don't find it boring—this endless round of dinner parties. It's what we do, since there seems to be nothing else. You're free to decline any invitation. Simply plead a headache. Well, almost any invitation. We don't turn down Smitty. Nobody does except in the most legitimate circumstances. But then nobody turns me down, either. Gladys and I are the *grandes dames* of the community."

"I have no intention of turning down any invitations. Remember, I came here to get away from what was."

"Only to find yourself getting into what is. Out of the frying pan."

"And into the fire? It's a lovely fire, Aunt Alice."

"It can be. It can also be a very hot one. Ah, here comes Helen with lunch."

THE MARLOWES' HOUSE was in the opposite direction from Creighton's and slightly farther down the hill. It was a large, beautifully appointed house, built, like all the others, for entertaining. Netty was standing in the doorway, ready to greet them when they got out of the Rolls. The sky was blue gray, tinted rose gold by the setting sun. Kaye wondered if Montego was ever anything but beautiful.

"Alice, darling," Netty cried as they approached the doorway. "You've managed for the first time in ages to arrive *after* Smitty. She'll be furious. Kaye, it's good to have you here."

"For me, infuriating Smitty is one of the few pleasures left in life," Alice explained. "I don't really enjoy it, but she does, and that makes me happy."

"Hello, Netty," Kaye said. "It's very good of you to include me."

"Don't be silly. You're family."

She led them into the drawing room, where the other thirty guests had already gathered for drinks. Although there were other people nearer to them, the first person Kaye saw was Creighton. He was standing on the far side of the large room, talking to a man Kaye had not yet met. As she watched him chatting cordially, their ride of the morning seemed miles away in some enchanted land she was afraid to set foot in again. Yet he was real. He seemed to glow, as if he had absorbed the warmth of the island sun that had turned his skin to bronze. He looked as if the island had somehow borne him. He was dressed in earth colors again—taupe and brown. He seemed unapproachable and mysterious, and she reminded herself this was a mystery of which she couldn't let herself be a part. She tore her gaze away from him.

All the "others," as she had already come to regard them, were there: Smitty and her guests, Amanda, Ellis, the Zimmermans. Sylvia and Herman waved to her from across the room, and she felt at home.

She was given a drink immediately, and it took half an hour for her to be introduced to the guests she hadn't already met. By the time the ritual was over, she was standing next to Creighton and the gentleman to whom he was talking. It was an effort for her to take her eyes off Creighton, but she managed it and stared expectantly at the other man. He seemed excessively British. He wore a safari jacket and khaki trousers; his face was ruddy and decorated with a bushy mustache with waxed ends; he had lively bright blue eyes, and he looked at Kaye with enthusiastic interest.

"Kaye, this is Barney Fairweather," Aunt Alice said. "He's an eccentric even by Montego standards, but he's a fixture, and we all love him. Barney, this is my niece, Kaye Belliston."

"I'm charmed, Miss Belliston," Fairweather said. "I've been living in a state of electric expectation ever since I was informed of your imminent arrival."

"Thank you, Mr. Fairweather," Kaye replied. "I'm delighted to meet you."

"Now that we've addressed each other as 'mister' and 'miss' once, I hope we can dispense with that formality. May I call you Kaye?"

"Of course."

"Good evening," Creighton said.

"Good evening."

"I predict you're going to be the highlight of every party," Barney said to Kaye.

"Barney is our resident soothsayer," Ellis Craig told her. Ellis had met Kaye twenty feet inside the front door and hadn't left her side for a minute. "Come and let me get you another drink."

"That would be lovely," Kaye acknowledged. She smiled at Barney and said again, "I'm glad to have met you." Then she turned away from Creighton without another word and crossed the room with Ellis.

When they had got their drinks, Ellis asked, "May I show you the garden? It's very beautiful, and it's Netty's pride and joy."

"Show me the garden . . . at night?"

"There's a moon. It will be lovely and cool and quiet."

She glanced over his shoulder and saw that Creighton was watching her.

"I'd love it," she answered.

They went outside. Whatever Ellis's intentions were, he was right about the garden. The sun had gone down, and it was hauntingly beautiful in the moonlight. The flower beds were laced with cobblestone paths, and as they walked, they could hear the distant sounds of the party wafted on the fragrant night air.

"I don't really give a damn about the garden," Ellis said. "I just wanted a moment alone with you. You're the most beautiful woman I've ever met."

"That's very extravagant of you."

"I hope you don't mind, but I've arranged with Netty to sit next to you at dinner."

"I don't mind at all. I'm flattered."

"I was afraid you'd think it forward of me."

"No, I don't. Oh, look at the sky! I don't think I've ever seen the stars quite so bright anywhere else in the world."

"Nights are always like this in Montego. Well, not exactly like this. The stars seem brighter, looking at them with you."

"That's very sweet of you."

"I've been thinking about you constantly since last evening. I've cabled London and told them not to expect me just yet."

"Ellis, you aren't staying on my account?"

"Yes, I am."

"You mustn't do that."

"I want to. You might be gone by the time I get back. I might never see you again."

Kaye didn't know what to say, and she said the wrong thing. She sensed he was being more romantic than even his words revealed, yet her question could have easily been interpreted as encouraging. "How long will you be in London?" she asked.

"At least a month. . .if I were going. But I'm not."

"You really mustn't put it off because of me."

"On the contrary, it's the one thing in the world I must do."

"Ellis. . . ."

"I'm sorry, I'm being forward. But I want so much to get to know you, really know you. I assure you that's more important to me than anything I have to do in London.''

"Ellis, I'm certain we can be very good friends, but it can't be anything more than that.''

"Would you mind terribly if I tried to change your mind?''

"I'd mind only because it would be futile.''

"The risk is mine, and I'm eager to take it.''

"That's very dear of you, and I'm highly complimented, but I've just been divorced, and I'm not ready for any kind of attachment. Not even a superficial one.''

"I wasn't thinking of a superficial one. It might be very good for you, Kaye.''

"No, it wouldn't. I'm sorry. Can we go back now?''

"Of course. If I promise you I won't make a nuisance of myself, may we see each other a bit?''

"Since we're in Montego, I'm sure we'll see each other inevitably, but I wish you wouldn't change your plans.''

"It really doesn't matter, and there are all sorts of things we could do. I could show you Kingston and Round Hill and Ocho Rios and...."

"Ellis, please. First of all, I came here to be with Aunt Alice, and I really shouldn't go running off without her. And second, it wouldn't work. You see, I don't want it to work. Not with anyone.''

"I can change your mind. I know I can. Just let me see you now and then.''

"We should go back.''

"Of course. Don't be angry with me.''

"I'm not angry.''

Dinner was served a few minutes after they got back to the house. Kaye was indeed seated on Ellis's right at dinner—and Creighton was on *her* right. She felt vaguely guilty about the seating arrangement, but she did nothing further for the moment to discourage Ellis's attentiveness. It made it possible for her barely to speak to Creighton during dinner. She realized shortly that he was making no great attempt to talk to her. After a while their joint attempt to avoid each other became worse than casual conversation would have been. She was grateful when Netty rose and announced that coffee would be served in the drawing room.

On their way from the table Kaye and Ellis encountered Lady Alice and Smitty.

"Alice, I believe your niece has been dodging me," Smitty said loudly enough for Kaye to hear.

"You're the last person in the world I'd want to avoid, Lady Smith-Croydon."

Smitty smiled at her and said, "I do understand. You young people should be together. You don't need old biddies like Alice and me."

"I am not an old biddy," Alice retorted. "A biddy is a chicken."

"You're certainly right about that, Alice. We're definitely not chickens—not in the modern slang sense of the word. Run along, children, while Alice and I sit down and knock back a brandy or two."

As the two ladies moved off, Ellis remarked, "'A brandy or two' is a nice idea. May I get one for you?"

"No, thank you, Ellis, but you go ahead."

Ellis went to the bar, and when Kaye turned around, Creighton was standing directly before her.

"Any bruises from this morning?" he inquired.

"None. No thanks to you."

"I don't know what you mean."

"I mean Wellington, the most dangerous horse in your stable."

"Oh, I am sorry. You were very convincing about

your ability as a horsewoman. Next time I'll arrange for
you to have a Shetland pony.''

"There won't be a next time.''

"I'm sorry about that. I rather enjoy baiting you.''

"I've noticed that. But I don't enjoy it. I might if it
were done in a spirit of fun, but you do it very crudely.
It isn't amusing.''

"It amuses me.''

"At my expense.''

"You might try being a good sport, Kaye. It mars
your charm when you're stodgy.''

"I'm not being stodgy,'' she answered. "I told you
the truth this morning. I expected you to accept it.''

"I have accepted it. I suppose I resent the fact you
didn't give me an opportunity to tell you the truth.''

"I don't know what you. . . .''

"Don't you realize you talk constantly about what
you feel? You've even gone so far as to presume you
know what *I* feel. Yet you've never given me a chance to
tell you that the moment I met you, I thought you might
be everything I've ever wanted in a woman. Don't you
know I wouldn't have paid such attention to you if that
hadn't been true? God knows, you're beautiful. And
you have style and character and breeding. But I don't
think you know anything about sharing. I don't think
you could ever share a man's life with him. Everything
would have to be your way, on your terms. I have to admit that the thought of sharing my life with you came
into my mind the instant I saw you on the veranda at
Traymore. I know now, though, that that wouldn't be
possible. You see, Kaye, I had all that once. I thought
for just a short time that I might have found it again.
Maybe that's too much to ask.'' He turned and walked
away from her.

As she stared after him, at least a little shocked, she

wondered if all he had said had been true. She knew only that she felt bereft as she watched him blend into the crowd. She felt alone.

"Is there something the matter?"

It was Ellis's voice. She felt absolutely incapable of dealing with Ellis at that moment, but she couldn't let her consternation show.

"I can't imagine what you mean," she heard herself saying.

"The expression on your face. You looked. . . I don't know—upset."

"Don't be silly. What would have upset me?"

"Possibly Creighton Jarvis?"

"That's even sillier. Creighton and I were talking about our ride this morning. That's all."

"Why do you think I'm silly? I may not be as mature as Creighton, but I'm not a child."

It took all her will, but she smiled at him, determined to make conversation and not be rude. She let Creighton go out of her view.

"I bet I can guess your age," she said.

"And I bet you can't," Ellis countered.

"I say you're. . . twenty."

"Well, actually. . . ." He smiled sheepishly. "Well, actually, you've hit it right on the head. But that makes you and me contemporaries."

"In terms of decades, yes. I'm six years older than you. A very important six years."

Aunt Alice approached them. "Kaye, darling," she began, "would you mind if we said our good-nights? I suddenly have a headache. By no means do you have to leave. Henry can take me and come back for you. There are any number of people who'd be happy to drive you home, if you'd prefer. Our house is on the way from here to Creighton's. He could. . . ."

"No, darling," Kaye replied. "I'm quite ready to leave. We'll find Netty and Harlan and be on our way."

"If you're quite sure."

"I am."

"All right, then. Good night, Ellis."

"Good night. Although I'm sorry to see you spirit your niece away."

"It's hardly forever, dear boy."

"Good night, Ellis," Kaye said.

He smiled at her sadly. "Good night, Kaye. Please think about my invitation."

"I will."

"My, my," Aunt Alice began as they walked away, "it's been only two days, and you seem to be virtually inundated with invitations."

"It's all very casual, and I told you, I'm invulnerable. I mean it. Even if I were as ripe as a plum, you'd have nothing to fear from Ellis."

"It isn't Ellis I fear. Ah, here's Netty. It was a lovely party, Netty. We must be leaving now."

"Already? It's the shank of the evening."

"The shank comes at different hours at different times of life."

"Well, I'll see you tomorrow at Smitty's. Kaye, I'm so glad you could come."

"It was delightful, Netty. Thank you for having me."

They stopped to say good-night to a number of people on their way to the door. Just before they reached it, they encountered Creighton.

"Good night, Creighton," Aunt Alice said. There was a slight coolness in her voice.

"Good night, Alice." He turned to Kaye. "Did you enjoy your walk in the garden?"

"Yes. Very much, as a matter of fact. Good night."

"Good night, Miss Belliston."

Kaye ignored the sarcasm, and they went outside, where Henry was waiting with the car.

When they got home, Aunt Alice went straight to bed. Kaye decided to have a walk in the garden before going upstairs. The night was still incredibly lovely. The sky was like velvet studded with bright jewels. The air was perfumed and heady. It had been only two days, Aunt Alice had said. Two days, and so much had happened. She looked at the dark branches of the trees surrounding the property, and in her mind she saw the trees of the forest rushing at her as Wellington galloped toward them, and she thought of Creighton. But what did she think of Creighton? What was this dreadful ambivalence she felt toward him? She could deny to everyone else the attraction she felt, but she could no longer deny it to herself. How could she dislike him so intensely and at the same time be so strongly drawn to him? Did she really dislike him, or was she merely pretending to herself she did, as a defense against him? She truly didn't know. The one thing she was sure of was that deep inside her she wished she had never come to Jamaica. Still, she had only to get on a plane in the morning to be away from the island forever. Yet she knew she wouldn't do it.

# CHAPTER TWO

SHE AWOKE THE NEXT MORNING to another glorious day. The scent of the flowers in the garden below wafted through her bedroom windows. For a moment she felt free and peaceful and calm. Then she remembered Creighton, and she was filled with a sense of anxiety. It would have been different if she'd been in New York, surrounded by its monumental concrete barriers. She could avoid him there. She could hide from him in the vast expanse and complexity of the city. But she was in Montego, and unless she became a recluse, she was going to see him—going to see him that very night. She could plead a headache, as Aunt Alice had told her she could. No. It was Smitty's party, and it was being given for her. She couldn't turn Smitty down. She felt as if she were caught in a web. She looked at the clock beside the bed. It was half past nine. She got out of bed and started for the shower.

When she arrived downstairs, Aunt Alice was sitting on the veranda having breakfast. There was a place set for her, and the table was laden with fresh fruit.

"Good morning, darling," Aunt Alice began. "You're up early."

"You're right about Montego. I slept like a top."

She kissed her aunt on the cheek and sat down.

"Wonderful. In spite of the parties and the late hours and the cocktails, we live a healthful life here. Perhaps it's the fresh fruit. You must have some. Helen will bring a pot of tea in a few minutes. You may have coffee if you prefer."

"Tea will be fine."

"You know, Kaye, I can't help feeling guilty."

"Guilty? About what?"

"You came here for a rest, for some peace and quiet, and you haven't had a minute to yourself."

"Aunt Alice, I think I'm glad of that. I mean, it wouldn't do for me to be sulking and mooning about by myself, would it? The truth is, I haven't had a minute to feel sorry for myself, and *that* is good. I haven't even had time to think about it. But I don't think I'd want it any other way."

"You're not just being polite to your old auntie?"

"I love you too much for that, Aunt Alice."

"And I love you. You know I've never had children of my own, and I've always regarded you as as much my daughter as your mother's. I suppose it's envy."

"Whatever it is, I'm grateful."

"Since there's not a great deal we can do about the social whirl, I can only hope you're enjoying it. Did you have a good time last evening?"

Kaye hesitated. "Yes, for the most part."

"Ah, what does that mean?"

"Well, it was a lovely party. Dinner was super."

"What wasn't?"

"I beg your pardon?"

"What wasn't super?"

"Ellis Craig for one thing."

"Ellis? He seems perfectly harmless to me."

"He is harmless to you. He took me for a walk in the garden, and I thought he was going to propose to me."

Aunt Alice laughed. "Poor Ellis. Believe it or not, I was young once, but I don't think I was ever as young as Ellis."

"And then, of course, there was Creighton."

"Oh, my," Lady Alice sighed.

"Aunt Alice, I think I need your help. I'm not a schoolgirl, and in spite of my unfortunate marriage I think of myself as a stable woman, but every time I see Creighton, I seem to feel...different about him. I know it hasn't been all that often, but...." Her voice trailed off.

"It hasn't been often, but it's been intense. Is that putting it fairly?"

"Yes. Yes, it is. One minute he's gentlemanly and helpful and courteous, and the next he's gruff and sarcastic. And just as quickly he can become as distant as if he were on the moon."

Aunt Alice was thoughtful for a long moment. "That's not like Creighton. Has it occurred to you it might be his reaction to you that makes him vacillate so?"

"His reaction to me?"

"You mustn't forget that these things are two-sided. You mustn't think only of what you feel. Try to remember that Creighton is feeling something, too."

"I do know that, auntie. That's the problem. We've discussed it, actually. We've told each other how we feel and what we want, and for a moment it's all very neat and tidy. Then we behave toward each other as if none of it had ever been said."

"It sounds as though you're both a bit out of control. And that's not like either of you."

"Maybe we are," Kaye said, looking across the veranda thoughtfully. "It frightens me, Aunt Alice."

"I don't think you need be frightened. I don't believe you and Creighton would deliberately bring any kind of harm to each other. However, you must be careful, both of you. You mustn't just let things happen to you."

"You're very wise, but I'm afraid that may be more easily said than done."

"Of course it is. You must never forget it, though, if you want to be happy. I've always found that happiness consists mainly in being in charge of your life."

"I've always felt I have been. . . until now."

"Take a long deep breath, my dear, and try to get hold of things."

"I'll try. I honestly will try."

"Creighton's coming by this morning." Kaye looked startled and alarmed. "In about an hour, I think. He telephoned early this morning and asked if he could see me. *That's* unlike him, too. My, things do seem topsy-turvy since you arrived, don't they? Well, no matter. Whatever Creighton has to say to me is private. You needn't even see him if you'd rather not."

"Would you prefer I didn't?"

"Kaye, I would prefer you did whatever is going to make you happy."

"Then I think that after breakfast I'll go to the pool and leave you and Creighton to your privacy."

"Whatever you like. Ah, here's Helen with our tray."

When they had had their tea and toast and fresh fruit, Kaye went back to her room and changed into a green one-piece bathing suit exactly the color of her eyes. When she got downstairs, she went out across the back terrace, avoiding the front of the house, where she knew Creighton would be when he arrived. She swam the length of the pool ten times, then lay on a mattress at the pool's edge and sunned herself. The air was deliciously warm, and she was soon drowsing. Her thoughts were of Creighton, but they were diffuse and vaporous, almost dreamlike.

"You look sublimely comfortable."

At the sound of Creighton's voice she opened her eyes

so quickly she was almost blinded by the sudden brightness of the sun. At first she saw only the great bulk of him standing over her. Then his features became clear. He was wearing a white pullover, riding pants and boots. He was hatless, and his hair shone in the sun. He looked younger somehow—and devastatingly attractive.

"Creighton," Kaye said. "I thought you were with Aunt Alice."

"I was. We finished our business, and I came back here to see you. You probably dozed off in the sun."

"Yes, I must have."

"The pool looks very inviting. Do you mind if I have a swim with you? There are always suits and towels in the cabana."

"No," Kaye said. "No, of course not."

"I'll be back in a minute." His smile flashed for a moment, and he disappeared into the white clapboard cabana at the end of the pool.

During the few minutes he was absent, Kaye closed her eyes again. Her drowsiness was gone, though, chased by the excitement of having him near. She tried desperately not to think of him, but it was no use. He was no more than fifty feet away, taking off his clothes. There would be a brief inevitable moment when he would be standing in a tiny room of the cabana utterly naked. She could not even pretend she wouldn't like to be there with him, looking at his nakedness in a mutually accepted intimacy, seeing his body as she could now only imagine it. She tried to put the image out of her mind, yet she couldn't. She got up and dove into the pool.

She was not actually swimming as she had been earlier. She was cavorting—surface diving and backstroking and treading water. But even in the flurry of her splashing about, she knew the exact moment at which Creighton came out of the cabana. She looked up and saw him standing at the edge of the pool. He was wearing white Lastex swimming trunks. For the first time she saw the tight lithe muscles of his body, which she had only seen previously rippling beneath the fabrics of his shirts and slacks. His body was a superb work of architecture, hard and firm and symmetrical and a deep glowing bronze. The hair on his chest was fine and of the same dark brown color as his mane. It closed to a fine line that went down his abdomen. She had had little doubt earlier, but she now knew for certain that he was the most beautiful man she had ever seen.

Suddenly his body was arched in the air, then straight as an arrow it knifed through the surface of the pool and disappeared into the water. In a few seconds she felt him brush against her, and his head thrust up into the bright air only inches from her own. For a moment they both treaded water and stared at each other silently and intently. Then his hands were on her shoulders, and even in the tepid water she could feel the heat his body seemed to generate. Without warning he kissed her, and as their bodies became rigid and motionless, they sank slowly beneath the surface of the water. It seemed to Kaye she had slid into another world, a warm liquid world away from the conceits and customs and the reality of Montego, a world in which she and Creighton were all that existed, a world in which anything might be allowed to happen. Her eyes were still open, and as she pressed against Creighton's nearly naked body in the watery ambience of the pool, even time seemed not to exist. For a moment she seemed lost to all that stood between them: her own resolution to be free, Creighton's need for a woman who would be docile and pliant. But the truth—or what she thought was the truth—came rushing back to her in the liquid silence. Frothy bubbles rose around them as she struggled to get away from his embrace. For a moment longer he held her with his great strength, then suddenly he let her go. Her body shot to the surface of the pool, and as she gasped for breath, Creighton surfaced beside her. His face was utterly calm, and he was not at all breathless.

"I told you...I didn't...want that...to happen again," Kaye said as she gulped the air.

"Words," Creighton replied.

"We've told each other...how we felt...and that's how it must...."

"Words. Just words. They're meaningless between us."

Without saying any more, she swam away from him to the side of the pool and climbed out. She didn't know how he could have managed it so fast, but by the time she stood up, he had shot up out of the pool and was standing before her. His tanned body was beaded and trickling with water that shone like tiny jewels against his skin. He put his hands on her shoulders as he had in the water.

"I'm telling you, it doesn't matter what we say. It doesn't change what we feel."

He kissed her again, and she wanted to melt into him, to be one with him. But she tore herself free.

"It matters to me. I meant everything I said to you, and I won't allow you to...to...."

"Seduce you?"

"All right, then, yes. I won't allow you to seduce me."

"You seem to think if I did seduce you, it would be a proposal of marriage. Nothing could be further from the truth. My wanting you doesn't mean I want a life with you. It's you who seem to think the two things are the same."

"Good Lord! Do you really think I'd go to bed with

any man who finds me attractive? Do you really think I'm so promiscuous?''

"Kaye, I didn't—''

"I can see now I was wrong in thinking you're a gentleman. You're an absolute cad. I wish to heaven I'd never set eyes on you.''

She turned away and strode across the lawn and into the house before Creighton could say another word. She ran up the stairs and went directly to her room. In that short distance she tried to put everything—which to her now meant Creighton—out of her mind. She thought she had done it. She dried herself with a luxuriously soft bath towel, dressed and read for a while, then decided she would take a nap. She took off her clothes and slipped between the sheets of the cool, freshly made bed. She soon discovered her eyes would not stay closed, for all she saw in the darkness was Creighton, his sun-browned body glistening in the golden light of the day. Each time the image came to her, she opened her eyes in an effort to chase it away. And each time she closed them again, it returned. She could still feel his body close to hers in the warm wetness of the pool. She could still feel his lips pressed to hers insistently. She could still feel the power and strength of his body as she struggled to get away from him. And she wondered if she could ever really get away from him.

Finally, almost in desperation, she got out of bed and took a long soothing shower. She put her pink silk blouse and white cotton slacks back on, then slipped her feet into a pair of straw sandals and went downstairs.

She found Aunt Alice alone in the little sitting room. Her face bore an expression of such unmistakable sadness that Kaye was alarmed. "Auntie, what's the matter?''

"Come and sit with me for a moment, dear," Alice said.

As Kaye sat down, Alice sighed deeply. She looked older than she had that very morning, and there was a weariness about her.

"Aunt Alice, please tell me what's wrong."

"I hope you understand that, in spite of the difference in our ages, Creighton and I are very close friends. I suppose it's because of the island. You see, my dear, Jamaica is a way of life, and Creighton has a fierce loyalty to it. How clearly I remember the day he first came here. He was so young and handsome and strong. His eyes shone with youth and excitement. If only Victoria had lived. Well, there's no good in wishful thinking. Kaye, you must promise to tell no one about this. I'm the only person on the island who knows. Creighton is going to put his house up for sale and go back to Australia for good."

Kaye was astonished. She stared at her aunt for a long moment. "But this morning he . . . ."

"Yes? What is it?"

"He just didn't behave as if he were planning to—oh, I don't know, Aunt Alice. I guess it's simply hard to believe he'd leave Montego."

"I'm afraid he would. He's tried to stick it out since Victoria's death, but the memories are just too much."

"But he's going to have memories wherever he is."

"I've told him that. I'm afraid I wasn't very convincing. I don't know what we'll do without Creighton. But then I loved Montego before he came here. Yet it's hard to remember what it was like without him. Well, life goes on. It must. It's going to be a great loss."

"I'm so sorry, Aunt Alice. How soon is he going to do it?"

"He doesn't really know. He mentioned six months

ago he was considering it. By this time I thought he'd given up the idea. But today he told me he'd made up his mind.''

"It doesn't—"

Aunt Alice waited for a moment. "What, my dear?"

"I suppose I don't know him well enough to say this, but his leaving that way, for that reason, seems at odds with my impression of him." It was as much as she could say, but what she meant was that Creighton's behavior toward her gave no hint he was planning such a dramatic change in his life. She wondered vaguely if she had in any way influenced his decision.

"I can understand that," Aunt Alice said, "He's very strong. Unless you had seen him with Victoria, it would be difficult to know how profoundly sensitive he is. He sometimes goes to great lengths to hide it." She smiled and went on. "Surprisingly enough, he has a passion for the romantic poets, and there are hundreds of novels in his private library, including those of the Brontës, of all people. And there are books by Goethe and Nietzsche and Plato—whom he reads in Greek. It's really quite remarkable for a man who grew up on an Australian sheep ranch. But then Creighton is altogether a remarkable man. How we shall miss him!''

"I guess all of that is a part of him I'll never get to know—if he really is leaving."

"If Creighton says he's leaving, he's leaving. It must be terrible for him to have had to make this decision— the place he loves most on earth, destroyed for him by memories of tragedy.''

"You're truly very sad about this.''

"Yes. I love Creighton. He's very much like a son to me—another of my surrogate children.''

"I guess that makes Creighton and me brother and sister.''

Aunt Alice smiled wryly. "Not quite."

"Well, children should be dutiful. I really should go upstairs and write to mother."

"Do give her my love, and tell her what joy your visit is giving me."

"I will, darling."

As she started out of the room, Aunt Alice said, "You do remember we're due at Smitty's at half past seven?"

"How could I forget?"

Kaye did not write to her mother immediately, although she had had every intention of doing so. She sat in her room and thought about what news there was to share with her mother. She made the mistake of wondering if she should tell her about Creighton, and from that moment on she didn't think about her mother or New York or anything or anyone but Creighton Jarvis. Creighton, at one minute charming, at the next sarcastic; at one minute attentive, at the next rude; at one minute hostile, then suddenly conciliatory, as he had been when she had encountered him that very morning. She had seen him four times in three days, and each time he seemed to be a different man. Maybe all these men were Creighton. And now there was this new aspect to him—the sensitivity that Aunt Alice had just disclosed to her. It should have been difficult to imagine, but somehow it wasn't. She believed there were great depths in him that she hadn't probed. And now she probably never would. He was leaving. She understood Aunt Alice's sadness, but why should she herself feel such a sense of loss? How, in such a brief time, could he have become in any way important to her? Was it the challenge of getting to know all of him—the gruffness, the gallantry, the sadness, the tenderness? At least life with Creighton would never be dull. Good Lord, what had prompted her to such a thought? *Life with Creighton?*

It was really quite simple. In some subterranean layer of her mind she was imagining what he must have been like when Victoria Penrose Jarvis had been alive. She saw him as he must have been in his happiness. She saw him as a loving protective husband. She saw his face lighted with laughter, then realized she had never heard him laugh. She wondered if she ever would.

Well, she would see him tonight at Smitty's, and that was her last waking thought. She fell asleep and dreamed about him. She dreamed about him as her lover. She dreamed about being in his arms. She dreamed about the ecstasy of his making love to her. But there was no ecstasy in the dream, because it had no reality. She had no real idea of what his body would be like, no idea of what such intimacy with him would be like. She awoke suddenly and with a sense of panic. And she awoke with a profound sense of sadness that she would almost certainly never turn the dream into substance.

Then the strong determined part of her began to catalog everything about Creighton she had found offensive. She thought about his sarcasm, his humiliating manner, about Wellington, and she tried very hard to hate him.

She forced herself then to write the letter to her mother. When she had finished, she read it. It was pure gibberish, but she knew she wasn't likely to do any better at a second attempt, and her mother would be very distressed at not hearing from her. She put the letter into an envelope and addressed it. She'd have to find out from Aunt Alice where to mail it. It occurred to her she had missed lunch, but she wasn't at all hungry. She started to get ready for Smitty's party—and for seeing Creighton.

Lady Smith-Croydon's house was grander and more

like an English country house than any Kaye had seen in
Montego. A butler opened the door and admitted them
to a marble-floored reception hall. They crossed it and
went into a large rectangular drawing room furnished
almost entirely with English antiques. There were perhaps forty people present already. Lady Gladys was sitting on a chintz-covered sofa with a man of about forty
whom Kaye had never seen previously.

"Good evening, Alice," Smitty said.

"Good evening, Smitty."

The man stood up, and Smitty said, "I want you to
meet Kevin Wright. He arrived today from London.
Kevin, this is Lady Armstrong and her niece from New
York, Kaye Belliston."

"I'm delighted to meet you," he said, smiling.

"It's a pleasure," Lady Alice replied.

"How do you do," Kaye said. "Am I right in assum-
ing you're Kevin Wright, the playwright?"

He smiled again and said, "How nice to be recognized."

"You have a new success in the West End, haven't
you?"

"Yes, I'm happy to say. I waited until it got fully settled in after the opening and came here for a rest. I
won't rest, of course. Like a fool I'll start another play
in my first idle moment."

"That's wonderful. I've always envied writers."

"We work harder than most people think we do."

"I'm sure of that. Are we going to have the pleasure
of seeing your current play in New York?"

"Probably. Negotiations are under way to bring it
over, but it will be some time before that happens. I expect they're waiting to see how durable it will be in London."

"I suppose that's practical, but your plays are always
successful," Alice mentioned.

"Not at all, Lady Armstrong. You just don't hear about the failures. May I get you something from the bar?"

"Thank you. A dry martini for me," Alice said.

"And for me," Kaye added.

"Excuse me." He went to the end of the room, where a uniformed Jamaican stood behind the bar.

"He's quite charming," Kaye said as she sat down.

"Oh, yes. I've known Kevin for years. I adore him. How are you, Alice?"

"Well enough, I suppose. . . for an old biddy."

"You won't let me forget that, will you?"

"It was very rude."

"I thought by now you'd have come to expect rudeness from me."

"Oh, I have. But I don't have to like it."

Kaye looked around and saw they were all there: Netty and Harlan, Barney, Ellis, the Zimmermans, Amanda and a host of people she had never met or had met only casually. There was no sign of Creighton.

By the time Kevin returned with their drinks, Ellis had already hurried over to Kaye.

"Good evening, Lady Alice. Hello, Kaye. You both look especially beautiful tonight."

"Kaye looks especially beautiful," Alice said. "I look ordinarily beautiful."

"Have you met Kevin Wright, Ellis?" Smitty asked.

"Oh, yes. We met through mutual friends in London."

Netty came over to them. "Hello, Alice. How are you?"

"I'm well, Netty."

"Kaye, come along with me for a moment. I want you to meet our houseguests. Will you excuse us?"

"Of course," Smitty said. "But don't subject Kaye to that crusty old Clarence Bonner for too long."

"All right," Netty answered with a laugh. "Come on, Kaye." She spirited the younger woman off, and soon Kaye was so deep in conversation she didn't see Creighton come in. She glanced over her shoulder at Aunt Alice, and Creighton was already standing there, talking to her and Smitty. With him was a black man who was obviously Jamaican. He was dressed like, but rather more conservatively than, most of the other men. He seemed about Creighton's age, and he was extremely handsome. Kaye excused herself from the presence of Netty and her houseguests and went back to Aunt Alice and Smitty.

"Hello, Creighton," she said from behind him.

He knew the voice immediately and turned to her. He smiled at her, and this time the smile reached the amber eyes.

"Hello, Kaye. How are you?"

"I'm fine. And you?"

"Fine. I'd like you to meet a very close friend of mine. This is George Montague. George, this is Kaye Belliston, Lady Alice's niece."

He smiled a bright warm smile and said, "Creighton has told me about you. Welcome to Jamaica."

"Thank you."

"Have you enjoyed your stay so far?"

"Yes, very much. It's enchantingly beautiful."

"May I say the same of you without being considered forward?"

"Yes, indeed. No woman would consider such a gracious compliment forward."

Kaye noticed that George's accent was primarily British, but the lilt of Jamaica colored it.

"George is a great force for good in our government," Creighton said. "He's been responsible for much of the recent progress—schools, roads, social programs."

"Don't be extravagant, Creighton. I've done what I can."

"Which is a great deal. Even Smitty will admit that."

"What do you mean, 'even Smitty'?" Smitty asked.

"It was said in jest," Creighton answered.

"Like many a true word, I suppose. There's not a non-Jamaican on the island who's done more for the people than I have, and I'm proud of it. Don't denigrate my efforts."

"You know I didn't mean to."

"No, I don't know that at all."

"He was joking, Smitty," George said. "Everyone is aware how tireless and generous you've been in trying to resolve the island's problems."

"Enough of that. This is a social gathering, not a political rally," she said. "You'd better get your drinks. Dinner will be served soon."

"All right, love," Creighton replied. "Can I get anything for anyone?"

"I haven't had my second martini," Aunt Alice noted.

"Well, we can't allow you to have only one," Creighton answered, smiling.

"I'd like one, too," Kaye added. "I'll go with you."

"You stay put," Ellis said. "I'll get it for you."

"Thank you, Ellis, but I'd like to circulate a bit. There are so many people I haven't met."

Before they could move toward the bar, Barney Fairweather descended on them. In his usual blustering way he took George by the arm and didn't bother to greet anyone else. "George, I'm glad to see you here. There's something I want to talk to you about. Let's find a quiet corner."

As the two men moved off, with Barney chattering animatedly, Creighton looked at Kaye. "Let's go and get the drinks. Excuse us," he added to the others.

Creighton ushered Kaye through the crowded room toward the bar. Without looking at her, he said, "Your departure from the pool this morning was rather abrupt."

"You gave me every reason to leave abruptly."

"I was trying to give you every reason to stay."

They had reached a suddenly quiet and empty spot in the room. Kaye stopped and gazed up at him. She was aware she couldn't betray Aunt Alice's trust by telling him she knew he was planning to leave Montego, but she had to make things clear to him.

"Creighton, stop tormenting me. You know as well as I do there's nothing in our lives that will allow us to be together. We weren't meant to be together, however strong the attraction between us may be. Perhaps you were right about my not knowing how to share a man's life. . . not your life at any rate, not a life on a Jamaican plantation. . . or an Australian sheep ranch. My life has always been New York and London and Paris. It's a fast-moving sophisticated life. It's what I know and what I want. You couldn't survive the tempo of my life-style, and I'd die of boredom in yours. Can't we let it go at that?"

"I don't believe a word you're saying, and neither do you. You're right about one thing, though: there's a great deal that stands between us. There's no need for you to make up things—such as all that gibberish about life-styles. I'm not a country bumpkin, and you're not a jaded wastrel of the jet set. We're two intelligent adult human beings—a man and a woman with all the usual reasonable expectations. But neither of us is looking for a mate. Don't you realize that makes us the safest combination in the world?"

"Safe? I feel a great many things when I'm with you, Creighton, but I don't feel safe."

"Good. It's the last thing I want you to feel."

Kaye laughed in spite of herself. "You're incorrigible. You're not even making sense."

"Maybe that's what's wrong with both of us," Creighton returned in a very serious tone. "Maybe we've both been trying too hard to be sensible, trying too hard not to make any mistakes—you in the throes of your divorce, me in my grief over the loss of Victoria. It might be a good time for both of us to throw caution to the wind."

"I wonder if you could be right."

"Why don't we try it and see?"

"Because. . .I guess because I'm afraid to try it."

" 'Faint heart never won fair lady'—or man."

"I thought we weren't trying to win each other."

"All right. A lark, then. Two carefree people out for a night on the town. Or a week or a month. What's the harm?"

Everything in Kaye wanted to surrender to him. She wanted that time on the town with Creighton. She wanted to break out the champagne. She wanted to throw caution to the wind. But an essential part of her held back, for she knew a casual trivial relationship between them was impossible. They already felt too much for each other.

"Oh, how wonderful it would be!" she heard herself saying. "But it *can't* be. It really can't."

"Kaye, don't be a fool. We could—"

"Aunt Alice will be thirsting for her martini. We should get back to them."

Creighton's face hardened again, and she hated seeing the boyishness disappear. She also hated being the cause of its disappearance.

They went to the bar, collected the drinks and returned to Aunt Alice and Smitty. The rest of the evening was not unlike the others Kaye had spent in Montego.

They went in to dinner at eight. The table easily accommodated the nearly fifty guests. Kaye and Creighton found their place cards, each one adorned with a tuft of peacock feather taken from the birds that roamed Smitty's garden. They were tacitly delighted to find they were sitting next to each other. Ellis was not delighted to find he was seated at the other end of the table. The dinner was elaborate. A horde of uniformed servants came and went, serving a cold soup, then roast pheasant and platters of green vegetables and parslied potatoes. A green salad followed that, and there was a savory before dessert—which was fresh fruit and cheese. Champagne was offered throughout the meal, and, as was the custom, coffee was served in the drawing room.

Kaye was talking to Creighton, George Montague and Kevin Wright shortly after dinner when Aunt Alice came to her.

"Darling, I'm very tired. I'm going to have Henry take me home, but I insist that you stay. It's much too early for you to leave. He can come back for you."

"No, auntie. I'll leave with you."

"Nonsense. I really insist you stay."

"Please do, Kaye," Creighton said. "And Henry needn't come back, Alice. I'll see Kaye home."

"Excellent. Have a good time, my dear, and for heaven's sake, don't worry about me. I'm perfectly capable of sitting in the back of a car and being driven home. I'll see you in the morning. Good night, Creighton. George. Kevin."

They all said good-night to her, and she left.

"Have you any idea how fond I am of your aunt?" Creighton asked.

"Yes, I think I have," Kaye replied quietly.

"We all are," George said. "She's a great lady."

Kaye stayed on for more than an hour, and she and

Creighton were at each other's side for every minute of it. There was somehow a congeniality between them that had never so fully existed previously. They laughed and chatted and drank with the other guests, and their togetherness escaped no one. Several times Kaye told Creighton that she felt she should leave, that she was concerned about Aunt Alice. It took very little persuasion on Creighton's part to keep her there. She didn't really want to desert either the party or Creighton.

Finally, in a rare moment of quiet, she looked up at him and said, "Creighton, I'm sorry, but I really must go now. Aunt Alice—"

"Alice is at home in her cozy bed, sound and blissfully asleep. She doesn't need—"

"I will not neglect her."

"All right," he said reluctantly. "You're a dutiful girl, and I admire a sense of duty. We'll go."

As they looked for Smitty, they encountered the others—the Marlowes and the Zimmermans and a sulky Ellis—and said good-night to them. They found Smitty holding forth in a corner of the drawing room.

"Thank you, Smitty, for yet another magnificent feast," Creighton acknowledged.

"You're most welcome, Creighton. I hope it won't be long before we have one of *your* magnificent feasts."

"It may not be," he answered. "I think I'm beginning to feel gregarious again."

"Splendid!"

"Good night, Lady Smith-Croydon," Kaye said. "And thank you so much for asking me."

"It will be the last time if you don't cease calling me Lady Smith-Croydon. From Alice's niece, indeed. You've been in Montego long enough to behave better."

"All right," Kaye said. "Good night, Smitty."

As they drove toward Traymore, the rich scent of bougainvillea was omnipresent. Kaye felt relaxed in the beauty and lushness of it all. The moonlight was soft and silvery, and the steady hum of the engine was soothing. Kaye was fully aware that the lovely, gay, untroubled evening with Creighton contributed more than anything else to her feeling of well-being. It was a profound and new delight for her to be with him during an evening unmarred and uninterrupted by bickering and sarcasm and doubt. Yet now, as she cast a sidelong glance and saw the chiseled profile in the diffuse light of the moon, the doubt and concern began to flow back into her. Of course it was pleasant when Creighton made an effort to be charming. No, that was unfair. It was pleasant when they *both* made an effort. But the pleasantness led to complacency, and her defenses came tumbling down, and that could only lead to her giving in to her desire for him, and that could only lead to. . . .

She looked away from him and told herself it could only lead to everything she'd been telling herself she didn't want. And what was worse, the more she saw of Creighton, the less sure she was she didn't want it. She would not, could not, let her heart tell her head what to do. Only children and fools did that, and she was neither. How she resented this confusion! She couldn't make any decision until her mind stopped flip-flopping. She wasn't used to indecision and uncertainty. She was used to composure and control, to having things on her own terms. She was not accustomed to obsessive desire, and her desire for Creighton made her angry with herself; its strength and persistence frightened her.

She could not have known that Creighton was experiencing much the same dilemma. In spite of his great strength of character and his iron self-control, he felt not only desire but a need for her. And he felt the same

resentment at his loss of balance Kaye felt at hers. He had
been unable to shake the sadness, the profound sense of
loss, at his wife's death. They had had nearly everything a
man and woman could want. When Victoria had told
him she was pregnant, he could hardly believe God could
see fit to bless them even further. Then Victoria had lost
the baby and died bearing it, and all of it was gone—all
the joy, all the wonder, all the perfection. The sudden
emptiness had staggered him, and soon the emptiness
was filled with a crushing sorrow that divested everything
else of meaning. He had gone on with his life, but without
purpose, without apparent reason, drifting in the echo-
ing hollowness of every day, indifferent to everything but
his loss. He was a survivor, everyone told him, and indeed he had survived. But for what? What good was it?
Even now the seeming recovery was superficial. Nothing
inside him had changed.

Now suddenly Kaye had brought the possibility of
golden sunlight. He told himself he didn't want it. He
told himself everything in life was temporary and it was
better to live with nothingness than to have everything
and risk losing it. He would not take the risk again. He
could not survive again.

The Land Rover made its way across the face of the
mountain toward Traymore. When they pulled into the
turnaround, the white-columned facade was bathed in
moonlight, which gave it a ghostly beauty. Creighton
turned off the ignition, and there was a vaulted silence as
the engine died. They sat without speaking for a brief
moment.

Kaye had intended to say, "Thanks for the lift." She
had rehearsed it in her mind as they drove home. But
without warning, as if someone else were speaking, she
heard herself saying, "It was a lovely evening. Would
you like a nightcap?"

Creighton didn't answer immediately. Then he turned to her and looked at her, his eyes filled with the lingering sadness she had seen in them previously. "I think not," he said, and Kaye had a sudden sinking feeling.

"A stroll through Aunt Alice's wonderful garden?"

He was smiling now, a smile of unexpected warmth. Kaye returned the smile, her heart suddenly lifting.

"All right," he said.

They got out of the Rover and walked toward the pool, beyond which the vast lawn and the garden lay drenched in moonlight.

"Do you know that Alice has the most beautiful garden in Montego? She's somehow managed to combine the serenity of an English garden with the natural wildness of Jamaica. It's really quite—" He broke off abruptly, stopped walking and speaking and stood for a moment like a towering marble statue. "Why am I going on about your aunt's garden? It has nothing to do with what I want to say. I'm a man, Kaye, a man of control and discipline. Yet when I'm alone with you, I can't even manage to make sense."

He looked down at her pale oval face framed by cascades of chestnut hair, and for a moment they stared into each other's eyes. Kaye turned away quickly and walked a few steps ahead of him.

They reached the end of the garden, where, beyond the low wrought-iron fence, the verdant land sloped suddenly and steeply down toward the bay. Far below them was the dark blue water in which two docked cruise ships lay at anchor, their hundreds of lights twinkling and reflecting on the water's surface. The faint music of steel bands wafted and faded on the soft breeze. They stood in silence for a long time.

"It's all so very beautiful, Creighton," Kaye said quietly.

"Yes. What I wanted to say is that I've been in this garden hundreds of times, but it's never seemed as beautiful as it is tonight. Kaye, I'm not a romantic; I'm not a poet. I'm a clumsy Australian sheep rancher. But for me, it's.... You make the garden, the sea, the moon, all of Montego, more beautiful than it's ever been without you."

"You are a romantic, Creighton. I know you try to hide it, but you can't fool me. Even in this brief time I know you too well. There's a poet beneath that crusty exterior—a kind, gentle, gallant poet. I wish you'd let me know *that* Creighton Jarvis."

"Do you?"

"Yes."

He felt his resolve flooding away. His mind reached out to check the recklessness of his heart, but suddenly there was nothing else but Kaye and the moonlight and the heavy perfume of the myriad flowers and the quiet surging and waning of the music from below them. He longed to feel her close to him, to feel the warmth of her body against his, but his arms seemed leaden at his sides.

Without warning all the sheer physical desire he had buried in the sorrow of losing Victoria rushed through his body. He had forgotten what it was to want a woman of grace and beauty and passion, and the unexpected uninvited rediscovery overwhelmed him.

Kaye, too, was paralyzed by her desire for him. She wanted to partake of his strength and his manhood. She wanted to give up her own strength to his, to let the mantle of cold resolve fall away forever and take her place in his protecting arms.

They stood looking at each other for a long moment, these unwilling lovers, trapped in their mutual passion, unable to speak their longing, yet seeming unable, too, to return to the cold emptiness they had known before they had met. Silently and slowly Creighton reached out and touched her hair. The touch of his large strong hand was as light as the whisper of the breeze. He could feel her trembling now. He bent to her and touched her mouth with his lips. His lips were full and warm and firm. His arms slipped around her, and she moved against him, embracing him. She had never before known such gentleness mixed with rushing male strength. It summoned deep inside her a momentary response of utter abandon, and they stood wrapped in each other's arms. There was no past, no sorrow, no memory. There was only now.

He released her as slowly and gently as he had embraced her. He looked down into her sea-green eyes and saw the tears flow slowly onto her cheeks. He took her chin in his hand, bent to her again and touched her cheeks with his lips. Nothing mattered to Kaye now except Creighton's closeness, the musky smoldering warmth of his body pressed against hers. There were no thoughts or doubts or arguments in her mind. There was only the feel of his mouth against her cheek, kissing away her tears and all her fears and sorrows with them. His arms went around her again, and their sinewy strength drew her to him. She felt as if she were melting into his body, as if they were becoming one being, as if her soft unblemished flesh and his rock-hard muscles were mingling in a communion of love.

As her arms reached to encircle his broad torso, her fingers dug into his back, clutching him even closer to her. He couldn't be close enough to satisfy her need for him. He kissed her again, and even though their open mouths were pressed together, tongues probing, even though his chest was crushed against her breasts and his bulging thighs were pushed against hers, it was not enough. She clung to him and felt like a tiny helpless doll against the massiveness of his body. She was enthralled by the feeling of being possessed by him, physically possessed and contained in his arms. If the rest of her life were to consist of only one prolonged moment, she would want it to be this one.

He kissed her forehead and her eyes and her nose. He pressed his face against hers, and his lips were next to her ear. She could feel the warm sweet whisper of his breath.

"Kaye," he murmured. "Kaye, come back to Penrose with me."

She didn't answer. She couldn't answer. He freed her from his embrace and took her hand. Gently he began to lead her back toward the Land Rover. Unable to resist the lure of him, she felt herself moving as if she were in a dream. She was trailing, floating behind him, when suddenly the reality of what she was doing flooded back to her. She stopped moving, feeling the strong pull of him against her resistance. He stopped, too, and turned to her.

"Creighton," she said. "I can't."

He stared at her, and even in the dim silvery moonlight, she could see that the expression on his face had hardened. "Why?" he asked. "For God's sake, why?"

"For all the reasons I've already told you. Creighton, you know I want to—more than anything in the world. But I can't."

She saw the gemstone eyes again, but now they weren't glowing with warmth; they were glinting coldly in the moonlight.

"Not more than two minutes ago you gave me every indication those reasons were a thing of the past."

"They don't...disappear...just like that," she said weakly.

"Mine did. My memories of Victoria, my . . . my fear of loving again—all of it became what it should be: part of the past. It still exists; it always will. But it was separate from you and me. I thought that had happened to you, too."

"So did I. For a minute, in your arms, close to you."

"For a minute? Is that all it meant to you?"

"Of course not. Creighton, please try to understand. . . ."

"There's only one way you can make me understand. Come back with me to Penrose."

"Creighton . . . Creighton, I can't."

"I'm sorry, Kaye. I misjudged you. I thought you were above playing games. I thought you were too honest, too decent, to toy with me. I can see now I was wrong. This walk in the moonlit garden was your idea. I tried to resist. You made yourself as beautiful and inviting as you could in this damned moonlight. I tried to resist that, too, and I couldn't. I was willing to throw everything aside for you—my pride, my caution, my judgment, my instincts. That's obviously all you wanted, because as soon as you saw you'd won, you turned away from me. I'm not easily hurt, but I don't think I'll ever forgive you for that."

He turned and strode across the garden to the Land Rover, disappearing into the darkness, and Kaye heard the sound of the engine as it roared into life, then faded rapidly in the distance.

As she stood there in the night, her heart ached with humiliation. Never had a kiss thrilled her as Creighton's had. Never had the closeness of an excited impassioned male body caused her such ecstasy. Yet she had clung to her resolve, not to Creighton's strength and masculinity.

She was filled with confusion as she ran across the

garden and went upstairs as quietly as she could so as not to wake Aunt Alice. She couldn't face anyone with her mind dizzied and the tears streaming down her face. She threw herself on the bed and wept until she could weep no more. She undressed and got into bed, where she lay for hours before she finally fell into a troubled sleep.

# CHAPTER THREE

KAYE WOKE UP shortly after dawn. The memory of what had happened with Creighton instantly shot into her brain and burned there painfully. She remembered his harsh words in the minutes just before he left her. They were branded like fiery script across the surface of her mind. At first she felt angry and misused, but as she heard the words again in her mind, she wondered if her behavior hadn't justified them. Slowly and with devastating certainty she was filled with remorse. She remembered the gently whispering touch of his hand. She remembered his warm full lips on hers. She remembered the heat and hardness of his body as it pressed against hers. Before she could check herself, she heard the words in her mind: *why, why did I reject him?* She wasn't ready to accept the total guilt for what had happened, and she answered her own question almost aloud: *because I don't want any man, and I mustn't let foolish romantic impulses lead me away from that sane idea.* She didn't convince herself at all.

She threw back the sheet and got out of bed. She went through the open French doors onto the balcony and looked down at the garden, flaming and glorious in the morning sun. For a moment she thought she saw herself and Creighton standing together in the distance. How ridiculous! They hadn't even been in the south garden but in the one on the other side of the house. She shook her head to try to ward off the memory. She turned and went back into the bedroom.

She hadn't slept well, waking periodically from wild, unpleasant, seemingly meaningless dreams. She was tired. She got back into bed and tried vainly to sleep. She kept hearing Creighton's voice and feeling his hands, his lips, his body. Each time she closed her eyes, she relived the whole experience in all its awfulness and all its brief passion. At last she threw off the sheet and got out of bed. As she paced the room, it suddenly all seemed clear to her. She hadn't recovered from the emotional devastation of the divorce. For perhaps the first time in her life she was vulnerable, and Creighton, deliberately or not, was playing on that vulnerability. Her only salvation was to stick firmly to her resolve, and to do that, she would have to leave Montego. She was afraid of what might happen if she didn't.

She went to the closet and took out a suitcase. She tossed it onto the bed and began stuffing clothes into it with unaccustomed wildness. When the first suitcase was filled, she took out another. She went back and forth frantically from closet to suitcase, dumping armfuls of clothing into the cases. There was a knock. She stopped her wild activity suddenly and looked toward the door. After a moment she said, "Yes?"

"Kaye, dear, it's Aunt Alice. I heard you stirring. Are you all right?"

"Yes, auntie. I'm all right."

"May I come in?"

Kaye hesitated. She could hardly say no, but she had wanted to break the news of her leaving to Aunt Alice slowly and gently, with some made-up excuse. This way it would be harsh and sudden. There was no help for it, though. She went to the door and opened it.

"Of course you can come in, Aunt Alice."

Aunt Alice took a few steps into the room and stopped, staring at the suitcases on the bed. She was silent for a moment. "Kaye, I'd like you to come downstairs. I want to talk with you." She left the room, closing the door behind her.

Hearing her aunt's words, spoken firmly and dispassionately, and staring now at the closed door, Kaye felt despondent. It seemed nothing she did was right. She showered hurriedly, dressed in slacks and a blouse and went downstairs. Aunt Alice was on the veranda with the usual breakfast tray before her.

"Aunt Alice?"

"Hello, dear. Do sit down here by me."

Kaye sat down and poured herself a cup of tea.

"I take it you're leaving," Aunt Alice said.

"Yes."

"Would you like to tell me why? I realize it's none of my affair, but . . . ."

"Of course it's your affair, darling, and it must seem terribly ungrateful of me to leave so suddenly."

"I'm not concerned about gratitude. Your visit in no way puts you in my debt. But I am concerned about your welfare."

"I'm all right, auntie. Honestly I am."

"I'm sorry, but I don't believe you. Kaye, I hope you'll believe I wasn't snooping, but last night when I came home, my headache worsened. I had trouble getting to sleep. I heard a car pull into the driveway, and it wakened me from my dozing. I still had the headache, and I thought some fresh air might help. I went out onto my balcony, and I saw you and Creighton in the garden—in each other's arms. I heard nothing. Then a cloud drifted across the moon, and I lost sight of you. When the moonlight shone again, I saw him turn and walk away—angrily, it seemed. And now this morning you're leaving. You're under no obligation to explain, but I would be happy if you did."

Kaye hesitated for a moment. "Of course I'll explain, Aunt Alice. And I'll be honest with you...perhaps more honest than I've been with myself. I told you when I got here that I wasn't on the rebound, and I meant it. Yet in spite of everything I've done to prevent it...in spite of everything we've both done to prevent it, even in the few times we've been together, I've found myself becoming involved with Creighton. It'd only just begun, and last night it ended, but I'm afraid of what might happen if I stay in Montego. You said yourself you wanted me to avoid him. That's impossible as long as I'm in Montego. So I'm afraid I must leave. I don't want to, auntie. I love being here in this beautiful place with you. But I don't see any other solution."

Aunt Alice was quiet for a while. "Where will you go?"

"I don't know. This would have been the perfect place if it hadn't been for...." She stopped.

"For Creighton?"

"Yes."

"I did tell you to avoid him, but I also told you not to shut out what life has to offer. Perhaps both you and Creighton are trying too hard to keep from getting hurt."

Kaye looked at her in astonishment. She had known it would be sad to Aunt Alice to have her leave so soon and so suddenly, but she had been certain her aunt would concur with her decision. Now she seemed to be on the verge of counseling her to stay. Kaye didn't understand.

"You surely don't think I should stay?"

"I don't know. I thought about it most of the night. I

wondered if I were selfish. You see, my dear, if there were an attachment between you and Creighton, it might keep *him* from leaving. It must be difficult for you to understand why it's so important to me that he stay. It's more than my affection for him. A number of people—people of what Smitty calls 'our society'—have already left the island. They're afraid—afraid the poverty and the political instability will lead to great trouble. It's entirely possible, of course, but in all truth we are a staple of the island's economy. Our leaving can only be detrimental to the welfare of the native Jamaicans, and in the long run it's nothing more than running away—which is cowardly. That wouldn't be Creighton's reason for leaving, but it would have the same effect. It is people like Creighton and George Montague who bring calm and stability to a potentially explosive situation, and losing them would be a loss to us all—native and alien alike. But finally I doubted that was the reason for my concern, and this morning when I saw you packing, I knew it. You see, my darling, I don't want *you* to run away.''

"Aunt Alice, I'm not—"

"Please listen to me. You've already run away once. I don't mean by divorcing Rod. I believe that was inevitable and psychologically healthful, and I believe it was a good thing for you to come here, even if it was an escape. But if you leave here without even a destination, you'll truly be running away. And you can't go on doing it endlessly. You've got to resume your life.''

"By staying here, where I'll be in constant contact with Creighton?''

"Perhaps. At least you'd be dealing with Creighton. You'd be dealing with what you feel for him—whatever it is—and what he apparently feels for you. Reject him if you wish, or. . . or accept him if you find that you love him.''

*"Love him?"*

"Kaye, I'm old, but I'm not blind. One can see and feel the tension between you when you're together."

"And that's what it is—tension. And I hope nothing more."

"You said you'd be honest with me."

"All right. I admit there's desire between us—an almost overwhelming desire. But is that enough?"

"Of course not. I've known you since you were an infant. I've watched you grow into a lovely girl and a beautiful young woman with poise and charm and dignity. You are not a wanton, driven by mindless physical need. If you have a burning passion for Creighton, it's based on something other than mere sex. Oh, don't be shocked to hear your staid old aunt say such things. Your Uncle Alex and I were physically intimate, passionately intimate, until the very end of his life. I'm simply saying you owe it to yourself and to Creighton— and he owes it to you and to himself—not to abandon whatever is between you until you're certain it's worthless or impossible or doesn't really exist at all."

"It exists, and I'm sure it isn't worthless, but it *is* impossible. I know that instinctively."

"Some things we *think* we know instinctively, only to find out later to our paralyzing regret that we were wrong. I know I urged you to stay away from Creighton as much as you could, but that was before anything happened between you. Now that it's begun, I beg you not to leave—not just yet. Don't leave, never to know what might have been. Face it. Let yourself be hurt, if need be. You may as well not live at all as go through life resisting all temptation because it might end in pain. Life without pain is only a kind of prolonged death."

Kaye had no answer for her aunt. Her wisdom was unmistakable, but her advice was hard. Somewhere in the distance, under Aunt Alice's words, she had heard the ringing of a telephone. Now Henry came onto the terrace and said, "The telephone call is for you, Miss Belliston."

"For me?" She turned to Aunt Alice, who sat staring at her with an expression of consummate calm. "Excuse me."

Kaye went into the drawing room and picked up the phone, filled with apprehension. She wasn't sure immediately whether she was relieved or disappointed to hear Amanda's voice.

"Kaye, dear, how are you?"

"I'm fine, Amanda. How are you?"

"I'm well, thank you. I do get a little bored sometimes with grandmother's endless string of guests, but aside from that, all is well. In a way that's why I called you. You're one of my paths to temporary freedom. You do remember that we have a standing date for Doctor's Cave?"

"Yes, of course."

"I'm not pushing you. I just didn't want you to forget." There was a pause, as if Amanda were hoping Kaye would say something.

"I'm looking forward to it, but I do want to spend a bit more time with Aunt Alice before I go running off on excursions."

"Of course you do. I understand perfectly. This was just a reminder. Give your aunt my love. I'm sure we'll see each other soon wherever the next dinner party's going to be."

Kaye laughed and said, "I'm sure we will. And we'll keep that date soon."

"Wonderful. Goodbye, Kaye."

As Kaye hung up, she thought the telephone call was somehow odd. Amanda seemed a bit more anxious than there was reason for her to be. Well, maybe she simply did want to get away from her grandmother's guests. There was nothing to be suspicious about.

When she reached the veranda, Aunt Alice looked up at her expectantly.

"It wasn't Creighton, auntie. It was Amanda. But it doesn't matter. I'm going to sit down with you and eat tons of that delicious fruit. Then I'm going upstairs to unpack. I'm going to stay, Aunt Alice."

"You're doing the right thing, my dear, and I'm delighted," Aunt Alice said.

They had a long leisurely breakfast during which Kaye seemed buoyant, perhaps because both she and Aunt Alice studiously avoided mentioning Creighton. After breakfast Kaye went up to her room and wrote letters. After completing her correspondence, she changed into a bright pink one-piece bathing suit and went downstairs again. Aunt Alice was still on the veranda, discussing menus with Helen. When she saw Kaye, she stopped talking in midsentence, and her eyes lit up.

"Now that's the ticket, my dear girl," she said. "Swim. Soak up the sun. Relax. I'm sure it will add to your pleasure to know we have no dinner engagement for tonight or tomorrow night or the night after that. We're as free as birds, and if you play backgammon, there won't be a dull moment."

"I play, and I love it. I warn you, I'm very good," Kaye said.

"Ah, we'll see about that. My blood actually thickens at the thought of an untried opponent. We'll have a game before dinner. Expect no mercy because you're my niece. I'm a gentle old lady in everything else, but I'm ruthless at backgammon. Go and have your swim, and I'll see you at lunch."

Kaye went to the pool and did all the things she had

expected to do since the minute she had left New York. She dived in and swam the length of the pool several times, her long slim body cutting the water without a splash. She climbed out and rubbed her body with soft luxuriant cocoa butter. She lay on a chaise longue by the side of the pool, letting the warm mild sun drench her. And she was alone. At last, she told herself, she was doing what she had come to Montego to do. She was alone.

But it was no good. She knew at every moment that thoughts of Creighton were with her. She felt as if she might never be truly alone again—ever. Her body shuddered, as though she were chilled, when a memory of his touch came back to her. She smiled in blissful privacy as she remembered the touch of his lips on hers. She pulled back her shoulders and thrust her face toward the sun to shake off his presence in her mind. None of it did any good. She dozed in the tepid air, half dreaming of him, and awakened startled, expecting to find him standing over her—and riddled with disappointment that he was not.

At twelve-thirty she went upstairs to bathe and change into a silk blouse and white slacks and sandals, to be ready to lunch with Aunt Alice. One thing she was sure of: she was looking forward to that and to at least three days and nights of being alone with her dear aunt without the intrusions and obligations dinner parties brought and without the heady consternation being with Creighton caused her. She did not know she owed this brief freedom to Aunt Alice, who had canceled two dinner invitations, pleading to her hostesses that she and her niece had had barely a moment together—which was an acceptable excuse. But more importantly it would give Kaye a breathing spell in which to collect her thoughts about Creighton. The hiatus could not last for

long, but Alice felt Kaye needed it, and she was as ferocious as a lioness protecting a cub.

They lunched long and peacefully in the shade of the
veranda and walked in the south garden afterward.
They reminisced about Kaye's mother and father, and
Alice told long enchanting anecdotes about London and
the days of Alex's courtship. The shadow of Creighton
was never far from Kaye, but Aunt Alice's soothing
presence seemed to make everything bearable. As they
had their martinis before dinner, Alice trounced her
niece at backgammon. She was every bit as ruthless as
she had promised to be. She won with undisguised joy
and relish, and Kaye enjoyed the victories almost as
much as Alice herself did.

The three days of freedom passed in this dreamlike
calm, haunted though they were for Kaye by thoughts
of Creighton. They never mentioned his name, but he
was with them—with them both—as surely as if he ac-
companied them on their walks and sat with them at
dinner.

On the fourth night they went to a dinner party at the
home of a couple who had just returned from a month-
long visit to London and whom Kaye had not met previously. She went to the party breathlessly primed for a
meeting with Creighton, but he wasn't there. No one
asked about his absence, and no one volunteered any information. Kaye found herself constantly looking over
her shoulder for a glimpse of him as he entered the
house, but he never arrived. She told herself it didn't
matter, yet her heart ached at not seeing him. As they
drove home from the party in the Rolls, Aunt Alice
talked idly about the food and the guests and Barney
Fairweather's eccentricities and Smitty's new diamond
brooch. She never once mentioned Creighton's name or
admitted she knew how deeply Kaye had missed him.

Early the next evening Aunt Alice came to Kaye in the little sitting room where she was reading and told her she had a slight headache and would like to have a dinner tray in her room. She was very solicitous about Kaye's being alone, and Kaye, of course, assured her it would be perfectly all right. Helen had fixed a dinner of cold soup and curried chicken and salad. People needed time to be alone, they both agreed.

Aunt Alice had not been in her room for more than half an hour before Kaye, sitting on the veranda with her book, heard the sound of an automobile engine. She looked up to see Creighton's Land Rover approaching the house. She saw it with a mixture of excitement and apprehension. What was he doing at Traymore? She had learned enough about Montego to know that people did not come by unannounced. Yet here he was without even a telephone call preceding him. The Rover stopped before the house, and Creighton got out. As he started up the stairs to the veranda, Kaye noticed that his polo shirt, which was stretched tightly across the taut muscles of his chest, was exactly the deep amber color of his eyes. He was wearing white cotton slacks and white patent loafers without socks—the formal uniform. He was ready for any occasion.

"Good evening, Kaye," he said. His tone was utterly casual.

"Good evening," she answered. They stood for a moment in awkward silence.

"Is Lady Alice about?" Creighton asked at last.

"I'm afraid she's retired. She has a headache. I wouldn't like to disturb her."

"I wouldn't want you to." There was the silence again. "Well, you might offer me a drink."

Kaye was disconcerted, but she steadied herself and said, "Oh, of course. What would you like?"

"Don't you remember?"

"It's...Scotch, isn't it?"

"Yes, with a splash of water, no ice. Look, Kaye, I know the house better than you do. I'll make it for myself."

She followed him into the drawing room and watched as he poured his drink. He turned to her and said, "Can I get something for you?"

"No. No, thank you."

He sipped his drink and stared at her over the rim of the glass. "Kaye, I'm afraid I was rude to you the other night. Let me make it up to you."

"Creighton, there's no need to—"

"Please. Lady Alice is indisposed, and obviously neither of us has dinner plans. Let me take you to Round Hill. It's a complex of privately owned cottages, but at its center is a wonderful inn and restaurant. They serve a beautiful buffet on the beach. Everything cooked over a charcoal pit. They have lobster and chicken and chops, cold crisp salads—and moonlight on the sea. I know you'll like it."

It was there again in her mind—the confusion and the uncertainty. And the temptation. She knew before she spoke she was going to accept the invitation.

"It sounds lovely."

"Well, let's go, then."

She held out her hands, palms up, and asked, "Am I dressed properly?"

"Properly and beautifully. It's quite casual, really—candles in hurricane lamps, soft torchlight, the sky and the stars. And there'll be a moon tonight. Shall we go, then?"

"I'd like to very much."

They chatted during the drive to Round Hill, each cautious not to say anything that would touch a nerve in the other. The result was a pleasant calm between them, as if their past storms had never existed. When they reached Round Hill, Kaye was fascinated by the place. It was a sprawling complex of cottages, some small and cozy, some large and elaborate. The road wound up the hill toward the hotel and restaurant, snaking through the scattered houses. At almost all of them people were having drinks and dinner on patios and terraces. It all seemed gentle and civilized and free from tension. Kaye felt relaxed and happy.

"Round Hill is very beautiful," she said.

"Yes. I lived here for a while. That is, Victoria and I lived here while our house was being built. It was almost a year, and we were very happy." He stopped abruptly, as if he were lost in a reverie.

Kaye waited for a long moment, not knowing what to say. When she did speak, there seemed to be an intimacy in her words. "You must still miss her very much."

He answered without hesitation. "I do. But I've learned something important since her death. I've learned the difference between when I'm feeling sad and when I'm merely feeling sorry for myself. It helps to know that."

"How wise of you."

"Oh, not really. Life goes on. Death, separation—" he glanced at her "—divorce—they're all just interruptions in the process of being alive. Being happy again can make you feel disloyal to the person you've lost, but that's a great mistake—a mistake I think we may both be making. Oh, here we are. They'll park the car for us. We needn't have a care in the world." He looked at her again, this time more steadily, and smiled. Kaye felt warm and comfortable and somehow reassured.

They climbed the steps to the sprawling main dining room of the restaurant. The maître d'. greeted Creighton by name and escorted Kaye and him to the terrace. They walked down the long flight of stairs to the beach. It was just as Creighton had described it. There were trestle tables laden with food and smaller tables covered with pale blue linen cloths. The entire scene was softened and mellowed by the flickering light of torches and candles. The music of stringed instruments wafted from somewhere in a grove of palm trees and mingled with the gentle sound of the surf. It was altogether enchanting.

A waiter showed them to a table, and they ordered drinks. They sat in silence for a moment until Kaye said, "Creighton, this is absolutely beautiful."

"I'm glad. I wanted you to like it."

"Did you?"

"Yes. It makes me very happy when you're pleased."

"I am pleased. . .with the entire evening."

"We should make a vow to keep it as it is. No harsh words. Agreed?"

"Agreed. On one condition."

"What is it?"

"Tell me the truth. Was it entirely coincidence that Aunt Alice was indisposed and that you arrived unexpectedly just in time to invite me to dinner?"

Creighton smiled shyly. "Not entirely. It was more collusion than coincidence. I hasten to add it was Alice's idea. I accepted the suggestion eagerly, but I didn't invent the plan."

"I think I'll have to speak sharply to my aunt."

"I don't think you will."

"No," Kaye agreed. "Not when the result of her scheming is so pleasant."

The waiter brought their drinks, and after a few minutes they went to the buffet tables and selected dinner. In a little while their plates, heaped with slices of cold meats and vegetable salads, were brought to their table. Creighton ordered a chilled white wine and they ate at a leisurely pace that seemed timed to the gentle rhythm of the surf.

As they were finishing their coffee after dinner, Creighton said, "How about a walk on the beach? Mild exercise after eating is just what the doctor ordered."

"I'd love it."

Creighton paid the check, and they started strolling along the shore. The moon was low in the sky and threw a streak of silver across the calm sapphire surface of the sea. When they had walked a few yards, Creighton took Kaye's hand. He didn't speak or look at her. He simply let their fingers touch for only seconds, then gently gripped her hand. She made no move to resist.

"I was thinking about you today," Creighton said after a moment. "I was riding Wellington out to a new sugarcane field, and I couldn't help remembering our ride together. Somehow it seems a very long time ago. Oh, I know it wasn't, but I've told you before it seems as if I've known you forever. That's what I was thinking about—how little I really know about you... where you were born, where you went to school, who your friends were... all the little details that make up a life."

"I have no secrets, Creighton," Kaye answered. "My life's been unspectacular. I'm not sure how well you know New York society, but you wouldn't have to know much to make up a fairly accurate biography of me. The schools, the clubs, the charities... even my marriage was predictable. My divorce, too, I suppose. I'm glad we met after all that nonsense was over. I think I like myself better now."

"I'm glad to have met you at your best."

They looked at each other for the first time since they'd begun their walk, Creighton down at her from his great height, Kaye tilting her head upward toward him. Their eyes met, and they smiled. There was a sudden intimacy between them that made them both feel shy. They turned their glances away and continued their hand-in-hand walk in another silence.

After a while, and without a word, Creighton disengaged her hand and slipped his arm around her waist. Kaye was in no way startled or surprised. She waited for a moment, then put her hand on Creighton's, which now rested on her hip.

In that instant it was all there again—the same electric warmth she felt whenever she touched Creighton's body, the same massiveness of his hand, which made her own hand seem like a butterfly perched on the trunk of a gigantic oak tree. Yet it was somehow different. Her will to resist him seemed to have fled. In the calm and beauty of the night she imagined what it would be like to give herself to him freely, without any thoughts of what was practical or reasonable. She imagined what it would be like to submerge herself in the sheer romance of being possessed by him, of loving him and being loved by him. The continuing silence was magical. Nothing interrupted her fantasy. It was caressed by the sound of the sea and the soft whisper of the breeze.

"Why don't you stop being Miss Kaye Belliston of New York and take off your shoes?" Creighton asked quietly. "You'd find it a lot easier to walk in the sand."

"And what would I do with them? It would be kind of awkward to carry them."

"Why must you be so bloody pragmatic? We'd leave them right here on the beach and pick them up on our way back. If we come back this way. And what if we don't? Does a pair of shoes matter? This night is unique; it can't come again. The shoes are expendable."

She looked up at him and smiled a wry knowing smile

that Creighton had never seen previously. She put her hand on his shoulder and said, "Steady me."

Perched first on one leg, then the other, she took off both shoes with surprising grace. She pinched them between her thumb and fingers and placed them neatly side by side on the sand.

Creighton looked at her, shaking his head. "That won't do at all." He picked up the shoes, kept one and handed one to Kaye. "Now you throw one, and I'll throw the other."

Her voice trembled on her laughter as she said, "Creighton, you're crazy. Why would we want to...?"

"Go on, throw yours first. There, toward the palm trees."

"I...."

"Go on."

She turned and tossed the shoe with all her strength, and suddenly, miraculously, she felt a sense of freedom she hadn't felt since she'd been a young girl.

"That's the way!" Creighton said, pitching the second shoe after the first. "There we go!"

Kaye stared after the lost shoes for a moment and asked, "Why in the world did we do that?"

"Does everything always have to have a reason?"

"I don't know. It always has for me."

"Too bad for you," Creighton said. "But if you need a reason, I'll give you one. We don't know where the shoes are, do we?"

"No, we certainly don't."

"And by the time we come back—if we come back—the moon may be paler...or gone completely. It will be very difficult to find the shoes. It will probably take us a very long time—all the more time for us to be together without your being able to come up with a single excuse for leaving my presence."

Kaye put her hands on his shoulders and said, "Oh, Creighton, I don't want an excuse for leaving your presence."

"Ever?"

"I don't know about 'ever,' but not for now. Not for tonight."

He put his arms around her and held her to him, not kissing her but encompassing her. Over his shoulder she saw the moon—a great pale disk hanging just above the sea. The warmth of his body, emanating through the thin cotton of his shirt and slacks, seemed to soak into her own body, and it thrilled her. She felt herself standing on the edge of an abyss— an abyss that contained all the joys and pleasures of life—and she felt ready to plunge into it without care, without caution.

Then the moon disappeared, and Creighton's open mouth was on hers, his warm firm lips trying to devour her. And she wanted them to. She wanted their bodies to be entwined, enmeshed and finally one. Nothing else mattered.

His mouth left hers and was suddenly pressed against her ear. It moved slowly, warmly, moistly along the side of her neck, then to her throat. Somehow, deftly and gently, he had undone the top buttons of her blouse. He slipped it off her shoulders as his mouth moved downward from her throat. His lips were eager as they kissed her breasts, yet his every movement was a caress, filled with tenderness. Kaye was engulfed by a sense of ecstasy she had never felt previously.

He pulled away from her, and she was looking at his face, all darkness with the moon behind him. She was startled and confused by his withdrawal. She could not see his expression.

When he spoke, his voice was quiet and breathless and throaty. "Oh, Kaye. I could have you now . . . right now, here. We both know that. I could take your hand and lead you into that grove of palm trees, and we'd lie down together on the long cool grass, softer than any bed man ever manufactured. For a short blessed time we wouldn't be Kaye and Creighton; we'd be one person. You must know there's nothing in God's world I want more. But I know now, as surely as that moon hangs in the sky behind me, that I love you, and I won't have you unless it's sanctified by your loving me, too. I won't cheapen what I feel for you. It's got to be us, together, against all the rest of the world. It wouldn't be any good any other way. But I want you to know I'll wait for that till the end of the world if I have to.''

"Oh, Creighton! My darling Creighton! I *would* have gone with you. You know that. But it's the Creighton who wouldn't take me that I want to. . . .''

"Say it. Don't hold back now.''

"That I want to. . . love. I don't know if I love you. Maybe I love you and am too afraid to admit it.''

"Afraid of what?''

"Of. . . the giving. . . of the involvement, of the commitment.''

"All right.'' He put his hands on her naked shoulders. "Be afraid of the commitment. Be afraid of saying you're mine, completely mine. Be afraid of doing anything that will bind you to me. But tell me the truth, once and for all. Just say it once, and I'll be content with that—for the time being. Just say it.''

She looked up at him, and the moon shone through the welling tears in her sea-green eyes. "I love you, Creighton. I do love you with all my heart, but—''

"Just that, no more, no buts.'' He kissed her then with the incredible gentleness that seemed to be a part of his strength. Then he pulled away and smiled down at her. "Now we can go and look for the shoes.''

It took them a while to find the shoes, and during the moonlit search they teased each other and laughed and touched each other casually and far more often than the search necessitated. It was a gay carefree time, and neither Kaye nor Creighton thought beyond the joy of the moment. Perhaps it was their holding the future in abeyance that made them so lighthearted.

Arm in arm they walked back along the beach to Round Hill. Their effervescent mood changed into a warm gentle calm. It had been a lovely untroubled evening, and they were both grateful for it.

They got into the Rover and drove back to Traymore in a glow of relaxation. They talked easily and comfortably, and even their silences were pleasurable. The Rover's engine died when they stopped in the driveway, and they got out and stood together in the velvet midnight.

"It's been a truly lovely evening, Creighton," Kaye said.

"Yes, it has. And yet. . . ."

"What?"

"It seems so fragile. I mean, I'd like a walk in the garden, but I'm afraid I'd be pushing our luck. I say to myself, 'Yes, it's been lovely. Let's just leave it at that. Don't take any risks.' "

"I'm not sure I understand."

"Kaye, every time we've tried to go beyond being just friends, something disastrous has happened between us—a fight, a misunderstanding, a falling out. Tonight has been nearly perfect. I'm afraid of ruining it."

"Yes, I understand that. Somehow the closer we get, the more dangerous it becomes."

"Exactly. In spite of what we've said to each other tonight—or perhaps because of it—it might be a good idea if we took some time to think things out. It's the perfect opportunity, actually. I didn't plan it this way, but I have to go to Kingston tomorrow with George Montague—a series of low-profile meetings with the prime minister. I'll be gone for a few days, probably a week. I don't want this separation, Kaye, but often what we don't want is what's best for us."

Kaye wasn't prepared for the profound shock this sudden announcement caused her. It was a moment before she saw the wisdom of what Creighton was saying.

"You're right of course, Creighton," she finally uttered. "But it is. . . sudden."

"I know, and I'm sorry. I wish you could know how much I'm going to miss you."

"It couldn't be more than I'll miss you."

"And you agree it's best."

Kaye smiled at him. "Painful, but best."

He took her in his arms and kissed her softly. The touch of him made her want to beg him not to go. She felt she couldn't survive without the warmth and strength and manliness of him, but she told herself it *was* right. She melted into his embrace and took advantage of the temporary haven.

He released her and said, "Good night, Kaye. I'll be back before you know it. It won't be long."

"It will *seem* long."

He kissed her again, and he was gone.

Kaye went directly to her room and put on a nightdress of white satin. She knew she couldn't sleep immediately, for the excitement of Creighton's recent nearness lingered and made her whole body tingle with desire. She went out onto the balcony and stood looking at the moonlit garden, filled with thoughts of Creighton and his words of love, which both thrilled her and frightened her. And she pondered his absence, brief though it would be; the reality of it flooded her being with a sense of loneliness. She was overwhelmed by a need to touch him just once more before he was gone from her. She wanted to run to him, to be with him, to keep him from leaving her.

Suddenly she was asking herself, *Where is that poised alabaster creature who arrived in Montego so determined in her aloofness?* And instantly the questions and the doubts were there again. Would she never gain control of herself again? Would she spend the rest of her life vacillating this way? She felt suddenly exhausted and started back into her room, but she paused and turned back toward the garden and the sea beyond. She looked at the moon—that same moon she had seen over Creighton's shoulder as he had held her close to him — and for a moment nothing mattered but that embrace and the sweet certainty that she would soon know it again. Soon? A week seemed an eternity.

# CHAPTER FOUR

ON THE DAY of Creighton's departure for Kingston, the social whirl began again for Kaye. She didn't want it to begin; she didn't want to be part of it. She ached for solitude. But she accepted the almost enforced gaiety for two reasons. First, she wanted to be a part of Aunt Alice's natural ambience, to add joy to it by participating in it willingly and happily. Second, she had to defend herself against the bruising loneliness she felt with Creighton gone.

And so she threw herself into the swirl of parties and dinners and luncheons with complete abandon. She saw Ellis and Amanda and Smitty and the Marlowes and the Zimmermans. She went to their galas and sparkled with wit and charm. And when Alice entertained, she was as much the hostess as her aunt, seeing to everyone's comfort and pleasure for every moment of the evening. She enchanted everyone and made each person feel he or she was the only one who mattered to her. No one knew that what she was giving of herself was superficial. It was no more than a ruse to cover the uncertainty that had begun again, in spite of her missing Creighton desperately.

There was no longer any doubt in her mind that she was in love with Creighton. She longed to be near him, to touch him, to feel his arms around her. She remembered vividly the feel and the warmth of his body, and whenever she slept, she dreamed of being close to him.

But was all that enough, she asked herself. The memory of the early days with Rod had blurred into vagueness, but she knew she had thought she was in love with him. Oh, there was never the wild physical excitement she now felt in Creighton's presence, but she could not honestly say Rod's courtship hadn't been romantic. He had never been anything but attentive and thoughtful. There had always been flowers and gifts and candlelit dinners. She had never questioned whether she and Rod were meant for each other. If she had been so wrong then, how could she be sure she wasn't wrong now?

By the time Creighton had been gone for five days, she had convinced herself she was on the brink of making a catastrophic mistake. She had to pull back from Creighton. She had to be true to what her intelligence had told her was best. She must not listen any longer to her heart but to her head. She knew she could not give him up entirely, yet she would have to resist the temptation to give herself to him totally. At the end of the week she was sure she was rationally, logically and stoically prepared for Creighton's return. She was wrong.

He arrived at Traymore unannounced, during a gold and mauve and pink sunset. He knew that no one of the "society set" was giving a dinner party that night and that Kaye and Lady Alice would almost certainly be dining at home, and he knew Alice's habits: dinner would not be served before eight-thirty, more probably not until nine. Neither of the ladies of the house had yet come downstairs when the Land Rover pulled into the drive, but Kaye had heard and recognized the sound of its engine. In spite of her resolve to be poised and controlled, she rushed downstairs and came out onto the veranda just as Creighton mounted the stairs. There was no restraint between them. They rushed into each other's arms, and Kaye felt the thrill she had been longing for.

Creighton was, if anything, more handsome than she remembered. He wore white linen slacks and a burgundy polo shirt that stretched tight across the muscles of his chest. She could feel the strength of him as he crushed her to him. They had no thought of decorum, of the servants or even, for the moment, of Lady Alice. They could think of nothing but each other and the feel of their bodies pressed close together, of their mouths touching eagerly.

When they were able to pull away from each other for a moment, Creighton said, "Kaye, how I've missed you!"

"And I've missed you," she answered. "Every minute."

They heard Aunt Alice coming through the downstairs hall then and disengaged themselves.

"Alice, how good to see you," Creighton said as Lady Alice came out onto the veranda.

"Creighton! What an unexpected pleasure. How was your trip?"

"Profitable, I hope. George Montague is a wonder. Even the prime minister treats him with respect—and caution. I think we may have accomplished a great deal."

"Wonderful! Well, you've arrived at an opportune hour. Will you stay and have cocktails and dinner with us?"

"I can think of nothing I'd like more—if you'll believe I didn't barge in like this looking for an invitation."

"I really don't care if you did," Alice said, "I'm just very happy to see you. I'll go and tell Helen you're staying."

As she turned to leave, Creighton said, "Alice, would it be inconvenient if I took Kaye away just now? No

more than forty-five minutes. There's something I want
to show her. I want her to see *my* part of Montego. Visitors don't usually see it, you know."

A whisper of concern crossed Aunt Alice's face, but it
gave way quickly to a smile. "It wouldn't be inconvenient at all—for me." She looked at Kaye almost questioningly, maintaining her smile. "There's plenty of
time."

Kaye was flustered, but she managed to say, "What
on earth is it you want me to look at, Creighton?"

"I'm certainly not going to tell you in advance. Come
along." He took her hand and started to lead her across
the veranda. Over his shoulder he called to Aunt Alice,
"I promise you we won't be long."

"I have absolute faith in your manners, Mr. Jarvis,"
Alice answered. "I'll arrange for dinner at nine. I'll expect you."

"And we'll be here," Creighton said. "In time for
drinks."

"That's entirely up to you," Alice said. "I assure you
I shall have mine with or without you," she added teasingly.

Creighton laughed and led Kaye down the stairs to the
Rover.

"Creighton, what is going on?" Kaye asked.

"Be quiet and get in."

Kaye obeyed with a sense of excitement and security
at being with Creighton.

As he started the car, he said, "Now please don't
talk. We'll be where we're going in a very few minutes."

"And where is . . . ?"

"Hush! This is one thing we must do my way. All
right?"

"Yes, yes. All right. I'll be still until I'm told to
speak."

There was an eager boyish smile on Creighton's face as he drove the Rover. Although Kaye had no idea where they were going, it was clear they were climbing farther up into the hills than she had ever been previously. She was content to bask in the glow of Creighton's enthusiasm, even when the primitive rutted dirt roads gave way to a mere single-laned track through the forest. As the Rover pulled abruptly to a halt, Kaye knew they had reached the peak, the very crown, of the hills.

Creighton smiled at her and said, "Here we are. Come on, now."

They scrambled out of the car, and Creighton took her hand. They left the track immediately, and it was rough going as he pulled her along through the wood, with its knee-high underbrush. Suddenly they broke out of the forest and into a clearing no more than twenty feet wide. It was as if a curtain had lifted. They were on the edge of a precipice, and before them, beneath the dizzying drop, was all of Montego Bay. The sky now was turquoise and pale orange, the clouds vividly colored with shades of purple and muted pink. Below them was the bay, a crescent sapphire jewel, the colors of the sky playing on it in constantly changing ripples. It was so breathtaking Kaye forgot for a moment even the touch of Creighton's hand on hers.

When she looked up at him, his smile was gone. He was gazing out over the panorama with a rapt expression, as if he were lost in the beauty of it.

Without glancing at her, he said, "This is what I wanted to show you. I've never stood on this spot with another human being except Victoria. I'm afraid I'm very selfish about it. It's always said that your Aunt Alice at Traymore has the best view in Montego, and I always agree; I never argue the point. But I know. It's rather like a man's wearing a solid-gold collar button. It doesn't show, but he knows it's there. That's an antique reference, but it says what I mean. You see, Kaye, this is my mountain. I own everything you can see, from here to that deep ravine to the west to that ridge there far to the east and all the way down to the bay. Kaye, I'm not a feudal baron; I don't own it out of a need for possession. I have plans for it. It's part of why I was in Kingston this past week. I want part of it for myself. I don't deny that. But think what much of it could be—a whole model community sprawling down that great hill, a community for the people, a symbol of what the entire island could be." He was quiet for a moment, and Kaye felt no need to speak. "I want all this to be ours, Kaye, not just mine. I was very busy in Kingston, but I managed to have a lot of time to think, mostly at night when I was alone. And I've come to a conclusion. We've had our ups and downs together. Sometimes I've been good and right and thoughtful—and sometimes I haven't. But that's been true of you, too. For the most part we've both behaved like children, and I think it's time we stopped. Kaye, I'm asking you to marry me. I want us to share our lives. And I don't mean for you to share my life or me to share yours. I want it to be one life... our life. I want us to be together every minute we can manage. I want you for the rest of our lives. Just say yes."

Kaye felt a moment of bright blinding happiness. There were no thoughts in her head. There was nothing but an emotional and physical excitement that turned her toward Creighton irresistibly, and she found herself in his arms. He kissed her passionately, the firmness of his full lips closing tightly on hers. She pressed herself against him, and the strength and hardness of his body at once thrilled and frightened her.

Quite wrongly, but with every reason, Creighton had taken Kaye's wild rush of emotion to mean her acceptance of his proposal. His own momentary happiness was unbounded. But even as his whole body throbbed with the vision of the life he had just found and the physical closeness of the woman who was that life, that woman's own bright vision was giving way to the velvety black reality of the dark night.

For Kaye nothing had changed—except that she now loved Creighton. Once she had loved Rod. Loving, she told herself, was not all there was to it. It was only a small part. . . not enough by itself. There was compatibility, life-styles, personal interests, temperaments. There was more to it than the intense burning desire she felt for Creighton. Oh, how she wanted him! But not at any price.

"Aren't you going to answer?" Creighton asked.

Everything began to swim in her head. The cascading mountainside Creighton had just offered her—along with himself and his life—went out of focus and rippled as if it were under water. Then she heard her own voice, as though from a distance, and when he spoke, Creighton's voice, too, seemed far away.

"I. . . can't marry you, Creighton," Kaye said.

"You love me! You said you did!"

"And I do."

"Then why can't you?"

"Creighton. It isn't enough, being in love."

"It isn't enough? What more is there?"

"Worlds more. I was in love with Rod when I married him—or thought I was—and it wasn't enough. There are so many other things that—"

"Damn it, Kaye! There's only one thing! We want to be together. I'd have that any way I could, anytime I could. But because of you, because there is nothing I wouldn't do for you, because you won't have me casually, because you've made me feel that way, too, I offer you my whole life, and all you can say is, 'it isn't enough'?"

"Creighton, you don't understand. I. . . ."

"You're bloody right I don't understand. I no longer have any idea what you think of me, but I assure you I don't go about asking women to marry me just on impulse. That you can treat the offer so lightly. . . that you can analyze it and evaluate it, makes me see you aren't at all what I thought you were. Perhaps I should thank you—for saving me from making a dreadful mistake. Come on, I'm taking you back to Traymore."

He turned and strode away from her. She followed and got into the Rover beside him. The engine roared as he started it, and he pulled out so fast the tires screamed and Kaye was thrown back in her seat. Creighton continued to drive quickly, but he drove so expertly there seemed to be no danger.

After a moment Kaye said, "Creighton, please try to—"

"Shut up, Kaye. I never want to hear the sound of your voice again."

Kaye knew he meant it. They drove back to Traymore without speaking another word. Kaye opened the car door herself, because she knew Creighton wouldn't do it for her. They walked up the stairs together, with Aunt Alice waiting for them, all unknowing. She greeted them with a smile.

"Alice," Creighton began, "I don't think I've ever been rude to you, but I have to refuse your offer of dinner. If you want to know why, I suggest you ask your niece. I'm sorry. Good night." He went back to the Rover and drove off.

Kaye and her aunt stood on the veranda in silence for

a long moment, watching the Rover disappear into the darkness.

"Well," Alice said, and drew in a breath, "Shall I ask you?"

"Oh, Aunt Alice!" Kaye cried, bursting into tears.

"Come here, darling," Alice beckoned with her ever present calm and poise. Kaye went to her, and Aunt Alice held her in her arms.

"You may as well tell me now," Aunt Alice remarked. "You know you're going to eventually."

"He—he asked me to marry him."

"And you refused."

"Yes."

"Good for you. You're not ready."

"Oh, thank God somebody...." Her voice trailed off.

"Understands? Of course I do. Oh, I know you love him. Just as I loved Alex—grandly and passionately. But we were lucky; everything else fell into place. Little things: our love of gardens, our passion for the theater, our love of people and entertaining them. I'm not at all sure you and Creighton have that much in common, and you're right not to rush into anything until you're sure you have."

"I know you're right, and yet...."

"Do you think I want to discourage you? Do you think I don't know what it's like to be in a man's arms under a Jamaican moon? But you're very dear to me, Kaye. I don't want to see you lose yourself in a mere affair. If, in time—good time—you decide you want to marry Creighton Jarvis, I'll be all for it, but I won't have you swept off your feet."

"You'll be all...for it?"

"Of course I will. You're a wonderful woman, and he's a wonderful man. That doesn't mean you belong together, but if you do. . . . Well, enough of that. Come on, let's have a cocktail before dinner." She glanced over at the driveway, where Creighton had so recently strode to his Land Rover. Her expression was wistful. "I was looking forward to the evening with Creighton. Oh, dear, how thoughtless of me! You were looking forward to it, too."

"Yes. Yes, I was."

Aunt Alice put her arm around Kaye's shoulders, and they walked to the wicker settee. Henry appeared magically, and they soon had their martinis.

In spite of Alice's continuous efforts to cheer her, Kaye remained glum. She was clearly preoccupied with thoughts of Creighton. After dinner the two women sat together on the veranda. Kaye's conversation became more and more desultory, until finally Aunt Alice herself fell into a blue mood. After a particularly long silence Kaye apologized for being such bad company, and they both went to their rooms, Alice to pace and worry, Kaye to fall into a troubled sleep.

She awoke quite early in the morning and knew she would be unable to go back to sleep. She bathed and dressed and went downstairs. She was surprised to find Aunt Alice already breakfasting on the veranda.

"Aunt Alice!" Kaye exclaimed. "You're up and about very early."

"Yes, I suppose we both had a restless night. Come and have some breakfast."

Kaye hadn't even poured her tea when a car raced along the driveway and stopped before the house. The car door slammed, and Amanda came running up the stairs.

"Good morning, Lady Alice. Good morning, Kaye," she said with the breathless air of a teenager. "Isn't it a lovely day?"

"Good morning, Amanda," Alice replied with less than warmth in her tone.

"I'm sorry to burst in this way, unexpected and uninvited, but I had a sudden moment of freedom, and I couldn't resist coming."

Aunt Alice smiled wryly and shook her head. "Not very good manners, my dear. No matter. You're here. Sit down and have some breakfast with us."

"I've already eaten, Lady Alice. I've come because— I know it will seem impulsive to you, but it's such a beautiful day I thought it might be the perfect time for me to show Doctor's Cave to Kaye. The water will be perfect, and the sun—"

"All right, Amanda," Alice said. "If Kaye wants to go to the beach, it's perfectly fine with me. As a matter of fact, it might be a very good idea, all things considered. Kaye, why don't you go along with Amanda? Get out of the house for a while."

"Auntie, I really don't feel—"

"Go on, now. It's just what you need."

Kaye smiled, knowing she had lost the battle. "All right, darling. Give me a moment to change, and we'll be off."

Kaye went to her room, slipped into sport clothes and was back on the veranda before Amanda was able to finish the cup of tea she had finally accepted at Aunt Alice's insistence.

Amanda jumped up from her chair and cried, "You're ready! Wonderful! Lady Alice, do forgive us for running off."

"Oh, do go on," Alice laughed. "Young people must have their time in the sun."

As hard as she tried, Kaye couldn't share Amanda's obvious excitement and enthusiasm on the drive to Doctor's Cave. Only Creighton was in her mind. Yet her persisting glumness didn't seem to daunt Amanda.

The beach was as beautiful as Kaye had been told, and the sea was a jewellike blue green color. The beach was dotted with round tables surrounded by chairs and protected from the sun by conical thatched roofs. Amanda led the way to a table she seemed to have chosen with predetermination.

"It's lovely and cool here close to the water," she said as she put her bag on the table.

They were both wearing bathing suits under their slacks and blouses. They peeled off their outer clothing, and Amanda spread a large towel on the sand. They rubbed themselves with suntan lotion and lay down.

"This is lovely," Kaye said. "The sun is delicious."

"Isn't it? We can bake for a bit, then cool off in the sea." She sat up and hugged her knees. She looked up and down the beach, anxious again.

After a few minutes a young man in bathing trunks came and stood gazing down at them. "Good morning, Miss Leyton," he began. "You're early today."

"Good morning, Danny," Amanda said. "Yes, I think it's the best part of the day. Kaye, this is Danny Riordan, one of our lifeguards. He's from the States, too. Danny, this is Miss Kaye Belliston."

"Hello," Kaye said.

"It's a pleasure to meet you."

Kaye judged he couldn't be more than nineteen. He was also an Adonis. His skin was the color of dark honey, and the ringlets of his blond hair were bleached from the sun. He had the body of a professional swimmer. His eyes were the color of the sea. When he smiled at her, it was the smile of an all-American boy.

"I'm a New Yorker," Kaye said. "What's your part of the country?"

"Promise not to laugh?"

"I promise."

"Cleveland."

"What's there to laugh about?"

"I don't know, but ninety percent of the people in the United States think Cleveland is funny. Phil Donahue is our only natural resource."

Kaye laughed, and Amanda asked, "Who's Phil Donahue?"

"A hugely successful talk-show host on television," Kaye explained: "He started his show in Cleveland, and now, with the possible exception of Johnny Carson, he's cornered the market."

"Wow! It's good to talk to somebody from home," Danny commented.

"Thank you," Amanda replied.

"Come on, I just meant it's nice to say, 'Phil Donahue,' and have somebody know who you mean. No offense, Miss Leyton." He grinned that boyish dazzling grin again. "Well...." He seemed embarrassed. "I'll be around."

"We'll shout if our lives need saving," Amanda said.

"It was nice meeting you, Miss Belliston."

"Same here," Kaye answered. "I do know what you mean. For the first time in two weeks I feel comfortable talking like an American."

"That's great. At the end of the summer I leave Montego," Danny remarked casually.

"Oh, you've been here previously?"

"This is my second year."

"And it's back to school in September?"

"Right on."

"Where?"

"Promise you won't laugh?"

"Is everything in your life funny?"

"*I* don't think it is, but other people do. I go to Grinnell."

"Iowa?"

"If I weren't a gentleman, I'd hug you. Yes, Iowa."

"Why is Iowa funny?" Amanda asked. "I'm sure it's lovely."

"Well...it's...."

"Corny," Kaye said.

Danny laughed, a robust uninhibited laugh. "You've got it. Iowa is corny. That's great."

"I don't understand," Amanda said.

Danny turned to her, his blue eyes glinting in the sun. "Corny in American English means rural, hicksville, small town. And Iowa is a corn state, agriculturally. It's a kind of a pun."

"Maybe when I go to the States, I'll visit Iowa. Then I'll understand."

"You sure will," Danny said. "I'd better get back to my post—in case anybody's drowning."

"It was nice to meet you," Kaye said. "Good luck at Grinnell."

"Thanks." He smiled at Amanda and walked away.

"What a nice young man," Kaye remarked.

"Yes, he is. Kaye, are you good at keeping secrets?"

"Superb."

"I feel very guilty. I'm afraid I've used you."

"Used me?"

"Yes, I used you as an excuse for coming here."

"Why did you need an excuse?"

"Because...I hope I can consider you an ally."

"Alliance between England and the States is a tradition."

"Yes, but I meant because you're young. You're the

only young person in our social set aside from Ellis, and I'm afraid I just don't feel close to Ellis.''

"And I'm afraid I feel closer to him than I'd like to. Never mind that. Go on.''

"Kaye, Danny and I. . . Danny and I are in love.''

"Oh, Amanda!''

"I needn't tell you how my grandmother would react if she knew.''

"No, you needn't. You and Danny. . . and Lady Smith-Croydon. Oh, God!''

"To grandmother he'd be just an impoverished midwestern American. No money, no family, no future.''

"I suppose that isn't so far from the truth.''

"Oh, Kaye, it is! He's bright and decent and wonderful. He comes here only to make money to help him pay for his education.''

"I don't doubt he's all you say he is, but, Amanda, think of your conversation of just a couple of minutes ago. You don't even know where Iowa is, let alone Cleveland. And I guarantee you you'd be like a fish out of water there. And how would Danny be in your social set in London?''

"Is that all that matters?''

"It's not *all* that matters, but it does matter. You're a rich upper-class English girl, and he's a poor middle-class American boy. It's oil and water.'' Amanda turned away and looked at the sea. "What's wrong?''

"I'm disappointed. I thought you'd understand. We love each other.''

And what was wrong with that, Kaye asked herself. They were just two kids who'd met and fallen in love. Who cared about their backgrounds? Wasn't truly loving each other enough? Amanda was right. She had every reason to be disappointed.

"Amanda, you and Danny are very young.''

"Yes, we are. And are we supposed to wait until we're middle-aged before we marry, just so everyone will be sure we're not making a mistake?"

There were tears in Amanda's eyes as she stared at Kaye. Kaye looked back at her for a long moment before she answered.

"No. No, you're not. May I give you some advice? If you're really in love, don't let anything or anyone stop you. Be proud of it. Don't hide it, and don't be foolish and run off together. Go to your grandmother and tell her. I'm sure she'll be horrified, but at least you won't be sneaking around behind her back. She's going to find out eventually, one way or another. Think how much better it will be if you just come out with it. Don't give her reason to think you're ashamed of loving him."

"That's all very well, except that she'd forbid me to see him. She'd send me back to England like a shot."

Kaye thought for a moment. "Yes, I suppose she would. Amanda, I'll be your ally. Please believe that. I don't want to be your ally in deceiving your grandmother, but I will be your ally in trying to find some happiness in life. If you promise me you and Danny *won't* do anything foolish, I'll help you in any way I can. Why don't you ask him to come over here? I suppose he can watch the swimmers just as well from here as from where he is now."

"Oh, Kaye, would it be all right?"

"Of course it would—as long as you're sure there's no one on the beach who knows you."

"I'm sure." Amanda waved frantically at Danny. It wasn't difficult to get his attention; he had hardly taken his eyes off her since he'd walked away. He jogged over to them immediately.

"Hi," he said. "Need something?"

"Yes," Amanda answered. "You. I've just told Kaye

about us." Danny looked perplexed. "It's all right; she's on our side. Can you stay here with us?"

Danny looked at Kaye questioningly. "Is it really okay?"

"It's okay with me, Danny."

He dropped to his knees beside Amanda, as if he were overcome with delight. "Oh, man, this is great." He reached out and stroked Amanda's hair, looking at her longingly. "You don't know how hard it is for us, Miss Belliston."

"Kaye. And I think I do."

"Sometimes we don't see each other for days at a time. I've asked her to tell her grandmother about us, but she says then we wouldn't be able to see each other at all, and I couldn't stand that."

"I know. I made the same suggestion, but I'm afraid Amanda's right. Danny, I've asked Amanda to make me a promise, and I'm going to ask you, too. If you swear to me you won't do anything rash or stupid—and I'm sure you know what that means—I'll help you to see each other."

"You're the greatest. All we want is to be together."

"Just don't be too together. Well, if there's no one from the enemy camp on the beach, why don't you two go for a walk? I doubt that your idea of being together includes me. Mine wouldn't if I were in your situation."

They looked at her, then at each other, as if she had just offered them an hour in the garden of Eden.

"Thanks, Kaye, we won't go far."

"I'd appreciate it if you didn't get entirely out of my sight—at least for now. I'll just sit here and try to figure out the best way to handle Smitty."

Danny gave her his glorious smile. "I've decided not to be a gentleman." He crawled past Amanda on his knees and hugged Kaye. "You don't know what this means to us."

"Oh, yes, I do. Now go on—before I try to steal you away from dear Amanda. You're altogether too attractive, you know. Too young but...hunky, I think, is the word."

"You're wonderful," Danny said. He stood and pulled Amanda up by the hand. They ran down to the water's edge and walked off hand in hand.

How to handle Smitty.... She had said it as if she had some idea of how to do it, and she most certainly didn't. To begin with, she was no more than a visitor to Montego society—a closely connected visitor, but a visitor nonetheless. And she was considering undertaking a confrontation with the most powerful woman in the community. Yet as she watched Amanda and Danny walking along the beach, it was crystal clear they were deeply in love—or thought they were. What, after all, was the difference? As to the problem of Smitty, Kaye realized her only hope was Aunt Alice. If she could convince Aunt Alice that Amanda and Danny belonged together, and if they would agree to wait until Danny had finished school, Aunt Alice might—just might—be willing to talk to Smitty. She was surely the only person who could have any influence with her. But if Aunt Alice disapproved, she might go straight to Smitty and ruin everything. How had she got herself involved in this mess? No, it wasn't a mess, she told herself as she watched them in the distance. Then she realized that what she felt more than anything else was envy. *Then* she reminded herself that what she envied was what she told herself was the last thing in the world she wanted. Or was it?

"Yes, damn it. It's the last thing in the world I want," she said under her breath. But that wasn't going to stop her from helping someone else achieve it, even if she didn't yet know how she was going to do it. She rolled over on her stomach, and in a few minutes she had dozed off.

When she woke up and realized where she was, she said to herself, *some chaperon you are*. She stood up and scanned the beach. Amanda and Danny had been only a hundred feet away, splashing about in the shallow water just off the shore. Apparently they could be trusted, but then, where could they have gone? It was broad daylight, and Danny was on duty. She realized she mustn't become so immediately trusting that she would arrange or even allow assignations.

They saw her after a moment and waved to her joyously. She waved back and sat down again. She continued to watch them for about twenty minutes. Then they came out of the water and ran across the sand and fell down at her feet.

"Oh, Kaye," Amanda said, "you've got to go into the water. It's super!"

"I will. I feel like a baked potato."

With the boundless energy of youth Danny sprang to his feet, pulling Amanda up with him. "Come on," he said. "We'll go with you." All three of them ran into the water.

They swam for fifteen minutes, then went back to the beach towel.

"I'm afraid we ought to start back," Kaye said. "They'll be worried if we stay too long, and I'll be burned to a crisp."

"It's been such a glorious time I hate to see it end," Amanda said.

"There'll be others," Kaye told her. "I'm very inventive."

"You're an angel of mercy!" Amanda declared. She

started to gather up their belongings like a child who didn't want to tax the patience of a lenient parent.

"You really are wonderful, Kaye," Danny noted quietly. "I hope you know I wouldn't do anything to hurt Mandy. She's my Mandy, and I love her, and I wouldn't even take advantage of the fact that you trust me. Not ever."

"I'm sure you wouldn't, and as one American to another, I hope you know I'd cut off your head if you did."

He smiled. "I'll just bet you would."

"Bank on it, buster." She offered a handshake, and Danny took her hand.

"Thank you," he replied, and he looked deeply grateful.

Amanda stood up and turned to him. In her eyes was a mixture of the joy of their time at the beach and the sadness of its ending. "I'll come back as soon as I can."

"You know," Kaye began, "I could tell Aunt Alice and Smitty *I* have a crush on a lifeguard at the beach and I need Amanda as an excuse to come here. That'd really confuse them." Amanda laughed, and Danny was convulsed.

"You're something else," he said when he had recovered.

"We've got to be on our way, Amanda."

"Yes. Goodbye, Danny."

"Goodbye, Mandy. I'll be waiting."

In the car they rode in silence for a while on the way back to Traymore. Then Amanda said, "What am I going to do, Kaye? I do love him."

"First of all, don't despair. There's a solution to every problem. I'm working on it. I have a basic strategy. Don't ask me to tell you about it, because I won't. Let's just hope something comes of it."

"Sometimes I think there's no chance at all we'll ever be married."

"Resign yourself to the fact that even under the best of circumstances that time is a long way off."

Aunt Alice was having tea on the veranda when they arrived at Traymore. Amanda paid her respects briefly and left for home. Kaye sat at the tea table, and her aunt studied her for a long moment.

"You seem rather perkier than you were last night," Alice commented.

"Only through a good deal of effort," Kaye replied.

"That's a good sign. At least you're trying. Keep it up. Keep going. Busy yourself. Let life go on."

Suddenly Kaye saw that this was the moment she had thought she might have to wait for. Her plan for Amanda and Danny—which had been vague at best—instantly sprang into completeness, and Aunt Alice had virtually invited it!

"I wonder. . ." Kaye began. She hesitated.

"You wonder what, dear?"

"I think Amanda was hinting this morning that she'd like to show me Kingston. I did nothing to encourage her, but now I wonder if it might not be a good idea. Something to do. . .to keep busy."

"Kingston? Why on earth would she want to do that? There's nothing in Kingston. Unless of course you have the curiosity of the tourist."

"I think maybe I have. But the point is, poor Amanda simply wants a chance to get out of Smitty's clutches for a while, to get away from the endless parade of guests. Just to be with someone closer to her own age."

"Still, two young women in Kingston alone. . . ."

"Auntie, don't you remember? I'm an old ex-married lady. I'd be more Amanda's chaperon than anything else. And it would be the perfect opportunity for me to do just what you suggested. It would be something for me to do, and...and it would get me away from Montego, away from Creighton.''

"Well...if you can get Smitty's permission—and I doubt that you can—it's all right with me. You'll have to fly, of course. The more I think about it, the more I think it's a splendid idea. I suppose I can tell you what to avoid at least. If you book yourselves into a decent hotel...the Terra Nova, I think...and take cabs. Or perhaps you should rent a car. You simply mustn't walk on the streets in the evening, and you mustn't go to those dreadful nightclubs. Yes, you might just have a splendid time. Yes, as a matter of fact, I'll talk to Smitty about it myself. She can hardly ignore a suggestion of mine.''

"You are a dear.''

But Kaye was wondering if Aunt Alice was dear enough to go a step further—perhaps several steps further. Would she go to Smitty on Amanda's behalf if she knew about Danny Riordan? Well, one thing at a time, she told herself. Now all she had to do was find out which day of the week Danny had off, and they'd pop over to Kingston together. Good Lord! She realized they'd all be in Kingston overnight. She really would have to be a chaperon. Nothing ventured, nothing gained.

She finished her tea and went to her room. She felt guilty about deceiving Aunt Alice. Dear Aunt Alice! She had understood Kaye's every problem and had comforted her. She had advised her wisely without intruding. She had been a true and loving friend. Yet at this very moment Kaye was concocting a plot of which her aunt would surely disapprove—and lying about it, as well.

She stopped unbuttoning her blouse, as if something had startled her. She stared blankly into space for a mo-

ment until the thought was clear in her mind. Aunt
Alice, at Kaye's age, would have done exactly what she
was going to do. Dear, romantic, practical Aunt Alice
would have schemed and connived for the young lovers,
just as she was doing. She couldn't do it—or even approve of it—in her present position, but in her youth she
would surely have helped Amanda and Danny. Kaye
suddenly felt much better.

The fragile balloon of well-being was soon punctured,
as it so often had been recently, by thoughts of Creighton. Where was he at this moment? What was he doing?
Was he longing for her as she was longing for him? She
remembered his anger with her when they were last together. "I never want to hear the sound of your voice
again," he had said. She was sure he had meant it. She
had destroyed whatever was or might have been. She
had been sure when she had done it. She was not sure
now.

# CHAPTER FIVE

AT THAT MOMENT Creighton was thinking of Kaye. He was sitting in his upstairs study, trying without much success to read. As he started rereading the same paragraph for the third time, he closed the book in dismay and tossed it onto the desk. He got up and went to a window overlooking the garden. He remembered standing in the garden with Kaye, but more vividly and more compellingly he remembered Kaye in his arms when, for a brief moment, he had thought she was his—his for the rest of their lives. And then. . . . Oh, he was still angry, damned angry—with Kaye for refusing him, with himself for being made a fool of. No. Perhaps he had made a fool of himself—which was even worse. The new world he had created in his mind, a world with Kaye at its center, had crashed. Well, he wasn't beaten just yet. He loved Kaye Belliston, and she loved him, and that was all that mattered—in spite of what she had said. This was a contest that was far from over.

There was a gentle knock on the study door. Knowing it would be Christian, his butler, he said, "Come in."

Christian, a tall elegant Jamaican, opened the door and announced, "There's a visitor downstairs, Mr. Jarvis."

"A visitor? I'm not expecting anyone."

"His name is Adrian James, sir. He says you know him and that it's urgent."

Creighton's tanned face paled, and the muscles of his

jaws tensed. It was a moment before he spoke. "Tell him to go away."

"I'm sorry, sir. I told him you were occupied, but he wouldn't leave. He insisted upon seeing you."

Creighton's eyes narrowed, and he said, "All right, Christian. Show him up here."

For the few moments it took Adrian James to reach the study, Creighton stood as if riveted to his spot before the window. Christian opened the door, and Adrian stepped inside. He looked exactly as Creighton remembered him, goldenly good-looking. He seemed never to age. Creighton knew he was thirty-five, but he looked no older than twenty-eight. His short blond hair was carefully styled, and his blue eyes shone brightly. His clothes were immaculately tailored.

"Hello, Creighton," Adrian James said.

"What do you want? What are you doing here?"

"Why, I came to see you, dear boy."

"Don't be any more unctuous than you have to be. Why are you here?"

"I've just told you. I came to see you."

"I warn you, Adrian. I'll brook no nonsense from you. Just tell me what kind of trouble you're in this time, and get out."

"There's no need to be rude."

"I'll be a great deal more than rude if you're not out of this house within the next five minutes."

"I'm afraid that isn't possible."

"It would give me great pleasure to throw you out bodily."

"Oh, I'm sure it would, but I don't think you will. I don't think you're prepared for the consequences." Creighton stared at him without speaking. Adrian smiled at him. "Aren't you going to ask me to sit down?"

"How much do you want?"

Adrian sat down in an armchair without the invitation. "I don't want money, Creighton. I want only your hospitality."

"You can't be serious."

"Oh, I assure you I am. Deadly serious. I haven't bothered you for a very long time, but now I need your help. I really do need it, or I wouldn't be here. And it isn't much to ask, Creighton. Just put me up for a few weeks."

"I'll give you as much money as you need to be on your way. I will not have you staying in this house."

"I'm afraid I have no place to go. Not safely, at any rate. Here I can just move about as part of your social set—an old friend from home, an old friend from Canberra. I won't be any trouble."

"You've never been anything but trouble. I want you out of here now."

"Ah, Creighton, don't make it necessary for me to threaten you. It's too unpleasant. Just resign yourself to having me as a guest. I won't stay any longer than is absolutely necessary."

"Someday I'm going to make you pay, Adrian."

"Yes, but not just yet. And once you're free to do so, you don't think I'd be fool enough to come within miles of you, do you?"

"Get out of this room. Find Christian and tell him to put you in the yellow room. And stay out of my sight."

Adrian got up. "You're going to have to treat me with normal courtesy. As I remember Montego, it's a tight little society. You can't keep me hidden for long, and it wouldn't do for your friends to think you were harboring a . . . an unpresentable guest, now would it?" He turned and went to the door. He paused for a moment, then turned back to Creighton. "Is the yellow room quite comfortable?"

"Get out!"

Still smiling, Adrian left the study and closed the door.

Creighton went to the desk and banged his fist on it so hard he felt a stabbing pain. The hatred in his heart seemed to poison his whole being. He felt it even on those rare occasions when he thought of Adrian, but to have him here in Montego and in this house was loathsome. His hatred had grown and festered through the years. Sometimes he wondered if he'd ever be rid of him. He knew he would, but there was nothing he could do to hurry that fateful day. The price was too high.

The telephone in the study rang, and although Creighton had no idea who was calling, his tone was barely civil when he answered. "Yes?" he barked.

"Well, you needn't bite my head off," a female voice said. "It's Sylvia."

"I'm sorry, Sylvia. How are you?"

"I'm fine, but I don't think you are." When Creighton offered no explanation, Sylvia Zimmerman went on. "Darling, I know it's quite short notice, but we're giving a very important dinner party on Saturday. Joe and Barbara Green have arrived from New York virtually without warning, and Saturday is the only night we're free. Say you can come. The Greens adore you, and they'd be very disappointed if they couldn't see you. Don't say no, Creighton. I know you're free, because if you were going to a dinner, we'd be going, too."

"I am free, Sylvia, but—"

"Please, no buts. For me."

"There's a small problem. I've suddenly acquired a houseguest of my own, and—"

"I know that. Since when has one more guest been a problem?"

"What do you mean, you know?"

"I know, that's all. The Greens were on the same plane as your guest, and they heard him tell his taxi driver to take him to Penrose. Very good-looking, Barbara said. Do I know him?"

"No. The last time he was here was years ago, before you and Herman arrived."

"Why so long an interval? I'm sorry. That's none of my business. But you will bring him, won't you?"

"Are you really giving this party for the Greens, or are you giving it to meet my guest?"

"Creighton! I would expect to meet any guest of yours eventually. I don't have to give a dinner party to do it."

"All right, I'll bring him. Thank you for the invitation."

"At seven?"

"We'll be there."

"Oh, what's his name?"

"Adrian. Adrian James."

"Even his name is attractive. I'm glad you can come, darling."

Sylvia hung up and looked at the phone quizzically for a moment. Then she picked up the receiver and dialed again. The telephone rang at Traymore, and Aunt Alice answered it in the drawing room.

As she came downstairs into the reception hall, Kaye heard her aunt speaking on the phone. Just as she stepped forward toward the veranda, Aunt Alice appeared.

"There you are, my dear," Alice said. "I realized just this minute that I've been presumptuous again. I keep forgetting you might have plans of your own. I've accepted a dinner invitation from the Zimmermans for Saturday night—for both of us, of course. Is it all right?"

"Of course it is, auntie. I wouldn't make any plans without consulting you, and with whom would I make plans anyway...now?"

"You've made friends other than Creighton since you've been here."

"Not the kind I'd be likely to make private plans with. I sometimes wonder if anybody in Montego ever makes private plans."

"I suppose we are clannish. You don't have to go on Saturday if you don't want to."

"Do you mean something specific by that?" Kaye asked, looking away.

"I didn't know if you'd want to see Creighton so soon after...."

"I want to see him more than anything else in the world, but I'm afraid to."

"He'll be at the Zimmermans', of course."

"I know," Kaye answered, "but there's not much point in my being in Montego if I'm just going to sit at home like a stick."

"That's the spirit, my girl. I haven't planned anything for this evening. Would you like me to ring up someone to come to dinner?"

"I'd be perfectly happy to have a quiet dinner with just the two of us."

"Would you really?"

"Really."

"Thank goodness. I'm getting a bit old for this constant round of parties. Perhaps you could fill me in on how your mother is doing."

"Why don't we phone her while we're having our drinks?" Kaye said. "She'd be delighted."

"A splendid idea. We'll do just that."

"I think I'll have a swim and a little nap before dinner," Kaye said.

They had their quiet evening at home, and it was a relief to them both. For Kaye the evening was punctuated by stabbing unwelcome thoughts of Creighton, but for the most part it was an evening of reminiscence and gentle humor. They called Kaye's mother, and the call was a delightful surprise to her.

The evening and all of the next day were so uneventful Kaye almost forgot she was in Montego. There were no guests, no social obligations, no telephone calls. But there was the constant presence of Creighton in her mind. During a solitary stroll in the garden she found herself standing on the same spot where Creighton had put his arms around her and kissed her. Nothing had changed. She felt the same memories of joy and anger. Trying to put it all out of her mind, she went up to her room and read herself to sleep.

The routine began again as she dressed for dinner at the Duckworths'. The Duckworths were very old and very genteel and lived in shabby elegance in a sprawling frame house farther down the mountain from Traymore.

The dinner party was not especially large—perhaps twenty-five people—and was held in the moon-bathed garden, where round tables for six had been set up. Kaye sat with Kevin Wright, Netty Marlowe, Herman Zimmerman, Mrs. Duckworth and Barney Fairweather. After dinner Mrs. Duckworth took her up to the second-floor veranda to see her fifteen Great Danes. Kaye asked Mrs. Duckworth if she showed the dogs.

"Oh, no, my dear! They're just my babies."

The incident seemed quite in keeping with the slightly eccentric personalities of the venerable Duckworths.

To Kaye's surprise there was no sign of Creighton, and no one seemed to ask about him. Kaye concealed her anxiety and waited until she was in the car with Aunt Alice on their way home. She tried to sound casual.

"Aunt Alice, I thought it was a cardinal sin not to invite Creighton to a dinner party, but he wasn't there tonight."

Aunt Alice chuckled. "Oh, I'm sure he was invited. I told you previously one can decline a dinner invitation simply by pleading a headache. The difference with Creighton is that he doesn't need an excuse. It's one of his privileges."

"I wish I understood why he's granted all these privileges."

"I would think you'd understand that better than anyone."

"Well, I don't. I wish you'd explain it to me."

"You find Creighton attractive. We all do. And we also find him necessary. Although you won't admit it, you do, too. When one is both attractive and necessary, one is granted privileges. One is granted them only so long as one doesn't abuse them. Creighton never does."

"Why do you suppose he wasn't there tonight?"

"I don't know. If you're implying it might have been because of you, I suppose you could be right."

"I hope I'm not. I have no right to move in among your friends and make things awkward for them."

"Creighton does not allow people to make things awkward for him."

When they reached Traymore, they exchanged a few pleasantries and went to bed with no more mention of Creighton.

The dinner party the next night at the Zimmermans' was as different from the Duckworths' as night from day. Kaye had begun to expect eclectic architectural styles in Montego, but the Zimmermans' house didn't seem even to belong in Montego. It was by far the largest house she'd yet been in. It was a huge rambling mansion of native stone and wood, which sprawled across at least an acre of the large estate. It was modern in tone and all on one level. The large entrance hall was covered in wallpaper of silver and canary yellow. It led into a room that was about a hundred and twenty-five feet square. The furniture in the room was all expensive, tasteful and relentlessly modern. It was arranged in seating groups spread like islands across a vast sea of beige carpeting. Along one wall was a series of tables set end to end and covered with white damask cloths, the whole easily able to accommodate the more than fifty guests. Everyone Kaye had met in Montego was there, and there were at least as many more whom she hadn't met. Much of the early part of the evening was taken up with introductions. Sylvia started the ritual, but there were simply too many guests for one hostess to tend to. It was soon clear to Kaye she was not going to meet anyone she didn't already know.

When she and Aunt Alice encountered Netty and Harlan, Netty said, "Kaye, isn't Sylvia's house fascinating?"

"Fascinating, indeed."

"I see Smitty hasn't arrived yet," Aunt Alice noted.

"Of course not," Harlan said. "She's probably lurking somewhere in the bush in her caravan of limousines, waiting until she's sure everyone else has appeared."

"Well, there's Creighton," Netty said, "with George Montague and the houseguest we've all heard about."

Kaye looked across the room and wondered why it was that every time she saw Creighton it was the same as seeing him for the first time. The thrill, the uncontrollable excitement, the physical tingling of her flesh were now just as they'd been when she had first seen him on the veranda at Traymore. It was quite simple, she told herself. It was because she loved him.

As if to disentangle herself from the reverie she said, "Houseguest?"

"Ah, we haven't *all* heard about him," Netty said. "His name is Adrian. . .Adrian what, Harlan?"

"I'm sure I don't know," Harlan answered.

"Adrian James," Aunt Alice said.

Netty turned to her with her eyebrows raised and asked, "Do you know him?"

"I met him briefly some years ago. I wouldn't say I know him."

"You met him here in Montego, Alice?" Harlan inquired with a note of curiosity in his tone.

"Yes," Alice answered. "He was Creighton's guest then, too. He's quite charming as I remember—in that dangerous way some men are."

"His visit seems memorable to you, Alice," Netty commented. "What happened?"

Aunt Alice shook her head as if to clear it. "I don't really recall that anything extraordinary happened, Netty. Except perhaps that Adrian James made. . .an impression."

"I can't wait to meet him," Netty said.

Before Sylvia had finished greeting Creighton, Smitty swept into the room with even more guests than she'd had the previous night. Creighton and everyone nearby were temporarily lost in the swarm. When Kaye saw him again, he was about thirty feet from her, introducing Adrian to the Duckworths. As Adrian kissed Mrs. Duckworth's hand—a gesture not often seen in Montego—Creighton looked across the room, directly into Kaye's eyes. He had obviously seen her and knew exactly where she was standing. He turned back to the Duckworths for a moment, then he and George and Adrian started toward Kaye and Aunt Alice.

"Hello, Kaye," he said, and she couldn't read the expression in his eyes.

"Hello, Creighton."

He and George said hello to Aunt Alice and the others, then he added absolutely tonelessly, "I want you to meet Adrian James."

There was no, "an old friend of mine," or "he's down from New York." He simply rattled off the names of the others, except for Aunt Alice, to whom he said, "Alice, you may remember Adrian."

"Of course I do," she replied with a faint smile. "How nice to see you again."

"I'm flattered, Lady Alice," Adrian said. He turned his attention to Kaye so swiftly and so intensely she was taken aback. "Kaye Belliston of the New York Bellistons?"

"I don't remember ever having been referred to in quite that way, but yes, I'm from New York. I'm here visiting my Aunt Alice."

"Ah, a modest celebrity," Adrian noted.

"Come on, Mr. James. I'm not a celebrity."

"Then the *New York Times* has been misled."

"What do you mean?" Kaye asked, genuinely puzzled.

"They seem to spend a great deal of time following you around."

"Oh, do you live in New York?" Kaye asked.

"I have at various times. I love your city. It may be the most exciting one in the world." Adrian smiled somehow wickedly as he said it.

"I agree," Kaye said. "It's so exciting that every now and then it does one good to get away from it."

"Yes, I've just done that," Adrian answered.

"A vacationer like me?" Kaye inquired.

"Kind of. I hadn't seen Creighton in such a long time, and Montego is so peaceful. I'd come here much more often if business didn't keep me away. Isn't that so, Creighton?"

Creighton merely nodded and turned back to Alice. Kaye did not miss the strange expression in the dark gold eyes—an expression she had never seen there previously.

"Will you be here long, Miss Belliston?" Adrian asked.

"I don't know really. And please call me Kaye."

"I'll be happy to, if you'll call me Adrian."

Almost inadvertently she glanced away from Adrian's sparkling blue eyes and saw that Creighton was looking at her. Now she could read his expression. It was stern and forbidding.

"And you, Adrian, will you be here long?" Kaye asked. She realized she was flirting with him, flirting with him solely because Creighton was watching her. It made her feel childish, and she was ashamed of herself.

"A few weeks, I think," Adrian answered, "if Creighton can put up with me."

She saw Creighton moving away toward Herman Zimmerman. It was perfectly natural for him to seek out his host, but there was something sudden and deliberate about his departure.

"Lady Alice," Adrian said, "I know it's a cliché, but you really haven't changed since I saw you so long ago."

"Nor have you, Mr. James. I remember you quite well."

"You had a houseguest at the time. A Miss . . . Sheila Brandon."

"You have an extraordinary memory."

"She was an extraordinarily beautiful woman—not easy to forget."

"She married Anthony Brewster. They live in London, but they come to stay with me from time to time."

"Would you be kind enough to give her my regards when you see her again?"

"Certainly. She'll be complimented."

"I feel compelled to say that as beautiful as Miss Brandon—Lady Brewster—is, she isn't half as beautiful as your niece."

"You're very extravagant," Kaye put in.

"Not at all. I like beautiful people. I've never shunned an ugly friend, but I prefer being with friends who are beautiful. I hope that doesn't sound superficial."

"It sounds honest," Kaye said. "And I'm sure you have many. Beautiful friends, I mean."

"Ah, beautiful and ready with a riposte, as well. I hope we'll see a great deal of each other."

Adrian saw to that immediately. He rarely left Kaye's side during the evening. He was constantly attentive, though not in the fawning way Ellis was or in the intense way Creighton had sometimes been. He was charming and witty and debonair. His presence was so unobtrusive Kaye sometimes was unaware of him. But when she needed a drink, Adrian was there with a fresh one. She didn't know whether it was coincidence or whether Adrian had taken steps to arrange it, but they sat next to each other at dinner. She could tell Creighton was watching from a distance.

Creighton's being there intruded into Kaye's consciousness. She was aware of him even without looking at him, wherever he was in the room. It seemed strange to her, until she realized she was also aware of him when he was miles away from her. She had been aware of him every minute he'd been in Kingston. She was aware of him moment by moment when he was at Penrose and she was at Traymore. His every absence was a palpable reminder of his existence. With him here, watching her, she had to make an effort to be casual and unself-conscious.

After dinner she and Adrian sat with a group of people, but Kaye couldn't shake the feeling they were together. Finally she turned to him and said, "I must find my aunt. I think she'll want to be going home now."

"You're very thoughtful," Adrian said. "Let me help you track her down."

They had gone only a short way through the huge room in search of Aunt Alice when Adrian asked, "Would you have dinner with me tomorrow evening?"

Kaye was startled. "Dinner? I don't know if—"

"There's a marvelous little restaurant overlooking the bay. At least there was. The people we know in Montego don't go there. It's authentic Jamaican food, and it's... unpretentious. I know you'd like it."

"It's very kind of you, but—"

"I know. You don't want to desert your aunt. We'll take Aunt Alice with us."

Kaye thought for a moment and, while she was thinking, saw Creighton quite by chance—or at least she thought it was by chance—looking at her from across the room.

How she wanted to go to him! Yet if she was to maintain any kind of control over her life, she couldn't run to Creighton every time she saw him at a dinner party. She was doing exactly what she should be doing: accepting the blandishments of an attractive newcomer to her life. That kind of behavior would put Creighton in perspective in her own mind. Yes. She had to go on trying to keep her balance.

"I think that would be lovely," she replied. "I'll have to ask Aunt Alice, of course."

"Of course. We can do that as soon as we find her."

Kaye looked up at him. "You really do mean to include her, don't you?"

He gazed at her as if in surprise and answered, "Certainly."

They found Aunt Alice talking with Smitty and the Marlowes. She was, as Kaye had predicted, ready to leave. On the way to the door Kaye extended Adrian's invitation. At first Aunt Alice looked distressed. Then she smiled uneasily and said, "I think it would be far more fun for you if you went without me. I'm really not up to such excursions."

"Please, Lady Alice," Adrian said. "We really would love to have you with us."

"It's very kind of you, Adrian, but I would prefer to stay at home."

He saw them to their car and went back inside. Creighton was waiting for him, just inside the door when he returned.

"Adrian, I don't know what your plans are, but if they include ingratiating yourself with Kaye Belliston, you'd better change them immediately."

"And what will you do if I don't?"

"There's a limit to my patience."

"Your patience, Creighton, has nothing to do with it."

"Don't overplay your hand."

"I can't. I have all the aces."


ADRIAN TOOK KAYE to dinner the following evening. He arrived at Traymore at seven in a rented car. After a drink on the veranda with Aunt Alice, he and Kaye set out for the Palms—the restaurant he had told her about. It was as authentic as he had said it would be. The waiters and the clientele alike were clearly surprised by their presence, but Adrian handled the situation with such aplomb and charm and confidence that he and Kaye were soon totally accepted. They were treated royally, and Kaye was impressed by Adrian's insouciance.

She could not keep from comparing him to Creighton. He was suave where Creighton was sometimes gruff. He was constantly attentive where Creighton was apt to be cavalier. He was openly romantic where Creighton hid his tender feelings.

It was clear to her Adrian was enormously fond of her, but he made it clear in such a gentle understated way that the entire evening was a compliment to her rather than a brazen flirtation. It wasn't until they had left the restaurant that there was any directness about his affection for her.

When they were outside, Adrian said, "I'd love to take a walk. Would that please you?"

"Yes, it would. People don't seem to walk much in Montego. They're either at home or traveling in cars. Or on horseback," she added wistfully.

"Have you been riding with Creighton?"

"Yes, once."

"Many people in Montego ride, but few of them keep horses. Creighton always seems to run against the pack."

"I'm not sure what you mean."

"Just that if nobody keeps horses, Creighton has a stable. If everyone has a staff, Creighton manages with two or three as help. If everyone gives elaborate dinner parties, Creighton gives a tea."

"I've been told it wasn't always that way."

"Ah, yes. Victoria."

"You knew her?"

"Very well. I knew her in Canberra before she and Creighton were married. I'm not really sure anymore—it was so long ago—but I think I was in love with her. Creighton won, as Creighton always does."

"I'm not sure I know what that means, either."

"It doesn't matter. He told me in fairly certain terms to stay away from you."

"He what?"

"You don't seem to know him very well. He's quite possessive."

"He has no right and no reason to be possessive where I'm concerned."

"That never matters to Creighton. I hope you've noticed I've ignored him."

"I'm glad you have."

"There's nothing Creighton or anyone else could say or do that would keep me away from you."

Kaye was surprised by the suddenness and the magnitude of the statement, and she was disarmed by its being as much against Creighton as it was for her.

"You are forthright."

"Kaye, I have not and do not live a sheltered life. I've known a great many attractive women, but you...I'm sorry. I'm being very forward."

"Are you going to make me take back what I said about your being forthright?"

He smiled at her and replied, "No. No, I won't. I haven't met a woman as lovely as you in a very long time. You must know without my telling you that you're very beautiful. But it's a great deal more than that. I knew the instant I saw you there was some kind of affinity between us. I'm afraid I'm being bold. The fact that I felt an affinity doesn't mean there was one. It doesn't mean you felt it, too. And there's another thing. I couldn't possibly know, but I sense you don't want any man to be intensely interested in you at this moment in your life.''

"That's—that's very astute of you.''

"But I'd like us to be friends. May we be discreet?''

"Of course, but I wouldn't want you to make the distance between us too great.''

"I'll try to gauge it carefully. However, I warn you, I think I may fall in love with you.''

"I suppose that's a risk we'll have to take.''

He took her hand then, and they strolled together through the narrow streets of Montego in silence. And as they walked, Kaye thought how much gentler, how much sweeter, how much more considerate than Creighton, Adrian was. She also realized that in making the comparison, she was thinking of Creighton. Why could she not experience the beauty of a sunset, the fragrance of a flower, the wafting of a breeze, the dappling of sunlight without interpreting them in terms of Creighton? Why couldn't she meet a man without comparing him to Creighton? She cursed herself for doing it, but it didn't stop.

# CHAPTER SIX

THE MORNING AFTER her dinner with Adrian Kaye left Traymore, with Henry driving her in the Rolls. She was going to pick up Amanda and go on from there to the airport for the flight to Kingston. They had been deliberately vague about their plans in talking to Aunt Alice and Smitty, partly because they didn't know whether Danny would be able to get extra time off from his job at the beach. All they knew so far was that Danny would catch a plane late that afternoon and meet them at the Terra Nova Hotel in Kingston. Even that small uncertainty added zest to the outing. Amanda seemed to glow with excitement.

When the plane was airborne, Kaye looked down and said, "My goodness, Jamaica is beautiful."

"Today it's pure paradise. Oh, Kaye, I'm so grateful! I hope Danny can stay through Wednesday, but if he can't, we still have tonight and all day tomorrow. It's a gift from heaven—from you and heaven."

"There's another gift from me you may not be so pleased about. I told you I wanted to make the hotel reservations myself. I was very careful about it. We all have separate rooms."

Amanda smiled at her. "I certainly didn't think you'd be so crazy as to put Danny and me in a double. I don't think we'd be very successful at keeping our promise to you if you'd done that."

"Neither do I. I was going to get a double for us, but

I thought that that would be kind of insulting to you. A promise is a promise.''

"Don't worry."

"I worry. Forgive me. I trust you, but I worry."

Amanda laughed and said, ''At least you're honest about it.''

"You be honest, and I can stop worrying."

For the rest of the trip they were as gay and light-hearted as schoolgirls on an outing. When the plane landed, Amanda rushed off in such a hurry that Kaye was left far behind her. Amanda had already got a taxi by the time Kaye caught up to her.

They hadn't gone far before Kaye realized how utterly different Kingston was from Montego. It was by comparison a bustling, somewhat seedy metropolis. There was no mistaking that one was in a tropical climate. The vegetation, the clothing, the architecture readily revealed that. To anyone of even limited experience it was obvious this was the Caribbean. Kingston was more sophisticated, more urban and somehow less exotic than Montego. It was also—for Kaye, at least—less attractive. If their mission had been merely tourism, she would have been disappointed, but since it was romance, she was content.

They arrived at the Terra Nova in time to have lunch on the terrace. As everywhere else in Jamaica, from the tops of the mountains to the shores of the lowlands, the vegetation was rife. Here in the island's largest city plants seemed to push their way up between the cracks in the pavement. Kaye was enchanted by this beautiful floral density, but Amanda kept looking beyond it, over it, around it, as if she expected Danny to pop up from behind a palm tree at any moment.

As they finished lunch, Kaye said, ''Amanda, at this moment Danny is sitting on his perch at Doctor's Cave.

He is not going to jump out at you in delicious surprise. His plane doesn't even leave Montego for another two hours."

Amanda fell back in her chair, suddenly relaxed. "I know I'm being silly, darling. It's just that . . ."

"You're not being silly, and I know what 'it's just.' Do you think I've never been in love?"

"I'm sure you have." She paused for a moment. "Are you?"

"Am I what?"

"In love."

"No. What a strange question."

"I'm sorry, I guess it's none of my affair."

"What's none of your affair?"

"Creighton Jarvis."

"Don't be idiotic, Amanda," Kaye answered more irritably than she'd meant to. "Creighton means absolutely nothing to me."

"I'm sorry, but I don't believe that. Oh, I know I have no evidence, but—"

"You certainly haven't."

"But something seems to happen between you when you're in a room together."

"That's preposterous."

"Even at a large dinner party." Amanda seemed determined to go on, even over Kaye's obviously heated objections. "I've watched you, Kaye. You're deep in conversation with grandmother or your aunt or the Marlowes, and Creighton is arguing with Barney Fairweather and George Montague. Or that's what seems to be going on. But two minutes never pass without you looking at each other."

"That's not true."

"Yes, it is. I've seen it."

Kaye looked away, as if to discourage pursuit of the

topic, then she turned back to Amanda. "I'm going to say this only once, then I want to hear no more about it. I consider you a friend, a very young friend caught up in a fervent romance. Don't attribute to me the feelings you're experiencing yourself. I've gone to a great deal of trouble to bring you here. I've done it at considerable risk to my own reputation in Montego. So you must realize that I understand what it is to be in love."

"Kaye, I—"

"Don't interrupt. So you must also realize that if I were in love with Creighton, if I were even interested in him, you would be broiling on the beach at Doctor's Cave, hopelessly eyeing your forbidden lover, and I would be sitting on this terrace with Creighton Jarvis. I've had some experience in these matters, and since I'm not sitting on this terrace with Creighton Jarvis, you may safely conclude I don't want to be. Is that quite clear?"

"I've offended you."

"You've annoyed me. It's one thing for me to help you in a love affair of which I so far approve. It's quite another for you to assume there's some kind of relationship between me and Creighton. May we drop the subject... permanently?"

Amanda looked down at the tabletop repentantly. "I'm sorry."

"There's nothing to be sorry about. Can we do some shopping while we wait for Danny? I'd like to find something for Aunt Alice."

"Of course."

When they had paid the check and started across the terrace, Kaye put her arm around Amanda's shoulders. "Will you forgive me? I'm afraid you hit a nerve."

Amanda returned the gesture and said, "Oh, Kaye, you are a dear."

"Come on, let's go and buy a surprise for Danny. I think a weird hat would be nice."

DANNY ARRIVED in Kingston at six-thirty, and Kaye and Amanda were waiting for him in the cocktail lounge of the hotel. He came across the room beaming, as though he were walking in an aura of Doctor's Cave sun that he had somehow brought with him. He was so unashamedly boyish and beautiful that Kaye was almost embarrassed.

As he approached, Kaye said to Amanda, "If you get up and throw your arms around him, I'll kill you."

Kaye thought it was above and beyond the call of duty that he greeted her first. "Hello, Kaye. You're wonderful."

"Hello, Danny. I didn't know you'd transferred your affections," Kaye said.

He grinned, and the grin faded to an expression of wistfulness as he looked at Amanda. "Hello, Mandy."

"Hello, Danny."

With great effort he pulled his eyes away from her and said to Kaye, "May I join you?"

"It would be a terrible waste of time if you didn't," Kaye quipped. Danny sat down. "How was the flight?"

"Boring. I couldn't wait to get here."

"Stop acting like a nineteen-year-old boy from Cleveland," Kaye teased.

"I *am* a nineteen-year-old boy from Cleveland."

Kaye looked at him laughingly. "Well, at the risk of a breach in international relations I'm going to leave the nineteen-year-old boy from Cleveland with the nineteen-year-old girl from London. It may be a painful bit of information for you both, but I'm joining you for dinner at nine on the terrace."

"We wouldn't have it any other way," Danny said.

"No other way at all," Amanda added.

"I don't believe you for a minute, but thank you very much." She got up as Danny got up, too. "Have a lovely time." She smiled at them and said, "And don't think I don't envy you." Then she turned and walked away toward the elevators.

She felt an inexplicable sense of sadness. She turned back in time to see Amanda and Danny hurrying across the front terrace of the hotel, their arms around each other's waists. Even without seeing their faces, she could tell how much in love they were from the way they touched, from the gentleness between them. She watched them go with complete faith in them.

Kaye decided to take advantage of the rare afternoon alone by doing nothing. And by doing nothing, she left herself open to thoughts of Creighton. She gave up resisting and let herself think about him—about how much she loved him, about how much she wanted him and, inevitably, about how wrong it would be for her to indulge her desires.

At eight she dressed and went down to the hotel terrace to wait for Amanda and Danny. She ordered a margarita, and before it was served, she saw them coming up the stairs to the terrace. They saw her, too, and hurried to her table.

"Hello, young lovers," Kaye greeted them. "How was your excursion?"

"Glorious," Amanda answered.

"Super," Danny said as he seated Amanda and sat down himself.

They immediately began glancing at each other furtively and smiling a great deal, as if they were trying to hide a guilty secret.

Kaye watched them for a few minutes, looking from one to the other. At last she said, "All right, you two. What's going on?"

"Haven't you noticed anything?" Amanda asked.

"Only that you're behaving like a couple of naughty children."

"Then you haven't looked very carefully," Amanda teased.

Kaye peered at them both. "You don't seem to me to have changed one iota since I last saw you."

"Oh, yes, we have," Danny replied.

Amanda held out her left hand, and Kaye looked at it, blankly at first. Then her expression changed to one of exaggerated alarm. There on Amanda's finger was a small modest diamond ring.

"Oh, no!" Kaye cried. "What have you done?"

"Just what it looks like," Danny told her.

"Are you crazy?"

"Oh, Kaye, be happy for us," Amanda said.

"Happy? When you've lost your minds? You can't be engaged."

"Why not?" Danny asked.

"Because—because...well, because of Smitty for one big reason."

"We're certainly not going to tell her," Danny said.

"Then what's the point?"

"We love each other," Amanda replied.

"I know that, but can't you love each other without being engaged?"

"It's just between us, Kaye," Danny said. "Nobody else but you is even going to know about it."

"Well...I guess I didn't mean to seem quite so shocked. It's just that...it's a rather big step."

"It hasn't really changed anything," Danny said. "We know we love each other, and we know we want to get married eventually. We also know we're not going to do it until I've finished school and can afford to get married. There's nothing wrong with long engagements, is there?"

"I'm all for them," Kaye said. "I suppose to all intents and purposes you were engaged anyway."

"Yes, we were," Amanda put in, taking Danny's hand and smiling at Kaye. "Now it's official, but only as far as we're concerned."

"Well, I guess it's champagne time." Kaye leaned across the table and kissed Amanda on the cheek. She turned to Danny. "You're very rash." Then she kissed him, too.

She summoned a waiter and ordered a bottle of champagne, and they had a lovely joyous dinner. Amanda and Danny were as happy as if they'd been sitting there discussing their wedding plans. Kaye realized it would be both painful and dangerous for them to talk too much about their uncertain future, and she admired them for being so sensible and so satisfied with their lot.

Suddenly Amanda looked puzzled. She said to Kaye, "Didn't you say something about there being nothing between you and Creighton Jarvis?"

"You know quite well I did."

"Then why do you suppose he just walked out onto the terrace and is looking straight at our table?"

Kaye's face went pale. She resisted her immediate impulse to turn around and look. "You must be joking."

"He's standing right by the French doors. He's undoubtedly going to come over here. How are we going to explain Danny?"

It was by no means Kaye's immediate concern, but she thought about it quickly. "He's a boy you met last summer at the beach, and we just happened to bump into him here in Kingston. I thought it would be nice if we had dinner together. There's no reason for him to be suspicious of that, but you'd better take off the ring."

Amanda let out a little gasp and took it off. Hurriedly she dropped it into her handbag.

Kaye's heart leaped as she saw Creighton coming toward them. Had Aunt Alice casually told him Kaye and Amanda had gone to Kingston? And had he followed her all the way just to be with her? She tried to make herself feel it was impertinent of him if he had, but what she really felt was it was rash and gallant and romantic of him—if he had. She couldn't change her heart; she hoped he was here because of her.

"Good evening, Amanda," Creighton said.

"What a surprise, Creighton," Amanda answered. "We didn't expect to see you here."

"Hello, Kaye," Creighton said, glancing at her. He then added to Amanda, "The trip came up suddenly."

"Hello, Creighton," Kaye said simply. There was no expression in either of their voices.

"Creighton," Amanda began, "I want you to meet a friend of mine, Danny Riordan. Danny, this is Creighton Jarvis, a neighbor of ours in Montego."

Danny stood up and extended his hand. "Hello, Mr. Jarvis."

"Two surprises in one day," Amanda said, smiling. "Danny and I met last year at Doctor's Cave, and lo and behold we just bumped into him this afternoon here in Kingston. He's American, of course, and he's waiting for some American friends to arrive. We couldn't let him have dinner alone."

"Are you having a pleasant stay?" Creighton asked them.

"So far it's been splendid," Amanda offered. "Kaye has never been to Kingston, of course, and I volunteered to show it to her. I haven't been here all that often myself, but I do know some of the places one should see."

"Alice told me," he said to no one in particular. "Kingston is so unlike Montego. Don't you agree, Kaye?"

"Yes." In spite of the empty chair at the table, Creighton, much to Kaye's relief, made no attempt to join them.

"I come here fairly often on business trips—with George Montague mostly, as was the case today. It is the capital, after all. It was nice to meet you, Mr. Riordan." He turned to Amanda and Kaye. "I hope you continue to have a splendid time. Good evening." Then he turned and walked back to the maître d's desk, where there was some discussion. Finally he was led to a corner table from which it was very difficult for the others to see him.

"He's kind of a cold fish, isn't he?" Danny said. "Or maybe I should just say he's cool."

"Sometimes I think he's both," Amanda declared. "And I don't think he believed a word I said about meeting you by chance."

"Why shouldn't he?" Kaye asked.

"I don't know. I just don't think I sounded very convincing. Of course, you can never tell what Creighton's thinking. Unless he wants you to know. Then he simply comes right out with it in no uncertain terms."

"I wouldn't be too concerned about his believing you," Kaye said.

"Why?"

"Two reasons. I'm sure that if Creighton suspected or even knew about you and Danny, he wouldn't go to Smitty. He isn't the kind of man to meddle."

"I think you're right," Amanda agreed.

"Second, since he was lying, too, I don't see why he should be concerned about your lying."

"Creighton? Lying?"

"Yes. Do you really believe he came to Kingston on political business with George Montague? If he did, where's George? Why aren't they having dinner together?"

"There could be a hundred reasons," Amanda said.

"Yes, of course there could."

"But, Kaye, why would Creighton lie about the reason for his being here?"

"For the same reason you did. He doesn't want anyone to know the real reason."

"Do you know the...?" Amanda's eyes opened wide. "Oh...oh! He knew we were here because Lady Alice told him. You think he came *because* he knew we were here, because he knew *you* were here?"

"I don't mean to flatter myself, and I certainly don't pretend to *know* why he came, but my instincts tell me it had nothing to do with George Montague and politics."

"Would you be pleased if you were right?" Amanda inquired.

Kaye looked in the direction of Creighton's table. "I don't know." She turned back to them. "It's too complicated to explain, and you don't want to waste your evening talking about Creighton Jarvis. That looks like a lovely garden out there beyond the terrace. Why don't you two go for a walk?"

"And leave you alone?" Amanda asked.

"No way," Danny said.

"Don't be noble. This whole trip was planned at great risk to us all so that you could be together. Now go on."

"You're some chaperon," Danny added, "always sending us off by ourselves. What would Grandmother Smith-Croydon say?"

"I shudder to think," Kaye replied, "but I want to be there the first time you call her that. Get out of here."

They walked across the terrace, careful not to touch each other because of Creighton's presence, and down the steps into the garden. Kaye watched them rather wistfully. What she wanted was not simply to be in love again—as she knew she was—but to be able to start over, to be nineteen and be in love for the first time. What nonsense, she told herself as she thought of Creighton sitting in the shadows across the terrace. She loved him at this moment, at her age, and there wasn't anyone else in the world she wanted to love.

"Excuse me. Would you join me and allow me to offer you a cognac?"

The voice was unmistakably Creighton's. She looked up to see him standing by her, unsmiling, the amber eyes hard and unyielding.

Kaye hesitated. "I'm not sure if I should."

"I don't see why not. We're simply a man and a woman who know each other and find themselves alone at separate tables on a hotel terrace. What could be more natural than my inviting you to join me?"

"Just a man and a woman who know each other, Creighton? Is that what we are?"

"It's what you seem to want us to be. I'm merely cooperating."

His sarcasm made her hesitate further. She was about to refuse his offer when a wry grin crept across his face.

"I'm only teasing," he added. "I really would like you to join me."

His smile made her feel free to do what she had wanted to do all along. "All right. Thank you."

He pulled back her chair and escorted her across the terrace to the small corner table. Two cognacs were already on the table. He seated her, then sat down across from her.

Kaye looked at the two brandies and said, "Creighton, forever confident."

"Not at all. I would have drunk the second one myself if you'd refused."

"And forever charming."

"I wasn't being sarcastic. I dislike waste. I would

have drunk the second one, but I would have been disappointed if you hadn't joined me."

"Would you?"

"You know I would. Amanda and her young man are an attractive couple."

"He is not her young man, and if by couple you mean simply two people, yes, they're an attractive couple. They're no more than that."

"I didn't mean to imply they were."

"I think you did."

"Why do you always argue?"

"Why do *I* always argue? You're the most contentious person I've ever met. And what's worse, you enjoy starting arguments over nothing."

"I suppose I'm just getting old and cantankerous."

"You are hardly getting old."

"Touché. We're beginning to sound like a mellowly married couple."

"If you're about to suggest that in that case we may as well *be* a mellowly married couple, I'm sorry I joined you."

"I promise you I'll mind my manners."

They were quiet for a moment, until Kaye said, "Creighton, why did you ask me to join you?"

"Obviously because I wanted to be with you—and because I want to tell you I must have been insane to say I never wanted to hear your voice again. The truth is, I'd be perfectly happy hearing nothing but the sound of your voice for the rest of my life."

"That's the most romantic apology I've ever had."

"You told me I was a romantic. You must have convinced me."

"Oh, Creighton, what are we going to do?"

"I have a suggestion," he said casually. "There's a club here I know you'd enjoy. We can make the ten o'clock show. Just a man and a woman who know each other out on a date. What do you say?''

Kaye actually giggled. "I'd love it," she answered.

"Wonderful!"

Creighton signed the check, and they grabbed a taxi in front of the hotel. They reached the nightclub just as the show was beginning. It was brash and loud and vulgar and irresistibly funny. They sat side by side at a tiny round table. The more they laughed, the more they had to laugh. They clutched each other in mirth and held hands in their quieter moments. They drank a bit more than either of them usually did, and neither of them cared.

On the way back to the hotel they reminded each other of various moments from the show and burst into laughter again and again like two children on the way home from a movie.

When they stepped out of the taxi in front of the Terra Nova and realized it was once again time to part, they became quiet. Finally Creighton broke the awkward silence.

"A cognac in the bar?"

"I don't think so, Creighton," Kaye replied.

"A cognac in my suite?"

"You can't be serious."

"Oh, yes, I am. I have a lovely bottle of Courvoisier and two snifters."

"As I said, forever confident."

"Why not, Kaye? After all, I'm not a brute. I'm not going to assault you. If we're not adult enough to have a nightcap together in a hotel suite, there must be something terribly wrong with both of us."

"I suppose you're right. Okay, Creighton, I accept."

The suite was comfortable and tastefully furnished. As soon as she entered it, Kaye wondered if Creighton had arranged the lighting deliberately in anticipation of their being alone there. There were four lamps, but they were turned so low they created a gentle romantic glow. The French doors that led to the tiny balcony were open, and a breeze stirred the curtains almost imperceptibly. Kaye sat on a sofa while Creighton poured the brandy. He handed a snifter to her and sat down at the other end of the sofa.

Raising his glass, he said, "Cheers."

"Cheers," Kaye answered, and they both drank.

"I'm so glad you enjoyed the show," Creighton remarked. "I wasn't entirely sure you would. It gets a bit heavy-handed."

"I haven't had such a good time in ages."

"It is a change of pace from Montego dinner parties."

"For which I thank God."

"Are you bored there?"

"Not really," Kaye replied. "But a change of pace *is* welcome."

"Oh, I almost forgot one of the reasons I wanted you to come up here. I want you to see the view from the balcony. Come on."

He took her hand and pulled her to her feet. He led her out onto the balcony, which was just big enough for a wrought iron table and two chairs. He took her to the low railing and extended his arm.

"There. I know it isn't spectacular; that isn't the point. Does it remind you of anywhere? Not the specifics. Forget the palm trees. Think of it only in terms of geometric shapes. Stare for a moment. I know it will come to you."

Kaye stared, almost squinting at the panorama before her. After a moment she said, "It looks like Paris—the Left Bank!"

"Exactly. I knew you wouldn't fail me." He bent to-

ward her and kissed her on the lips without otherwise
touching her.

The contact of his lips on hers couldn't have lasted
more than three seconds, but it thrilled Kaye as much as
if he had taken her in his arms. She struggled to regain
her poise.

"You know Paris?" she asked—idiotically, it seemed
to her.

"Very well. I've told you I'm not a country bumpkin.
Victoria loved Paris. We kept an apartment there while
we were married. We'd run off every now and then, if
only for a weekend."

"You never cease to amaze me, Creighton Jarvis."

"Why do you say that?"

"I'm sorry, but I can't quite picture your running off
from Montego for a weekend in Paris."

"Don't underestimate me. And remember, I was in
love—as I am now."

"Creighton. Oh, darling Creighton."

He took her in his arms, and as always, his touch was
as gentle as the breeze that caressed them. His kiss was
gentle, too, for a moment, but the touch of their mouths
was too violently exciting. Kaye's arms went around
him, and the fingers of one hand wound into his hair as
she pressed his head closer to hers. His arm around her
waist felt like a band of steel, and he pulled her whole
body against his, as if she weighed no more than a
feather. For a long moment they stayed locked in each
other's arms, everything forgotten except their physical
contact. The feel of their thinly covered flesh pressed so
closely was intoxicating. Kaye drew back and looked
into his eyes. In the moonlight they were the color of
topaz, and they shone with love and desire.

"Creighton, I shouldn't have come here."

"Yes, you should have. You belong here. You belong

with me." She began to pull away, but he held her firmly. "Don't go before I tell you what a cad I am. I told you that I wasn't a brute, that I wouldn't assault you. But I haven't been above luring you into my web for my own purposes. And here's my purpose."

He reached into a pocket of his jacket and took out a tiny velvet box. Before Kaye could speak, he lifted the lid and held the box before her. It was the simplest, most beautiful diamond ring Kaye had ever seen: a single glittering stone in an exquisitely delicate Tiffany setting. She drew in her breath involuntarily at the sight of it.

"It was my grandmother's engagement ring...and my mother's. It's meant to stay in the family. I'm offering it to you."

"Creighton—"

"Let me finish. I know very well how you feel about marriage. All I'm asking is that you become engaged to me. It isn't a commitment to marriage. You can end it anytime you want simply by taking off the ring. There's no wedding date. There are no plans for the future. There's only—forgive the old-fashioned word—a troth between us, a tangible expression of our love, a bond for as long as you want it to last. I want you to be mine, if not forever, at least for a while."

Kaye couldn't help it. She had begun to cry as soon as she had seen the ring. Now the tears were streaming down her cheeks and she could hardly speak.

"Oh, Creighton, I love you so much!"

He started to pull her back to him, but she held him away.

"I can't accept it. It *would* be a commitment. It *would* be a promise of marriage. At least it would be to me. And I can't do that to you."

"Give me that much, Kaye. I won't beg you."

She heard the steely hardness creeping into his voice.

Could she do nothing but hurt him? Could she do nothing but make him angry when she loved him so desperately? She turned away, her face buried in her hands.

"All right," Creighton said. "I want to tell you something. When Alice mentioned you were going on an excursion to Kingston with Amanda, I was furious—furious you could shrug off what had happened between us and just go off on holiday. I decided to follow you, to seduce you with every romantic trick I knew. I wanted to bring you to the very point of going to bed with me so I could reject you at just that moment. I wanted to hurt you, Kaye. I was at the front door of Penrose with the car waiting in the driveway and my whole brain seething with anger, and I stopped right there with my hand on the doorknob. And all the anger, all the resentment flowed out of me; all that was left was my deep love for you. I went back up to the safe in my study and took out my grandmother's ring, knowing that I could never hurt you, knowing that I wanted you, needed you, even on the precarious terms I offered you just now. I don't know why you make our love a battlefield, but you do. All right. You've won the battle. The victory is yours. I'm not used to the taste of defeat; perhaps that's why it's so bitter to me. But one thing I do know: you'll never hurt me again. I'm sure you're capable of finding your way back to your room. Get out, Kaye. Just get out."

She turned back to him and started to reach for him. He was looking out over the city, his chiseled profile proud in the moonlight. She could think only that she had lost him irrevocably. She started to speak his name but couldn't. She turned away, still crying as she crossed the room, and closed the door of the suite behind her.

She ran to her room and threw herself on the bed, sobbing until there were no more tears left. For a long time she lay in the darkness, with her face buried in the

pillow and her head flooded with contradictory
thoughts. She got up from the bed and dabbed her eyes
with cool water. She looked at herself in the mirror. Her
confusion was so great she felt she might as well have
been looking at a stranger.

She went out onto the small balcony and looked out
over the moonlit rooftops of Kingston, as she had a little
while ago with Creighton. Creighton—the iron-willed
iron-muscled Australian who was able to see Paris in the
rooftops of Kingston. Creighton—the sometimes harsh,
sometimes gentle giant who had tenderly offered her his
grandmother's ring and an engagement on her terms. It
was no wonder she was confused. She had never known a
man of such extremes. She never knew what to expect
from him. How could she ever share a life with someone
so unpredictable? How could she—

She stopped in midthought and looked up at the
moon, that pale disk that was said to drive men mad.
Well, it wasn't going to drive her mad. She was going to
face her situation for once and for all, and she was going to begin by asking herself what it was she had to face
and why her need to face it was so insistent.

Creighton had offered her a good and gentle and gallant proposal of marriage. She loved him, and he loved
her. Yet she had refused him. She decided she had better
examine her reasons and make sure they were good
ones, and she swore to herself that if they weren't, she
would go to him and give him her life, the way he had
offered his to her.

Immediately she remembered a conversation with
Aunt Alice about husbands and wives having things in
common. What did she and Creighton really have in
common aside from their love and their passionate
desire for each other? *Good,* she said to herself, *I'm listening to my head instead of my heart. Love and desire*

may be enough for a wild fleeting affair, but are they enough for a lifetime together? "No," she said aloud, shaking her head. Oh, there would doubtless be an idyll, maybe brief, maybe prolonged. But it would end. What then? Another part of her now overactive brain told her she was being asked to live in a physical paradise with the man she loved and who loved her. Why must the idyll end? She answered that only schoolgirls believe that kind of ecstasy lasts forever. When it ended, as it must, what would there be? Montego *was* a paradise, but could she bear the tropical sameness day in and day out for the rest of her life? The dinner parties were novel and amusing—for a time.

Jamaica was Creighton's adopted country, and he loved it, but she had no such feelings for it. What would happen when she became bored with the endless routine? What would happen when she began to long for New York and Paris and Rome?

Creighton was right, of course. He was no country bumpkin. He had gone to Paris with Victoria. But he had been more resilient then and less dedicated to his land and to the politics of his adopted country. She could see the scenario for the future. She could see her suggesting to him that they go abroad for a while. He would agree immediately, to please her. He'd say a fortnight abroad would do them both good. Then she would explain she hadn't meant a fortnight. She didn't want them to go to London for a week and Rome for a week like two tourists, then come right back to Montego. She would want to spend some time in New York with her mother. She would want to stay in London long enough for Creighton really to get to know her many close friends there.

Surely they could arrange to be gone for two or three months—at least. Perhaps they could even establish a routine of six months a year in Montego and six months a year traveling. They might even maintain apartments in their favorite cities. Almost everyone else did it. Smitty circulated regularly between Montego, London and Cannes. The Zimmermans split the year with three months in New York, three in the Hamptons and six in Montego. The Marlowes' schedule was even more flexible. They traveled when they felt like it, stayed in London when they liked and came back to Montego for as much of the season as they wished.

Only the seasoned veterans—Aunt Alice, Creighton, the Duckworths, Barney Fairweather and a handful of others—stayed the year round. And there was the rub. For Creighton, Montego was a way of life, not a temporary retreat. He had planted roots there, and there he would stay. If he had ever had wanderlust, he had now lost it. She never would. She and Creighton had less in common than even—than even—Amanda and Danny.

The thoughts struck her as immediately and incessantly as hailstones. *She* had been counseling Amanda? She, in all her uncertainty and confusion, had been advising two young lovers? And advising them to do what? To stay together in spite of everything—in spite of the fact Amanda was an extremely wealthy upper-class English girl who had no doubt been presented at court, who routinely spent weekends in the stately homes of England, whose social activities were chronicled in the London press, whose family could be traced back to the sixteenth century, and Danny was a middle-class American boy with an uncertain future, whose family tree became vague after three generations of tracing and who was inextricably bound to the American way of life.

If, by some elaborate miracle, they were ever able to marry, where would they live? How would they live? Danny would never live off Amanda's fortune, and

Amanda would applaud that—in the beginning. If they lived in London, Danny would be ill-equipped to work there. If they lived in the States, on Danny's twenty thousand dollars a year, what of the luxuries Amanda already took for granted? She, Kaye, was leading them into the very trap she herself was trying to avoid. She would have to go to them tomorrow and tell them how wrong she had been.

Just then she turned away from the maddening moon. Quite inadvertently she looked along the row of balconies that jutted from the wall of the hotel. In the distance she saw Creighton's massive figure bathed in moonlight. He was standing on his balcony, casually holding a drink. He had been watching her. Her hand had already started out in a gesture toward him, when he disappeared into the living room of his suite.

She stood alone, looking at the distant, empty, moonlit balcony, where she had so recently stood in Creighton's arms. She felt again the closeness, the strength, the warmth, the power of him. She felt his mouth against hers. She felt his arms pressing her to him in mutual necessity. She felt her being melt into his.

All the practical, objective, rational gibberish she had been forcing through her mind seemed to vaporize. *Go to him,* she told herself. *Go to him and give yourself to him wholeheartedly and without reservation!*

She went into her room and crossed it without knowing she had done so. Her hand was on the doorknob before she caught herself. She knew then she would not go to him—and she knew why.

Creighton was everything she had always wanted in a man. He was a man capable of, above all else, willfulness and dominance, yet overflowing with gentleness and kindness and love. He had offered himself to her, first on his terms, then on hers. With all his manliness and dignity even humility was not beyond him. She knew this was a mark of his great strength. What more could she want? He was perfect.

No, it wasn't Creighton who was at fault. If there was any fault to be found, it was with her. Finally she was able to admit it: she was afraid. She was afraid of failing again. She was sure now that all the things she had told herself about her relationship with Rod were excuses. She had been too demanding, too exacting. She had expected her marriage to be exactly as she had pictured it. She believed now she had browbeaten Rod. Creighton would never allow her to do that to. . . .

There it was again. She was picturing a life with him, all the while telling herself why it wouldn't work. She couldn't think anymore. She would take a warm bath and try to stop thinking about it altogether. After a good night's sleep she'd be able to sort it all out.

But she did not have a good night's sleep, and she did not sort it all out. She hardly slept, and when she did, she dreamed of Creighton—the same sensuous, erotic, passionate dreams that had plagued her in the past. The last one woke her just after dawn, and she realized there was no point in trying to sleep again. She put on a robe and went out to the balcony, where she sat pretending to herself she was not hoping to catch a glimpse of Creighton. She sat there until nine with guarded impatience, but he did not appear. She wondered if he had left during the night. Then—it seemed almost suddenly—it was time to meet Amanda and Danny for breakfast.

They were waiting for her at a table on the terrace. She saw them before they saw her, and she paused for a moment, watching them in their uncomplicated joy. How different it was for her and Creighton, she thought as she watched them laughing and touching in utter innocence. Why couldn't it be that way for her? She found the answers obvious. Because she and Creighton were older. Because she and Creighton had each been married. Because she and Creighton had become cynical from the experience of love. Or was it only she who had become cynical? She braced herself and walked across the terrace to the table.

"Good morning," she said. "Mind if I join you?"

Danny stood up and replied, "Of course we don't mind. We've been waiting for you." He pulled out a chair for her. "But I wish you'd stop calling us children."

As she sat, she said, "I apologize, Danny. I'm just beginning to realize being a child has nothing to do with chronological age."

It was already clear to both Amanda and Danny that something was wrong with Kaye. She was making an obvious effort to be cheerful. She was working at being pleasant. It soon became too obvious to ignore.

"Kaye, is there something wrong?" Amanda asked.

"Wrong? Of course not. What could be wrong?"

"I don't know. You seem...distant is the word, I suppose."

"Nonsense. I've never felt better. Now how are you two going to spend your day?"

"We haven't decided," Danny replied, "but whatever we do, we wish you'd come with us."

Kaye smiled. "Danny, that's very sweet of you, but you don't want me traipsing along."

"Do come with us," Amanda urged.

"Absolutely not," Kaye answered. "We came here so that you could have some time together. And as a matter of fact, I wouldn't mind having some time alone. I can have a swim; I can lunch at the pool." She paused for a moment. "I have some things to think about."

"Are you quite sure?" Amanda asked.

"Quite sure. You go on and have your day together. But remember, since Danny couldn't get anyone to work for him, we have to go back tonight. There's a ten-o'clock flight. I'll call Aunt Alice and have Henry meet us at the airport with the car. Once we land, you'll have to make yourself scarce, Danny. We don't want Henry to see us together. I don't know if he gossips, but we mustn't take any chances. And do remember to take off your ring, Amanda. If there's nobody we know on the plane, Danny and I can switch seats so that you can be together a little longer."

"We have to be careful about that," Danny said. "I told Mandy, but I haven't told you that Mr. Jarvis was on the plane I came in on."

Kaye's face paled at the mention of Creighton's name. She tried to maintain her composure, but she couldn't think of anything to say.

"I suppose we should be going," Amanda said. "Are you sure you won't. . . ."

"I'm sure. You run along. I'll see you at dinner."

When Amanda and Danny had gone, Kaye had her swim. Then she went shopping and bought a lace stole for Aunt Alice and presents for the servants. She had lunch. She window-shopped. She did everything she could to keep her mind off Creighton. To some extent she succeeded, but fragments of memory kept breaking through her defenses. She didn't allow them to linger. By the end of the afternoon she was exhausted from her effort.

She took a taxi back to the hotel and had a nap and a long bath, after which she dressed and went downstairs to meet Amanda and Danny. Once again they were waiting for her on the terrace. She interpreted their punctuality as a mark of respect and gratitude, and she was right.

"I hope you had a wonderful time today," she said as Danny pulled out a chair for her.

"We did," Amanda answered—rather too intensely.

"Your enthusiasm tells me it must have been quite special," Kaye remarked.

"Quite special," Amanda echoed.

"Well," Kaye began, "shall we celebrate again?"

"Celebrate what?" Danny asked.

"Your glorious holiday together."

"You mean the end of it," Danny said glumly.

"That, young man, is a negative attitude. Would you rather not have had it at all?"

"Not on your life."

"There you are, then. Be happy and thankful for what you've had, not gloomy and depressed because it has to end. And *remember*, if we pulled it off once, we can pull it off again. Well, if we're going to get that plane, we should order."

"It's funny," Amanda said. "Ever since Danny and I got back to the hotel, I've been putting things off. I brought practically nothing, but it took me ages to pack. I dawdled for half an hour before getting dressed to come down to dinner. Now I don't feel like ordering. I guess it's just a futile attempt to keep things from ending. But I do so hate to see it end."

"You'd hardly be human if you didn't."

"I know we've thanked you earlier, but 'thanks a lot' doesn't seem to be enough to cover what you've done for us," Danny said. "You did it to make us happy, so maybe it'll be some kind of repayment for you to know that it was, hands down, the most wonderful time of my entire life."

"If there's a debt, that pays it," Kaye replied.

"It was blissful," Amanda said. "Thank you, dear Kaye."

They had a very pleasant dinner, but the air of festivity gradually diminished as their departure time neared. Amanda and Danny sat together on the plane, and sitting alone, with no distractions available, Kaye's thoughts turned inevitably to Creighton. Her salient feeling was one of confusion. The truth was creeping up on her. The plane was taking her back to Montego, back to Traymore, back to Aunt Alice, but more than anything else it was taking her back to Creighton.

Amanda and Danny said their goodbyes on the plane—which was fortunate, because the first person they saw upon disembarking was Henry.

It was after eleven thirty when Kaye got to Traymore, but Aunt Alice was waiting up for her. As usual, they went into the sitting room for a chat before going upstairs.

"It's good to have you home," Aunt Alice said. "I've missed you."

"I've missed you, too, auntie."

"Did you have a good time?"

Kaye found the question ironic, and for a moment she considered sharing the irony with Aunt Alice, mentioning she had seen Creighton. But since she couldn't tell her what had happened, she decided there was really no point in revealing it at all.

"Yes, it was very pleasant. Amanda showed me the sights, and we went to the Blue Boar for lunch. You were right; it's charming." She made a mental note to tell Amanda she had said that. "I do think one visit to Kingston is enough. I mean, you don't find there what you have in Montego. I bought you a present, but I'm not going to give it to you until I unpack—which will be tomorrow."

"That was very thoughtful. Kaye, you look tired. Did you overdo your little holiday?"

"I think perhaps I did. With all my alleged sophistica-
tion, I turn into a tourist every time I arrive in a city I've
never been to previously."

"I think that's wonderful," Aunt Alice remarked.
"If you can manage that for the rest of your life, you'll
never be old."

"Ah, that's your secret."

Alice smiled wryly, a thousand memories flickering in
her mind. "Part of it," she said. "Did Amanda have a
pleasant time?"

Kaye was instantly alarmed. It was exactly what Aunt
Alice would say if she knew about Danny. It was typical
of her grace and charm. On the other hand, it may have
been no more than an idle question.

Kaye pulled herself up and said, "I think so. I think
she rather enjoyed showing me the town.... If you
don't mind, darling, it's off to bed for me."

"And for me."

They went upstairs and, after a loving hug, went to
their rooms. Kaye was more tired than she had realized.
In fact, she was nearly exhausted. She got into bed and
after a few troubled thoughts fell into a deep uninterrupted slumber.

She woke the next morning feeling refreshed by her
sound sleep. The events of Kingston came back to her in
a kind of miasma, a kind of foggy mixture of memories
and emotions. She was angry with herself for her feeling
of inertia. For the first time in her life she was allowing
circumstances, other people, accidental events, to dominate her life. She felt like a tiny bit of flotsam being
tossed this way and that. Her ambiguous feelings toward Creighton, her sense of disloyalty to Aunt Alice
and Smitty, her keeping all of it from Aunt Alice while
accepting her unlimited hospitality and kindness, all
crashed in on her and dizzied her. She felt defeated by

the simple dilemma of wanting to go downstairs to be with Aunt Alice, yet being unable to until she had somehow pulled herself together. Finally she threw everything else aside and walked down the stairs to find Aunt Alice writing letters in her cherished little sitting room.

"Good morning, Kaye," Aunt Alice addressed her cheerfully. "I thought a good sleep was exactly what you needed, so I decided not to disturb you. You look radiant. You must have slept well."

"I slept absolutely mindlessly—which was, indeed, just what I needed."

"Splendid. Now summon Helen, and we'll get you some breakfast."

"All I want is some juice and a cup of tea," Kaye replied.

"Are you sure that's enough? You must keep up your strength if you're to continue the strenuous life you've been leading."

"Strenuous life?" Kaye repeated, astonished at Aunt Alice's astuteness.

"Well, you have our usual round of dinner parties to deal with, and you have poor Ellis panting after you. You're hardly back from an overnight trip to Kingston, when Adrian James is on the telephone inquiring after you. And—"

"Adrian called?"

"At ten this morning. Of course, there's the extra burden of having Creighton follow you to Kingston." Kaye looked at her in amazement. "Darling, the servants are as much a part of our society as we are ourselves. Christian, Creighton's butler, is Henry's half brother. Helen is married to Smitty's cook's first cousin, and their son is engaged to one of the Zimmermans' maids. It's endlessly entangled, and whether we like it or not, it creates a grapevine that keeps us all informed of one another's comings and goings. Montego is no place in which to try to be circumspect. Do, sit down, dear.''

"I'm sorry. I'm kind of astonished." She was not only astonished, she was afraid—afraid for Danny and Amanda. Under these circumstances how could they hope to keep their relationship secret?

There was a brief respite from the tension when Helen arrived to take Kaye's breakfast order. When she had gone, Aunt Alice said, "If Creighton went to Kingston to see you, I'm sure he succeeded."

"Yes, he did."

"I certainly won't ask you to tell me about the encounter, but you must understand that any involvement between Creighton Jarvis and a member of my family is a matter of great concern to me."

"Aunt Alice, there is no involvement, and there never will be."

"It's unlike Creighton to pursue women. There must be some substance to whatever is going on. For the moment I will ask no questions. However, I hope you would want to keep me informed of any developing attachment."

"You're angry with me."

Aunt Alice looked up from her writing. "Oh, my darling, no. Please try to understand. This is not New York, where there are so many people that liaisons can go unnoticed."

"Liaison is certainly not the proper word to describe whatever relationship there is between Creighton and me."

"Now you're angry with me."

"I could never be."

"We'll say no more about it for the moment. It's up to you if you wish to return Adrian's call. He seemed . . . eager to talk to you."

"I do wish to. I'll do it right now."

As she started toward the telephone in the drawing room, she realized there was a possibility Creighton would answer. She told herself she didn't care and, with a sense of defiance, dialed the number. Christian answered.

"Mr. Jarvis's residence."

"This is Miss Belliston. Is Mr. James there?"

"One moment, Miss Belliston."

Adrian came on the line. "Kaye. How good of you to return my call."

"Not at all."

"I'm afraid I'm a bit embarrassed about all this."

"Embarrassed? About what?"

"I wanted to ask you here for lunch and an afternoon by the pool, but when I asked Creighton about it, he forbade my doing so. I suppose that's neither here nor there, but I can't just go on not seeing you. Would you think it terribly rude of me to suggest that I might come to you? Would you give a poor starving wretch lunch and a swim one day?"

Kaye was startled by the proposal, but it immediately seemed attractive in a number of ways.

"Certainly. I'd be delighted. How about today?"

"You're an angel."

"Let's see. It's almost noon. Why don't you just come ahead when you're ready?"

"That's delightful. I'll be there within the hour."

Aunt Alice didn't seem enthusiastic about the plan when Kaye announced it, but she made no objection. Adrian arrived shortly, driving Creighton's Porsche—which for some reason puzzled Kaye. She and Aunt Alice were sitting on the veranda, and Kaye went to the top of the stairs to greet Adrian.

"This is very kind of you," Adrian began as he mounted the steps. "I'm sure you must think me a clod."

"Not at all. Come and have a drink before our swim."

Adrian came onto the veranda and said, "Lady Alice, how good to see you again. You must think me terrible, begging invitations."

"No, no, you're quite welcome at Traymore." It was an almost institutional greeting, considering Aunt Alice's usual warmth, but it was in no way offensive.

"We're having a rum punch that's a specialty of Henry's," Kaye said. "But you can have—"

"That sounds perfect."

Kaye poured him a drink from the pitcher on the table and asked, "Now would you like to have lunch and then swim, or the other way around?"

"It's entirely up to you."

"Why don't you just go to the pool and have your drinks, your lunch and your swim all together? I haven't nearly finished my correspondence, and I'd welcome the opportunity to do so. Don't think me rude, Adrian, but swimming is one of the few things I've been forced to forgo in my dotage."

"Dotage, indeed," Adrian said. "You're a mere child."

"And you're a flatterer. Go on to the pool, you two."

They had a long refreshing swim, during which Adrian kept up a witty patter. When they had finished, they dried themselves and sat under the arbor. They sipped another rum punch and looked down on the bay, blue and serene in the low distance. Helen brought them lunch.

When she had gone, Kaye said, "Adrian, I suppose it's none of my business, but would you tell me something?"

"Certainly."

"You obviously don't like Creighton very much, and

he seems to restrict your social mobility in Montego. Why do you visit him?"

"I'd be happy to tell you, but I doubt if you'll believe me."

"Try me."

"All right, but you must promise never to tell Creighton any of what I'm about to say."

"I promise."

"Creighton and I knew each other long ago in Australia. Our families' ranches bordered on each other's. It's a very lonely life when you live it as seriously as our families did. We didn't even have the advantage of school and school friends. Our families jointly engaged a tutor, who gave us a quite decent education—decent enough that when our time came, we were qualified for higher education in England. In the meantime, he and I were the only children for miles around, and we were inevitably thrown together. We literally grew up together. That kind of thing forms a bond that lasts a lifetime. I hope you won't think me disloyal for saying this, but Creighton was always a dour lonely person. He was never much fun to be with. Oh, I'm sure you've heard all this Montego business about Victoria's death and Creighton's withdrawal, about the gay parties and the blissful life they led. They did live that way, of course, but it was all Victoria's doing. Creighton hated it. He was deeply wounded by Victoria's death, but he didn't withdraw because of it. He simply returned to the life he would always have preferred anyway—a somber reclusive life in which he needn't incur any obligations through friendship."

"But everybody in Montego seems to adore him. They're very close to him, Smitty and Aunt Alice and—"

"And who? Does he ever have anyone to the house? Are the Marlowes or the Zimmermans or anyone else

frequent visitors? Creighton is fiercely loyal. I'll give
him that. The friendships he made during Victoria's life
he has continued to honor. And I suppose he loved Victoria in his way. You must remember that whatever accounts you've heard of their marriage were from people
who knew them only after they came to Montego. And
they came only because Victoria begged him to come.
He wanted to stay on the ranch, hundreds of miles from
the nearest social center, where frail, gay, vivacious Victoria would have withered. Well, anyway, they came.
The reputation Creighton now enjoys sprang out of Victoria's infectious gregariousness. Those who will tell
you how merry and outgoing Creighton was during
those years don't really know him. He pretended because Victoria wanted him to, and he was very good at
it. He's almost diabolically devious. I seem to have
strayed from the subject. I come to see Creighton because I simply cannot abandon that ancient friendship. I
come to see him out of gratitude for it."

"That's very generous."

"There's nothing noble about it, but somehow
Creighton does seem less lonely during my brief stays
with him. He won't acknowledge it, of course, but we
sit up till the wee hours reminiscing. There isn't really
anything to reminisce about, except that it takes him
back to the life he'd still like to live."

"Surely he could go back to Australia if he chose to,"
Kaye said guardedly, remembering what Aunt Alice had
told her about Creighton's plans.

"It's too late. That whole world, that way of life have
changed. Besides, I think he's become addicted to Montego. The addict doesn't usually like the drug to which
he's addicted, but there's nothing he can do about it.
I'm afraid Creighton is a very twisted person."

Kaye was surprised at this comment, but said nothing. They swam for a brief time, then lay in the sun by the pool. Kaye dozed for a moment, and then, without warning, she felt Adrian's lips on hers. Although she was startled, she did not resist. She did not respond, but she did not pull away. When his lips were gone, she heard his voice.

"I know I shouldn't have done that, but you looked so irresistible. I told you I might fall in love with you, and I think I have. I also told you I'd keep my distance, and I will. Just allow me to be with you."

"It's not a matter of 'allowing' you, Adrian. I like being with you."

"Then we *will* be friends?"

"Yes, we will."

"Could that begin with a return trip to our little restaurant?"

"I'd love it, but I don't want to leave Aunt Alice so soon after my Kingston trip. Why don't you stay here for dinner?"

"If that wouldn't be inconvenient, I'd love to."

"It's settled."

"I won't say it again until I know you want me to, but I do care about you very much."

For the next several days Kaye and Adrian saw each other almost every day and every evening. When they weren't attending the same dinner party, Adrian dined at Traymore or he and Kaye went to a restaurant in Montego. Creighton was present at the dinner parties, but it was possible, even easy, at gatherings of such size for two guests to avoid each other. And Kaye and Creighton did just that. Upon entering a drawing room, each of them would scout it to see where the other was and would then go in another direction. If one saw the other inadvertently nearing, he or she would drift away to other people. When they did meet, which was inevitable, there would be no more than a nod and a hello before one of them would move off. Montego hostesses were uncannily astute. Their guests were not seated at dinner at random. And although it was not openly discussed, it was common knowledge Kaye and Creighton did not welcome each other's company and Kaye and Adrian did. Kaye and Creighton were never seated within conversational distance of each other. However, the ritual did the reverse of what was intended. It drew attention to the mysterious thing between them.

Even veterans of Montego life felt the necessity now and then of easing the social regimen, and when this happened, dinner parties were suspended for two or three days. During such a period, just as Kaye and Aunt Alice were finishing a quiet dinner on the veranda, they saw the lights and heard the engine of an approaching car. It was only seconds later when they recognized Creighton's Land Rover. Neither of them spoke. The Rover stopped before the house, and Creighton got out and climbed the steps to the veranda. His expression as he neared them was even stonier than usual.

"Good evening, Alice," he said formally.

"Good evening, Creighton."

"I'm very sorry to intrude like this."

"*You* can never intrude at Traymore."

"I've come to speak with Kaye privately. It's important."

"Obviously," Aunt Alice said.

"I'm sure there's nothing you can have to say to me that you can't say in Aunt Alice's presence," Kaye cut in.

"Don't be foolish, girl. Go on into the garden."

"Aunt Alice—"

"If you don't, I'll go into the house."

"I won't inconvenience you," Kaye said. She got up

and crossed the veranda to the stairs. Creighton followed her. Kaye turned toward the back garden. She had almost reached it before Creighton caught up with her.

"I know you're far from happy to see me," Creighton said, "but however contradictory it may seem, I've come out of concern for your welfare."

"How touching."

"Don't be snide, Kaye. This is truly in your own interest. You've got to stop seeing Adrian."

Kaye ceased walking and looked up at him aghast. "You really are unbelievable. First you tell Adrian to stop seeing me, and when that fails, you tell me to stop seeing Adrian."

"He told you that, of course."

"Yes. Who do you think you are, Creighton, to go around managing other people's lives when your own is such a shambles?"

"My life may not be a happy one, but it isn't a shambles. At least it wasn't."

"Until I came into it?"

"None of that is important. What counts is that you stop seeing Adrian. You don't know him. You don't know how dangerous he is. I know all about his charm and his attractiveness to women. I may have hurt you. Adrian will destroy you."

"Such drama!"

"Don't mock me. I can't put this strongly enough. I don't know what he's told you, but I must make you aware that Adrian has never spoken a sincere word in his life. He has no regard for truth. He's amoral and vicious."

Kaye started walking again, shaking her head in disbelief. "You've come here thinking that Adrian has told me some truth about you, and your only defense against that is to tell me he's a constitutional liar. Really, Creighton."

"I've come here in your defense, not mine. I don't give a damn what you think of me."

"And I don't give a damn what you think of me. . . or of Adrian. My life is none of your business."

"All right. I've warned you, and you won't listen. It's like you to misinterpret kindness. But if Adrian hurts you—and he will—he's going to pay. You needn't bother to tell him that. I already have."

He turned and walked away from her, striding across the garden and around the house. He started to get into the Land Rover, but he hesitated. Turning abruptly, he came back to the foot of the stairs leading to the veranda, where Aunt Alice was still sitting, and looked up at her.

"Make her leave Montego, Alice." Without waiting for a response, he went back to the Land Rover and drove away.

When Kaye returned to the veranda, Aunt Alice could see it was no time to talk to her about anything. Kaye was pale and making a visible effort to control her trembling. She sat down on the wicker settee next to her aunt, and Alice put her arm around Kaye's shoulder. Kaye could no longer hold back the tears.

"There, there," Aunt Alice said. "Go on and cry."

"I don't want to cry, Aunt Alice."

"Sometimes there's nothing else to do."

"I think this is one of those times. Oh, auntie, I've made such a mess of things. . . for myself, for you, for—for everybody."

"No, no. I'm sure it seems that way to you just now, but you haven't made a mess of anything."

"I have. I know we haven't spent a great deal of time together, but you know me better than anyone else in the world. I've always been in control of myself. I've always faced problems head-on, and if I've made the wrong decision, I've been willing to face the consequences. But now.... Oh, Aunt Alice, what am I going to do?''

"First of all, you're going to go and wash your face and brush your hair. Then, while Henry is clearing things, you're going to spend a few minutes thinking calm thoughts. There's no point in our talking when you're in such distress. And we must talk. When you've—what is that marvelous expression Smitty has taken to using? Oh, yes. When you've got your act together—I don't really know what it means—but when you've got your act together, come back here to me, and we'll have coffee and cognac—which is simply a loftier version of tea and sympathy.''

"Oh, auntie, you're so wonderful.''

"We shall see about that. You may not like some of the things I will probably say when you return. Go on now, and do as I say.''

Kaye did exactly as Aunt Alice had said, and, as simplistic as the solution sounded, it worked. There was hardly a thought in her head when she came back to the veranda. Aunt Alice was sitting on the settee, calm as a prioress. On the small glass-topped table before her were two tall white candles, a silver tray and coffee service and two translucent bone china cups and saucers. She looked up at Kaye as if there had been no trouble at all.

"There's my girl,'' she said. "You look absolutely splendid. Let's get down to business. Tell me what's wrong with you.''

"Everything,'' Kaye replied as she virtually fell into a chair next to Aunt Alice.

"That is not a practical answer.''

"I know, but it's true. Literally everything seems to be wrong."

"Everyone, with the possible exception of Smitty, thinks I'm a bit fey. I can afford to be, because beneath the pixie quality I am supremely organized. We must categorize. You came here from New York on the rebound from what we have agreed was not an extraordinarily unpleasant divorce. You were determined to be free of any kind of emotional attachment. You immediately fell in love with Creighton, and—"

"Aunt Alice! How can you. . . ?"

"If you're not going to be honest with me, we can stop this conversation and talk about local gossip. Tell me in one sentence that you're not in love with Creighton."

"I loathe him."

"That's not what I asked you." Kaye looked away. "All right, you fell in love with Creighton, and Creighton fell in love with you. I don't say that is good or desirable or easy, but it is the first and the essential fact with which we have to deal. Do you know he asked me tonight to make you leave Montego?"

Kaye looked back at her aunt as if startled into attentiveness. "No, I didn't know that."

"The signs of love are not gifts of diamonds or candlelight dinners or unexpected midnight phone calls. Those are superficial. But the willingness to sacrifice the love itself for the benefit of the loved one is a profound act of love. That is what Creighton did tonight."

"I don't understand."

"Yes, I know that. Creighton, loving you as he does, was willing to have me send you away rather than have you hurt by Adrian. It's also possible, I suppose, that Creighton thinks his position with you is hopeless. But I doubt it. Creighton doesn't give up easily."

"But what could he have meant about Adrian?"

"I don't know, but if he warned you, there must be danger."

"He said Adrian is a liar. He said he's vicious and amoral."

"Then it's probably true."

"Adrian is one of the most charming thoughtful men I've ever met."

"Charming men can be dangerous."

"I know that, auntie, but isn't it possible Creighton wants to discredit him in order to...." She couldn't finish.

"In order to clear the field for himself? How can you know so little about Creighton? He's a man of absolute honor. He would never do such a thing. If he advised you to stay away from Adrian, I think you should do it. But it's your life. Yet it isn't Adrian we're concerned with. It's Creighton. I know I've advised you to leave Montego and I've advised you to stay. Solutions change as problems change. If you love Creighton, you should go to him and say so. If you don't, I think you should leave."

Kaye looked out over the front garden thoughtfully. "I don't know, Aunt Alice. I do know I've never felt about anyone the way I feel about Creighton, but every time I'm with him, every time it seems we're going to get on together, something happens and we end up at each other's throats."

"My, it does sound like love."

"It isn't right to say, 'something happens.' It isn't by accident. Either he does something to infuriate me, or I do something to infuriate him. And it always somehow seems deliberate."

"As I said, it does sound like love," Aunt Alice replied wistfully. "Love in its first throes at least. But you can't go on like this, darling. It's unfair of both of you to put each other through this agony. Make a decision and stick by it, but under no circumstances go on with this—this vulgar hurtful charade. It's beneath both of you."

"I give you my solemn word that whatever happens, I will not allow things to go on as they have been."

"That's enough for me. I'll hold you to your promise, though."

"Auntie, there's one other thing."

"Oh, my. What is it?"

"I'm taking a great risk by telling you this. I know how deep your friendship with Smitty is, and I know your first loyalty is to her."

"You're quite right. I can't imagine what you're talking about, but if it in any way involves my betraying that friendship, you'd best be careful."

"I'm going to trust my instincts."

"All right. Go on."

"It's about Amanda."

"Amanda?"

"Yes. She's in love with a very decent young man of whom Smitty would never approve."

"If he's a very decent young man, why wouldn't Smitty approve?"

"Because he's a middle-class American boy with no money, no position, no name."

"And in spite of the fact he's very decent, you think these things would matter to Smitty?"

"Wouldn't they?"

Aunt Alice was silent for a moment. "All right. Probably. It would depend entirely on the young man. This is very distressing, Kaye."

"But you won't just go directly to Smitty and tell her."

"You don't seem to have a very high regard for either Smitty or me."

"Oh, darling, I wouldn't have told you even this much if I hadn't known you were incapable of doing anything but the wisest kindest thing. I became involved in this matter absolutely inadvertently, and now I don't know what to do. You're the only one who can help me...and Amanda."

"I will not in any way become involved in a conspiracy to deceive Lady Smith-Croydon."

"I wouldn't dream of asking you to."

"As long as that's understood, we can proceed."

"I've met the young man, and he's absolutely above reproach. He adores Amanda and treats her with the utmost respect. There's not the slightest question of their doing anything rash. He's in school in the States. They're serious enough to be talking about the future, but they talk about it in only the most sensible terms. Danny—his name is Danny Riordan—"

"Oh, dear. Considering we're dealing with Smitty, one wishes it were Algernon Montcrief! Well, it can't be helped."

Kaye couldn't help laughing. "Your sense of humor must have saved your life a thousand times."

"Two thousand. Do get on with it."

"Danny wants nothing more than to have Amanda present him to Smitty."

"He's obviously very decent and mad as a hatter."

"The only thing that's prevented it is Amanda is certain Smitty would immediately ship her off to England and she and Danny would never see each other again."

"It's fortunate one of them is sensible. That's precisely what Smitty would do. You seem to have omitted something. If this young man, Danny—couldn't we at least call him Daniel?"

"Never. It would be ludicrous."

"Is there nothing favorable about this situation?"

"Not much. Except that Danny is, as virtuous a man as Amanda could ever hope to find."

"That's no little asset. However, if he's in school in the States, and, as far as I know, Amanda has never been to the States, how did she meet him?"

Kaye could not control the sheepish expression that spread across her face. Aunt Alice shuddered.

"She met him here in Montego last summer. At Doctor's Cave. He. . . ."

"You may as well say it."

"He's a. . . a lifeguard."

Aunt Alice closed her eyes and put her hand to her forehead. "Are you proposing that we present a penniless middle-class American lifeguard to Lady Smith-Croydon as her prospective grandson-in-law?"

"I'm afraid so."

"Give me a moment. I'm trying to picture it. She will immediately go into either cardiac arrest or a rage of majestic fury. I am also picturing something else—something that disturbs me deeply. I see now the purpose behind that excursion to Doctor's Cave. I fear a web of deviousness and deceit in which you may be involved."

"It's true. I asked myself what you would have done when you were my age and a sweet dear friend like Amanda had come to you, begging for help, and I decided you would have done exactly what I did."

"How high-handed of you. You couldn't possibly know what I would have done."

"Would you tell me what you would have done."

"I would, like you, have been torn between the two loyalties. You must remember it would have been long ago, in a society utterly different from yours. . . . Oh, I suppose I would have behaved just as you have. It hardly seems important. I have one more question. The young man was undoubtedly with you and Amanda in Kingston."

Kaye hesitated. "Yes. He was."

"That is unforgivable."

"Aunt Alice, it was the only—"

"Have you no respect for me whatever? You could have come to me before you took so drastic and foolish a course."

"I know I should have, but, Aunt Alice, I was with them virtually every minute. And they were so innocently and divinely happy. It was the first time they'd ever been able to be alone together."

"And therefore there was no basis on which you could predict their behavior."

"Except their fundamental decency. And that I'll defend forever."

Aunt Alice sighed deeply. "All right. What's done is done. I don't quite understand what you expect of me."

"Your advice. Your counsel. You're the only person on earth who knows Smitty well enough to know what to do under these circumstances."

"Which is a gentle way of asking me to intercede with Smitty on behalf of Amanda and—and Danny. You must be mad as a hatter, as well."

"There's no hope for them if you don't."

"What makes you think I have the power to persuade Smitty of a course of action that is against her every value? And if I should present this young man to her, *I* would be part of a conspiracy against her. I would risk wrecking a friendship that has endured for four decades. You're asking a great deal."

"Aunt Alice, I'm simply saying that if Danny is presented to her with your nominal approval, he'll have at least half a chance of gaining hers."

Aunt Alice sighed again. "All right. I will do this much: I will meet the young man. Bring him here to dinner with Amanda. Smitty must know that she's dining here. It must all be as aboveboard as possible under these wretched circumstances. We have no plans for tomorrow evening. That would be as good a time as any. Will you see to it?"

"Oh, yes! Aunt Alice, trust me. You won't regret this."

"Do you think I'd do it if I had the slightest doubt about that?"

"No. No, you wouldn't."

"Kaye. Don't think for a minute that my agreeing to this scheme is tacit approval of the young man. I dislike sitting in judgment, but that's the position you've put me in. And remember, I will be judging by my standards, not Smitty's. They are essentially the same, but there are idiosyncratic differences, which I will take into consideration. I will present him to Smitty only if I find him to be an entirely desirable and suitable fiancé for Amanda. If I do not find him so, I will go directly to Smitty and tell her that this—this liaison exists, and she will deal with it accordingly. If those terms are acceptable to you, we'll go on. If they are not, I will do you the courtesy of considering that you have never spoken a word to me about any of it."

"I wish I were you."

"What?"

"I hope that some day I'll find the way to your dignity, your sense of humor and goodness and your impeccable standards."

"You don't *find* the way, my dear; you *make* the way. And it is not easy. The secret is simple: integrity has to matter more than anything else. Now go and call poor Amanda. She must be on tenterhooks."

"I love you very much, auntie," Kaye said, and went into the drawing room to the telephone.

As usual, Smitty's butler answered the telephone and went to find Amanda. She was on the line very quickly.

"Kaye. How are you?"

"I'm fine. I have news. I want you to pick me up here tomorrow at eleven on the way to Doctor's Cave. I don't care how you arrange it with your grandmother, but we're invited to dinner here at Traymore tomorrow night—all three of us."

"All three— You mean...?"

"That's exactly what I mean. It's the first step. I can't guarantee it'll do any good, but it's a beginning."

"Kaye, you're a wizard! A wonderful, wonderful wizard! I'll be there on the dot."

"Good. That's all I can tell you now. I'll see you in the morning."

Amanda was early the next morning, and she was bubbling with excitement and curiosity by the time they were on their way to the Cave.

"Calm down, darling," Kaye said. "There's no point in my going through it all twice. I'll tell you all about it when we reach the Cave."

Danny joined them as soon as they appeared. They sat at one of the tables under a thatched roof, with Amanda and Danny leaning forward, silently begging Kaye to tell them what was going on.

"Look, the time in Kingston was wonderful, but that kind of thing isn't going to do you any good in the long run. We've got to deal with the problem of your grandmother's approval. I told you I'd try to help. Well, the only way I know how to do it is through the one person in the world who might have some influence on Smitty: my aunt. I've told her about you, about—"

"Kaye! You didn't!"

"I had to. I admit it was risky, but she reacted just as I'd hoped she would. I told her about your meetings here at the Cave, even about Kingston. She agreed to—no she insisted on—meeting Danny. If she approves, she'll present him to Smitty with her blessings. If she doesn't, she'll go to Smitty and tell her the whole truth."

"Oh, no!" Danny said.

"There's another alternative. If you don't want to go through with it—I mean, if you don't want to meet Aunt Alice and risk her disapproval—she'll just forget the whole thing and not mention it to Smitty. It's up to you."

"What are we going to do?" Amanda asked, almost wailing.

"Kaye, let me get this straight. If your aunt approves of me, she'll introduce me to Mandy's grandmother?"

"Yes."

"If she doesn't approve of me, she'll tell Mandy's grandmother about us and wreck the whole thing?"

"Yes."

"But if I don't meet her at all, things will just stay as they are?"

"Yes. She obviously made the last offer to save my neck. She's very dear."

"And I'm scared to death. I don't know what to do."

"Haven't you any faith in yourself?"

"What if I'm not good enough?"

"Danny, you are! You know you are," Amanda said.

"I mean good enough for them. I think I'm good enough for any respectable girl, but we're talking about their standards, not mine. What if I blow it?"

"You won't, Danny," Amanda said.

"Look, Mandy, if we don't go through with it, we'll have the rest of the summer and, as far as I can see now, next summer, too. But if I go to meet them and they don't approve of me, it'll be all over right now. You'll be on a plane to England before the week's out, and we'll never see each other again."

"That's the risk, Amanda. You'd better think about it carefully. I'll leave you alone to talk it over."

Before she could get up, Amanda said, "Don't go, Kaye. You're as much a part of this as we are."

"What do you want me to do, Mandy?" Danny asked.

"I want you to meet Lady Armstrong."

"*Lady* Armstrong? Oh, man!"

"I want you to go to Traymore knowing that nothing and nobody is ever going to keep us apart forever. If they send me away, I'll wait till I'm twenty-one. Then nobody can stop me from coming to you."

"That's almost two years, Mandy. Two years in which we wouldn't even see each other. A lot can happen in two years."

"If you think I wouldn't feel the same way after two years of not seeing you, we're wasting our time talking about it."

It was the most adult, conclusive, womanly thing Kaye had ever heard Amanda say.

Danny smiled at her. "Okay, toots. It's off to meet Lady Armstrong. God help me."

Amanda threw her arms around him. "Oh, Danny, it's going to be all right."

"Hey! Stop it! What if somebody sees us?"

"It doesn't matter now."

He thought for a moment and said, "It doesn't, does it?"

"Not a bit. It's all or nothing."

"Okay. How about a crash course in how to behave in the presence of titled English ladies?"

"There'll only be one tonight," Kaye said.

"It'd be all the same to me if I were being presented at court. What do I do? What do I say? What do I wear?"

"Just be yourself," Kaye answered.

"I'm going to feel as if I were on the slave block. At least tell me what I'm supposed to call your aunt."

"Lady Armstrong, at first," Kaye told him. "She'll probably suggest you change it to Lady Alice, which, under the circumstances, she would consider quite familiar. Don't be frightened, Danny. She's the dearest woman on earth. Save your being frightened for your first appointment with Smitty."

"If I get that far. No kidding now, what do I wear?"

"Do you have a sport jacket?"

"Of course I have a sport jacket. What do you think I am, an urchin? It's a blue blazer."

"Perfect. And slacks and a shirt and... yes, and a tie, I suppose."

"A *tie*? In Montego?"

"On this occasion, yes. You may smoke."

"I don't smoke—although I might start."

"You'll be offered a drink, and only one."

"Do I look like an alcoholic?"

"Don't be surprised when my aunt knocks back a couple of dry martinis."

"What do I talk about?"

"I'll take care of that. At least, I'll lead the conversation... when Aunt Alice doesn't. And remember, although she's a British subject, she's an American."

"An American? You didn't tell me that. That's great."

"If I hadn't told you, you wouldn't have known from meeting her. She went to England more than thirty-five years ago when she married Lord Alex, my uncle. She's been indelibly English ever since. Still, her being American is in your favor. And for goodness' sake, don't be fashionably late. Be punctual."

"Will we have something unrecognizable for dinner? Something I won't know how to eat?"

"Stop underestimating yourself. If your future didn't depend on this dinner party, you'd behave perfectly naturally and be a complete success."

"Yeah, but it does."

"You've had two summers in Montego. You must have met dozens of worldly people."

"Oh, sure. The other lifeguards and Mandy."

"Well, we'll be rooting for you."

"I'll need all the help I can get."

When Kaye came downstairs just before seven-thirty, she went straight to the veranda, expecting to find her aunt there. It was empty, so she went into the drawing room. Aunt Alice was sitting in the great wing chair, which was more or less reserved for her.

"I thought you'd be on the veranda," Kaye said.

"Do you think I'm going to be that easy on the young man? Anyone can behave acceptably on a veranda. A drawing room tests the mettle."

"You won't be too hard on him, will you, auntie?"

"I won't be anything, actually. I'm simply giving a small dinner to meet a young man and get some impression of his character. I won't be putting him through his paces. He'll be going through them, of course, but not at my behest. The trouble with this sort of thing is that the guest is always fully aware he's being evaluated and is on his best behavior. Well, I'm not easily fooled."

"This guest will certainly be on his best behavior. He's scared to death."

"Of me?"

"Of course. You've got to remember that as far as Danny is concerned, his whole future depends on this meeting."

"That's putting it a bit strongly."

"Probably, but that's how Danny sees it."

At that moment Henry came into the drawing room

and announced, "Mr. Riordan is here, Lady Armstrong."

Danny followed Henry into the room. Kaye wasn't sure if it was good or bad, but she had never seen a more typical all-American boy at his best. By those standards he was almost breathtakingly handsome. Kaye knew he must be terribly nervous, but he appeared completely composed.

"Hello, Danny," she said, getting up to greet him.

"Hello, Kaye," he replied, smiling.

Kaye took his arm and gave it a little squeeze of encouragement. "Aunt Alice, I'd like to present Danny Riordan. Danny, this is my aunt, Lady Armstrong."

Danny took one step forward, bowed almost imperceptibly and said, "How do you do? I'm very pleased to meet you, Lady Armstrong." It was just right, Kaye thought. She was glad he hadn't said "honored to meet you" or made an attempt to kiss Aunt Alice's hand. His manners showed just the right combination of decorum and informality.

"How do you do, Mr. Riordan? I always find it refreshing to make the acquaintance of young people." *Ah,* Kaye thought, *she's going to try to put him at his ease. That's encouraging.* "Do sit down. May I offer you a drink?"

"Thank you. I'd enjoy a gin and tonic."

Henry had retired to a corner of the room, anticipating the order for drinks. "Henry, would you see to it, please? Are you having a martini, Kaye?"

"Yes, thank you, darling. Did you save any lives today, Danny?"

He looked a bit sheepish and replied, "That's a very embarrassing question."

"Embarrassing?" Kaye repeated, rather in alarm. "Why?"

"Through all of last summer and so far this summer I've sat on the beach every day and watched everybody having a nice safe time, and I've felt useless. And on the one day I do something, I'm asked that question."

"Well, don't be modest," Kaye said. "What happened?"

"It wasn't anything spectacular. It was just before five. I was getting ready to go off duty, and I saw a girl out beyond the sandbar. I still haven't figured out how she got out that far without anybody's seeing her, but there she was, and she was obviously in trouble. She was waving her arms and yelling, so I swam out and brought her back."

"You actually saved her life?" Kaye asked.

"Well...I suppose so. She was pretty tired by the time I got to her. She might have made it back by herself."

"Nonsense!" Kaye replied. "Tell us more."

"By all means, Mr. Riordan," Aunt Alice said. "It isn't every day we entertain heroes."

"Somehow I don't think it's heroic when you're getting paid for it."

"A life is a life," Aunt Alice declared.

"I have to admit I felt...gratified. She was only about twelve years old. I honestly don't think she could have made it back on her own. She needed mouth-to-mouth resuscitation."

"And did you do that, too?" Aunt Alice asked.

"Yes."

"I must say that's exciting," Aunt Alice remarked. "Do you know who she was?"

"I think her name was Brent. Jennifer Brent."

"Why, that would be Agatha Landsbury's granddaughter," Aunt Alice exclaimed.

"I don't know," Danny said. "We just got her name

and age for the record. She was with some adults who took her home."

"How careless of them not to have watched her more closely," Aunt Alice stated.

"How careless of me not to have seen her sooner. The light gets strange at that time of day, and sometimes it's hard to see people out by the sandbar."

"She was very fortunate," Aunt Alice declared.

"How can you be so calm," Kaye asked, "when a little more than two hours ago you saved someone's life?"

"I'm not calm inside," Danny said, smiling. "I was more scared than she was. I guess I didn't realize it right away, but back on the beach when we knew she was all right, I started to shake all over."

"I would think so," Aunt Alice said. Henry brought the drinks, and Aunt Alice raised hers. "A toast to you, Mr. Riordan. It was a very brave and noble thing to do."

Danny was blushing even through his tan. He was thoroughly embarrassed, and it did not escape Aunt Alice's notice.

Amanda arrived then. She was more nervous than Danny, and it showed. The whole life-saving tale was recounted, and Amanda flushed with excitement.

When Aunt Alice finished her martini, she summoned Henry. "Henry, I think we'd all like another cocktail."

"I think this is enough for me, Lady Armstrong," Danny said.

"Nonsense. If I'd been through what you have today, I'd get roaring drunk. I insist you have another gin and tonic." She was sure he'd been instructed to have just one drink, and she wasn't going to allow it. "Where is your home in the States, Mr. Riordan?"

"In Ohio. Cleveland."

"We have distant cousins in Cleveland, Kaye. I don't think you know them. Have you family, Mr. Riordan?"

"Yes. There's my mother and father—dad has a small automobile business, a dealership—and there's my younger brother, Richard, who's seventeen. My sister, Cathy, is fourteen, and that's all of us."

"And you attend college when you're not here in Montego saving the lives of hapless swimmers?"

"Yes, Grinnell College in Iowa."

"I seem to remember that many years ago I had a beau who attended Grinnell. Do you intend to return to Cleveland when you've finished your education?"

"Only for a long visit with my family. The father of a classmate of mine is a partner in an investment firm in New York. Mr. McBride seems willing to take me into his firm when I've graduated."

"That sounds very promising. Are you sure you want to live in New York?"

"I know I want to try it, Lady Armstrong. I'm afraid I wouldn't be content being a big fish in a little pond."

"Admirable. You must call me Lady Alice in exchange for my being able to call you Danny. It makes me feel very old to call young people by their surnames. How is your grandmother, Amanda?"

"She's fine, Lady Alice. She sends you her love."

"I hope she'll continue to be of a disposition to do that."

Henry came into the room and announced dinner. The meal was blessedly simple and went very smoothly. The conversation never lagged, and although Danny was careful not to be intrusive, he made a genuine and welcome contribution to it. When they had finished, Aunt Alice adjourned to the veranda for coffee. Although cognac and liqueurs were offered, only Aunt Alice had a brandy.

"Are all your houseguests still with you, Amanda?" Aunt Alice asked.

"Oh, you know grandmother. The guests come and go. The Morrisons left this morning, and the McTavishes arrived this afternoon. Sometimes it's like living in a very good hotel."

"How does Smitty do it?" Alice wondered. Turning to Danny, she said, "Are you coming back to Montego next summer, Danny?"

"Yes, but that's a long way off. I do plan to come back, though."

"I should think that after today they'd welcome you with open arms," she commented.

"Yes," Kaye agreed. "You must be the fair-haired boy of Doctor's Cave."

"I was just doing my job, after all."

"Ah, modest to the end," Aunt Alice said.

"It's time for me to be going," Amanda indicated, seemingly with no reluctance at all. She knew Aunt Alice would think it presumptuous if she stayed on in the hope of getting a report on her reaction to Danny.

"All right, dear," Aunt Alice said. "It was lovely seeing you."

Amanda said good-night to Kaye and Danny, went out to her car and drove off.

"I would have Henry drop you," Aunt Alice remarked to Danny, "but I see your car in the driveway."

"It's the car I drove here in, but I'm afraid it's not mine. I wish it were. I borrowed it from a friend. All the people who work at the Cave are very good about that kind of thing."

"Do you have lodgings there, Danny?" Aunt Alice asked.

"Yes, they put us up as part of the contract. It helps make the job practical economically. It was a wonderful evening, Lady Alice. I'm grateful for having been invited. It was very kind of you."

"I thoroughly enjoyed meeting you, Danny. I hope you'll come again."

"Good night, Kaye."

"Congratulations on today. Come on, I'll walk you to the car."

The car was very near the veranda, and Kaye had time enough to say only, "I think you were a smash. You certainly were as far as I'm concerned."

"I was as nervous as a cat. Did it show?"

"Not a bit. I'm sure Aunt Alice liked you a great deal. We'll come to the Cave as soon as we can and give you a full report."

"Don't make it too long, or I'll die of anxiety."

"All right, Danny. Good night."

"Good night. We'll never be able to thank you enough, no matter what happens." He got into the red Triumph and drove off.

Kaye went back to the veranda and sat down again. "Thank you, Aunt Alice, not only for agreeing to meet Danny but for being so completely fair and helpful to him."

"How do you know I've been fair? You don't know what I thought of him."

"You don't have to agree with me to have been fair, darling. You tried and succeeded in making him feel comfortable and secure so that he could put his best foot forward. You could have been very intimidating if you'd wanted."

"Did you expect me to be?"

"No. Smitty would have been, but not you."

"Oh, yes. Smitty, if she ever has the opportunity of meeting him, will probably try to destroy him." Aunt Alice looked very thoughtful for a moment. "I somehow think she might not succeed. He's no weakling, your Danny Riordan."

"Then you did like him?"

"You knew I would, and you know I did. I think he's an entirely respectable, well brought-up young man. He's intelligent and certainly most presentable, and, thank God, he is courteous without being courtly. I liked him very much indeed. I'd like to help him and Amanda. I'm not sure I can, and I'm not sure how I should proceed—if at all. I'll have to think about it. In the meantime, your secret is safe."

"Thank you, Aunt Alice. Thank you so much."

"Well, I think I'll go upstairs now. I suppose you'll want to call Amanda."

"I don't know. We have to be circumspect on the telephone. There are so many extensions at Smitty's house."

"Come on, Kaye. Smitty's eccentric, but I doubt she's taken to eavesdropping on her guests."

"It could happen quite by accident, and it needn't be Smitty herself. It could be a gossipy guest."

"I suppose so. Use your own discretion. Good night, dear."

"Good night, Aunt Alice. Sleep well, and thank you again."

Kaye waited a short while to be sure Amanda would have got home, then went to the drawing room and telephoned her. It happened that she answered the phone.

"Hello, Amanda, it's Kaye."

"Kaye, how wonderful of you to call! I've been going crazy."

"I thought you would be. I can't say very much, of course, but Aunt Alice was enchanted. So far everything is perfect."

"Oh, Kaye, what heavenly news!"

"We'd better not talk now. Can you manage to go to the Cave tomorrow?"

"I don't know. I'll try my damnedest."

"If you can, just ring and come by to pick me up."

"I'll manage it some way. And thank you, Kaye."

"It isn't me you have to thank."

"Oh, yes it is. It wouldn't have happened if it hadn't been for you."

"All right. Try to get a good night's sleep. God willing, I'll see you tomorrow. Good night."

"Good night."

Amanda called the next day and stopped by at the usual hour. Kaye was just coming down the stairs as Amanda walked into the house.

"Good morning," she said, smiling broadly. "It is a good morning."

"You're even worse than I am," Kaye said. "All this happiness is a bit premature. We haven't even approached the real problem yet."

"Yes, but we may be a step nearer," Amanda answered.

"I'm certain of that."

"Where's your aunt? She'd think it odd if I dropped in and didn't take time to thank her for dinner."

"She's in the little sitting room. Come on."

"Amanda's here, darling," she said as they entered.

"Good morning, Amanda," Aunt Alice replied as Amanda went to kiss her cheek.

"Good morning, Lady Alice. Thank you for that lovely evening last night."

"You're most welcome. I have a feeling that isn't all you'd like to thank me for. I suppose we can stop being circumspect. I liked your young man very much. He's quite nice."

"Oh, thank you, Lady Alice. And thank you so much for having him. I'm sure he was delighted and grateful."

"He said as much as he was leaving, diplomatically allowing me to choose for myself whether he was thanking me for my hospitality or for something more. A very wise young man, I think."

"You are a darling."

"Kaye tells me you and Danny are determined not to do anything headstrong. As long as that's the case, I'll consider what I might do to help you. It's useless to plunge into an argument about anything with your grandmother. She must be...handled. Give me some time to think about it."

"Thank you, thank you," Amanda said. "I'm terrified of what she might say or do."

"I'm afraid you have reason to be, my dear. But there's no sense in worrying yourself to death about it. Go on to the beach, and do give my regards to Danny."

"He'll be thrilled."

Danny was keeping a very watchful eye on the bathers, but when he saw Amanda and Kaye, he rushed across the beach to them. They sat at a table.

"You seem very eager about something this morning, Danny," Kaye remarked.

"Come on. Tell me what your aunt said."

Kaye laughed. "You passed with flying colors. Aunt Alice adored you!"

"Oh, thank God! I thought I behaved like an idiot."

"You were wonderful," Amanda declared.

"Aunt Alice thinks you're respectable, courteous, intelligent and very presentable. The last means she thinks you're beautiful."

"Scared as I was, I thought *she* was beautiful. I guess she's the loveliest lady I've ever seen. And don't think I didn't notice she went out of her way to make me feel at home. She's something else."

"She sends you her regards," Amanda told him.

"Really?"

"As we were leaving, she said, 'Go to the beach and give my regards to Danny.'"

"That's wonderful."

"She's being very open about it now," Kaye said. "She approves of you and Amanda and is trying to think of the best way to approach Smitty. If I know my aunt, she'll come up with something."

"And if I know my grandmother, it can only mean trouble."

"I think your chances now are certainly better than they were."

"It's really wonderful of your aunt even to consider doing this for us," Danny remarked. "I really like her. I guess I'd like her even if she didn't approve of me."

"In that case, you'll adore Smitty," Kaye said.

"Now just a minute," Danny said haughtily, "I'm very popular around Montego this morning. About an hour ago a uniformed chauffeur came marching across the beach and handed me this."

He gave Kaye a small white envelope. She turned it over and looked at the printed return address.

"It's from Lady Agatha Landsbury," she noted with no small degree of wonder. She opened the envelope and read the note aloud:

"Dear Mr. Riordan,
Our gratitude for your having saved my granddaughter's life is beyond all expression. You are a fine brave young man, and we will be forever in your debt. It would be a great honor to me if you could come to dinner here on Wednesday the twenty-first at seven-thirty. If that is inconvenient for you, please let me know, and we will arrange an alternate date that will suit you. I would never for-

give myself if I did not meet you and offer you my undying thanks.

With warmest regards,

Agatha Landsbury"

"Danny, that's wonderful!" Amanda exclaimed.

"It means I'm practically a member of Montego society," Danny stated, smiling and knowing, of course, that it meant nothing of the sort.

"Not quite," Kaye said. "But what it probably does mean is that you're going to meet Smitty a great deal sooner than you thought."

"Oh, no!" Amanda burst out. "I didn't think of that!"

"What are you talking about?" Danny asked.

"This could be an intimate family dinner at which Lady Agatha can offer you her thanks in person," Amanda said, "but it's much more likely to be a 'do' given solely in your honor. In that case, virtually everybody in Montego will be there, most certainly including my grandmother."

"Oh, God!" Danny said. "Why didn't the kid start yelling help five minutes later? I would have been off duty, and Kenny could have saved her."

"There's nothing we can do about it. We'll just have to wait and see if my aunt and Smitty get invitations to the dinner," Kaye concluded. "Who knows? This could be the plan Aunt Alice has been looking for. Let's go for a swim."

Amanda dropped Kaye at Traymore at three o'clock, and as she entered the house, she encountered Aunt Alice crossing the front hall.

"Ah, Kaye, I'm so glad you're home. I completely forgot to tell you the dressmaker is coming at five for the final fitting on your Juliet costume. It will interfere with tea, but some price must be paid for Smitty's idiosyncrasies. Is that inconvenient for you?"

"No, darling, not at all."

"Goodness, it seems so short a time ago that we were in the sitting room on the day you arrived and I told you about the ball, and here we are and the ball is on Saturday. So much has happened since that day."

"Much too much," Kaye said. "Let's sit on the veranda for a little while. I have things to tell you."

"I hope they aren't exciting. I've had quite enough excitement the past few weeks."

As they walked to the veranda arm in arm, Kaye began. "Auntie, I'm afraid I've created the excitement, and I'm afraid I've been a terrible nuisance to you."

"Don't be silly, my girl; I secretly love it. But in my day we were supposed to pretend to be fragile, whether we were or not. Most of us were as sturdy as oxen and more durable than the men. I suppose the pretense was never shed." They sat down on the veranda, and Aunt Alice said, "Now all the news."

"First of all, Danny was thrilled at meeting you. He said you were the most beautiful lady he'd ever seen."

"He's had a sadly limited life."

"No, he hasn't. You are beautiful, and you know it. And he was.... I don't know the right word. Relieved? Happy beyond measure? All of that, I guess, that you liked him. Don't worry, auntie. We all agreed it was no more than a first faltering step toward Smitty's approval, but Amanda and Danny couldn't help being encouraged. Something else has happened, though."

"Oh, my."

"Lady Landsbury sent a note to Danny this morning at the Cave. She is, understandably, deeply grateful to him for having saved her granddaughter's life. She's invited him to dinner to offer her thanks in person."

"And so she should. She might better put twenty thousand dollars in trust for him to assure his education, but I suppose that would be vulgar."

"What kind of dinner do you think it will be?"

"I don't know what you mean."

"If it's a private little family dinner, that will be one thing, but if it's a big bash, everybody will be there—including Smitty. You know Lady Landsbury. What do you think she'll do?"

"Darling, I haven't the faintest idea. If she means merely to thank Danny, Agatha will keep it private. If she means to pay him tribute, it will be a bash. I should think we'll know soon enough. I must say, it would be an auspicious way for Danny to meet Smitty."

"I thought of that, and I wondered how you'd feel about it."

"I have no control over it, but I may be able to incorporate it into my plans. We'll see when we know what Agatha has in mind."

Henry appeared on the veranda. "Excuse me. There's a call for you, Miss Belliston."

"Oh? Do you know who it is, Henry?"

"It's Mr. James, miss."

"Thank you, Henry." She didn't get up immediately. Aunt Alice said nothing. "I suppose I may as well take it."

She went into the drawing room and picked up the phone. "Hello."

"Kaye, it's Adrian. How are you?"

"I'm fine, Adrian, and you?"

"Splendid, thank you. I hope you won't think this forward of me, but I've heard through the extraordinarily efficient Montego grapevine that you and Lady Alice are going to Smitty's ball as Juliet and her nurse."

"I thought it was a secret."

"Perhaps it was, but it isn't anymore. I've arranged to go as Romeo, and I thought it might amuse you both if we went together."

Kaye hesitated. She hadn't decided how she was going to handle Creighton's warning. Her first impulse was to ignore it—not because she took it lightly, but because, in spite of her loving him, she resented his interference in her life. Adrian might be the perfect tool with which to demonstrate to Creighton she was utterly serious about her determination not to marry him. She didn't want to hurt him in any way, but she had to make him understand she meant what she had said to him.

"That sounds marvelous, Adrian," she replied. "Of course, I'll have to see what Aunt Alice's plans are."

"Of course. Why don't you call me this evening and let me know?"

"I'd—I'd rather not. Can you call me at six?"

"Certainly. I do hope it can be arranged."

"So do I. I'll talk to Aunt Alice. Goodbye, Adrian."

She went back to the veranda and sat down. "Adrian is going to the ball as Romeo," she said. "He wants to know if we might all go together—Romeo with Juliet and her nurse."

"And how did he know what we were wearing?"

"The grapevine."

"Ah, there are no secrets anymore in Montego."

"Do you want us all to go together?"

"No. The question is, do you?"

"I don't know."

"Are you going to go on seeing him in spite of Creighton's warning?"

"You think I shouldn't?"

"I think you should do as you like, but I think if you're going to see him, you should do it with caution."

"I'll be careful, auntie, but I've got to make Creighton see that I'm still absolutely independent."

"I understand that, though I'm not sure I approve of your using Adrian to accomplish it."

"I'm not using him, darling. He wants us to go to the ball with him, and I want to. I didn't wangle the invitation. It was entirely his idea."

"All right, if that's what you want. Creighton will understand that it's your decision. After all, he warned you, not me."

"I don't want to cause trouble between you and him."

"You won't, my dear."

"All right. I'm going to go and have a nap and a bath before the fitting."

"Very well. I'll see you at five."

The fitting took place at exactly five o'clock in Kaye's bedroom. The seamstress—a tall, thin, handsome Jamaican woman—was something of an artist. Kaye's Juliet dress fit so perfectly that nothing more had to be done to it. The high-waisted bodice of pale blue satin was encrusted with seed pearls, and beneath it flowed a full six-layered skirt of pure white organza. A skull cap of white satin and seed pearls completed the costume, and Kaye looked radiant in it. All three women were pleased and greatly excited as the fitting progressed, and Kaye was reluctant to take the gown off when it was over. There was much praise and a generous bonus for the departing seamstress.

Kaye had just hung the dress in her closet when the telephone rang. It was six, and she was sure it was Adrian. The phone was answered downstairs after the third ring. She waited a moment and picked up the bedroom extension in time to hear Henry saying, "Just a moment, Mr. James."

"Thank you, Henry," Kaye cut in. "I've got it. Hello, Adrian."

"Tell me it's good news."

"Aunt Alice and I would be delighted to have you accompany us."

"Wonderful! Why don't I drive over to you at about nine-thirty?"

"Perfect. I'm looking forward to the evening."

"So am I," Adrian replied softly.

When Kaye hung up, Aunt Alice said to her, "Well, it's done, is it?"

"Yes, it's done."

"I suppose it's a bit late, but I'm beginning to wonder if Creighton really *will* understand."

"Oh, Aunt Alice, I know he will."

"We'll see."

# CHAPTER SEVEN

SINCE THE NIGHT in Kingston with Creighton, Kaye had been using every device she could find to keep herself from thinking about him—and about what she had done to him. Each day at tea with Aunt Alice she talked a great deal and laughed a great deal. She occupied herself with the simple occasion of tea to prevent her thoughts from straying to Penrose and its inhabitant. Aunt Alice saw through it, of course, but held her tongue.

Tea was by no means Kaye's only device. The telephone became a necessity. She called Amanda at least twice a day. She called the Zimmermans and the Marlowes just to ask how they were. Danny's heroism and his invitation to the Landsburys' were a godsend to her because they involved her completely and left her free of her unwanted thoughts. When she ran out of such social involvements, she began to invent things to keep her busy.

She came down to breakfast one morning and asked Aunt Alice—quite unnecessarily—if it would be all right for her to have Henry drive her into Montego to do some shopping. It was all right, of course, and just before noon she started into town in the Rolls.

She filled her mind with idle thoughts and bought things she didn't need and window-shopped at every storefront she encountered. For a full five minutes she stared into the window of a jewelry shop that contained not one piece she would have wanted to own. She pulled herself away finally, and as she did, her eye was caught by a brass plaque glinting in the sunlight on a building front. The words were, in simple Roman lettering: GEORGE MONTAGUE—BARRISTER. She was standing there, astonished at the coincidence, when she suddenly saw Creighton framed in the doorway of the building.

For a moment in which lightning seemed to have struck they stared at each other, unable to speak. Their eyes were locked in the now familiar embrace, and neither of them wanted to be first to pull away.

It seemed an eternity before Creighton uttered, "Hello, Kaye."

"Hello, Creighton." She didn't know she was going to say it, but suddenly the words were there. "I hope you don't think I was loitering about George's office building hoping to bump into you. As a matter of fact, I didn't know until thirty seconds ago that this was George's office building."

Creighton frowned at her, and his face looked like the coming of a storm. "There you go again. I've said nothing but hello; I've made no accusations, yet you feel obliged to start an argument by defending yourself against imaginary charges. You're hopeless, Kaye."

He turned away and started along the narrow sidewalk.

Kaye's eyes followed him, and she heard herself call out. "Creighton!" He stopped and turned back to her, the frown still fixed on his face. "Please. I want to talk to you."

There was a moment of absolute immobility, a moment in which Kaye truly didn't know what Creighton was going to do. Just when she was sure he was about to turn again and walk away, he moved toward her.

"All right, Kaye," he said softly. "I'm a reasonable man. If you want to talk, I'll listen. Come on," he added, taking her arm and leading her along the twisting street.

Neither of them said anything more until Creighton had ushered her into a tiny, cool, sunless restaurant. As they were seated, he said, "This is one of my favorite places. The food is superb—not that I think you care any more about the food than I do. I'll order something refreshing to drink."

Kaye found it difficult even to glance at him while he gave the waiter the order, but when he had finished, she knew without looking at him that he was staring at her. She forced herself to gaze up at him. His eyes, despite their luminous color, were as hard as stones.

"Creighton, it's not going to be easy for me to say what I want to say."

"Perhaps you should spare yourself the discomfort. I doubt it could make any difference."

She looked away and said, "I know I deserve that, and that's exactly why I must talk to you." She paused and looked back at him. "When I returned to my room that night in Kingston, I went out to the balcony, and I saw you standing on your balcony in the moonlight."

"I know that," he replied harshly. "I saw you, too."

"But what you don't know is that I started back to you. I got as far as the door of my room, and my hand seemed to freeze on the knob. I couldn't go any farther."

"It's probably just as well. I hope you haven't chosen to go farther now."

"I only want to explain."

"You did that in Kingston."

"No. No, I didn't, because I didn't tell you the truth. But I didn't know the truth until I was alone again in my room. That's when I realized that everything that's happened between us—the wrong things, I mean—have been my fault."

"I hope you don't expect me to disagree with you."

"I suppose you have a right to be cruel," Kaye said, looking away again.

"I'm not being cruel. I'm being honest."

"Then let me be honest, too."

"I'd welcome it," he said.

"I...I don't think I can say it here. I feel so...so closed in in this tiny place."

"Yes, I understand that. This place was designed for lovers, not for enemies—or whatever it is we've become."

"Not enemies, Creighton, never enemies."

He frowned again briefly. "There's a small park just down the street. Maybe you'd be more comfortable there."

As they walked the short distance to the park, Kaye was acutely aware that Creighton neither looked at her nor took her arm. She was suddenly afraid she had lost even his friendship.

They went into the park and, after strolling silently for a time, sat on a shaded bench. The silence continued for long moments.

"Kaye, I do wish you'd say whatever it is you have on your mind and get it over with," Creighton declared, at last breaking the silence.

"All right. First of all, I love you very much."

"For God's sake, Kaye...."

"It's true, and it's part of what I want to tell you. Nothing has changed. I still can't marry you. But I want you to know the real reasons why. I told you I wasn't ready yet, and that's true. But I'm not ready because of me, not because of you. Creighton, we've talked about pride previously. My pride makes it difficult for me to say this. I'm going to say it because I love you. I...I think my marriage to Rod failed because of me. I think it was totally my fault.''

"Kaye, you don't have to—"

"Please listen. I think I had a preconceived idea of what Kaye Belliston's marriage would be. There was none of the adventure of two people starting out in life together. There was none of the give and take that is part of beginning and sharing. There were only my needs and my demands and my standards and my expectations.'' She looked away wistfully. "Poor Rod, I think I smothered him with my selfishness. Do you know what would happen to us if I tried to do that to you? It would be a nightmare. But I'm not sure yet that I might not try to do it. I'm not sure I know any other way.'' She paused again, and there were tears in her eyes. "Dearest, dearest Creighton. I know your love could mean a lifetime of happiness for me. I just want time to be sure I can bring that to you. I think I failed Rod. I don't want to fail you. I don't want just to have a go at it and spoil our one lifetime chance because I don't know how to handle it. I want to be certain I'm worthy of you.''

For a shadow of a moment there was the frown again on Creighton's face. Then gradually the devastating smile began to spread across his full sensuous mouth. He took her in his arms and kissed her. She pulled away from him in alarm.

"Creighton! This is a public park!''

"Yes, but like the restaurant, it was designed for lovers. If a man and woman don't kiss in this park, it's considered a sacrilege.'' He kissed her again, and she yielded completely. They stayed in each other's arms until time seemed not to exist.

"Will you do me a favor, darling?" Creighton said.

"Almost any favor," Kaye answered.

"Will you accept my grandmother's ring? I don't ask you to wear it. I don't expect you to brandish it as a badge of our love for each other. I simply want you to have it until you decide whether you're ready to marry me."

"You are the dearest, most generous man I've ever known. I will accept the ring. And I won't fail you, Creighton. No, I won't fail *you*."

"I'm not sure I know what that means, but it doesn't matter. I love you; that's all that matters. Kaye, it will probably seem adolescent to you, but. . . well, I grew up on rituals. People who live so far away from civilization, as we did in Australia, need rituals to keep them in touch with the outside world. I'm sure that seems strange, but—"

"It seems absolutely sensible to me."

He smiled at her and said, "Yes, it would. Then you won't mind if we do this my way."

"I won't mind in the least."

"Good. I want you to come back to Penrose with me. I have to get the ring."

"All right, darling."

"And I want to give it to you on the hill, not at the house. On our hill. All right, it's not *our* hill just yet, but it may be someday. I want you to come with me."

She smiled at him tenderly and wryly. "If you promise you'll drive me home, I'll dismiss Henry."

Creighton smiled back and said, "It's a promise."

As they drove toward Penrose, Kaye saw once again the boyish smile on Creighton's face. He seemed young and eager and almost embarrassed by his passion for her. And for the first time she felt a sense of commitment to him. Oh, it wasn't really the first time, but she felt it now sincerely and without reservation. She would take his grandmother's ring, and she would cherish it. However, she would accept it not on the tentative terms on which he had offered it, but as a token of their love for each other. And she knew—somehow she knew—that one day she would wear it, wear it at once humbly and proudly as the future Mrs. Creighton Jarvis.

She caught herself in midthought. Creighton had offered her the ring without entanglements. She had accepted it on that basis. She would find a special place for it in a drawer of her desk, and there it would stay until her confusion was over. From the corner of her eye she glanced at Creighton and wondered how she could go on resisting him.

They pulled into the driveway at Penrose, and Creighton stopped the Rover in front of the house. He turned to her and kissed her cheek. "I'll only be a moment."

He got out of the car and started for the house. He stopped, though, came back to the car and leaned on the door at the bottom of Kaye's open window. "You do understand I'm not being rude."

"I don't know what you mean."

"By not asking you in. The time will come very soon when I'll show you Penrose, but I want it to be an occasion. I want to show you all the little things that make it dear to me. . . all its secrets, all its peculiarities. It will take time, and I want it to be unhurried."

She smiled again. "I love you. Go on now, and be quick about it."

He was back in less than five minutes. He got into the driver's seat without speaking and with a sly grin on his face, and he drove back to the road and started up the mountain. Kaye recognized every foot of the way—the flowers, the trees, the winding rutted dirt road. She felt as if she were going home.

Creighton stopped the Rover at the exact spot at which they had stopped previously. Still not speaking, they got out of the car and walked to a point from which they could see all the way down the hill to the sea.

"There isn't really any need for words," Creighton began. "I want you to have this. That's all."

She put out her hand, and he put the unopened velvet box in her palm.

"I want to have it, Creighton. It will be as sacred to me as it has been to the others who've worn it."

"I know it will."

He took her in his arms and held her close to him without kissing her. It was a different feeling for each of them, different from what they had experienced for each other in the past. The overwhelming passion was still there, devastatingly the same, but it was tinged with a sense of peace and security and calm. Kaye felt so safe in his arms, and Creighton felt sure of her and confident and supremely masculine. He twined his fingers in her hair and gently tilted her head back. His look was different so close, although it wasn't, it seemed to Kaye, the first time she had been so near the smoldering amber eyes. Then she saw the difference with a startling clarity. It was the first time he had allowed her to see into them, to see behind the mask of them into the depths of the Creighton Jarvis who was hidden from everyone else, into the Creighton Jarvis who could now be hers if she had the strength to accept him. This was how it could be forever—the oneness, the gentleness, the sureness of their love.

"If I can't have a lifetime, may I at least have the rest of this one day?" Creighton asked.

"Oh, yes!"

"Look down there, all the way down to the sea. That beach is mine. No one ever uses it. I'll have the kitchen at Penrose fix us a picnic lunch, and we'll spend the afternoon on the beach together. Would that please you?''

"I can think of nothing that would please me more.''

"We can swim and sun and eat cold chicken and salad and sip chilled white wine.'' He grinned suddenly. "And we can argue about what to do with the rest of the day and night.''

"Us? Argue? Don't be silly. We never do that.''

"We may never do it again.''

"Oh, Creighton!''

He kissed her again long and lovingly. Then he held her at arm's length and said, "Come on now, back to the house to get that picnic for us from the kitchen and a bathing suit for you from the cabana.''

As Creighton drove to Penrose, Kaye felt a sense of excitement and adventure she hadn't experienced in years. She knew Creighton felt it, too, and the private intimate sharing made it all the more ecstatic.

When they got out of the car, Creighton led her into the drawing room and firmly sat her on a down-cushioned divan.

"Now you stay there, young lady, while I supervise. I meant what I said about showing you Penrose. There'll be no roaming about, no exploring on your own.''

"I won't move an inch.''

"Good. I'll be back. Can I get you a drink or something?''

"I'm already intoxicated.''

He smiled. "If you change your mind, the bar's over there in that armoire. Miss me while I'm gone.''

"I will. Every second.''

Kaye did not change her mind. She sat quietly marveling at the beauty of her surroundings. *This is Penrose,* she kept saying to herself as she examined the exquisitely appointed room. There were Queen Anne chairs and sturdy sofas. Oak paneling flanked the bookcases. There were damask draperies at the French windows. She suddenly realized the room was a delicately balanced blend of Creighton and.... And what? A quiet unobtrusive feminine element. It was a blend of Creighton and Victoria Penrose Jarvis. Of course. *She* had done the room. She had done it for Creighton, adding subtle touches of herself, just as she must have done in the rest of their life together—in their parties, in their social life, in their jaunts to Paris...and in their bedroom. Could she do it, she wondered. Could she insinuate herself into Creighton's life so inconspicuously that she would color it without making any attempt to dominate it? That was what sharing a life was all about. Creighton would respond to her efforts tacitly, with a loving protectiveness.

But could she do it? Could she share any man's life on a fifty-fifty basis? Or would she again demand more of the man than he was prepared to give? Not with Creighton, she told herself. He would....

He was back in the room wearing a grin worthy of Danny Riordan. He had a wicker picnic basket in hand, which he held up before her.

"Here it is—full of cold chicken, white wine and a dozen surprises. I hope you like surprises."

"I do, darling, that kind anyway."

He lowered the basket to his side, and his smile faded.

"What does that mean?" he asked.

"I've had another surprise just now. Penrose. Sitting in this room, I felt that...."

"Go on, say it."

"I felt that Victoria was virtually here. The room is so filled with her presence."

Creighton put the picnic basket on the floor beside

him. He knelt on one knee before her with casual gallantry. "My dear Kaye. You've got to understand something. This *is* the house that Victoria and Creighton
built. I loved her. Some part of her will always be here—
for me certainly, but in a curious way for you, too. She
was a part of my life, just as Rod—and for that matter,
Aunt Alice and your parents and your friends—have
been a part of yours. But things change. Friends drift
apart. Children grow up and leave their parents; they
marry and start lives and families of their own. And
people die. . . as Victoria did. She was a part of my life,
and I will not deny my love for her; you wouldn't want
me to. But she's gone now, and by some miracle you're
here. . . here in my life, and I love you. My having loved
Victoria doesn't diminish my love for you any more
than my loving you could diminish my having loved her.
The past is part of all of us. But this is now, and I'm in
love with you and will be for as long as we live. I want
you to share this house with me—with all its memories—because it's all part of me, the me I hope you
love."

She put her hand on his dark hair and said, "Oh,
Creighton. There is no part of you or your life that I
don't love. I love everything you are."

"That's my girl. Come on now. Here's your swim-
suit. Go and put it on, and we're off to our own private
beach."

She went to the downstairs powder room to change.
Her heart sang at the idea of spending the rest of the day
and evening with Creighton. And the night? The night
would come, and. . . and they would have to part, she
told herself. It was understood now. They would hold
their love in abeyance until she was sure—not of Creighton, but of herself. She found herself hurrying. As she
adjusted the shoulder straps of her suit, she did a last-

minute check of herself in the mirror. Satisfied with what she saw, she pulled back her shoulders and returned to the drawing room and to Creighton.

He was waiting for her, wearing a denim shirt and khaki trousers. She noticed immediately that he was barefoot.

"Well, you're casual enough, Mr. Jarvis, but I thought we were going to swim."

"I've put on my bathing trunks and covered them up with street clothes."

"And no shoes?"

"I'm sorry, but I get a great sensuous thrill from driving a car barefoot." He paused and squinted at her. "Do you understand that, Kaye?"

"I think so. You're a very physical man, and you like physical satisfactions."

"And there's no greater one than being near you." He was very close to her now, so close that they could feel the warmth of each other's bodies. They stood for a long moment in a silence so intense that the buzzing of a fly in the enormous room sounded thunderous.

"There's no point in putting ourselves in harm's way. Let's go," Creighton said.

Hand in hand they ran—not walked, but ran like excited children—out of the drawing room, across the entrance hall and out to the Rover. Once in the car, they fell into one of their customary silences. But this one was underlined with a mutual quiet contentment.

"'The greatest joy is the expectation thereof,'" Creighton proclaimed quite unexpectedly.

"What?"

"Someone—I don't remember who—said that to me when I was just a child. I've always remembered it and found it to be true. Sometimes it doesn't even matter if what you're expecting turns out not to be all you hoped

for. The anticipation becomes so great a joy in itself
that it makes up for the loss.''

"Dear Creighton, the farmer, the aristocrat, the poli-
tician, the romantic—and now the philosopher.''

"I *was* being a bit philosophical, wasn't I? You see,
you bring out the best in me.''

"And that's why you love me.''

"It's as good a reason as any.''

Creighton drove the Rover right onto the beach and
parked it in the shade of the palm trees that began their
growth thirty feet from the waterline. They got out of
the Rover and stood on the warm sand. In seconds he
had peeled off his shirt and khakis and stood next to her
in only his blue bathing suit. His body was magnificent.
He had the look of a statue, yet his buoyant spirits made
him seem a mere boy. He took Kaye's hand.

"I'll bow to your preference, Miss Belliston, but I
have a standard procedure. A swim first, then lying in
the sun until one is very warm, then another swim. How
about it?''

"If you'll just let me put out the beach towels, we
can—''

"No, no. In ten seconds we start running, and we
don't stop until we're neck-deep in the sea.''

"But—''

"No buts. Six, five, four, three, two, one. We're
off!''

Still holding Kaye's hand, Creighton pulled her across
the beach and into the cool refreshing water. They
romped in the low waves, splashed and dunked each
other, as if they hadn't a care in the world, as if they
weren't involved in a love affair that might destroy them
both.

After fifteen minutes of frolicking in the water, they
walked back onto the beach. Kaye got the beach towels

from the Rover and spread them on the sand. They lay down side by side with beads of seawater trickling along their bodies. They held hands for a long time without speaking, and the sun toasted them and dried their bodies. It was like being in a private world, together in a magic place apart from everything and everyone else who existed. This was their moment, their time in the sun, away from care and obligation and intrusion.

The moment was too sacred to tarnish with words. They lay for at least an hour without speaking. There was no more between them than the touching of their hands, but that contact was so exquisitely intimate there was no need for anything more. The tiniest movement of a finger, the gentlest squeeze of their palms communicated more than any words could have. It was an hour of the deepest togetherness.

Kaye had fallen into a sensuous doze, aware of the sun's warmth and of Creighton's touch, yet drifting in a viscous dreamlike world. Suddenly she was aware of his mouth against hers, gentle and tender. His lips were radiant with the heat of the sun, and almost lazily her own lips responded to his. There was no need to hurry, no need to plunge into the depths of passion.

Without taking his lips away from hers, Creighton said, "We have all this, and there's still the evening."

Kaye felt his mouth moving against hers as he spoke, and she spoke back to him without retreating. "As long as we're together, nothing else matters."

"Nothing in the whole bloody world."

As he kissed her again, the passion could no longer be avoided. Their desire for each other kindled inside them. The flickering tongues would soon be a holocaust. It was Creighton, in his strength and honesty and dedication, who pulled away.

"We still have to decide about the evening," he said.

"Yes, I know."

"I have an idea. If you hate it, you must tell me."

"I promise, but I know I won't hate it."

"I am by no means a chef, but I make the best cheese omelet in Montego—perhaps in the world. I'd like to take you back to Penrose and place you securely on the terrace, with the same rules as earlier about snooping. I'll make you a lovely rum cooler, then disappear for half an hour. I will send the servants off—they won't have a hand in this meal. When I reappear, I'll be carrying my triumphant omelet, with a green salad and a bottle of Bollinger. I suppose what I'm saying is that I want us to spend the evening together in complete privacy. Just us."

"It sounds like pure heaven."

"We'll do it."

They had another swim, then packed up the towels and the picnic basket and drove back to Penrose. Kaye telephoned Aunt Alice and explained that she was having dinner with Creighton at his house. Aunt Alice's immediate reaction was one of extreme surprise. Very few people were invited to Creighton's even for a drink; a dinner was a rarity. Her surprise quickly turned to happiness as she realized that things between her niece and Creighton had indeed taken a fortunate turn.

The butler showed Kaye to a bedroom suite, where she bathed and changed back into her clothes. Creighton was waiting for her at foot of the staircase. He led her through the drawing room and onto the terrace. Her rum cooler was ready, frosted and decorated with a sprig of mint. He seated her in a cushioned rattan chair.

"Remember the rules. I'll be back before you know it."

Kaye sat looking out over the lovely garden—a garden Victoria had probably designed. She knew then that the thought of Victoria was no longer troublesome. Creighton, in his sweetness and wisdom, had put Victoria in proper perspective, not only for himself, but for Kaye, as well. In the cool blue of the approaching twilight, she felt serene. She was so deep in thought that she lost track of time. Creighton startled her when he came back carrying the dinner tray.

After one glance Kaye decided Creighton was some kind of culinary wizard. It was all there on the tray: the omelets, the salad, chilled champagne glasses, the champagne in a bucket of ice.

"Did you really do this yourself?" Kaye asked as Creighton put the tray on a coffee table.

"I hope you don't think I'd deceive you. I'm a man of my word."

The food, the champagne, being with Creighton, the Jamaican twilight falling softly on the beautiful garden gave Kaye a sense of security, of belonging, and she was plagued again by the thought of a lifetime of such moments.

When they had finished the meal and were still sipping champagne, Kaye leaned back in her chair and said, "That may have been the most wonderful dinner I've ever had."

"It needn't be the last one," Creighton replied. Then, as if having read her thoughts, he added, "We could have this for the rest of our lives."

"You mean, if I'd say yes."

He shrugged. "I guess this is my own clumsy way of wooing you. The Australian outback doesn't breed graciousness."

"But it has bred something I like very much. It's given me you."

"Then accept me."

"Oh, Creighton, I—"

"I'm sorry. I shouldn't have said that. I must learn to be content to leave things as they are—at least for the moment."

"It may not be a long moment."

He grinned at her again and added, "Don't encourage me in my folly."

"It isn't folly. I love you."

"And I love you. Now, it may be the most difficult thing I've ever done, but it's time for me to take you back to Traymore."

"You do know it's just as difficult for me."

"Yes, I suppose it is."

"One day, my darling, you'll reach for my hand and feel your grandmother's ring on my finger."

"I won't take that as a promise, but I live for the day."

"Please be patient."

"I will—but not forever."

They said no more after that. Creighton escorted her to the Rover and drove her back to Traymore. His arm was around her waist as he took her to the foot of the veranda stairs.

"I love you, Kaye," he murmured as he put his arms around her, "but I meant what I said. I won't wait forever."

"I won't make you wait forever. I swear it."

He kissed her gently. "Good night, my sweet girl. Sleep well."

"Good night," she replied. "I love you."

She waited, listening to the familiar sound of the departing Rover. She knew she wanted to hear that sound again, coming toward instead of going away from her. Then she turned and went into the house.

# CHAPTER EIGHT

THERE WAS A LARGE DINNER PARTY the next night at the Marlowes' and another the night after that at the Duckworths'. Everyone talked about the ball. They theorized and guessed about one another's costumes, and a game was devised in which the participants were to suggest the Shakespearean character the others might most appropriately represent. The only general agreement was that Barney Fairweather should come to the ball as Falstaff. For Kaye, the salient feature of both parties was Creighton's absence. She knew she shouldn't ask about it, so in spite of her great anxiety she restrained herself. She didn't even inquire of Adrian, who surely knew, even though he was at her side at almost every moment.

In the car on their way from the Duckworths', Kaye broke the silence. "Aunt Alice, do you know why Creighton wasn't at dinner either last night or tonight?"

"No, my dear, I don't. I made discreet inquiries and received exactly the answer I expected. He was invited, but he said he was unable to attend."

They rode the rest of the way in silence and said goodnight without their usual late-night chat.

The next few days were languid and uneventful. There appeared to be no need now to convince Creighton of her sincerity, but he was being careful, discreet. He made no attempt to contact her. Apparently he was resigned to the conditions they had agreed upon.

The day of the ball seemed to arrive suddenly. She

found herself hurrying to be prepared to leave when
Aunt Alice was. They met in the downstairs hall just as
Adrian got there, and after a token drink they were
ready to go.

The ballroom of Lady Smith-Croydon's house was
used infrequently. Only two or three times a season did
she give parties large enough for it to be called into service. This occasion, of course, was the kind for which it
had been created, the kind Smitty loved.

The ballroom had been transformed into the great
hall of a medieval castle. It was lit entirely by candlelight. The three massive chandeliers had been turned off
and fitted with white tapers for the evening. Between the
pilasters that lined the walls, six-foot candlesticks
holding tall candles five inches in diameter had been set
up. The pilasters themselves were wrapped in garlands
of laurel that had been dotted with flowers. Dozens of
great urns had been filled with native English flowers
flown in from London. Twenty-five feet above the
floor, the walls were lined with escutcheons bearing
sixteenth-century English coats of arms. Between every
two candlesticks was a suit of armor standing under
crossed lances. There were tapestries and velvet wall
hangings. A large orchestra dressed in Elizabethan
minstrel costumes played at one end of the room. Smitty's entire staff and the one hundred extra servants hired
for the ball were attired in green and gold sixteenth-
century livery.

The eight pairs of French doors lining the west side of
the room had been thrown open to the garden, where
minstrels strumming lutes and singing ballads strolled
among the guests. In the middle of the lawn an enormous tent—a replica of the exterior of the Globe
Theatre—had been erected. The canvas had been expertly painted to heighten the illusion, and atop the

short spire rising from the dome, green and gold pen-
nants flew in the breeze.

Inside the tent were long, planked, wooden tables
heaped with food. There were huge roasts of beef, sad-
dles of lamb, suckling pigs, roast pheasants and quail
and partridge. There were casseroles of Yorkshire pud-
ding and immense bowls of mixed salad. Great white
tureens holding soups and vegetables dotted other
tables. Yet another was laden with fresh fruit and cheese
and trifle and pastries of every description. And Smitty
was true to her word. In one corner of the tent a huge ox
turned on a spit over an open fire.

Outside the tent were tables holding lighter fare for
those with less hearty appetites. There were platters of
roast chicken and turkey and lobster and poached
salmon. There were fruit salads and aspics and cold
cream sauces for everything. From yet another table servants circulated with silver trays offering beer and ale
and red and white Bordeaux, and champagne flowed
endlessly. Under a towering oak tree was a traditional
bar for the diehards. It was surely the party of the
season, and it would be talked about for many seasons
to come.

The ballroom was already crowded with dancers
when Aunt Alice and Kaye and Adrian arrived. The costumes, which were extraordinarily elaborate, were not
meant to, and for the most part did not, totally disguise
their wearers. Neither did they aid one in finding one's
immediate friends. There were Henrys of all numbers
and Calibans and Banquos and witches and Rosalinds
and Portias and Shylocks and Caesars and Antonys and
Cleopatras and Lears and a host of lesser characters.
Nor were the costumes restricted to characters in the
plays. There were Elizabeths and Raleighs and Drakes
and Marys and Darnleys and Frobishers. Kings met

paupers; heroes met villains; ladies met rogues, and
whole families congregated. It was spectacular.

Kaye, Aunt Alice and Adrian set off in search of
Smitty. They had little trouble finding her. She was
seated on a gilt throne on a dais opposite the French
doors. She was by far the grandest Elizabeth of the half
dozen or so present. Her gown was of garnet damask
encrusted with rubies and sapphires and pearls. She
wore an enormous ruff of white organdy from which
hung yard-long ropes of pearls. Her gown was also studded here and there with diamond brooches, and her
fingers were covered with diamond rings, the genuine-
ness of which no one questioned—they were Smitty's
own. Crowning the whole glorious affair was a carrot-
red wig wound through with ropes of pearl and topaz.
She reigned over the ball as Elizabeth I had reigned over
her realm.

"Your majesty," Lady Alice cried as she approached
the throne with a deep curtsy.

"Is it Juliet's nurse I see there?" Smitty said from a
great height, physically as well as in manner. "Nurse
Armstrong?"

"It is, Your Majesty, and here is my mistress, Juliet
Belliston, and her adorer, Romeo James."

"Ah, yes. A sad case that," Smitty commented. "No
matter. Tonight is a night for merrymaking. Be gay!"
she commanded. She leaned far forward and whispered
to Alice, "I'll see you about if I ever get off this damned
uncomfortable throne."

Alice laughed, and they began to move away. They
had gone only a few feet when they spotted Netty and
Harlan dancing at the edge of the dance floor. They had
come as Macbeth and his lady. Their costumes were
elaborate and authentic in design. They approached the
new arrivals arm in arm.

"Kaye, you look absolutely exquisite," Netty said. "You *are* Juliet."

"Have you seen the garden?" Harlan asked. "The tent is a replica of the Globe—and almost as big."

"I can't wait to see it," Kaye remarked.

"And the food!" Netty exclaimed. "It's unbelievable!"

"We may as well start toward it," Alice put in. "It's going to take us some time to get all the way around the dance floor and through the crowd. Certainly everybody in Montego is here."

"Not to mention the hundred or so guests Smitty flew in from London and the south of France," Harlan noted. "Oh, there's a New York contingent, too, Kaye. Perhaps you'll know some of them."

"I must investigate."

They had got a quarter of the way around the rectangular dance floor when they saw a hugely rotund, bald-pated, heavily masked friar approaching them. He obviously knew them, but none of them recognized him.

He greeted them in a high rasping voice. "Good nurse, watch for the full moon lest your young charge be driven mad."

"I will watch, dear monk, but methinks I know you not."

"A little more time in chapel, dear lady, and perhaps thou wouldst," the mysterious friar replied. "And thou, Romeo, wouldst not be so gay if thou knew what fate holds for you."

"In the company of my love," Adrian replied, "I would be gay in the face of any fate."

"Ah, all the young are fools." Then in his own voice Barney Fairweather said, "I haven't had a drink since I got here."

"Barney!" Alice cried. "You're a complete success. Your disguise is foolproof."

"Thank you, Alice. Made it myself, of course. Even the bald pate. Some thin rubber sheeting and a little hair from my goat."

"You're a genius, Barney," Kaye said, adding, "We're on our way to the garden."

"I'll come with you, if I may. The food's there."

Thus augmented, the group continued toward the French doors. They finally reached them and stepped out onto the terrace overlooking the garden. They stopped in awe.

"Isn't it fantastic?" Barney declared.

"I don't believe it," Adrian said. "It *is* the Globe. Old Will himself might step out of it at any moment."

Aunt Alice was smiling. "Ah, Smitty. It's all so Smitty. Who else would give an authentically Elizabethan party on a tropical island?"

They went into the tent and were overwhelmed by the rather smoky aromatic reality of it all. Some of the minstrels had wandered in, and one of them was singing a bawdy song to the accompiament of a lute.

"The ballroom is magnificent," Alice began, "but this is sheer magic."

"It's the work of a wizard, a Merlin," Barney put in.

Across their line of vision came a tall, emaciated, white-robed Lear, wisps of white hair trailing after him like the smoke from the ox fire. He was made all the more impressive by·his unfeigned doddering. On his arm was an incongruously withered Regan with a plain but beautifully designed gown of pale green silk. It was the Duckworths.

"Maude," Alice called out to Mrs. Duckworth, "come and say hello."

The· Duckworths looked slightly and mutually star-

tled. When they were together, all their reactions
seemed to be the reactions of one person. Then they
both smiled and came toward Alice.

"My dear Alice," Maude said. "You look charming.
Who are you?"

"I'm Juliet's nurse."

"Oh, of course, and your dear niece is Juliet. Who is
this fat friar?"

"An old friend in disguise, madam," Barney rasped
in his altered voice.

"Oh, it's Barney," Maude said immediately. "Very
nice costume, isn't it, Phillip? Alice, I did so want to
bring one of my dogs—there should always be dogs in
*Lear*—but I was afraid he'd turn playful and wreck
Smitty's party."

"It was a wise decision, Maude," Alice said.

They helped themselves to plates of food, and when
they had finished, they walked out into the crowded
garden, Kaye and Adrian bringing up the rear of the
party.

Adrian said, "Kaye, it is a ball after all; wouldn't you
like to dance?"

"I'd like it very much."

"Will you excuse us?" Adrian said to the others.
"We're going to go and take advantage of the dance
floor."

They made their way to the French doors and inside
to the ballroom. The orchestra was playing a waltz.
Adrian took Kaye in his arms gently but firmly, holding
her very close to him. Kaye didn't know quite what was
in her mind or heart as she felt him pressed so close to
her, the movement of their bodies making the contact
all the more intimate. Then she made the inevitable admission. She knew exactly what was in her mind and
heart: Creighton. Being in Creighton's arms was being

in another world, a world she had never known before she had met him. It was a world to which they alone had admission, a world in which they alone existed. It was a magical fairyland.

Even though she was now close to Adrian, there was a distance between them. She wondered if the distance had been created by Creighton's warning or simply by her love for him. It was a bit of both, she decided. One thing was certain: she was in Adrian's arms, thinking of no one but Creighton and wondering why he had not yet arrived.

When the waltz ended, they were near the edge of the dance floor. "We've been here for almost an hour," Adrian said, "and we haven't had any champagne. Shall I get us some?"

"I'd love some."

He took her hand. "Come with me." He led her off the dance floor. "Wait here, just by Smitty's throne. I'll only be a minute."

As soon as Adrian left, a young splendid Mercutio approached her. "Hello, Kaye."

"Ellis! How handsome you are!"

"And you're beautiful!"

"Thank you."

"Why have you been avoiding me?"

"Ellis, I haven't been avoiding you. Truly, I haven't."

"I haven't seen you for days."

"Everybody seems to have been busy getting ready for Smitty's ball. There haven't been many parties or—"

"You were at dinner at Netty and Harlan's, and we barely spoke half a dozen sentences to each other. You spent the entire evening with Adrian James, just as you are this one."

"You must believe I didn't avoid you intentionally."

"Why should I?"

"Because it's the truth. Things have just happened that way."

"I know I have no right to ask, but is there something between you and Adrian?"

"You're right; you have no right to ask. But I'll tell you anyway. There's nothing between me and Adrian or anyone else, and I don't want there to be. I've told you that previously."

At that moment Adrian came back with two glasses of champagne. "Here you are, darling," he said. "To Shakespeare. . . and to us." He sipped the wine. "Hello, Ellis. How are you?"

"Good evening, Adrian, I'm fine. And you?"

"Very happy."

"Adrian, Ellis and I are going to dance. Would you hold my champagne for me?"

"Now I'm not so happy. But certainly. I'll be right here. No, I'll be at that little table back there in the alcove. And I'd better get it while it's unoccupied."

When their dance ended, Ellis escorted Kaye back toward the alcove. As they were about to break through the edge of the crowd, Kaye saw George Montague standing a few feet from the table. He wore draped robes of pure white bordered with narrow strips of unmistakably Jamaican fabric and sported a meticulously trimmed beard, with a gold earring in one ear. He was a tall, black, elegant Othello. George, like everyone and everything else in Montego, made her think of Creighton, and she began to scan the room with a breathless excitement, hoping for a glimpse of him. Then, with an electrifying suddenness, she saw him near George. His back was toward her, but she knew instantly it was Creighton. He wore a motley full-sleeved tunic, black trousers bloused below the knee and loose black leather boots. His shining dark hair was hidden by a wide-brimmed felt hat adorned with three long pheasant feathers. He looked altogether enchanting. Even through the crowd and from the distance she knew it was Creighton, and she knew he was Petruchio.

For a moment she didn't realize she had stopped at the edge of the dance floor, paralyzed by the sight of Creighton. His good looks had been made all the more glorious by his assumption of the role and the character of Petruchio. She knew then that in her heart she wanted him to tame her as Kate had been tamed. She knew she wanted him to take her away and shape her into the kind of woman he wanted her to be—and, she knew just as certainly, into the kind of woman she wanted to be: his kind of woman. . . his woman.

She heard Ellis's voice and realized she had forgotten she was at his side. "Are you all right, Kaye?"

"Yes. Yes, of course," she replied.

"You're as pale as a ghost."

"It must have been the dance and the champagne."

"Or the sight of Creighton," Ellis said.

"Don't be ridiculous."

"All right, then. Let's go and talk to him."

As she and Ellis neared the table, George saw them. He smiled and was about to speak when they heard Creighton's voice, barely audible above the music and the voices of the throng.

"This is the last time I'm going to warn you, Adrian."

"Good evening, Kaye," George said more quickly and more loudly than was necessary. "Pardon me—Juliet."

Creighton turned around immediately upon hearing Kaye's name. It was perfectly clear George had warned him of her approach.

"Ah, my lord Othello," Kaye said. "How striking you are, George."

"Thank you, and you are the fairest Juliet of them all. Good evening, Ellis."

"Hello, George," Ellis said.

Creighton had turned but still had not spoken to her. He was staring at her with his usual inscrutable expression, tinged, it seemed to Kaye, with anger. "Good evening, Kaye," he said at last. "You look very beautiful."

"Thank you, Creighton," Kaye acknowledged. "And you look very handsome."

"Since we're such an attractive couple, perhaps we should dance—that is, of course, if Adrian doesn't mind."

"Of course I don't mind, dear boy," Adrian said with an almost proprietary air that made Creighton seem to cringe.

As Creighton took her in his arms, Kaye knew her judgment when she had been dancing with Adrian had been sound. There was nothing in the world like Creighton's embrace. Even in the precarious state of their relationship the thrill remained unchanged.

"A penny for your thoughts," Creighton whispered with his mouth close to her ear.

"I don't believe you'd like them," Kaye answered. "I was thinking about how much I love you."

There was a moment of silence before Creighton spoke. "After our last meeting I decided it might be best if we didn't see each other too often—being near you is almost painful. But when I saw you tonight, saw those mysterious green eyes, that irresistible mouth, I saw the woman I loved, and I decided that to deny myself your company would be foolish indeed. So here I am with my arms around you."

"Blessedly, my darling."

The frown she had come to know so well darkened his face. "But you're here with Adrian," he finished.

"Adrian came with Aunt Alice and me," she corrected. "I did not come here with Adrian. There's a difference."

"Still, I mustn't usurp too much of your time," he said, smiling at her wryly.

The dance ended, and he led her back to the table. He seated her in the only empty chair—which put her very close to Adrian.

"I hope we'll have another dance," he said. He glanced at Adrian without expression, and he was gone.

"Creighton makes a smashing Petruchio, don't you think?" Adrian commented.

"Yes, smashing," Kaye agreed. "Adrian, it may be none of my business, but what was Creighton saying to you as I came back from dancing with Ellis?"

Adrian leaned back in his chair and sighed. "Oh, the usual; he was telling me to keep away from you."

Kaye found it curious, but she felt none of the resentment she had experienced on first hearing of Creighton's intrusion upon her friendship with Adrian. There had been something deeply serious in his expression, and the amber eyes had flashed for an instant with unmistakable fury.

"But why?"

"Kaye, don't you see how simple it is? He wants you for himself, and he thinks I'm a threat. And even if he can't have you, he wants no one else to. It's so typical of him. He doesn't care a damn for your happiness. He cares only about himself and his own selfish pride. I know that as yet there's nothing serious between us—at least on your part. But what if there were? What if we were falling in love? Creighton would destroy that if he could, regardless of what it would mean to you. Beneath the seeming nobility, he's a very greedy man."

For the first time Adrian had said things Kaye did not

believe. She could not disprove them, but she felt she knew Creighton, and Adrian seemed to have a chip on his shoulder. Yet she was suspicious of instincts, her own or anyone else's, so she tried to shake off the feeling of unease she was now experiencing. She liked to act on decisions made on reason and objectivity, and she was afraid that whatever she now felt was likely to be unreasonable and nonobjective. The old confusion returned, but shake it she would, she decided, if only for the moment.

"Well, we mustn't let it ruin the evening," she said.

"I wouldn't dream of it. Besides, Creighton's ravings mean nothing to me. Would you like to dance?"

"I think I'd like to go back to the garden."

"All right." He started to get up just as Ellis came by.

Virtually ignoring Adrian, he said, "I don't suppose there's a chance of my having another dance with you, Kaye?"

"Not just now. We're going back to the garden. Won't you come along?"

Ellis smiled very appealingly and with great pleasure. "That's very thoughtful. I'd love to join you."

As they made their way to the French doors, Kaye wondered if they'd ever find Aunt Alice again. The garden was a sea of Elizabethiana. The thought of trying to find one human being in the costumed reveling throng was at best discouraging.

But luck was with them, and from the terrace they spotted Aunt Alice. She was still with the Duckworths, but Barney had gone off somewhere. The Zimmermans had joined them, and Kevin Wright was there, too, costumed as Henry IV. Kaye wasn't sure who else was in the immediate group, for people were almost shoulder to shoulder now.

"Hello, good nurse," Ellis said. "I've brought your ward to you."

"Thank you, Ellis. My, aren't you handsome in your doublet and hose."

"Thank you, Lady Alice. I must say, you make quite a fetching nurse."

Kaye asked, "Aunt Alice, have you seen Amanda?"

"Yes, briefly. Look for a beautiful Ophelia. She's wearing a white gauze dress with garlands of weeds and wild flowers in her hair. She looks quite appropriately mad. Oh, there she is, floating across the terrace like a wraith."

Kaye looked toward the terrace and saw her standing at the top of the stairs. "She'll probably be gone by the time I get there, but it's worth a try. Excuse me."

By using her elbows judiciously, Kaye made her way through the crowd and reached the terrace before Amanda left it. She approached her from behind and put her hand on the girl's shoulder. As Amanda turned, Kaye said, "Aunt Alice was right. You look quite crazy."

"Isn't it delicious? I've always wanted to play Ophelia. Are you having a good time?"

"Yes, I suppose so. Are you?"

"No. Not without—"

"Now none of that. You've got to learn to be reasonably happy when you're away from him. What are you going to do next winter when you're in London and he's at Grinnell?"

"I'm sure I don't know."

"At least you're certain he loves you, and you can write to each other."

"And have grandmother intercept the correspondence?"

"Don't be a ninny. Have you never heard of a post-office box... or whatever it's called in London."

"Of course."

"If you're going to conduct a secret affair, you'll have to learn to be more resourceful."

"Oh, Kaye," Amanda said dreamily, "we talked about the ball. We talked about how wonderful, how secretly and sweetly wonderful it would be for him to come as Romeo and me to come as Juliet without anyone's knowing. We could do the whole ball scene from the play, pretending not even to know each other and falling in love for the first time. We almost did it. It would have been bliss."

"It would have been disastrous. I'd like to know which one of you finally decided against it."

"Danny. Oh, I knew it could never be, but I was more reluctant to give up the fantasy than he was."

"That sustains my faith in him. Well, whether we're having a good time or not, you must admit your grandmother knows how to give a party."

"It is spectacular, isn't it?"

"Only your grandmother or Cecil B. De Mille could have managed it. Let's stay together, Amanda. I'm sure we'll both have a better time that way."

"I'd love it."

"Let's go down into the garden and join Aunt Alice—" Kaye looked at her with humor "—and Ellis and Kevin and the Duckworths and Adrian—"

"And all the other new and exciting people," Amanda finished.

They both giggled, and Kaye said, "Come on. It's better than nothing."

They ran down the terrace steps and had got no farther than ten feet into the garden when Kaye was caught by the arm so firmly that she was immobilized. She looked up to see Creighton standing beside her.

"Amanda," Creighton said, "I'm going to borrow Kaye for a short time. Don't tell anyone."

Before either Amanda or Kaye could object, Creighton had taken Kaye by the hand and was leading her across the lawn.

"Creighton, what in the world are you doing?" Kaye cried as she was swept along in Petruchio's wake.

"Don't for a minute think I'm going to ask you to accompany me. I am taking you with me, and unless you're not as bright as I think you are, you can see there's nothing you can do about it."

He pulled her across the lawn, but he knew better than to try to take her through the house when he was virtually kidnapping her. Instead he took her around the house, first onto a kind of meadow, then onto the front lawn and the driveway. He signaled for his car to be brought, all the time holding Kaye so tightly that she couldn't escape him. She didn't want to escape him, but she was not prepared to admit it.

"Creighton, where are we going?" she demanded in mock anger.

"To my car."

"To your car? We can't leave the ball."

"Why not? It'll only be for an hour."

"It would be extremely rude."

"Nonsense. Who'll miss us?"

Somehow they reached the car without being approached. Creighton seated her very firmly and got in beside her. Without a word of explanation he started the engine. In minutes it was perfectly obvious to Kaye that they were driving down the mountain.

"Creighton, you're heading toward town."

"Yes, that's quite true."

"But why?"

"Because that's how we have to go to get where we're going. That's a very odd sentence."

"It's not as odd as what we're doing."

"It's not odd at all. I simply want to show you something—a secret I've kept from you."

"Right now? Right in the middle of Smitty's party?"

"It was an impulse, and I believe in acting on impulse. . . within reason, of course."

"You're a complete contradiction," Kaye said with an exaggerated sigh. "Will you please tell me where we're going?"

"No, as a matter of fact. Just be quiet, and I guarantee you you'll be glad we made the trip."

Kaye was thrilled by Creighton's impulsiveness, but she decided not to give him the satisfaction of knowing it just yet. She pretended to pout as they drove the circuitous road into town.

They had driven halfway around the crescent-shaped bay before either of them spoke again.

"Creighton, we've come miles. Where on earth are—"

"Never mind, we're here."

He made a turn and pulled the car up to the end of a long lonely quay. The other docks closer to the center of the crescent were crowded with every kind of sea-going craft, but this one seemed almost deserted. Creighton got out of the car and opened the other door for Kaye. He kept possession of her arm once she was out of the car and led her a few feet onto the dock.

"There she is," Creighton said, and she could see his radiant smile even in the pale moonlight.

"There *who* is?" Kaye asked.

"My boat, the *Eos*."

She didn't know how she could not have seen it long before this—perhaps it was because she had been looking at Creighton—but there it was, listing slightly at its moorings. It was a lovely, trim, slender, two-masted sailboat, glistening immaculately in the moon's silver light.

"Oh, Creighton, she's beautiful!"

"I knew you'd know about boats."

"I've been sailing since I was five years old."

"Then you can see that she's yare."

"She's perfect. Oh, Creighton, could we go aboard...just for a minute?"

"Why do you think I brought you here? She has a diesel, so we won't have to sail her."

Kaye was flabbergasted. "You're not thinking of taking her out? You can't be."

"The *Eos* is always in a state of absolute readiness, and since you're a sailor and can handle the lines, we'll be cruising within five minutes. Come on. No arguments." He took her by the hand, and they scrambled aboard.

"She's yours, isn't she?" Kaye said. "I mean, really yours."

"Yes. I know it sounds pretentious, but I created her. I designed her, outfitted her, supervised her construction.... I'm sorry to sound so foolish."

"It isn't foolish at all. She may be the most beautiful boat I've ever seen. But you are devious, Creighton Jarvis. You knew that once you got me on board, I wouldn't rest until I'd seen you run her."

"I want to see *you* run her. Oh, I don't mean tonight. But I want to see you run her; I want to run her with you—just the two of us together, under sail."

"What a joy that would be!"

"*Will* be. Come on, let's get her started. Stand by to cast off those two stern lines when I start the engines."

"Aye, aye, sir."

Within minutes they were on their way out of the harbor. The engines were the quietest Kaye had ever heard. They made no more than a gentle soothing hum. Now that her nautical duties were over, she went and stood behind Creighton at the wheel. She put her arms around his chest.

"I hope we're not headed for the open sea," she said.

"I don't think you trust me," Creighton answered.

"Not for a minute. If I left you to your devices, I'd probably end up in Europe."

"She could make it, you know."

"Yes, I know very well."

"We'll hug the coastline and stay in the shallows." There was a pause. "Kaye, I just wanted to be alone with you here on the *Eos*."

"I can't think of any place in the world I'd rather be."

After twenty minutes Creighton cut the engines and threw out the anchor. There was a sudden quiet and tranquillity that Kaye knew happened only on an anchored boat, but the sensation was heightened by her being alone with Creighton in this luxurious and restricted space. It was like the isolation of being in his arms—which she knew she soon would be.

He came back from the bow after having dropped the anchor, and they stood on the aft deck, staring at each other for a long moment. Then he took her in his arms and kissed her gently.

As he pressed her to him, over his shoulder she could see the streak of moonlight lying on the surface of the sea. There was a light mist, which made the shoreline vague and uncertain. It was an absolutely magical moment.

"I'm trying neither to bribe you nor persuade you, but this is what it could be like. Together, just us together, we could sail her to Puerto Rico, to the Bahamas, to Bermuda. Or we could go west to Mexico, or south to Caracas. Nothing but the sea and the silence and us."

"You're very persuasive for someone who isn't trying to be persuasive."

"It may have something to do with my loving you."

"Oh, Creighton, it would be paradise! But my reasons can't just disappear."

"Neither can mine."

They stood on the deck for a long time in each other's arms, bathed in moonlight and silence and lulled by the gentle swaying of the boat. It was a moment neither of them wanted ever to end.

"I love you very much," he whispered.

"And I love you," Kaye answered. "Oh, Creighton, what am I doing to you? I wish I had the courage to leave Montego. I don't want to go on hurting you."

"Your leaving would hurt me more than anything else. And it wouldn't do any good. I'd follow you."

"You would, wouldn't you?"

"Anywhere in the world."

He tightened his arms around her and kissed her again. Kaye felt the ecstasy she had come to know so well and to cherish. She snuggled against him, feeling tiny and helpless in the presence of his strength. She wished she could stay right there forever, but her sense of obligation nagged at her.

"Creighton, we've got to get back," she said at last. "I don't want to; you must know that. But we can't just run out on the party completely."

"Of course we can't," he answered. "Want to run her back?"

"I'd love it! If you're sure you trust me."

"I wouldn't offer if I didn't. Start the engines while I pull up the anchor."

When the anchor was secure, Creighton gave her the compass reading. She was like an excited child as she ran the graceful, incredibly responsive boat along the moonlit coastline. Creighton stood beside her, offering encouragement and occasional instructions and enjoying the whole thing fully as much as Kaye was.

When they tied up the *Eos* at the dock in Montego, Creighton embraced her again and kissed her.

"Creighton, thank you for showing her to me. I love her already."

"Will you promise to come out with me for a whole day?"

"You know I'd love it."

"I'd like to make the invitation for overnight, but... well, I don't entirely trust myself."

"Just the two of us, alone on the *Eos* overnight? I wouldn't entirely trust you, either."

They laughed then and scrambled off the boat and back into the car. The first person to see them return was Smitty, who, contrary to their predictions, had missed them. She immediately collared Creighton and began to scold him. Adrian was the second person to spot them, and he had certainly been aware of their absence.

"Well, you had quite an extended excursion," he said to Kaye as Smitty led Creighton away. "You owe me a little walk in the garden."

They took one of the winding paths that led to a partially wooded part of the back garden. It was deserted, and they walked out of the subtle artificial lighting of the lawn into pure pale moonlight. They strolled for a while in silence, then Adrian stopped and took both her hands in his.

"Kaye, may I say something to you?"

"Of course," she answered nervously.

"I told you in the beginning that I'd keep my distance, and you can't deny that I have. Oh, certainly we've been together—perhaps more than you've wanted—but I haven't pressed you or been in any way obtrusive."

"No, you haven't, Adrian."

"I also told you I might fall in love with you." He paused. "I have. I love you very dearly and very deeply."

"Adrian...."

"Please hear me out. I'm sure that nothing has changed for you, but I can't help it if it has for me. I want you to understand one thing: everything except my feeling toward you will remain the same. I will not be insistent or demanding. I will not in any way force myself on you. I will expect nothing of you but the sweetness and courtesy that's so much a part of your nature that you couldn't be otherwise. I ask only that you don't commit yourself to anyone else without telling me first, that you don't suddenly leave the island, that you don't move out of my life abruptly and without warning. Please, Kaye. I beg you for just that much."

"All right, Adrian. I promise."

He took her in his arms and kissed her gently. She felt his passion growing as the kisses became less gentle, but at the first sign of her resistance he released her.

"I do love you, Kaye. Now let's go back."

When they emerged onto the lawn, Kaye saw Creighton standing at the foot of the terrace stairs. He was alone, holding a glass of whiskey and staring at them. She couldn't tell if he had stationed himself there or was there by accident. He made no move as they crossed the lawn toward the place where Aunt Alice and Smitty were standing together with at least a dozen other people.

It was perhaps twenty minutes later when she heard Creighton's voice just behind her. It was calm and quiet.

"Kaye, I'd like to speak with you for a moment. It's important."

She turned to him and looked up into his troubled amber eyes. "Of course," she said.

He took her arm and led her to the far end of the garden, where there were no people but where they were in plain sight of the other guests, though a good distance from them.

"Kaye, I know that what has been between us has not always been pleasant, but it has been for me far deeper and more meaningful than anything I've felt for a very long time. I care for you very, very much. I'm going to tell you something only a handful of people in the world know. I'm going to tell you at a dreadful risk to myself—a risk that nothing in twenty years has tempted me to take. I can do it only on your solemn promise that you will tell no one what I'm going to say. No one. Not Alice, not Amanda, not your closest friend, not your mother, and above all not Adrian. Will you promise me on your honor as a woman and as my trusted friend?"

"Yes, I promise you."

"All right. It's the only way I can convince you that what I've told you about Adrian is not self-seeking or false or said out of jealousy or rancor. It's the only way I know of making you see it's the truth."

"Creighton, I give you that trust because I believe you trust me. I won't betray it."

"That's all I wanted to hear. Once I've told you, you must not ask me any questions. Agreed?"

"Agreed."

"You can believe the things I've told you about Adrian because I know him better than anyone else in the world. Because his name isn't Adrian James, it's Adrian Jarvis. Because he's my brother."

There was nothing in the silence and the moonlight but a quiet involuntary gasp from Kaye.

"If you tell anyone else what I've just said, the consequences to me would be...would be beyond my bearing."

"Oh, Creighton. You can trust me with your life."

"I just have. We should go back now." He touched her hair once with his massive hand in the same incredibly gentle way he had earlier, then he took her arm and led her back toward the others.

# CHAPTER NINE

IT WAS TEN O'CLOCK in the morning when Adrian burst into Creighton's study without knocking. One look told Creighton that his brother was greatly agitated. His eyes were narrowed with anger, and his jaw was so tightly set that the flesh covering it was white.

"What have you told Kaye Belliston?" Adrian demanded.

"I don't know what you're talking about," Creighton replied, turning back to his book.

"Yes, you do. What have you said to her about me?"

"Aside from my having told her she would be wise to stay away from you, you've never been a topic of conversation between us. Talking about you has always bored me."

"Don't be flippant. That won't get you out of it."

"Out of what?" Creighton asked calmly.

"That's what I'm trying to find out. You've said something to discredit me with her, and I want to know what it was."

"Don't be a fool."

"You'd better be careful, Creighton. There's an end to my patience. You know I can always—"

"That's why you're being a fool. Why do you think I'd suddenly take the risk I've been avoiding for so long?"

"I don't know. I *do* know I don't trust you, and I know you're clever."

"I don't remember ever having asked you to trust me," Creighton said. "It would be useless, since you don't know the meaning of the word and you would be the first to point out that I've never been as clever as you. You have nothing to fear from me."

"I've always had something to fear from you, ever since we were children."

"That's your imagination. I was always protective of you as a child . . . until I realized how little you needed anybody's protection. It's other people who need protection from you."

"You're evading the issue."

"There is no issue, Adrian. I advised Kaye to stay away from you some time ago. Obviously she's ignored my warning. That's the end of it."

"Then why has she been avoiding me for the past few days?"

"I'm sure I have no idea. Why don't you ask her?"

"I have."

"Then why are you troubling me with this nonsense?"

"Because Kaye said there was nothing wrong. It's just that she's been neglecting her aunt, and she feels she should spend more time with her."

"That seems a reasonable answer."

"In the past when Kaye wanted to be with her aunt, I was frequently invited to join them. Lady Alice is quite fond of me."

"That's an assumption."

"Are you implying it's Lady Alice who has come between Kaye and me?" Adrian asked.

"I'm not implying anything. I despise you so much that I sometimes forget the person I despise—the real Adrian Jarvis—isn't the person other people see. Perhaps you've succeeded in deceiving Alice the way you have most people. Yet I'm not sure you're that clever."

"And you insist you've told Kaye nothing about me?"

"Adrian, after what I've allowed you to put me through for twenty years, would I go to Kaye and place myself in jeopardy?"

"You might...if you were in love with her. And you are. You're in love with her, and you're trying to drive her away from me."

"Could I afford to do that, Adrian, after all you've cost me?"

"You certainly could, but there's nothing I can do about it just yet. Don't ever forget, though, what I *can* do about it when I'm ready."

"I won't. Not for one minute. But don't forget that your resources will inevitably run out. It's sure as death itself."

"How subtle of you, Creighton."

"And don't forget that the more you make me pay now, the more danger you'll be in when that day comes."

"Ah, but that's all the more reason for me to take what I can while the taking is good," Adrian said.

"Yes, but my day will come. I would live in dread of it if I were you," Creighton answered.

"I will be prepared."

"Will you? It could come very suddenly. And considering the nomadic nature of your existence, I might be aware of it before you are."

"It's unlikely. I've covered myself on that."

"But it's possible."

"Don't threaten me, Creighton."

"That's the one thing I can do safely."

"I warn you again. Be careful. I'm going away for a day or two. I'm bored to death with Montego and its old stale people."

"How pleasant for me. Where are you going?" Creighton inquired.

"To Kingston. I'm told there's some very eclectic entertainment there. I'll be leaving on the noon plane."

"I don't care when you leave. Just go."

Adrian turned and exited from the study, leaving the door open behind him in a gesture of contempt.

Creighton waited only until he saw Christian drive off in the Land Rover, taking Adrian and his luggage to the airport. Then he called Kaye.

When Henry got her to the phone, Creighton said, "Kaye, I have to see you—today, if possible."

"It sounds urgent."

"It is. I hesitate to ask you this, but would you care to come here? We could ride for an hour or so this afternoon. I promise to keep Wellington in the stable."

"I'll come only if you promise to let me ride Wellington."

"It's a bargain. Two o'clock?"

"Perfect."

Kaye went back to the pool, where she had been sunning and where Aunt Alice had been sitting under an umbrella, reading. Alice glanced up expectantly.

Kaye looked at her for a moment, then said, "It was Creighton."

"Oh?"

"He wants to see me. It seems to be important. He's invited me to go riding this afternoon."

"And you're going?"

"Yes."

"All right, my dear. I hope you won't come back in a state of discomposure."

"I won't."

"Very well. We'll have lunch before you leave."

Henry drove Kaye to Penrose, and she arrived just after two. Creighton had obviously heard the car and came down the steps to greet Kaye in the driveway, just as he had on the first morning they'd ridden together. He helped her from the car, and they walked around the house to the stable. The same two horses, Wellington and Caligula, were saddled and waiting. There was little preliminary conversation. They simply mounted and rode off in the direction they had taken previously.

But there was a difference. The tension, the hostility, the sense of challenge of that first morning were gone. The silence between them was not one of contention but almost of mutual trust.

Creighton, who was leading the way, looked back at her over his shoulder. "How does Wellington feel to you?"

"Different," Kaye answered. "More...cooperative."

"Perhaps he senses we're friends this time."

"Perhaps."

They rode in silence at a gentle trot, breaking into a canter whenever the terrain would allow it. They passed the spot where Kaye had fallen, but neither of them mentioned the incident. They came to an open field, and Creighton turned back to her again. "Want to have a run?"

"Yes," she called to him.

Creighton put Caligula into a gallop, and Wellington followed suit. He was a much faster horse than Caligula, and soon Kaye was riding abreast of Creighton, then ahead of him. When they came to the other side of the field, Kaye reined Wellington in and slowed him immediately to a walk. When Creighton caught up, Kaye said, "He's a wonderful horse."

"Yes, he is, and he knows when he has someone who can handle him. I think we're all four in better spirits than the last time."

Creighton led the way onto a path that entered the

woods on the far side of the field. They came to a wide glade, and Creighton brought Caligula to a halt.

"This is a lovely spot," he said. "Shall we dismount for a while?"

"All right."

They dismounted and tied the horses to a tree. Kaye sat on a low mound of earth and leaned against the trunk of another tree. Creighton sat beside her.

"Kaye, Adrian came to me this morning, complaining that you were avoiding him."

"Yes, I have been."

"I'm sure it seems to you that I do nothing but meddle in your life, but I'm worried."

"About what?"

"Adrian is convinced I've told you something derogatory about him."

"You have."

"I've told you only that he's a man of little character and that you should beware of him."

"And that he's your brother."

"I didn't know that was derogatory."

"It isn't, but it certainly had the effect you wanted it to have. It's curious, though. I don't quite understand why I should consider it devious of Adrian not to have told me that without considering it devious of you, as well, not to have told me."

"But I did tell you."

"Rather late along the way."

"Nonetheless I told you. Adrian never would have."

"Creighton, I don't understand any of this. Obviously I'm not supposed to. Can't you just tell me what Adrian has done to make you so wary of him?"

"If I could tell you that, it would solve the whole problem."

"Why can't you? I'm afraid I don't see any point in

our having conversations like this one if you're to know what they're about and I'm not.''

"This discussion has a purpose."

"Then I wish you'd just tell me what it is."

"I know this is hard to understand, but I must ask a favor of you. I want you either to tell Adrian flatly you don't want to see him again, for whatever believable reason you care to give him, or...."

"Or what?"

"Or go on seeing him from time to time."

Kaye was aghast. She could not believe Creighton had said it.

"Go on...seeing...him?"

"Yes."

"You can't be serious."

"I'm afraid I am."

"For weeks you've been telling me to stay away from him for my own good. Now, when I've decided to do just that, you want me to go on seeing him. I've had enough of this...."

She started to get up, but Creighton took her arm and pulled her back beside him.

"Listen to me, Kaye. Adrian is not just going to go away. For the time being he *can't* go away."

"Not *more* mystery."

"If you can convince him you simply don't want to see him for your own reasons, he'll let you alone without doing any damage to me. But if he continues to suspect you're not seeing him because of something I've told him, he will eventually attack me...with disastrous results."

"And in the meantime I'm supposed to do whatever you ask to protect you from him?"

"It isn't like that."

"Isn't it? Ever since the first day I met you, Aunt

Alice and everyone else who know you have spoken to me of your strength, your integrity, your nobility. And now, in spite of all that's gone on between us, you come to me and ask me to go on seeing your apparently contemptible brother, to keep him from attacking you. Is that strong? Is that honest? Is that noble?"

He turned toward her and took her by the shoulders. "Damn it, Kaye, do you think I like being reduced to helplessness? Do you think I like squirming and begging and crawling at Adrian's every command? Do you think I enjoy being robbed of my manhood and my power and my honor?"

"Then why do you stand for it?"

"Are you blind? Can't you see Adrian has a hold over me I can't break? Can't you see I—I can't say any more."

Again Kaye started to get up, and again Creighton pulled her down. This time she did not fall back against the tree; she fell back onto the slight slope of grassy earth behind her. She saw Creighton looking at her, his dark topaz eyes filled with pain and longing. Then he rolled over on top of her, pinning her arms to the ground above her head. He pressed his mouth against hers so hard she could feel his teeth against her lips. She struggled as he pushed against her, kissing her with an insatiable hunger. At last her body went limp and she gave way to him. He released her arms and they went around him, pulling him closer to her. She was conscious of everything around her as Creighton continued to cover her mouth with his. She felt the warm moist air like a great sea enveloping them both. She heard the quiet steady drone of insects and the occasional snort of one of the horses. But all she felt was Creighton, his warm body heavy upon her, the muscles of his thighs against hers, his chest crushing against her breast.

Her lips were against his ear now, and she said, "Oh, Creighton! Creighton, I want you so much! But it can't be like this, with no certainty between us. I couldn't bear for it to be like this!"

He took her chin in his hand and pulled her face beneath his. He kissed her again, and his mouth was warm and soft as an opening flower. Then he rolled over on his back and lay beside her.

"I'll do what you ask," Kaye said. "Adrian has told me he loves me. I'll convince him that that is exactly what I don't want and that I can't see him that way. He'll believe me. I'll make him believe me."

"Do you believe he loves you?"

"I—I don't know."

"He's never loved anyone. He'd marry you in a minute, and two years later he'd leave you, and you'd find yourself penniless. That's Adrian's style. I know you don't think he could do that to you. You think you're too protected by trusts and attorneys and family. But he could. . .and he would. You shouldn't be involved in any of this, and you wouldn't be if it weren't for me."

"Don't think about me," Kaye said, "think about yourself. This can't go on for the rest of your life, can it? You couldn't bear it."

"No, it won't go on for the rest of my life. But I should have told you earlier. Would you like me to ask you to wait until it ends, until I'm free of him—without knowing why or what it is I fear, without knowing when it would end? And if you became part of me, you'd also become Adrian's victim, just as Victoria nearly did. There's no hope, no hope at all."

"There's always hope."

He made a sound like a laugh, but it was no more than a grunt.

"Not for me there isn't. We must go back now.

Adrian has gone to Kingston. God knows what new plan he'll have when he gets back.''

He got up and took Kaye's hands and pulled her to her feet, and he put his arms around her and kissed her. His kiss was unique. No lips had ever felt to her like his; no mouth had ever been so dear, so wanted. Yet every time she felt that mouth on hers, it seemed to be in a kiss of farewell. She wondered if it would ever be different.

He helped her to mount, then he climbed up on Caligula, and they started back toward Penrose.

They left the horses with a groom at the stable and made their way to the front of the house. The Land Rover was parked in the driveway. They walked over to it, and Creighton helped her in, then got behind the wheel. He hesitated for a moment, looking at the house. Without facing her, he said, "Some day I want to show you Penrose. I can't bring myself to do it just now. Do you understand?''

"Yes.''

He turned to her and smiled sadly, then he started the engine, and they drove off.

When they reached Traymore, Aunt Alice was sitting on the veranda, having tea. Creighton escorted Kaye up the stairs.

"Hello, Alice,'' he said.

"Creighton, I'm delighted to see you. Won't you stay and have tea with us?''

"I'll be happy to stay for a few minutes. It's always refreshing and strengthening to be with you.''

They sat down at the table, and Aunt Alice inquired, "Did you have a pleasant ride?''

"It was lovely, auntie, and I rode Wellington with complete success.''

"Good for you! You may not believe it—even Creighton wouldn't remember—but there was a day when I could have ridden Wellington.''

"I don't doubt it for a minute," Creighton answered swiftly. "And Kaye is her aunt's niece. She handled Wellington splendidly."

"Ah, me. Would you believe that Smitty and I used to ride, cantering up and down these treacherous hills?"

"Did you really?" Kaye asked.

"Oh, yes. Then the passage of time forced us to give that up. I took up tennis and Smitty, golf. Now it's croquet, and even that's becoming strenuous. Creighton, we haven't had a good Sunday afternoon croquet match for ages. We must do that. The back lawn is still in perfect level shape."

"I'd love it."

"You wouldn't think a man of Creighton's strength and power would be good at croquet, but he's a marvel. We always connive to be on the same team against Smitty and Barney Fairweather. Barney plays croquet the way he does everything—irascibly."

"You must admit, Alice, he's quite good," Creighton commented.

"Oh, he is! We have fierce battles, Kaye. People have been known not to speak to one another for weeks over a croquet dispute. We can gossip and backbite and snipe at one another socially, and all is immediately forgiven. But croquet is altogether a serious matter."

As Kaye listened to Aunt Alice and Creighton talk, she saw a world that seemed not to exist any longer. It had been tranquil and filled with innocent joy and leisure. Now she saw only strife and discontent, strife and discontent in which she felt she had a hand.

"Well, thank you for the tea, Alice," Creighton said, getting up. "I've got to start for home."

"You're welcome. I wish you'd come by more often."

"Goodbye, Alice."

"Goodbye, Creighton."

"I'll see you to the car," Kaye said.

They walked to the Rover together, talking quietly. "I'll keep my promise, Creighton," Kaye said. "I'll see to it that Adrian is out of my life with no trouble."

"Adrian is always trouble," Creighton said.

She didn't want to talk about Adrian. "Thank you for the ride. I hope we can do it again."

"Perhaps. I'll have some time to think in the next day or two. Maybe I.... Goodbye, Kaye."

She went back to the veranda and sat with Aunt Alice.

"You don't seem a bit discomposed," Alice said. "A little sad, perhaps, but in control."

"I don't feel in control, auntie. Anything but."

"Is it something you can talk about?"

"No, I'm afraid not. There's nothing I'd like more than your advice, but it's a matter of necessary secrecy for the moment. Please don't worry. I'm all right. If you must worry, worry about Creighton. I want so much to help him, and I can't. At least there's no more rancor between us. We've become very close friends."

"No more than that?"

Kaye remained silent.

"I have a vague premonition that disturbs me."

"I'm sorry, Aunt Alice. I didn't mean to—"

"It has very little to do with you and everything to do with Creighton. I've felt it for a long time. Whenever things seem to be better, they inevitably get worse. Do you know what's troubling him? I'm not asking you to tell me; I'm asking if you know."

"No, not exactly, and I'd betray his trust if I told anyone what little I do know."

"I wouldn't have you do that for anything in the world."

"I won't. Have faith in me."

"I've always had faith in you. Well, since we can't

talk about Creighton's problems, let's talk about Amanda's. Today I received my invitation to Lady Landsbury's dinner party. Apparently everybody is going to be there."

"Poor Danny."

"Yes, it will be a formidable group. At least he'll be facing it under auspicious circumstances. My original plan was to go to Smitty before the dinner, but upon further thought I feel the thing to do is catch her at her own game."

"What do you mean?"

"No one in Montego is a hero until Smitty says so. She'll make a great show of giving her stamp of approval to the brave young American boy. She'll behave as if his having saved the child's life is incidental to gaining her seal of approbation. Once she has made a public flurry of doing that, we can present the boy as her granddaughter's fiancé. Oh, she'll be in a quandary. Smitty would rather be publicly flogged than embarrassed. Of course, she'd rather be embarrassed than have her granddaughter marry a middle-class American boy. But she is going to be caught. We'll see what we can make of her predicament."

"Auntie, you're wonderful."

"I didn't make the plan. I'm just taking advantage of circumstances. But you see, my dear, Smitty will be much easier to handle once she's committed herself to championing Danny's strong character and general worth—if she's to be handled at all, that is. Oh, I can hear her saying it. 'Of course I want my granddaughter to marry a man of strong character, a well-placed *Englishman* of strong character.' She *can* get out of it. Well, we'll just have to wait and see. I'd consider it great fun if Amanda's happiness weren't at stake."

On Kaye's and Amanda's advice, Danny did not wear

his blazer and shirt and tie to the Landsburys' dinner party. Even at a dinner party honoring a hero the usual attire of sport shirt and slacks was in order. Danny wore a dark green shirt and gray cotton slacks with white loafers. He was perfectly dressed for the occasion.

He was also very nervous. He had received a communication from Lady Landsbury, which had arrived with his formal invitation, requesting him to come half an hour earlier to meet her privately. Again he borrowed the red Triumph, and now he was parking it in the driveway of Lady Landsbury's great white mansion.

A young Jamaican man opened the car door and smiled at him. He asked him to leave the keys in the car. As Danny approached the front door of the house, the Triumph was driven away, presumably to be parked in a guest parking space. Danny rang the bell, and a butler answered the door immediately.

The butler smiled respectfully and asked, "Mr. Riordan?"

"Yes, good evening."

"Good evening, sir. Lady Landsbury is in the library."

Danny followed the man through a large reception hall to double doors. The butler knocked and opened the doors. He stepped in and slightly to the side to allow Danny to enter.

"Mr. Riordan, Lady Landsbury."

Lady Landsbury was sitting on a flowered chintz settee in the moderate-sized book-lined room. She wore a floor-length mauve gown with a shoulder-to-shoulder ruffle at the neckline. She was a tall woman in her late sixties with a very good figure. She had white marcelled hair and a pince-nez hanging from a black ribbon around her neck. She was formidably elegant, but there was a gentle expression on her handsome face. Several other people were in the room, including Jennifer Brent, the girl whose life Danny had saved. Lady Landsbury stood up as Danny approached her.

"Mr. Riordan," she said, extending her hand. "I'm so happy you could come."

"It was gracious of you to ask me," Danny replied.

"I'd like you to meet my daughter, Cynthia Brent, and her husband, Phillip. They're Jennifer's parents."

"How do you do?" Danny replied.

Mrs. Brent took Danny's hand in both hers and said, "How can we ever thank you, Mr. Riordan? You must know what it means to us. Jennifer is our only child. She's our life."

"You don't owe me any thanks, Mrs. Brent. It was a very rewarding experience for me."

Mr. Brent extended his hand. "Good show, old chap. We're forever in your debt."

"You know Jennifer, of course," Lady Landsbury said.

Jennifer came to him rather shyly and murmured, "Hello, Mr. Riordan."

Danny stooped to her. "If I can call you Jennifer, you can call me Danny, all right?"

"Yes." She smiled and added, "Danny."

"We're going to be more careful at the beach from now on, aren't we?"

"Oh, yes!" Jennifer agreed.

The others thought it was a charming display of adult manners toward a child. In truth, Jennifer was the only person in the room with whom Danny felt even remotely comfortable, and he was even a little nervous with her.

"This is my sister, Lady Armbruster."

A woman remarkably similar to Lady Landsbury smiled at him from her armchair and said, "I'm delighted to meet you, Mr. Riordan."

"And my niece, Miss Sarah Armbruster."

Sarah was a pretty girl a bit older than Amanda. She extended her hand and smiled. "We're all terribly grateful, Mr. Riordan. I'm very pleased to meet you."

"Thank you," Danny replied.

"Do have a chair here by me," Lady Landsbury said. "Would you like something to drink?"

"Yes, thank you. A gin and tonic."

"Phillip, would you? Mr. Riordan, I'm sure you're modest enough to feel you were simply doing your job when you brought Jennifer in from the sea, and I'm sure that an endless display of our gratitude would only embarrass you, but you must understand what it means to us. I thought it only fitting you should meet the family and let us have this brief time together to express our deep, deep thanks to you."

"Lady Landsbury, I can tell you only that the reward in saving a life is in the act itself. Not that I'm a veteran. I've never rescued anyone before this. I'm grateful that I was there and that I saw Jennifer in time to do something about it."

"You're even more modest than you ought to be," Lady Landsbury commented.

"Here's your drink, old man," Mr. Brent put in.

"Tell us something about yourself, Mr. Riordan," his hostess began. "I know little more than you're an American college student."

"There's not a great deal more to know. My family lives in Cleveland, Ohio—my father and mother and a younger sister and brother."

"Would you be kind enough to give me their address before the evening ends? I must write to them and tell them how proud they should be of you. I'm sure they already have reason to be, but this achievement mustn't go unnoticed. Is this your first time in Montego?"

"No, I was here last year, too. I love it here."

The easy conversation went on for half an hour. Danny had a second drink. Lady Landsbury and her family made every effort to make him comfortable, and they succeeded. The formality about them was an accumulation of generations of courtly manners, beneath which were a great warmth and civility. As the conversation went on, there were pleasant little jokes, and Danny became more a participant than a target of the gathering.

At 7:33 the double doors of the library opened, and the butler announced Lady Armstrong and Miss Belliston. Aunt Alice had decided there was a faint chance Danny would need moral support and had taken advantage of her long-standing friendship with Lady Landsbury to intrude on the private meeting.

"Agatha, how good to see you," Aunt Alice began. "I thought I'd come a bit early to chat with you before the horde arrives."

"Alice, you're looking wonderful," Lady Landsbury remarked.

"May I present my niece, Miss Kaye Belliston. She's visiting from New York. Hello, Danny."

Lady Landsbury's surprise was so great that before she even acknowledged Kaye she said, "You know Mr. Riordan?"

"Oh, of course," Alice answered blithely. "My niece met him at Doctor's Cave and was so charmed by him that she asked him to dinner at Traymore." It was a very strategic move, aimed not at Lady Landsbury but at Smitty. Alice wanted to give the impression that Danny was already—to some degree, at least—a part of Montego society. There was some risk, of course, in that Smitty might find out Danny had been to dinner at Traymore even before she herself knew of his existence.

It would be clear evidence of a conspiracy, but that evidence would come out eventually anyway.

Lady Landsbury was able then to turn her attention to Kaye. "How delightful to meet you, Miss Belliston." She introduced her to the others.

It was time for Lady Landsbury to begin receiving the rest of her guests. She led everyone into the reception hall and stationed herself on the side of the room opposite the double doors. Danny stood beside her, and there he stayed as the guests came in and paid their respects to the hostess. Danny was carefully and rather proudly introduced to everyone. They all already knew who he was and why he was there. There were many comments: "You must be very proud, young man." "We're very fortunate to have such brave and skilled young men at Doctor's Cave." "We're all very grateful to you, Mr. Riordan." "Ah, this is the man of the hour, is it?"

He met all the people he'd heard Amanda and Kaye speak of: the Marlowes, the Zimmermans, the Duckworths, Ellis Craig, Kevin Wright, Barney Fairweather, all of them—and finally, because she was, as usual, last of all to arrive, Smitty.

He knew who she was the instant he saw her coming through the doorway, her flowered crepe gown flowing, her monocle in place. She strode across the room directly toward him. She was peering at him through her monocle even as she greeted the hostess.

"Good evening, Agatha. This is our hero, is it?"

"Lady Smith-Croydon, may I present Mr. Daniel Riordan."

Danny's heart was pounding. Lady Smith-Croydon ought to have been no different from any of the others, with whom he had already acquitted himself well, but not only was she the grande dame of Montego, she was also his grandmother-in-law to be, the woman upon whom his future with Amanda depended.

"I'm proud to meet you, Mr. Riordan," Smitty said.

"How do you do, Lady Smith-Croydon?"

"Dear boy, has Lady Agatha kept you standing here all evening? Agatha, the poor young man must be exhausted from saving lives all day. You must let me take him away and sit him down next to me while I get to know him."

"Of course, Smitty," Lady Landsbury said.

Before poor Danny could say a word, Smitty took his arm and led him across the room. She found an empty settee and almost pushed him into it, then she sat down beside him. One by one her entourage came by, and Smitty introduced them. Suddenly Amanda was standing before him.

Before Smitty could introduce her, Amanda said, "Hello."

"Hello, Miss Leyton," Danny replied.

"You know each other?" Smitty asked with undisguised astonishment.

"I've seen Mr. Riordan at Doctor's Cave."

"Oh, of course."

"Everyone is very proud of you, Mr. Riordan," Amanda remarked.

"Thank you. I don't really deserve it."

"Of course you do!" Smitty countered robustly. "I wonder how many of our own Montego men would have the courage and strength to swim out to sea and save a young girl. Well, the courage, I suppose. But the strength and the skill? I doubt it. I'm going to look into this matter and see if there isn't some official commendation we can give you. If there isn't, we'll establish one. We cannot let such valor go unrewarded." Smitty was falling into the trap beautifully. "Creighton! Creighton, come here."

Danny's heart sank. All Creighton had to do was mention he had met Danny in Kingston with Amanda and Kaye, and Danny's hopes would be dashed. And why wouldn't he?

"Creighton, this is the young man who saved Agatha's granddaughter from drowning. Daniel—or do you prefer Danny?"

"Danny."

"This is Danny Riordan. Creighton Jarvis."

"How do you do? You're deservedly something of a hero, Mr. Riordan."

"Thank you. Thank you very much, Mr. Jarvis." Creighton knew what he was being thanked for, and Danny knew he knew it.

"Now you must tell me about yourself, Mr. Riordan. Oh, I must call you Danny, and I insist you call me Smitty. Everyone does. Where in the United States do you live?"

"In Cleveland, Ohio."

"How very American. You have family?"

"My mother and father and a younger brother and sister."

"How proud of you they must be! You've cabled them, of course."

"Well, no. It didn't seem to me to be—"

"What? You're the toast of Montego, and your family doesn't even know it? We must cable them immediately. Or perhaps that would alarm them."

"I'm afraid it would."

"Well, then, tomorrow I will compose a letter, and we'll have everyone in Montego sign it. Your relatives must be made fully aware of your valor."

Most of the rest of the evening was like that. Smitty had taken Danny under her wing, and it was a position from which one did not easily escape. By the time dinner was served, Smitty knew almost as much about him as Amanda did. At dinner, Danny was seated on Lady

Landsbury's right, and Smitty was seated on his right. It wasn't until after the meal that she finally released him. By that time she had reintroduced him to all the guests, virtually claiming him for her own.

Aunt Alice seemed greatly amused at first, but she soon saw that things were going too far. Smitty was making a much greater fuss than even she had expected. Things might get unpleasant when the truth came out.

Kaye came to her after dinner and said, "Well, the plan certainly worked."

"Far too well, I'm afraid."

"What do you mean?"

"There's going to be the devil to pay when Smitty discovers she's been tricked."

"But, Aunt Alice, no one's tricked her. No one arranged Jennifer Brent's near drowning, and no one forced Smitty to make such a hero of Danny."

"And no one told her before she did about the connection between Danny and Amanda. That will not sit well with her. I am deeply concerned."

"It's done now."

"Yes, I know."

"Is this a conference, or may I join you?" It was Creighton.

"Oh, Creighton, do stay and talk to Kaye," Alice said with some urgency. "I'd better go and speak with Smitty or she'll think I'm avoiding her." She started across the room toward her friend.

"How are you, Kaye?" Creighton asked quietly when Alice had gone.

"I'm all right, Creighton. How are you?"

"Lonely. Would you like a walk in the garden?"

"All right."

Lady Landsbury's garden was large and lovely and reminiscent of the other gardens Kaye and Creighton had been in together. As they walked along one of the winding brick paths, Kaye said, "I take it that since Adrian isn't at this party, he's still in Kingston."

"As far as I know. I haven't heard from him, but I don't think he planned to stay this long."

"You've never told me why he went in the first place."

"No, and I don't intend to."

"Out of loyalty?"

"I owe Adrian no loyalty, but I see no reason to defame him, either."

"You're a very kind man."

"No, but I live by a code."

They were quiet for a while. "Have you done your thinking?"

"Oh, yes. Not to much avail, I'm afraid. Kaye, what are you going to do when you leave Montego? I no longer feel I can ask you to stay."

"I realize that," she noted sadly. "I also realize that I have no life to return to."

"Start a new one."

"I should be starting a new life, but I keep telling myself I'm not ready."

"No one knows that better than I."

"I suppose I'm not even trying. You almost gave me a reason to leave once."

"*I* did?"

"Yes. The night you drove me home from Smitty's dinner party and we walked in Aunt Alice's garden."

"A night I prefer to forget. I've never forgiven myself for some of the things I've done."

"I, too, was to blame, but I was so upset that the next morning I started packing with every intention of getting a plane that very day."

"What stopped you?"

"Aunt Alice. You couldn't possibly know it, but she saw us in the garden that night. She didn't see all of it. She saw us in each other's arms, and she saw you walk away. She also saw me packing and convinced me I was simply running away."

"Thank God for Alice."

"Would it have mattered to you? Then?"

"Yes, a great deal. Perhaps I didn't realize at that time how much it would have mattered, but I knew it would have. Now I know it would have...."

"Would have what, Creighton?"

"It would have left a permanent scar on my life."

"I don't understand."

"You're the only woman I've met since Victoria died, who's made me feel alive again, the only woman I've wanted. If I'd driven you away, I would never have forgiven myself. My life would have been over, and I would never have known what might have been." He looked down at her, and even in the moonlight he could see she was smiling.

"That's what Aunt Alice told me."

"What?"

"That if I stayed, at least I'd be dealing with what I felt for you, but if I left then, I'd never know what might have been between us."

"My dear wise friend, Alice."

"Will we ever find out, Creighton?"

"I don't know." He stopped walking and took her in his arms. He kissed her, and the memory of his mouth became a reality again. It was as if it held her to him, welded them together in tenderness and an immediate awakening of passion. Then he put his face next to hers and said quietly, "Will you believe me if I tell you I'm going to do everything I can to clear the way for us to discover what there might be for us?"

"Yes, I believe you."

"Will you trust me and wait for me until I'm free to come to you if I promise to try not to make it too long a wait?"

"I'll wait for as long as I have to."

He kissed her again, and the hint of his passionate loving was already in the kiss. They both knew it was foolish not to stop it then, but they went on, drawing each other even closer, their mouths locked together, the contours of their bodies molded into a single entity. Their unfulfilled—and, at the moment, unfulfillable—desire became unbearable. Creighton took her by the shoulders and held her before him. She felt like a doll in the strength of his grasp.

"I won't fail you, Kaye. I swear it."

"I know."

They walked through the garden arm in arm and went back into the house.

The guests had begun to leave, none of them failing to seek out Danny, as well as their hostess, to say goodnight. Kaye was happy Aunt Alice was ready to leave. She felt drained by her fruitless desire for Creighton's continued nearness, and to stay would have been painful for her. She and Alice said their good-nights.

"Danny, the party was a great success, and so were you," Aunt Alice remarked. "You deserve the adulation."

"Thank you, Lady Alice. It was easier for me because you were here."

"Good night, Danny," Kaye said. "You've got to stay on till the bitter end, you know."

"That much I figured out. I'm glad you were here."

"Smitty practically devoured you. Did you like her?"

"You know, you may not believe it, but I liked her a lot!"

Kaye and Aunt Alice laughed. Kaye hugged Danny furtively, and they were off.

Smitty stayed true to form and was the last to leave. She swept up to Danny and said, "Well, young man, you've had a well-deserved tribute. I will see to that letter in the morning. I trust you will soon honor me with your presence at a dinner of mine. You'll hear from me. Good night."

"Good night, Lady Smith-Croydon."

Amanda hung back at the end of Smitty's retinue so that she could have at least a few private words with Danny, which she had not been able to manage during the evening.

"Danny, I was so proud of you," she said, taking his hand.

"Were you, Mandy?"

"Oh, yes!"

"I confess I was a little proud of myself. I was afraid I'd behave like a dunce, but I don't think I did."

"You were wonderful. I've got to leave now. I'll try to see you tomorrow." Then she whispered, "I love you."

He smiled at her and watched her leave. He turned and saw that Lady Landsbury was saying good-night to the last of her guests. They went out, and he and she were alone in the drawing room.

"Good night, Danny Riordan. I hope your life is always enriched by the knowledge that someone lives who wouldn't, had it not been for you."

"Thank you. I think it will be, Lady Landsbury. And thank you for an exceptional evening. Good night."

# CHAPTER TEN

SEVERAL DAYS WENT BY quite normally for Kaye—except that she neither saw nor heard from Creighton. There were the usual dinner parties, but Creighton was at none of them. She inquired discreetly of her various friends, but none of them had seen or talked to Creighton, either, except to be told by him or his butler that he was not available for a dinner party. She had not expected such a withdrawal, and she didn't know how to interpret it.

Creighton had shut himself away to turn all his strength and all his intelligence upon solving the problem that had plagued him for two decades. It was no use. No matter how he approached it, the end was always the same: a stone wall. There were no negotiable elements in his dilemma, nothing with which to bargain. Nothing was variable; nothing changed. He was like a man trapped and looking for a door in a doorless room. There was no way out except to blow up the room and himself with it. But he would not be the only one destroyed in the explosion.

He was in his study around midnight one night, pacing and struggling as he had done every night since the last time he had seen Kaye, when he heard an automobile in the driveway. He waited for a few minutes, thinking that Christian would come up to the study to announce the unexpected visitor. When nothing happened, he started down the great curved staircase. From the top of the

stairs he saw Adrian entering through the front door.
Adrian did not look up, did not see him watching. He
simply dropped his suitcase in the hall and went into the
drawing room. Creighton came down the stairs and followed him.

When he walked into the room, Adrian was pouring
himself a large whiskey from a crystal decanter. He
turned at the sound of Creighton's entry, and Creighton
knew immediately he was drunk.

"My dear Creighton," he said in his most unctuous
way. "You've come to welcome me home. How touching."

"You stayed rather longer than you'd expected."

"Ah, yes. It was a very good trip—quite diverting.
I'm afraid I spent rather a lot of money. But that's not
important. When I need financial assistance, my dear
brother always comes to the rescue."

"I want to talk to you."

"Wonderful! I'm in the mood for a good chat." He
threw himself onto a sofa in a slouch.

Creighton remained standing. "I want to make a bargain with you."

"A bargain? How interesting. And what, pray tell,
have you to bargain with?"

"The thing you want most in the world—money."

"How can you think me that crass?"

"Adrian, let's dispense with the sarcasm. This is
deadly serious."

"I can see that, but you can hardly expect me to
change in five minutes the charming personality I have
so carefully cultivated through the years. I'm afraid you
must deal with me as I am."

"I want you to leave Montego."

"Don't be silly, Creighton. I'm very happy here. Besides, I can't leave. I am, as they say in American films, a wanted man."

"What is it this time?"

"Does it matter?"

"Yes, if it can be fixed."

"You, Creighton? Offering to extricate a guilty criminal from his unhappy predicament? How unlike you."

"Tell me what you've done."

"I'd rather not."

"You must, if there's to be any bargain."

"I don't remember saying I wanted a bargain. Things are very much to my liking as they are. I don't think you can make an offer attractive enough to persuade me to change them."

"I think I can," Creighton replied.

"Then do."

"After you've told me what trouble you're in."

"You are tiresome. All right. There is a lady in Paris, a lady of uncertain age and questionable beauty. But she is extraordinarily rich. I'm afraid she'll have to remain nameless for the moment. In any event, she's a bit dotty, and she became inordinately fond of a certain Sir Roger Buckminster. Sir Roger is a man of infinite talent but scant morals, and he is not always what he seems. In this case, he appeared to be the scion of a very old, respectable, wealthy English family, a family chosen with great care by Sir Roger. The family does indeed exist. It is a family of octogenarians. They are so socially remote that it's virtually impossible to find anyone who has a personal acquaintance with them. Everyone knows *of* them, but no one actually knows them. One could say, for instance, that they have a huge country estate in Scotland—which they have—and no one would dispute it because no one knows enough about them to dispute it. On the other hand, one could say they have a huge country estate in Kent—which they haven't—and no one knows enough about them to dispute that, either. You do see the advantage of having studied such a family through every available public record, don't you, dear Creighton?''

"Yes. Get on with it." Creighton had already lost patience with this sordid recital, but he knew it was the only way Adrian would tell the tale, and he was determined to hear him out.

"Well, you must also see it would be entirely possible for one to say that he is the issue of a troublesome marriage between one of the three surviving Buckminster males and a Scottish girl of little reputation and that the marriage was quietly and secretly dissolved but its issue taken into the family bosom. That issue, of course, was Sir Roger, and no one knows the Buckminsters well enough to dispute it. Are you following?''

"Yes."

"Well, Sir Roger presented himself with just those credentials. The lady was immediately most sympathetic, because, of course, Sir Roger was most winningly pathetic. He was in dire need. The lady was in need, too—though it was a need of a different sort, a need that Sir Roger was eminently equipped to fulfill.''

"You are disgusting."

"Oh, no, Creighton. It was like every civilized business transaction. I had something to sell that the lady wanted to buy. Strictly on the up-and-up.''

"You've never done anything honest in your life."

"Perhaps, but at least what I've told you thus far is honest. Unfortunately, as time went on, I acquired some financial obligations that were extracurricular as far as the relationship was concerned. Even you, Creighton, wouldn't expect me to spend all my time with a...let's say 'mature' lady. And I do like to gamble. It was at about that time that the lady's family became aware of my existence. They did not approve of me. In spite of all their wealth and power I had the upper hand, as I had planned to have all along. They were willing to spend a goodly sum to save their aging relative from social disgrace.''

"If they paid you well, why are you here?''

"Poor Creighton, you will never understand. I have already spent it. In any event, I had to flee from France. They were planning to bring a legal—I think 'criminal' is the right word—action against me. Or against Sir Roger.''

"And do they know that Sir Roger Buckminster is Adrian Jarvis?''

"I didn't stay long enough to find out. I suppose they do by now.''

"That doesn't mean you can't leave Montego.''

"No, but I am safe here. Wherever I go, there is risk, and there are the aliases, the secrecy, the inconvenience. No, Creighton, Montego is too comfortable for me to leave.''

"I'll give you enough money for the rest of your life.''

"And how much money is that, Creighton?''

"You tell me.''

"You don't have that much money.''

"I have enough that you could go on living your profligate life without ever scrimping until the day you die.''

Adrian studied him for a long moment. He got up and poured himself another drink, then sat down again, erect and attentive now.

"There is something missing from this bargain. My leaving Montego isn't enough to warrant so extravagant an offer. I think you haven't told me the full terms under which I must leave.''

"May I take that to mean you're considering the offer?"

"I consider every offer that is made me. What are the terms?"

"That you take the money and got out of my life—and out of Kaye Belliston's life—forever."

"And what am I to be paid for this permanent departure?"

"I told you to name the price."

Adrian looked up at him thoughtfully, then gazed down at his drink and asked, "Would it be worth everything, Creighton?"

After a moment Creighton replied, "Yes."

"Are you sure you understand? I mean *everything*: this house, this estate, all your cash, all your holdings and all the land and other investments in Australia."

Creighton did not even wince. "Yes, everything."

Adrian began to chuckle, then the chuckle turned into a full robust laugh. When it had subsided, he said, "Oh, Creighton, you're more of a fool than even I thought you were. What makes you believe I'd stay away from you even if I had all that?"

"There'd be no reason for you to come back. I'd have nothing left for you to take."

"In all these years you still haven't seen the truth, have you? Let me show you the whole picture from my point of view. Yes, it's time you knew. You see, I assumed you had figured it out for yourself. If I had thought for one minute you didn't know what I'd been doing, I would have told you long ago. Creighton, you're like a nice safe bank to me. You don't know what it's like to spend money. I can go through in a month what you live on in a year. Oh, I don't mean that you're parsimonious. Far from it. You simply don't have any big appetites. Do you have any idea how much

money you've 'given' me through the years? I'm sure
you have a record of it somewhere, but I know in my
head. It's almost a million dollars. If you'd given it to
me all at once, it would have been gone in a year, but
this way I can hit you for twenty-five or fifty thousand
and live just as I please until it's gone. Then I can come
back for another twenty-five or fifty thousand. Back to
my bank. Back to Creighton. You're as safe as having a
trust. But there's more to it than that. I don't do it just
for the money. I do it out of my deep everlasting hatred
of you. I do it to punish you, to torment you. And I
won't give that up, Creighton. I would punish you for
the rest of your life if I could, punish you for turning
father against me.''

"You did that yourself."

"Oh, no. Only later, when he already despised me,
did I do anything to turn him against me. But long before that, as long ago as I can remember, you were
everything he wanted in a son. You were serious and in-
dustrious and strong and oh so virtuous. You were
never frivolous. You never made mistakes.''

"I made many. You were so busy with your own you
never noticed them.''

"Clever, Creighton, but you can't change any of it.
Whatever I tried to do, you did better. Wherever I failed,
you succeeded, until I was nothing but a worthless fool in
his eyes. That's when I made the big mistake. I almost got
away with it. I would have if it hadn't been for you. One
more thing I have to punish you for. I realize that what
you've suggested giving me runs into tens of millions of
dollars, but I don't need tens of millions. I don't want
this bloody house or your bloody estate. I'd be happy
never to see Montego again, and I wouldn't give you a
cent for all of Australia. Aside from living well, I want

nothing more from life than the pure joy of torturing you."

"I should have known better than to try to deal honestly with you."

"Yes, you should have. It was stupid of you. And in addition to being stupid, you're very shortsighted. I know why you made the offer. With me out of the way there'd be nothing to prevent your marrying Kaye Belliston. But if you did that, there would be something for me to come back for: the Belliston fortune. I'd do that, Creighton. You know I would."

"Yes, I know. But you won't have the chance." He started out of the room.

"Creighton, you aren't going to marry Kaye Belliston under any circumstances. I won't let you. You're never going to have that happiness. Not ever. By the time I've lost my power over you, it will be too late."

Creighton left the drawing room without uttering another word.

TWO DAYS LATER Kaye received a telephone call at Traymore that she considered very unusual.

"Kaye?" a mellifluous voice said when she answered.

"Yes. Who's this?"

"It's George Montague, Kaye. I hope I'm not intruding."

"Not at all. It's nice to hear from you, George."

"If it's at all possible, I'd like to speak with you on a matter of some importance."

She was completely taken aback. "Why—why, of course, George. When would you like to meet?"

"At your convenience, of course, but the sooner, the better. I'm in Montego now; however, I'll be leaving for Kingston tonight."

"Can you come up to the house now?"

"Yes. I was hoping you'd suggest that, but I didn't want to seem demanding. I can be there within half an hour."

"That's perfect. I'll see you then."

She couldn't imagine why George Montague would want to talk with her. Beyond some pleasant conversation at dinner parties she'd never spoken to him. They were always very cordial to each other, and she was quite fond of him, but calling their relationship a friendship would have been an overestimation. It had to be something to do with Creighton, she decided. She determined to put it out of her mind until George arrived, but she couldn't stop thinking about it.

George got there exactly half an hour later. Kaye was sitting on the veranda, and she went to the top of the steps to greet him.

"George, this is something of a surprise—a very pleasant one, but a surprise nonetheless."

"I know. It's very gracious of you to see me, especially on such short notice."

"Come and sit down. Can I get you anything? A drink?"

"No, thank you, Kaye."

They sat in white wicker chairs opposite each other. George seemed reluctant, or perhaps uncertain, as to how to begin.

"Kaye, I hope you won't think I'm overstepping the bounds of propriety, but I don't know what else to do."

"What is it, George? You sound worried."

"I am worried. I'm worried about Creighton."

"He's all right, isn't he?"

"Oh, he's not ill or anything like that, but something's very wrong, and I don't know what to do about it. I don't know if there's anything I can do, but I must try. Being a friend of Creighton's doesn't give one much experience at being helpful. I've never known him to need assistance with anything."

"I'm sure that's true."

"I suspect he's not very good at accepting aid even when he needs it."

"I'm absolutely sure that's true. He's a very proud man."

"Perhaps too proud sometimes."

"George, please tell me what's wrong."

"Did you know that Creighton is leaving the island?"

"Aunt Alice told me some time ago he was considering it."

"He's no longer merely considering it. He's found a buyer for the house and has already begun packing some of the few things he's taking with him—books, papers, that sort of thing."

"You mean it's that definite?"

"According to Creighton, it's final."

Kaye looked puzzled. "I don't understand. I suppose if he's been considering it for as long as he has, it isn't really sudden. But it seems so—so unexpected."

"It is unexpected and calamitous. Creighton loves Jamaica—Montego particularly. No one but me knows how much he's done for the island and its people. . . my people. From the time I was a child, I've wanted to be part of the Jamaican government. It seemed an impossible dream then. Oh, Creighton wasn't here when I started my unspectacular climb, but later he was always available when I needed him. And I've needed him often. He's used his money and his influence again and again, not merely to help me, a friend, but to help the people of the island. This has been Creighton's home for more than ten years. He pays no attention to the 'season.' He's here year round, except for an occasional necessary trip. Creighton, more than any other non-native I know, with the possible exception of Lady Alice, *lives* here. His life is here.''

"Do you know why he's leaving?"

"I'm not sure. I thought you might.''

"No.''

"Kaye, you must have realized from my tone on the telephone that I was hesitant about coming here.''

"I sensed it.''

"I'm hesitant to presume upon my friendship with Creighton, which I assure you is a deep one, and I'm hesitant to interfere in your private affairs. After all, we barely know each other. But we both know Creighton... and care for him. He's told me very little, but I know he loves you.''

Kaye was startled and somehow embarrassed. "How could you know that?"

"I know Creighton. I knew him when he was married to Victoria. I've known him in his grief. I know when he's angry or delighted or enthusiastic, even though he shows little emotion. I've never seen him the way he's been these past weeks. He's more open with me than with anyone else, yet I've been unable to figure out what is going on in his head and his heart. Kaye, if I'm going to help him—if we are going to help him—we must be close and honest with each other. You do know that he loves you?''

"Yes.''

"Forgive me, Kaye. Do you love him?"

"Yes, very much.''

"Then it may be that you're the only one who can save him.''

"Save him from what?"

"I don't know. From leaving the island, if nothing else. But he wouldn't leave the island if something weren't driving him—something dark and mysterious and, I think, dangerous. Have you any idea what it could be?"

"I know who it is, but not why."

"Adrian?"

"Yes."

"What do you know about him?"

"Nothing...nothing I can tell you. I'm sure it wouldn't help anyway, but as a matter of honor I cannot tell you."

"What frightens me, Kaye, is that it must be something quite terrible if Creighton himself can't handle it, if it is so strong that he will allow it to drive him away from his home."

"Perhaps he has no choice."

"There must be a choice. I cannot stand by and see my dear friend uprooted. I cannot stand by and see Jamaica deprived of so valuable an ally. Yet I feel hopeless—so hopeless that I am driven to extremes. You must believe that, because I am going to ask you to do something I have no right to ask. I want you to go to him. If there is anything that can keep him here, it is your love."

Again Kaye was startled and confused. George had no way of knowing the depth or extent of Creighton's love—of hers, either. She didn't know that herself. How could he be so sure that that love might make a difference?

"George, you must believe me when I tell you there's nothing I wouldn't do for Creighton, but my going to him won't help."

"It can't do any harm. Will you try?" Kaye got up and walked to the edge of the veranda. She stood looking out over the garden. "If it changes nothing, you will at least know that you tried."

She turned and faced him. "All right. I'll go to him."

"Thank you, Kaye. It gives me hope. He's in town for the day, attending to business connected with his leaving, but he will be at home tonight. Can you go to him then?"

"Yes. What about Adrian?"

"Adrian will be traveling to Kingston this afternoon. I have friends who will require his presence there. They are not friends I like to call upon, but this time they will serve."

George got up, and Kaye crossed the veranda to him. "I hope you will forgive my intrusion. It was brazen of me to come to you, but my love for Creighton is very deep."

"I know that. I promise you I'll do everything I can."

"I know you will. Let us both pray it will help, and my everlasting thanks to you."

Kaye was deeply troubled when George left—troubled by many things. She had her lunch but ate hardly anything, then she sat on the veranda and let all the disturbing thoughts run free in her mind. Her greatest concern was that Creighton was leaving. Everything George had said was true. Whatever was driving him away from his home had to be terrible. She did not know how or why, but in her heart she was certain it had something to do with her. She couldn't tell George any of that, but she knew now she would have gone to Creighton even if George hadn't asked her to. But why hadn't Creighton told *her* he was leaving? Perhaps it was because he knew she'd try to stop him. But surely he wouldn't have left without seeing her. It was all a muddle to her. She wanted desperately to see Creighton, yet she dreaded the coming night.

She walked in the garden for half an hour; it succeeded only in heightening the vividness of her thoughts and memories of Creighton. She went to her room and tried to read, but her mind would not stay focused on the book. She threw it aside and went back downstairs again. As she stepped out onto the veranda, the Rolls pulled into the driveway and Aunt Alice got out. She looked very young and stylish in the dress she had worn to go out to lunch, and once again Kaye realized how much she loved her.

"Hello, Aunt Alice," she said as her aunt mounted the steps. "How was lunch?"

"As exciting as a club meeting," Aunt Alice replied cheerily. "Why we go on doing it, I do not know. I suppose it's to prove we're not housebound old ladies. Maude Duckworth talked incessantly about her dogs. Vanessa Carruthers talked incessantly about her ancestry. Cornelia Bracefield talked incessantly about her dead husbands. The only thing Smitty and I did incessantly was listen—which for Smitty is at once an ordeal and a triumph. I want only to sit down and recover. You had some lunch, I trust."

"Yes, though I wasn't very hungry."

"Now that I'm comfortable, you may tell me what's wrong."

"There's no fooling you, is there?"

"Not at my age. What is it?"

"It's Creighton. He's definitely leaving. He's found a buyer for the house, and he's in the process of packing."

Aunt Alice's face darkened. "I was afraid it would happen. Did he telephone?"

"No, George Montague came by and told me."

"George Montague?"

"I know it seems strange, but he wanted me to know."

"Of course you should know, but he seems a strange courier."

"He asked me to go to Creighton."

"Why?"

"To try to dissuade him from leaving."

"I don't think that will be possible."

"Neither do I. I think I'm part of the reason he's leaving."

"Yes, that may well be. Are you going?"

"Yes, tonight. Do you disapprove, auntie?"

"No, I think you must go. I pray that somehow you'll be successful."

"I'll try, Aunt Alice."

"No one can ask more than that."

Kaye had a swim and a nap and a quiet dinner with Aunt Alice. She deliberately postponed her visit to Creighton until it was dark. She had decided against telephoning him beforehand. This was too important to consider mere manners, and she was sure he would forbid her to come if he knew of her visit in advance.

After dinner she said, "Aunt Alice, does the Morgan in the garage still run?"

"Like a Swiss clock. Helen's son tinkers with it constantly and somehow manages to keep it in running order. Do you want to take it?"

"Yes, I don't want the fuss of Henry and the Rolls. I know the roads well enough now to drive them, and I'm a very good driver—even on the left-hand side."

"I'm sure you are, my dear. When are you going?"

Kaye looked at her watch. It was almost ten o'clock. "Now, I suppose. I've been telling myself I've been putting off leaving for tactical reasons—which is nonsense. I've been putting it off because I dread it. I have no idea what I'm going to say or do. I may succeed in making Creighton angry, and I don't relish the thought of that."

"I don't think I've ever seen him angry."

"It's impressive, to say the least, especially if the anger is directed at you. I survived it before; I suppose I can survive it again."

"I'll ring for Henry and get you the key to the Morgan."

Fifteen minutes later she was on the road, driving the Morgan as if she had grown up with it. As she approached Penrose, she could see that the house was essentially dark, with only little islands of light here and there. She got out of the car and noticed a light go on in the downstairs hall. By the time she had started up the stairs to the house, she could see Creighton's tall broad figure silhouetted in the doorway. She could not make out his expression, and in a way she was glad.

"Kaye! What in God's name are you doing here?"

"I've come to see you, obviously."

"There are telephones."

"You wouldn't have let me come if I'd telephoned."

"No, I wouldn't have."

"Now that I'm here, may I come in?"

After a moment Creighton stepped aside, and Kaye went into the reception hall. "Why are you here?" he repeated.

She could see his face now; it was stony and unreadable. The dark topaz eyes were inscrutable.

"I have to talk to you."

"About what?"

"About your leaving Montego."

There was a pause. "I don't know how you know about it, and I guess I don't much care. . . except that I wanted to tell you myself. You do know that I would have."

"Yes, I know."

"Well, I am leaving, and now you know. I want you to get back into the car and go home."

"No, Creighton. I've come to talk to you, and I'm not going until I've done so."

"Do you want to make me put you out?"

"If that's what you must do, yes."

"Damn it, you know I can't."

"No, I don't know it. I was only hoping."

The expression in his eyes softened almost imperceptibly. She thought for a fleeting moment he was going to take her in his arms. But he didn't; he stood looking at her for a long time.

"Come upstairs to my study. We won't be disturbed there."

"Disturbed?"

"The servants will be curious, but no one intrudes there except Adrian, and he's gone to Kingston."

George was a man of his word, she thought. Then for the first time she noticed that Creighton was not impeccably attired, as he usually was. He was wearing a white long-sleeved shirt, unbuttoned to the waist, and a pair of beige cotton trousers that were uncreased and that hugged the muscles of his legs. He was obviously dressed for the chores of packing and sorting the possessions he was taking with him. It made her sad and made her mission seem more futile.

He reached out almost tentatively for her hand. She put her hand in his, and he led her up the curved staircase. She was too lost in touching him to note the magnificence of the house. At the top of the stairs he took her along a picture-lined corridor. At the end of it was the door to the study, which had been left open.

He ushered her into the room, which had obviously once been a paragon of order but was now total chaos. There were packing cartons everywhere, along with half-empty bookcases and stacks of papers on every flat surface. It was the first real physical evidence of his departure, and it stunned her. She looked around the room as if in wonder.

"Did you think I was dissembling?" Creighton asked, seeing her expression.

"No, it's just that your leaving was all an idea earlier... no more than a rumor, but this... this makes it real."

"It is real, Kaye. I'm leaving."

"Why? Why, Creighton?"

"Because I must. Do you think I'd leave if there were an alternative?"

"There must be."

"There isn't."

"Is it in any way because of me?"

"Don't ask me that."

"I am asking. I have to know."

"The only thing you have to know is that it almost happened between us. The one essential miracle of life was almost ours. I reached out for it, and so did you, but it wasn't ours to take. We have to resign ourselves to that."

"Will you tell me one thing? If I left Montego for good, would you stay?"

"No. Perhaps I'm being greedy. I want you *and* Montego. One without the other is meaningless."

They stood looking at each other in a kind of helpless stupor until Kaye said, "Take me with you."

Creighton's expression softened further and revealed to Kaye a man she had never seen previously. He was a gentle giant of whom she need have no fear.

He took her in his arms and covered the back of her head with his hand, holding her face to his shoulder.

"I was wrong about you and Montego. It wouldn't matter where we were: Montego, Paris, Canberra, New York, Rome. You're my Eden. It isn't a place or a situation or a condition. It's being with you, anyplace, anytime. I love you, Kaye.''

"And I love you. Oh, Creighton, isn't that all that matters?''

"No, it isn't. Whatever might have been is lost. It doesn't belong to us. It never did.''

"It does! It always will! Let's take it before it's too late!''

"It's already too late. Go home, Kaye. Let's say goodbye to each other now. This is nothing but torture for us both.''

"Let me stay with you.''

"No.''

"Are you afraid? Are you afraid that if I stay with you, you won't be able to let me go?''

"Nothing could make it more difficult than it is already.''

"Then let me stay. Let me have that at least.''

He held her at arm's length for a moment and looked into her eyes, then he slipped his arm around her shoulders and led her across the room toward a door between two bookcases. He opened the door and ushered her through. She realized instantly she was in his bedroom. The only light was from a small lamp on a night table by the bed. The room was like Creighton himself—handsome and sturdy and masculine. There were campaign chests with brass hardware that gleamed in the dim light. There were two leather armchairs. The carved oak bed was enormous. Yet it was a comfortable room, and Kaye was comfortable in it—perhaps because of the security of Creighton's strong arm around her.

He pulled her close to him again and kissed her. His body appeared to possess some mysterious energy that jolted through her like electricity when he held her. She could feel his strength even from his mouth. It was warm and firm and seemed to hold her lips in its grip. She felt the warmth and safety of his lean strong body against her own. She knew this was what she had longed for—perhaps for her whole life. All her pride and defiance fell away from her, as if she had dropped them like an abandoned robe. It was as though she stood naked, as she knew she soon would, in Creighton's arms, free at last to be a woman—and to be his. All decisions would be made, all courses determined, all havens constructed by Creighton and his love for her. She was comforted and protected from all harm. For the first time in her life she was a woman. She wanted nothing else but to give herself, her total self—her body, her heart, her mind, her life—to Creighton. She wanted nothing but the sweetness of surrender.

She stood, her body utterly relaxed, her arms at her sides, waiting. She felt Creighton's gentle hands caressing her hair, stroking it with a gossamer tenderness. Then his hands, smooth and hard as polished stone, cupped her face and tilted it up toward his own. He kissed her again, and the kiss was as soft as the whisper of a breeze. His mouth opened against hers and engulfed her lips. She opened her mouth, not in the clutching way in which she had kissed him previously but simply, in communion. His arms went around her again, and he pulled her body tight against his. After a moment she felt his fingers at the buttons of her blouse. Unhurriedly and nimbly he began to unbutton them. She made no move to help him. There was no uncertainty, no fumbling, in his movements. He slipped the blouse off her shoulders and let it fall to the floor. Her skirt was fastened at the side of the waistband with a single clasp. He undid it, too, and let the skirt drop around her feet. He embraced her again, and through the cotton of his shirt she felt the muscles of his chest against her naked breasts. He released her and quickly removed his shirt while she stepped out of the skirt and slid off her white silk panties. For a moment he didn't touch her but stood looking at her, as if in wonder. It was not an evaluation. He was drinking in the sheer beauty of her: the firm rounded breasts with the nipples erect now, the plateau of her torso as it fell to the gentle mound of her belly, the darkness between her slender thighs and hips, the long line of her legs. The sun had turned her smooth fair skin the color of honey except where her breasts and abdomen had been protected. There it was the color of pale ivory. It was thrilling to her to have him look at her so leisurely and with such longing and joy. She gently pulled back her shoulders and stood absolutely still, allowing him to bathe her body with his gaze. He took a long time, as if there would be no end to their loving, as if time itself had ceased to exist.

Slowly and easily he pulled off his loafers and his trousers and shorts. Still he stood before her, both of them naked now, his eyes traveling up and down the length of her body. Then he reached out with his open arms, and she went to him. His skin was hot, and all the muscles of his body seemed to be tensed at once. He took her hand and led her to the bed. He pulled back the bedspread, and she lay down on the cool white sheets. In a moment he was beside her, and she could feel the heat of his body radiating across the short distance between them. Then she saw his face hovering above hers.

"I love you, Kaye. I want you, all of you."

"And I want to give myself to you the way I've never given myself to anyone. I'm yours, Creighton. Take me. Take all of me."

He kissed her with an almost frenzied passion, his mouth grasping at hers. She threw her arms around his neck and pulled his head down hard to her. He caressed her neck and shoulders and breasts with his mouth and hands. He touched her everywhere, stroking her hips and thighs until her desire for him grew wild. Then, with unbelievable gentleness, he was inside her, and the world became a new place for her. Now it was a world that existed only in their oneness, a oneness made complete by her own desires melding into his, her own will joined to his will, to the very rhythm of her body moving with the rhythm of his. Her joy, her ecstasy seemed eternal.

His loving was a fluid thing, flowing slowly, slowly in an ever increasing rush that swept her along in its passion until she herself knew a passion that was wild and alien and sweet with pleasure. It went on and on until suddenly there was no time, no place, no existence outside the engulfing wave that rocked them both at the same seemingly endless moment. Then the joy of it lingered like the wafted scent of a flower.

He lay beside her again, their bodies touching and their fingers entwined. The silence between them was as palpable as their lovemaking had been. Gradually the sadness of reality began to return to them like spilled water spreading on the surface of a stone.

"Will you stay the night?" Creighton asked quietly.

"Yes. I'll stay forever if you ask me. "

He turned his head and kissed her hair, which was feathered across the soft pillow, but he didn't answer her.

She wanted his answers to all the questions that were welling up inside her again. She wanted to know that tonight was the future for them. Somehow she believed it could be no other way—not after what had been between them, not after the love that had poured from them both and made them one. There could be no future for either of them without the other—not now. Separation may have been possible, may have seemed inevitable, when she had pulled the Morgan into the driveway before the house, when Creighton had assured her he was leaving Montego forever, but now their being apart had no reality, no possibility. She wanted to hear him say it. She had given herself, and he had taken that gift. He could not now give back what he had taken, any more than she could take it back from him.

Yet she couldn't bring herself to say any of these things. As they lay basking in the glow of their love, it seemed wrong, blasphemous, to talk of anything.

Creighton switched off the lamp, and soon, in the darkness, a sense of calm began to come over her.

"I love you, my darling," she whispered.

"And I love you—more than I thought I could ever love."

In a short time Kaye was asleep. Creighton lay watching the rise and fall of her breasts in the deep steady breathing of slumber. He did not sleep; he did not even close his eyes. He lay thinking until the stars were gone and the black sky at the window had begun to fade to a lustrous pearl gray. Even then he did not doze but watched Kaye, who had nestled in his arms during the night.

It was eight before she stirred, and she awoke to a gradual awareness of Creighton's presence. Then she remembered it all, and the whole world seemed miraculous. She felt a pure happiness she had not known for years, perhaps had never known previously.

"Good morning," Creighton said. "You slept soundly."

"And so peacefully. Good morning, my darling."

He kissed her, then threw back the sheets and got out of bed. His nakedness startled her. He put on a robe and went into the bathroom. Kaye stretched deliciously and propped herself up against a pillow, pulling the sheet up to her neck. Quite suddenly she remembered Creighton's imminent departure, and her happiness clouded. She remembered, too, last night's feeling of happy abandon, of not wanting to think about it or talk about it and not having to. But now it was time—or soon would be. What would he say? Everything had changed now.

There was obviously a dressing room adjoining the bathroom, for Creighton came out fully clothed, in a white pullover and brown slacks. He carried a white terry-cloth robe, which he laid beside her on the bed.

"This will be a few sizes too big, of course, but it will do." He sat on the edge of the bed and took her in his arms. He kissed her once and held her for a long time in silence. "I love you very much." Then he got up. "Come downstairs and have breakfast," he said, and he was gone.

Kaye was a little frightened by his reticence, but she sloughed it off. She took a long relaxing shower and got dressed. She went along the corridor, glancing at the pictures she had ignored the preceding night. Creighton came out of the drawing room, carrying a sheaf of papers, as she came down the stairs. He looked up and smiled at her.

"You're beautiful," he said. "Breakfast is ready on the terrace. Come on."

He took her hand and led her through a formal library with French doors that opened onto a terrace overlooking a spectacular garden. Before her was a table set with coffee cups and plates of fresh fruit. Creighton pulled out a chair and seated her, then sat opposite her.

"How do you feel?" he asked.

"Very well—and happy . . . terribly happy."

"Have you given any thought to what you're going to tell Alice?"

"No, it doesn't require any thought. I'm going to tell her I spent the night with you. She knows I'm here—or at least that I came here last night."

"Are you sure she won't object?"

"Quite sure. Have you any idea how fond she is of you?"

"Yes, we've been very close for many years. I'm deeply fond of her, too. But I don't see what that has to do with her approval or disapproval of our sleeping together."

"Aunt Alice is not a prude."

"I'm aware of that.

"And we are in love, aren't we?"

"Yes, as deeply in love as it's possible to be. But that doesn't change anything."

"It doesn't change—you can't be serious."

"Kaye, none of the circumstances of yesterday and the preceding days have changed one iota."

"Our whole life has changed. We love each other. There's no more fencing between us, no more deviousness. What are we to do, throw away our love, our life together? Don't you want us to have a life together?"

"More than anything else in the world. I'd like to go back to Traymore with you and announce our engagement to Aunt Alice. I'd like us to be married and living together in a matter of days. But it can't be. I don't think it can ever be."

Kaye was stunned into near speechlessness. Somehow she'd thought that everything *had* changed. How could it have not? They were in love—genuinely, deeply, in love—and that could change anything. It was more important than anything else in the world.

"Are you telling me that—that you're going through with your plans to leave the island?"

"Yes."

"Without me?"

"If I could leave with you, I wouldn't have to leave at all. Kaye, you don't understand."

"No, I don't understand at all. I assume you're going to explain it to me."

"I can't. I can tell you only that our marrying, even our having an affair, would bring you desperate unhappiness. And it would bring me worse than that."

"But how?" Her voice was plaintive, pleading.

"Kaye, you've got to trust me."

"Trust you to what? Just to leave me...without a reason, without an explanation?"

"There is a reason."

"And by trusting you, you mean I'm to accept that without knowing any more about it? How can you ask me to trust you when you won't trust me enough to tell me why you're destroying us both?"

"I'm trying to keep from destroying you and myself, as well. My darling, everything in this situation could change overnight, but there's nothing I can do to change it."

"But when might it change?"

"I don't know. Kaye, it could be years. That's why it's hopeless. Do you want me to stay here if we're unable to see each other alone...virtually unable to touch each other, unable to marry, unable to make love? We'd both go mad."

"But tell me why it must be that way."

"I can't. But you've got to go on, Kaye; you've got to leave me behind, out of your life."

"I won't! I love you!"

"That's why I must leave and get out of your life. If

there were merely some technical reason why I couldn't marry, I'd ask you outright to live with me."

"And I would."

"But that isn't the problem. We can't be together in any way at all."

"It's Adrian, isn't it?"

"It doesn't matter whether it's Adrian. But it's as I told you. If you were to go to him and mention any of what I've said to you, it could have the direst consequences for me."

"This is insane, Creighton! Why can't we go away somewhere together? I don't care where we live. We could run away so that no one would know where we were."

"We'd be found. Even if we weren't, could I ask you to live that way—in hiding like a hunted criminal? And if we succeeded in disappearing, the harm would be done anyway."

"Creighton, don't you see what you're doing to me? If you'd let me share whatever this burden is, maybe I could understand, maybe I could deal with it somehow. But this way you're asking me just to accept the fact that you love me yet are simply walking out of my life. How am I supposed to be able to bear that?"

"It will be easier than bearing the consequences of our marriage."

"It couldn't be! Whatever those consequences are, we'd bear them together. I haven't minded being alone, but now that there's us, I don't think I could stand it. Creighton, I didn't ask to fall in love with you. God knows, I did everything I could to avoid it. But it couldn't be helped. It couldn't be stopped. How can you throw it all away now, just when our happiness is within reach?"

"But it isn't, Kaye. I've never wanted anyone as

much as I want you. I've never loved anyone the way I
love you. After Victoria died, I was resigned to spending
the rest of my life alone. I didn't think I could ever love
anyone else. Then you came to me, and even though I
fought my feelings desperately, it did no good; the love
was too strong. For a brief, brief time I thought we
would have a life together. And then. . . . Kaye, just believe me. There's nothing in the world I wouldn't do for
you. I'd give up my life for you without a thought. But
there's no hope for us.''

She wanted to go on fighting this blackness, this mysterious unknowable enemy, but she knew it was useless.
She knew Creighton's strength, and she loved him for it.
She could see now that that strength was working with
all its power in this situation—working against her, it
seemed. Yet she knew he loved her and that whatever he
was doing, he was doing for her, to protect her against
some awful harm he couldn't reveal.

''When will you leave?'' she asked hesitantly.

''As soon as I can get things in order. It will take
some time—at least a week or ten days, possibly
longer.''

''Where will you go?''

''I don't know. . . probably to Australia.''

''I don't know if I can bear to see you, even if we can
arrange it.''

''I know. I'm afraid it would only make things more
difficult for both of us.''

''I've got to leave now. Let's not say goodbye just
yet.''

''All right. Whatever happens, please remember that
I love you with my whole heart.''

''I will. I love you, Creighton.''

They stood up, and he took her in his arms. They
walked through the house and out onto the driveway in

silence. He went to the car with her and kissed her once more. Then she got into the car and drove off.

She had managed the roads better in the dark than she did on the drive back to Traymore. The bitter tears flowed without a sound, and it seemed to her they would never stop. She had found all that she wanted in life—a great love—only to have it snatched away after one ecstatic night. The farther she got from Penrose, the more unreal it all seemed to her. In the somber reality of Creighton's presence, hearing the words of sadness and despair in his deep quiet voice, her loss seemed a tragic certainty. But once away from him it became as elusive as mist. She feared things would always be that way. She feared that when he was gone, it would be like having lost him to unbelievable death. Nothing in her life had ever filled her with such unbearable sadness.

She managed to hold back the tears when she greeted Aunt Alice in the sitting room, nevertheless it was perfectly clear she had been crying. Aunt Alice was terribly alarmed, but she tried to remain calm.

"Do you want to sit down and tell me what's wrong, my dear?"

"Yes, as much as I can." She sank down on the small sofa next to Aunt Alice. "I was with Creighton last night, as I'm sure you're aware."

"Yes. I'd hoped it would make you happy."

"Oh, it did, Aunt Alice. I love him so very much, and he loves me. After all we've put each other through, it's finally come to our loving each other as much as any two people can. And yet... he's going away."

"He's going away even in the face of your loving each other?"

"Yes."

"But why?"

"I don't know."

"Surely he offered some explanation?"

"Only that marriage was impossible for us, that it could bring us both only unhappiness and misery. Our being together in any way—and I would live with him, Aunt Alice, anywhere, any way that we could—would have the same consequences."

"But he can't expect you to accept that without knowing any more about it."

"Something or someone has a hold on him so powerful and so terrible that even his telling me about it might cause him some awful harm. I know how much he loves me and how much it's costing him to do this. I can't be angry with him, not even for keeping all this a mystery. What am I going to do, Aunt Alice?" Now the tears came again, unchecked and uncontrollable.

"I don't know, my darling. I don't know. Creighton doesn't make decisions quickly or lightly. He doesn't go off half-cocked. But once he's made a decision, his will is like granite. He won't change his mind." She put her arm around Kaye's shoulders. "There, there, my dear. I know how difficult this must be for you."

"Nothing will help. Creighton is leaving, and I'll never see him again."

"Kaye, you may not approve of what I'm going to do, but I am going to do it nonetheless. I am going to see Creighton."

"Aunt Alice, I don't want him to think that I—"

"It isn't a matter of what you want. Creighton owes me an explanation—not because of you, but because of our friendship. One cannot buy friendship; one can only give it and accept it. But it doesn't come without obligations. It creates debts, and I am going to collect this debt from Creighton."

"I don't think it will change anything."

"Neither do I. But he may tell me things he could not tell you. We'll see."

"I think he's probably at home now, if you want to call him."

"I'm going to break a few rules. I am going to him right away, unannounced. I'm not fool enough to think that taking Creighton by surprise will create an advantage, but it will impress him with the gravity of the situation. Would you ring for Henry, please, and tell him to bring the car around? It will take me only a few minutes to change."

Half an hour later the Rolls pulled into the driveway at Penrose. Henry helped Aunt Alice from the car and escorted her to the front door of the house. It opened before she could ring, and Creighton stood in the doorway. His expression was not impenetrable now; he was clearly worried. In such a serious situation these two good friends did not waste words. This was not the time for the customary amenities of Montego society. Their mutual interest was to get to the heart of the matter and have it done.

"Hello, Alice," Creighton said as he stepped back to admit her.

"Hello, Creighton."

"Come into the drawing room," he said. When they were in the room, Creighton closed the door and turned to her. "Do sit down, Alice."

"Not until I've heard the answer to my first question."

"All right."

"There's been an affinity between us since the first day you set foot on this island. We are old close friends. Leaving Kaye aside for the moment, you owe me an explanation for your leaving Montego."

"I know I do, Alice, but I can't give you one."

"How many times have you and I joined forces, openly or conspiratorially, to foil some silly social project of our friends? How many times have we had secret meetings with George Montague here or at Traymore to bring about some social reform for the island's people or to block some venal move by members of the government? How many times have we put our individual welfare and reputation in each other's hands without the slightest fear of betrayal?"

"Countless times."

"And now you display this utter lack of trust in me?"

"It isn't a lack of trust, Alice."

"Either you trust me, or you don't. You are about to do the most drastic, the most unaccountable thing you've done in all the years I've known you. Can you actually believe that if I knew your motives, I'd betray you?"

"I know that you would under no circumstances betray me. You don't know what disloyalty is. But you must trust me. Won't you accept the fact that there are valid reasons for my leaving and that those reasons must remain secret, even from you?"

"I can accept that only believing that your faith in me and in our friendship has diminished."

"Even if your knowing would threaten to ruin my life?"

"It could do that only if you felt I'd reveal your secret or in some way use it against you. Is that what you think of me?"

"You know what I think of you, but it's a risk I can't take."

"A *risk*? Trusting in my honor is a risk?"

"If you knew all the facts of the matter, you would want me to behave exactly as I'm behaving."

"Tell me the facts, and let me be the judge of that."

"I can't. It's impossible."

Lady Alice looked at him with a sternness he had seen displayed previously, though never directed at him. "All right. We'll say no more about that part of it. And what of Kaye?"

"Everything I've said to you applies to Kaye, as well."

"Do you love her?"

"With my whole heart."

"And last night you slept with her, only to dismiss her this morning like a common harlot?"

"Alice, you can't think that."

"Friendship and honor demand a great deal of one. Love demands a great deal more."

"Damn it, Alice, I'm doing what I'm doing because love demands it—my love for you, my love for Kaye and my. . . . There's nothing more I can say."

"I admit Kaye has been difficult. There has been great tension between you. But you are treating her shabbily. For God's sake, Creighton, tell her what's going on!"

"I can't."

Alice, tiny though she was, pulled herself up to her full height, and the effect was regal. "You have denied me the honesty on which our friendship has been based. You have treated my niece, who loves you, with a callous and cruel lack of regard. You have demeaned both my friendship and her love. I am saddened beyond measure. You are no longer welcome at Traymore. Good day."

Lady Alice turned and walked out of the room. Creighton made no attempt to escort her. He knew it would have been useless. In one morning he had lost everything dear to him, and no one believed he had lost it out of love.

Kaye was waiting for her aunt when the Rolls pulled up before Traymore. Her heart sank when she saw her getting out of the car and approaching the steps of the veranda. She appeared tiny and old and defeated. There was no need for questions.

Aunt Alice paused for a moment at the top of the stairs. She looked at Kaye with a great weariness in her eyes and said, "It *is* hopeless. I've suffered a great loss—perhaps not as great as yours, but I'm too old to be dealt such a blow. It is extremely unlikely Creighton will come here again, but if he does, you are not to receive him. I'm going up to my room now. At dinnertime I'll have a tray there. I'll make my excuses to the Marlowes by telephone; however, I think you should go. You should start over without pause...it's easier. Forgive me, my darling, I tried."

"It's you who should forgive me. If it hadn't been for me—"

"Don't blame yourself. It's not your fault."

Aunt Alice disappeared into the house, and Kaye wondered how long it would be before she saw her again.

# CHAPTER ELEVEN

KAYE SPENT THE AFTERNOON in a state of utter consternation. Nothing she did or tried to do gave her respite from thoughts of Creighton and his leaving. She put on a bathing suit and went to the pool, hoping that after a swim she could doze in the warmth of the afternoon sun. The swim did nothing to refresh her, and as she sunned herself, her eyes refused to stay closed long enough for her to become sleepy. She gave up the project in less than half an hour. She put on a robe and sat in the shade of the veranda, trying to read. She was unable to concentrate for more than a few minutes at a time. She started for her room, but turned around in the downstairs hall and went for a walk in the garden instead. It was the last place she should have gone to try to be free of thoughts of Creighton. After that she found her mind wasn't functioning at all. She couldn't decide between a cup of tea and a drink, so she had neither. She picked up the telephone twice to call Netty Marlowe to say she was unable to come to dinner, but both times she hung up without making the call. Finally, at the end of the afternoon, she went to her room and drew a tepid bath. She lay in the tub for a long time; the bath seemed to soothe her.

It was not only thoughts of Creighton that preyed on her mind. She was terribly worried about Aunt Alice. She had never seen her look as pale and worn as she had on her return from Penrose, and for her to retire to her room at midday and take supper there, as well, was so unlike her, was so far removed from her fighting spirit and her resilience, that it alarmed Kaye. Yet she could not intrude upon her privacy to inquire after her. She asked Helen to look in on her, but Helen reported she was not allowed entry into the room.

All of this dismay was compounded by Kaye's feeling that she was to blame for everything. If she had kept her distance from Creighton from the beginning, as instinct had told her to do, there would have been no relationship between them to blossom into love. She knew Creighton was leaving because of her, both because he was afraid for her and because he knew neither of them could bear to be in such constant proximity and be kept apart by this unnamed threat that hung over them both. And if they weren't in love and he weren't leaving, whatever had happened between him and Aunt Alice wouldn't have happened.

What had taken place between them that morning, she wondered. It wasn't really difficult to imagine. Aunt Alice had asked him to tell her why he was leaving, and Creighton had refused. Aunt Alice had taken this as a slight and forbidden him to come to Traymore. So it was she, Kaye, who had wrecked that long-standing deep friendship. All of it was her fault. All the trouble, all the pain to everyone was her fault.

And her meddling in Amanda's and Danny's life was unforgivable. What good had it done, beyond providing them with a little time together in Kingston? It had probably goaded them into facing Smitty prematurely. It had helped put Smitty in a position that would eventually make her look foolish, and it had put Aunt Alice in a position that might eventually lead to an end of her old and deep friendship with Smitty. Oh, if only Aunt Alice hadn't prevented her from leaving Montego that morning so long ago! None of these terrible things would have happened then. What a blind, meddling, selfish fool she was. She thought of getting out of the bath and packing to go that very night. But she couldn't leave Aunt Alice, and she couldn't leave Creighton. It was too late now.

She thought once again of calling Netty. Something told her, though, that Aunt Alice wanted her to be at the dinner party. Perhaps it would help disguise the importance of what was happening if one of them attended. For whatever time was left, she must do what little she could, if not to undo the wrongs she had done, then to ease the pain those wrongs had caused.

She got out of the bath and took a great deal of time dressing and preparing herself. When she had finished, she went downstairs and made herself a martini. It was unlike her to drink alone and before a dinner party, but the whole world seemed unlike itself. She sat on the veranda, toying with the drink until it was time to go, then she put the three-quarters full glass on the table before her and went upstairs again.

She knocked gently on the door of Aunt Alice's bedroom. After a moment she heard her voice. "Who is it?"

"It's Kaye, darling. May I come in?"

There was a pause. "Yes, of course."

Aunt Alice was in bed, propped up against the pillows. She looked frail and tired, and her sweet smile seemed to be an effort for her.

Kaye went to her and took her hand. "I just thought I'd look in on you before I left for the Marlowes'. Are you all right?"

"Perfectly, my dear. You run along and have a good time."

"Auntie, I don't really want to go. I thought for some reason you wanted me to."

"I do. I think you should be there for a number of reasons."

"Let me stay here with you. I'd so much rather."

"I won't hear of it. I'm just a little tired, dear. I won't deny that this morning upset me a great deal, but I'll soon be myself again. You go on, and give my love to Netty and Harlan."

"All right, if you insist."

"I do."

"I won't be late. Shall I look in on you when I get back?"

"If there's a light visible under the door, do stop in. If not, you'll know I'm fast asleep. Good night now, and try to enjoy it."

"I'll try. Good night."

She went downstairs, got into the Morgan and drove off toward the Marlowes' house.

There was another lone guest about to make his way to the Marlowes' at that moment. Adrian had returned from Kingston late in the afternoon and was now dressed and ready to set out from Penrose for the dinner party. As he came down the stairs, jaunty and whistling, he saw Creighton standing in the hall outside the drawing room.

"I'd like to talk to you before you leave," Creighton said. Without waiting for an answer, he turned and went into the drawing room. Adrian hesitated, then followed him.

"You're not going to the Marlowes'?" Adrian asked as he entered the room.

"No."

"Well, I am, old chap. I'd appreciate it if you didn't make me late." He went to the table and poured himself a whiskey.

"You're going to have to leave, Adrian."

Adrian looked at him impatiently and said, "I've told you. I can't leave."

"I'm selling the house."

Now the surprise in Adrian's eyes was evident. "You're what?"

"The new owners won't be moving in until the season starts in December, but I'm letting the servants go and closing the house until then."

"And where will you stay? Not that you wouldn't be welcome in any house in Montego."

"I won't be in Montego. I'm leaving the island. . .for good."

Adrian stared at him in astonishment. "Now just a minute, Creighton, I think you'd better explain this to me."

"I don't have to explain anything to you. I'll give you as much money as you need. Then you're to get out of this house and out of Montego."

"I'm afraid that isn't convenient for me. Oh, I'll get out of the house. What good is it without servants? But I don't want to leave Montego just yet, as I've said. I'm sure that when it becomes known that your hospitality has been sold out from under me, someone will come to my rescue with an invitation. If not, there are always the hotels. And I *do* have some unfinished business here. . . ."

"If your unfinished business is Kaye Belliston, you're wasting your time."

"You *have* told her something about me. I warned—"

"I've told her nothing."

"Then why are you so sure that—" Adrian's angry expression faded, and he smiled. "Ah, I see. Not only are you in love with her, she is in love with you, and therefore I am out in the cold."

"You may think anything you want. It's enough for me that I can leave knowing she's safe from you."

"But you wouldn't blame me for trying, would you, Creighton? It is a very large fortune, you know, and after all, with you gone and dear Kaye bereft, I might get her on the rebound.''

''You're disgusting. But you're not going to have everything your own way this time. Just make the arrangements to be out of here as soon as possible.''

''You're leaving that quickly? Of course, you would be. It's really very touching. I won't let you have Kaye, and you can't stand being near her without—well, you know. And so you remove yourself from the scene of torture. It's really too easy. I'd much rather have you stay on and suffer, but I suppose you'll be suffering in any case. That's quite good enough for me. Where will you go?''

''I don't know.''

''You surely wouldn't leave me without a forwarding address?''

''When I decide where I'm going, I'll get in touch with you.''

''Promise, Creighton?'' Adrian said playfully, knowing that Creighton had no choice.

''Go on to the party. And remember, if you haven't made arrangements to get out by the time I close the house, I'll throw you out and lock up.''

''All right. I'll scout around tonight at the Marlowes'.'' He put down his glass and started out of the room. Stopping at the door, he turned back to Creighton. ''This really is working out very nicely. Good night, Creighton.''

The only unusual thing about Netty's and Harlan's dinner party was that Smitty had been the first to arrive. She had written the letter to Danny Riordan's family and was still in the process of getting the signatures of all the members of Montego society. She was going at it all with her usual ferocious energy, and no one, of course, was allowed to refuse. She accosted Kaye in the doorway of the drawing room before Kaye had even had a chance to say hello to her host and hostess. It was first things first with Smitty, and whatever her greatest interest was at the moment was first.

"Kaye, darling, you haven't signed my letter to Danny Riordan's family," she said, letting the monocle drop from her eye as she thrust the pale blue stationery at Kaye.

"I'm not really a resident, Smitty. Do you think I—"

"You were here when the valorous incident occurred. You were, therefore, a slightly removed witness to it. You must sign it, of course." She peered past Kaye like a cat looking for a bird. "Where's Alice?"

"She wasn't feeling very well. Just a little tired, I suspect. She sends you her love."

"Are you sure she's all right?"

"Of course. She's having a tray in her room. I think she enjoys an occasional night off from the general round of parties."

"Alice always has had good sense." She looked around conspiratorially and whispered, "If *I* had any sense, I'd do the same thing now and then. Come, sit down here at this table and sign." She thrust a pen into Kaye's hand.

Smitty's attitude made Kaye feel as if she were being forced to sign a confession of some kind, as if there would be a severe penalty for disobedience. But it was for Danny, after all, so she signed willingly. Yet she was also reminded of the coming confrontation between Smitty and Danny. It should not be a confrontation, but it would, and Smitty's boundless enthusiasm for Danny was going to make it a more difficult one. There was nothing to be done about it now, thanks in part to her.

"There," she said, handing the paper and pen back to Smitty. "I'm sure the Riordans will be deeply touched and very proud."

"And so they should be," Smitty declared. "They have a fine young son. Excuse me, my dear. There are the Duckworths. They haven't signed yet." She scurried off across the reception hall.

Kaye saw the Marlowes across the room, talking to Barney Fairweather. She approached them and said, "Good evening."

"Kaye, how good to see you," Harlan said.

"How is Alice?" Netty asked.

"I think she's just a bit tired. It's nothing to worry about."

"Kaye, you don't have a drink," Harlan remarked. "Let me remedy that."

"Thank you, Harlan. I think I'd like just a plain Perrier."

Kaye turned to watch Harlan leave and saw Adrian coming into the room. She frowned, but quickly changed her expression. She was going to have to be very careful with Adrian. He started toward her immediately, but since she was standing with their hostess, Kaye could not be sure if he was coming to her.

"Good evening," Adrian said. "Netty, you're very kind to include me in your lovely dinner parties."

"Not at all, Adrian. You're a most welcome addition."

"Hello, Kaye."

"Hello, Adrian."

"Creighton hasn't changed his mind about coming, I see," Netty commented.

"Creighton never changes his mind," Adrian answered. "He's very busy."

"Busy? Busy with what?"

"Oh, just the details of running the house, I suppose."

Harlan returned with Kaye's drink and said to Adrian, "I saw you come in, so I brought you a drink. Whiskey, right?"

"Right and very thoughtful."

"Would you excuse me?" Kaye put in. "I have something to tell the Zimmermans."

"Of course, dear," Netty replied.

Kaye started toward the corner, where the Zimmermans were standing with a group of guests. She had gone only a few steps when Adrian was at her side.

"Kaye, could you spare me a moment sometime during the evening? I'd like to talk to you."

"Oh, of course." Kaye didn't want to talk to Adrian, and she certainly didn't want to be alone with him, but if she was going to hear what he had to say eventually, she thought it would be better to have done with it now than have it hanging over her head all evening. She said, "I suppose the Zimmermans will be here all evening. Why not now?"

"Splendid." He looked around the room. "It's awfully crowded in here. Do you suppose we could go into the library?"

"Is it that confidential?"

"Not really, but it would be difficult to get anything said at a dinner party when one is with so beautiful a woman. We'd be interrupted constantly."

"All right," Kaye replied, not acknowledging the compliment.

They left the drawing room and walked down the carpeted hallway to the library. Adrian followed her into the room and closed the door.

"I didn't mean to make this seem so cloak-and-dagger, Kaye, but since Creighton seems to have chosen to tell no one about it, I felt I should be discreet and make every effort not to be overheard."

"Creighton has chosen to tell no one about what?"

"He hasn't told even you?"

"I can hardly answer that question until you tell me what you're talking about."

"Perhaps in the interest of discretion I shouldn't tell you." Kaye waited. "It's just that I was so certain he wouldn't make so important a move without telling you."

"I don't see why you think I'd be privy to the details of Creighton's private life."

"Oh, come now, Kaye. Taciturn as Creighton is, it's impossible to be living in his house day after day and not see perfectly clearly that—"

"That what?"

"That he's in love with you."

"That can be nothing more than an assumption on your part."

"Yes, but I took the liberty of mentioning it to him, and he didn't deny it. I also assumed, therefore, that he would have told you he's leaving Montego—selling the house and leaving."

"Yes, he told me, but hardly for the reason you're suggesting."

"Why did he tell you then?"

"Because of Aunt Alice, I suppose."

Adrian smiled at her as he had always smiled previously, but for the first time Kaye saw the invidiousness beneath the charm of the smile, and she wondered how she could ever have been attracted to him.

"Dear Kaye, surely he could have told Alice without telling you."

"Adrian, I really don't see what all this has to do with me—or with you, either, for that matter."

"Kaye, my feelings for you haven't changed. I realize I had a rival in Creighton, but now all that will be changed. Creighton will be gone, and there'll be only you and me."

She wanted to strike him. She wanted him to be fully

aware that her mild feeling of affection for him had turned to contempt. It was clear that Adrian was interested only in what *he* wanted, and no one else mattered. She didn't know how deeply Adrian was involved in Creighton's unhappiness, but she was sure he played a part in it. She hated being in the same room with him, yet she was afraid to alienate him completely, afraid he'd retaliate by hurting Creighton further.

"Adrian, I've already told you I'm not ready for an involvement with anyone. You're a charming and attractive man, and I enjoy being with you, but there can be no more to it than that."

"Perhaps. We'll see. I realize that, to some degree at least, you return Creighton's feeling for you. But he'll be gone soon, and I can see to it that you're not lonely." He came to her and put his hands gently on her shoulders. Her body stiffened. "If you'd let yourself, I promise you'd find my attentions entirely agreeable." He bent to kiss her.

She tried to pull away from him, but the gentleness of his grip belied his strength. He kissed her on the mouth, and the kiss was hard and aggressive. His mouth lingered on hers until he was finished with her, then he let her go. She stepped backward, holding the back of her hand against her lips.

He looked at her suspiciously. "You didn't pull away from me that night in the garden."

"I—I. . . . It's just that it would be wrong for me to lead you on. I'm. . . perfectly willing to see you, but it—it can't be anything more than a friendship."

"Friendships have a way of blossoming into romances. I can wait, Kaye, and I'll be patient. With Creighton gone, there'll be no need to hurry."

"I'd like to go back to the drawing room now."

"Of course."

Kaye was miserable for the rest of the evening. She was not very good company for the few people she spoke to, and she spoke to them mostly because Adrian was at her side at every minute. She was thankful they were not seated near each other during dinner. After dinner she found a seat on a small settee next to Netty. It was a successful defense against Adrian's presence. When she saw Adrian move across the room to get a brandy, she told Netty she was concerned about Aunt Alice and felt she should go home. Netty understood completely, and Kaye was able to leave the party without seeing Adrian again.

There was no light in Aunt Alice's room when Kaye got back to Traymore, and she was relieved. She was glad that Aunt Alice had apparently been able to sleep and that she herself wouldn't have to make conversation. She went directly to her room. She stood on the balcony for a long time, staring at the starlit sky and wondering if Creighton was awake at that moment. She wondered if he was thinking of her and longing for her as she longed for him. She remembered Aunt Alice's telling her it would be better to deal with Creighton than never to know what might have been. If this was all that was to be—this crushing loneliness, this aching desire—perhaps Aunt Alice had been wrong.

She lay awake for a long time, thinking of nothing but Creighton. When she finally did sleep, it was only to dream of him. The dreams were vague and filled with anxiety. She felt the touch of his hand on her hair, then felt it withdraw as he called to her, his voice fading into an ever increasing distance, until it was gone altogether into darkness. She awoke from such dreams frequently during the night, the last time with dawn's light at the windows. She slept again then and didn't awaken until midmorning.

She bathed and dressed and went downstairs to find

Aunt Alice sitting on the veranda, looking quite rested.

She kissed her and said, "Good morning. You look fully recovered."

"I feel somewhat better. I've made myself feel better, actually. It seemed to outsiders that girls of my era and class were coddled. We were in many respects, but we were never allowed to give in to afflictions of the spirit. Depression was considered both weak and sinful. I don't believe that now, of course, but the discipline has seen me through many a difficult time."

"You're being modest, auntie. You have the spiritual strength of a saint."

"Oh, goodness, no! I've simply found that giving in to hopelessness is far more painful than just to continue hoping. Helen is bringing your breakfast."

"Thank you."

"Another thing I've learned in my many years is that there's nothing like a new problem to take your mind off an old one."

"That sounds ominous."

Helen appeared with Kaye's breakfast tray and put it on the table before her.

"Thank you, Helen," Kaye said. "What's the new problem?"

"I'm afraid it's more my problem than yours. An invitation arrived this morning from Smitty. It's to a dinner she's giving in further honor of Danny Riordan."

"That is a bit much."

"The problem is, we can't let her do it."

"What do you mean?"

"It's quite bad enough that we've allowed her to lionize him as much as we have without telling her about Amanda and Danny. She's already going to feel foolish. Smitty can tolerate a great many things, but seeming a public fool is not among them. The one thing for which she and all of us have less tolerance is betrayal. I'm afraid she's going to see the whole thing as a conspiracy against her—and not without cause. The longer we let it go on, the worse it's going to be. She must be told about Amanda and Danny before the dinner party, and what's worse, she must be told that you and I knew about it even while she was praising him and displaying him at Agatha Landsbury's dinner and collecting signatures for her letter to his family."

"Aunt Alice, she doesn't know Danny was here to dinner; she doesn't know you knew anything about it, and there's no reason why she has to know. If she has to be told, let Amanda and me tell her. There's no reason why you should risk your friendship over this."

"It wouldn't be a friendship worth risking if I didn't. There is no such thing as a friendship based on deceit. I'm quite sure I could keep my involvement from her indefinitely, but I would never again feel I was her friend if I did."

"You wouldn't be lying to her, you know. It would be only a sin of omission."

"I would keep anything from Smitty that I thought would hurt her unnecessarily, but I could never keep something from her to prevent my being hurt myself. No, it simply wouldn't do."

"You make me feel so unworthy."

"Don't be silly."

"It's true. Here I am trying to persuade you to desert the principles you've lived by all your life. I should be ashamed of myself. And I am."

"Principles grow on and in you as you age. Don't be harsh on yourself. The problem now is how to approach her."

"No one could know better than you."

"I *don't* know, Kaye. I could go to her privately and

confess the whole thing. Or you and Amanda and I could go to her. Or the three of us could take Danny to her. No, that would never do. We could have her here and present Danny to her. No, no. That's too conspiratorial, and there's been enough of that. You see, my dear, I'm trying to do this in the way that will give Amanda and Danny the best chance of getting Smitty's approval and at the same time save face for you and me, to whatever degree possible. It may be that the simplest way will be best. What if you and I didn't know anything about Amanda and Danny, and what if they decided they couldn't go on with the deception? What would they do?''

"I don't know.''

"Of course you do. What would you have done at nineteen in the same situation in New York?''

"Well, I would have invited Danny to the house, and he would have asked for my hand.''

"Exactly. It would be far better if it were Danny who tried to spare Smitty embarrassment. It would be far better if Danny, driven by conscience, went to her and told her he could not allow her to go on expressing public approval of him, thus entrapping her when he asked for her private approval. He would express his deep remorse at having let it go even this far, at having conducted a secret relationship with Amanda at all, however innocent it was. After the fact is plenty of time for us to involve ourselves, and after the fact we could vouch for the innocence of the relationship—which would not only bolster her faith in Amanda and Danny but would take some of the onus off us. We allowed it to go on only because we knew there was nothing illicit about it.''

"Aunt Alice, you're a genius.''

"No, I'm not. I'm just trying to help two dear young people and save my own skin at the same time. There is absolutely no guarantee it will work. As a matter of fact,

I doubt it will achieve either objective. But I believe it's the best, the only way to do it. Beyond that we can only pray.''

"I've known this had to come, yet now that it's here, I'm frightened. What about the timing?''

"I hope I'm not pushing, but now that we've decided on a course, I think the sooner, the better. Can you call Amanda? I don't suppose one more tiny deception is going to do any harm. Tell her you'd like to go to Doctor's Cave for lunch.''

"She won't believe it. It's Tuesday—Danny's day off.''

"Splendid! Do you know how to get in touch with him?''

"I think so. I don't know if he'll be there, but why do—''

"Kaye, we're being a trifle high-handed. We say *we've* decided on a course. It's really up to Amanda and Danny. We must get them here and propose the plan. Then the decision will be theirs.''

"I'll call them both right now.''

She went into the drawing room and dialed Smitty's number. Amanda was summoned from her late breakfast.

"Kaye, darling, how are you?''

"I'm fine. Could you come over here for lunch? I haven't seen you for ages.''

"Ages? You saw me last night at Netty's and Harlan's.''

"Don't be a dunce. Come to lunch.''

"Of course. I'd love to. What time?''

"I don't care what time, you ninny. Just come.''

"What's going. . . . All right. I'll be there at noon.''

"Good.''

She hung up and dialed the number for the employees'

residence at Doctor's Cave. After a moment she heard Danny's voice. "Hello."

"Danny, it's Kaye."

"Kaye! Great! How are you?"

"I'm fine. Can you come up to the house no later than noon?"

"Wait a minute. What's happening?"

"Aunt Alice and I want to talk to you. It's about you and Amanda and Smitty, of course. Amanda's coming, too, but she doesn't know why. You've got to come, if it's at all possible."

"Of course I'll come. I'll come right now if you want."

"As long as you're here by noon. Can you borrow a car, or shall I pick you up?"

"It'd be safer if you picked me up. I'm never sure about being able to borrow a car."

"I'll be there shortly. Goodbye, Danny." She hung up, feeling excitement now mixed with her foreboding.

When Kaye returned with Danny a short time later, Amanda hadn't arrived. As they came up onto the veranda, Danny said, "Lady Alice, it's really so good to see you again."

"It's good to see you, too, Danny. Do sit down."

"Well, I've delivered this half of the package," Kaye said. "Now if the other half would arrive, we could get down to business."

"Would it be all right if I asked what business we're going to get down to?" Danny questioned.

"There's really no point in going through it all twice, my dear young man. Amanda will be here at any minute. I've ordered lunch for us. Would you like something to drink?"

"No, thank you, Lady Alice."

"I'm going to have a rum punch, and I suggest you have one, too."

"I think you mean I'm going to need it. That's scary."

"There is really nothing to be anxious about," Lady Alice reassured him.

As Henry was serving the rum punches, Amanda drove up to the house. She started up the stairs before she saw Danny. She stopped, openmouthed, at the top of the stairs. She would have run into his arms if Danny hadn't been there long enough to be in firm control of himself. He went to her and kissed her on the cheek. "Hello, Mandy."

"Danny! What... what are you doing here?"

"I was invited."

"Oh, I'm sorry, Lady Alice. I'm just so... surprised. How are you?" She went to her and kissed her on the cheek.

"I'm fine, my dear. Would you like a rum punch?"

"No. No, thank you." She looked bewildered.

"Do you both know that Lady Gladys is giving a party in Danny's honor?"

"Yes," Amanda answered.

"Oh, no!" Danny said.

"Your invitation should have arrived this morning," Amanda told him.

"We don't get our mail until noon at the earliest," Danny explained. "Why is she doing that?"

"For the same reason Lady Landsbury did," Aunt Alice replied.

"I didn't save Lady Smith-Croydon's grand-daughter."

"No, you certainly didn't," Kaye remarked.

"Curiously enough, that irony is exactly why I asked you here," Aunt Alice said. "You see how... awkward it would be if you were to go to Smitty to ask for Amanda's hand *after* allowing her to give a party in your honor without telling her your circumstances."

"Yes," Danny agreed emphatically. "I do see that."

"I'm afraid Smitty has unwittingly forced your hand," Aunt Alice told them. "Kaye mentioned that you didn't say anything to her earlier because you were afraid she'd send Amanda away, and I'm sure she would have. If none of this had happened, you could have gone on waiting until the last possible moment—next year, the year after that. But I'm afraid that's impossible now. Once she gives the party, you will be in deep trouble. You couldn't possibly come back next year and expect to get her approval. You'd be very unlikely to get it this year."

"Why did she have to do this?" Danny moaned.

"It's done, and we have to deal with it," Aunt Alice replied. "I am in no position to tell either of you what to do, but you have sought my help, and I'm willing to give it. I've given the matter a great deal of thought, and I believe there is only one thing to do. Amanda, you must invite Danny to the house—oh, probably for tea. This is not to be a surprise; there are going to be enough surprises. You must tell your grandmother you've invited him. She'll think it odd, but you can handle that. You, Danny, must ask to speak with Lady Smith-Croydon privately, with only Amanda present. Then you must tell her what's been going on. Tell her that you realize you have compromised her by allowing her publicly to extol your virtues while you and Amanda have been deceiving her and that you want to put an end to the situation immediately. That, unfortunately, is the moment at which you must ask for Amanda's hand."

There was absolute silence.

"I—I can't do it," Danny answered weakly.

"I'm afraid you must," Aunt Alice asserted. "I'd be happy to hear alternate suggestions."

"Lady Alice, I thought there was the possibility of your going to Lady Smith-Croydon and—"

"That would infuriate her to such a degree that there'd be no hope for any of us—for you and Amanda or for my friendship with Smitty."

"Couldn't we invite her here? Then all of us could—"

"Lure her into the conspirators' den like some unsuspecting prey? No, Amanda. I'll have no part of that."

"Aunt Alice is right," Kaye said.

There was another silence, which Danny finally broke by asking, "What do you say, Mandy?"

"I—I guess there's no other way."

"Good," Aunt Alice said. "I think you should do it tomorrow."

"Tomorrow?" Amanda shrieked.

"You've got to give Smitty time to call off the dinner party. I mean, she's either going to go ahead with the party in Danny's honor and simultaneously announce your engagement—which would, happily, make it seem as if she knew about it all along—or she'll refuse your request, in which case she'll have to cancel the party. You owe her the choice."

"Lady Alice, do you really believe this is the only thing to do?" Danny asked.

"Yes."

"It seems to me you've covered all the bases." He looked at Amanda sadly. "Am I invited to tea?"

"I suppose you are."

"Good! Chin up now. Take comfort in the fact that you're doing the right thing."

"Lady Alice, what do you think grandmother will do?"

"I don't know, Amanda."

"What would you do if you were she?"

"I'm not."

"Please tell me."

Aunt Alice thought for a long time. "I think I would be

furious with both of you...and I think ultimately I would give you my blessing. But I'm not as proud as your grandmother. She's going to be deeply hurt, and she's going to feel betrayed by us all. If she can deal with that within herself, there's a chance. It won't be easy for her."

BEFORE DANNY ARRIVED for tea the next day, Amanda asked her grandmother if she might be present, at least at the beginning of the meeting, and the request was granted. Danny arrived at five in his formal uniform: slacks, blazer, shirt and tie. The butler showed him into the sitting room, where Lady Smith-Croydon and Amanda were waiting for him. Tea had already been set out. Smitty's facade of impishness had been abandoned. She was warm, amiable and dignified. Her successful attempt at hiding her curiosity put her at a certain distance.

"Mr. Riordan," she said as Danny entered the room, "how nice to meet you again."

"It was very gracious of you to see me, Lady Smith-Croydon. Hello, Miss Leyton." Immediately he felt ill at ease and confused. He had just addressed his unofficial fiancée in a way that could only deceive Smitty further. He was sure nothing he did could be right.

"Hello, Mr. Riordan," Amanda replied, compounding the dilemma.

"Do sit down and have some tea," Smitty said. "I trust you received my invitation to dinner."

"Yes, I did. Thank you very much."

"I hope further lionizing won't embarrass you, Danny," Smitty began. "I also hope it won't turn your head," she added teasingly. "I got the letter off to your family. I'm sure they'll be proud."

"That was very kind of you, Lady Smith-Croydon."

"Smitty."

"Smitty. You must be wondering why I asked to see you."

"Needless to say." Her tone hardened just a bit.

"I don't really know how to put any of this. I guess you don't care about being articulate until the time comes when you wish you were."

"Amanda, perhaps you'd better leave us."

"I think it would be better if Amanda stayed." Smitty looked puzzled but said nothing. "However I phrase it, it's going to sound... blunt, but I don't know any—your granddaughter and I met at Doctor's Cave last year, and... and we fell in love." He might as well have been speaking to a statue. There was not a whisper of reaction from Smitty. "We're still very much in love, and I've come to ask your permission for us to become formally engaged."

Smitty stared at the young man imperturbably. She did not even glance at Amanda. "I take it you have not come here on a sudden impulse."

"No."

"Then I may further assume that you and my granddaughter have been seeing each other... privately... since last year."

"Yes, we have."

"And neither of you has seen fit to inform me of this situation?"

"We were afraid you'd disapprove and send Amanda away."

"I was under the impression we have been honoring you for your bravery. Is there some reason I should disapprove?"

"No, Lady Smith-Croydon, there isn't."

"Then I fail to understand your reluctance to have come to me before this. If there is truly no reason for my disapproval, you ought to have had nothing to fear."

"We thought you might think I was unworthy of Amanda."

"Are you unworthy of her?"

"No, I'm not."

"You can't be very confident of that. If you believe yourself to be worthy, surely you could not think I would feel otherwise."

"It's possible that. . . that your standards are different from mine."

"Yes, it's possible. But before we discuss that, would you kindly tell me the circumstances under which you and my granddaughter have been seeing each other."

"We've seen each other only when Amanda could come to Doctor's Cave."

"You've seen each other at the beach? That hardly seems a sound basis for an engagement."

"We were away from each other for months, and when we saw each other again, nothing had changed. We've known each other for a year."

"Known each other? A few furtive meetings on a beach under public scrutiny and then a separation of several months, and you think you know each other?"

"We do, Lady Smith-Croydon. We know each other and love each other very much."

"Considering the facts of the matter, I do not believe that is possible. You do not know each other's friends or families. You know nothing of each other's lives or customs or backgrounds. Your brief and insular meetings on a beach could not possibly have given you such insights."

"From what we do know, we're sure we're in love. We simply want your permission to see each other openly and freely so that we can learn all there is to learn about each other."

"I think you've waited rather too long to ask. And if you were to learn all there is to learn about each other, you would find that my granddaughter is an English girl of the upper class, who is accustomed to the comforts and privileges and luxuries that rank affords. No doubt she is willing at the moment to forgo them in the future. Such assets are easily given up when one has no knowledge of life without them. But perhaps I am presuming. Are you in a position to give Amanda the kind of life to which she is both entitled and accustomed?"

"No. As you know, I'm still in college. But I have an offer of a well-paying job with a brokerage firm in New York when I graduate. My prospects for a very successful future with that firm are excellent. Of course we wouldn't even consider marriage until such time as I was settled in that job."

"You have come upon a difference in our standards. We are not accustomed to giving our female children away in marriage to men who have only 'prospects for the future.' We expect them to be secure in the present. You must know that upon coming of age Amanda will come into a great deal of money."

"I hope you aren't suggesting that—"

"I am not suggesting for one moment that you are a fortune hunter. I do not believe you are. I do not believe Amanda's fortune is of any consideration to you. I merely wish to point out that a wealthy wife and a financially struggling husband are basically incompatible. In fact, I do not believe there is a single recognizable area in which you *are* compatible—except that you love each other, a consideration that is not to be overlooked. However, the kind of love that overcomes all obstacles is the kind that comes out of long and intimate association, and you have not had that. I should like to know more about the association you have had. Am I really expected to believe that in the time you've known each other, you have never been together except at Doctor's Cave?"

Without meaning to, Danny and Amanda exchanged glances. The exchange did not escape Smitty. They both knew that an outright lie at this point would destroy whatever meager chances were left.

"We were together once recently...in Kingston," Danny answered.

"With Kaye," Amanda added hastily, hoping to prove the innocence of the meeting.

Lady Smith-Croydon stiffened. Her face was set as if it were granite, and she turned to Amanda for the first time since Danny had come into the room. She stared at her implacably for a moment, then turned her gaze back to Danny. She did not speak.

Amanda went on. "Grandmother, Kaye was with us almost every minute, and when she wasn't with us, we went for long walks together through Kingston. We all met again for dinner, and afterward we retired to our separate rooms. There was no more to it than that. You pointed out yourself that we couldn't have got to know each other sitting on the beach at Doctor's Cave. We *had* to have some time alone together. We had to."

"I don't suppose it's worth much now," Danny said, "but we both hated deceiving you, and I certainly couldn't have accepted the honor of your dinner party without your knowing the truth."

Smitty looked at them both again, turning her head slowly from one to the other. "I have never understood why confessed liars expect to be believed forever from the moment of their confession."

"We aren't lying, grandmother," Amanda pleaded. "Even Lady Alice will vouch for Danny's honor and truthfulness in this."

Smitty's head jerked toward Amanda, and her face flushed fiercely. "What does Alice know of this?" she demanded.

"She knew nothing until recently. Kaye asked her to

invite Danny to dinner at Traymore so that she could meet him and see that he was all the wonderful things Kaye said he was."

"And Alice did this?" Smitty asked slowly and quietly.

"Yes."

"When?"

"It was on the evening of the day Danny saved Jennifer Brent."

"I see," Smitty said. She stood up then, and Danny stood up with her. "I would have been reluctant to give my approval to this engagement on the basis of your utter incompatibility. I would have been further inclined to withhold it in consideration of your background and financial insecurity, Mr. Riordan. Your deceiving me about your meetings at Doctor's Cave is unspeakable. Your illicit tryst in Kingston, arranged by Kaye Belliston, and your flagrant underhandedness and defiance of what you knew to be my wishes are unforgivable. But your enlisting the aid of my dearest and oldest and most cherished friend in your filthy conspiracy is despicable and contemptible beyond my comprehension. You, young man, are to leave this house at once, and you are never to see or speak to my granddaughter again. I assure you there is no use in your resorting to any of your treacherous methods; she will be in England within forty-eight hours. I will thank you to get out."

Danny looked helpless and defeated. He glanced at Amanda for a moment, then turned and left the house.

"Grandmother—"

"I will never forgive you. Now come with me."

KAYE AND AUNT ALICE were in the sitting room, listening with great intensity to a local news report on the radio. Neither of them had spoken since the newscast had begun. The voice on the radio was entirely calm and controlled.

"The storm, which has just reached hurricane pro-
portions, is now located approximately six hundred
miles southeast of Jamaica. It has winds of up to one
hundred twenty-five miles per hour and is traveling
northwest at a speed of fifteen miles per hour. On its
present course it is expected to pass seventy-five
miles southwest of the island some time between
8:00 A.M. and noon on Friday. Its course is not
entirely predictable. Any deviations in its direction
will be reported immediately. And now a report
from. . . ."

Aunt Alice switched off the radio.

"That sounds threatening," Kaye said.

"Possibly. As a rule they pass either to the northeast or
the southwest of the island, so we don't usually get them.
They are treacherous, of course. They can change direction very quickly and very erratically."

"Wouldn't it be safest, then, to get off the island?"

"Oh, dear me, no. Actually, I mean yes it would be
safest. But if we ran for Florida every time a tropical
storm came by, we'd turn into commuters. In any event,
we have plenty of time. That is, you have."

"I don't understand."

"If there were the slightest danger, I would expect you
to get on a plane for Miami, but I'm among the diehards
who sit them out."

"You mean you'd stay here in Montego even if you
knew a hurricane was going to hit?"

"Oh, yes. In all my years here there's been only one
that we felt was really dangerous. Alex was alive then,
and even he couldn't talk me into leaving. *He* was staying, of course, but he wanted me to go. We argued for
three days. We were still arguing when a palm tree came
crashing down on the house, and then it was too late to

leave. It was very frightening, but we had a gay old time—Alex and I and the servants, all huddled in the—"

At that moment Smitty burst into the room, her face set in a grim expression. Amanda was just behind her, looking pale and agitated.

"Smitty!" Alice said in astonishment.

"Do you know why I'm here, Alice?"

"Yes, I think I do."

"Then you also knew that Danny Riordan was having tea with me today?"

"Smitty, sit down and—"

"Did you or didn't you know that?"

"Yes, I knew."

"Then I am to believe everything I was told today?"

"I don't know what you were told. If you would sit down—"

"I will not sit down. Simply tell me one thing: you've known about this...liaison between Amanda and the Riordan boy since the day the Brent girl was rescued at Doctor's Cave?"

"Yes, Smitty, I knew."

Smitty looked sad suddenly. "If there is some reason why you haven't told me, I will listen to it."

"I was as shocked as you must have been when I was told what had been going on. But I have the utmost faith in my niece, and—"

"In your niece—who arranged the shoddy lovers' meeting in Kingston?"

"It was not a shoddy lovers' meeting."

"Oh? Were you there? Do you know?"

"I was not there. I didn't know about it until after it had occurred."

"I am happy to hear that."

"But I know that Kaye would not arrange an illicit meeting between two young people, particularly when one of them was the granddaughter of my dearest friend, and I am entirely satisfied that the incident was utterly innocent and free of any wrongdoing."

Smitty smiled bitterly and said, "Sufficiently satisfied that you saw fit not to tell me of it."

"Smitty, I agreed to have the young man to dinner on the condition that if I found him wanting in any way, I would go to you and inform you of the entire affair."

"Thereby usurping my privilege of deciding with whom my granddaughter should or should not consort."

"Yes, I suppose I did do that."

"And having, in the most high-handed manner, given your approval, you did not even come to me and tell me that. You allowed the affair to go on behind my back. By what prerogative of friendship did you come to that decision?"

"Smitty, the life-saving incident had already happened that very day, and while I was trying to decide what was best to do, Danny was suddenly made a hero. I did and I do approve of him. I think he's a fine young man."

"He's a liar and a cheat and a deceiver."

"Only in the name of love."

"I have never known you to believe that the end justifies the means. That two infatuated adolescents could be led to such low behavior is almost understandable—that is, if one disregards principles. But that you could have had a hand in it—this I find unbelievable... and inexcusable."

"It was all my fault," Kaye said.

"I would be the first to agree with that. But this is now between your aunt and me. I will thank you to keep out of it."

"Will you believe," Alice added, "that I did what I did out of love for you?"

"No, I will not believe that, Alice. You betrayed me. It

is quite bad enough that you allowed me to make a fool of myself lionizing a young man you knew was seducing my granddaughter behind my back, but that you could put your own silly romantic notions and your own opinions above your duty and your loyalty to me has wounded me more deeply than I could have ever believed possible. Aside from my incessant gadding about, for which I care nothing, I had nothing left in life except our unquestioned and unquestionable friendship, and you have destroyed that. I will not deign even to offer an opinion of your niece's invidious behavior. I do not ever wish to see you again, Alice. Goodbye.''

She turned and left the room, and Amanda followed without a word.

''Oh, Aunt Alice! This is all my—''

''Hush, Kaye.'' Kaye could see the tears in her aunt's eyes. ''Everything Smitty said is just, and I deserve every word of it. She's right. It has nothing to do with you; it's between her and me. But I'm afraid it may kill her...and me, as well. I'm going to my room now.''

# CHAPTER TWELVE

THE EVENING YAWNED before Kaye like a chasm. Aunt Alice was in a state of private agony upon which she could not intrude, an agony to which she had contributed a significant amount. She was not such a fool as to accept the total blame for what had happened—much of it had been pure accident—but she had brought Aunt Alice into the situation, and that had caused the confrontation with Smitty, and for that much she had to accept the blame and the guilt.

But her great concern now was for Aunt Alice. When Smitty had taken away her friendship, she had somehow also taken away Alice's strength. She had to help her, but she sensed that Aunt Alice was in seclusion from her as much as from anybody. Her only possible ally was Helen.

She started to ring for her, then thought better of it. She went through the hall and into the kitchen. Helen looked at her with an astonished expression.

"Helen, may I speak with you, please? It's very important."

Helen looked at the two girls who were the kitchen staff, then followed Kaye through the hall and out onto the veranda.

"Helen, I'm very worried about my aunt."

"Yes, she is not good."

"You probably know her better than I do. What should I do?" Helen was not accustomed to being asked for advice in such matters, and she seemed embarrassed. "Please tell me."

"I don't know. I think she is sick inside, in the spirit."

"Yes, you're right. Should I go to her?"

"No, not yet. I will give her some soup tonight—soup with herbs. I will try to fool her, but she will know. She will eat it because I will insist. If she is better, you should come and see her. If she is not better...."

"What, Helen?"

"You call the doctor, Dr. Burgoyne from Montego. He comes to her when she needs him."

"Shouldn't I do that now?"

"No, it is too soon. The soup will make her sleep. If it is the same in the morning, you should call Dr. Burgoyne."

"But if she's ill, Helen, maybe I should start trying immediately to get her to a hospital—here or in Miami."

Helen's face clouded, and she looked away from Kaye, out over the garden toward the bay and the sea.

"She would not go to Miami now, and soon it will be too late for Miami." She pointed in the direction in which she was looking. "You see?"

Kaye turned and gazed out over the bay. There was a rim of blue-gray just above the horizon. It was not a cloud or a mist. It was simply a thin line of color, different from the clear azure blue of the sky.

"The storm," Helen said.

"Yes, I know about the storm, but it's supposed to pass south of us."

"It will do what it wants. Soon there will be no boats, no airplanes."

"Then I have to get my aunt out of here. I have to—"

"She won't go. We must wait until after the soup. Then I will come to you and tell you how she is."

"All right, I'll do whatever you say."

"Do not worry. Lady Armstrong has courage."

"Yes. Yes, she has. Thank you, Helen, thank you very much."

She watched Helen go back into the house, grateful that she was there. Then she turned and looked out over the sea again. That band of blue-gray rimmed the horizon, and she noticed for the first time that the sea had changed color. It was no longer the dazzling sapphire blue that had greeted her every morning. It had darkened to a dull gray, the color of metal, and it was dotted with tiny peaks of white froth. The boats anchored in the harbor far below bobbed something less than gently, as if they were annoyed by the water that lapped at their hulls. She could not remember being so lonely and depressed.

Suddenly she thought of Creighton. She turned and almost started into the drawing room to the telephone, but she realized that that, too, was useless. "Let's not say goodbye just yet," she had said. Maybe there was yet to be a goodbye, and maybe there wasn't. He might already be gone, for all she knew. *How I want him!* she said to herself, folding her arms across her breasts and hugging herself against the despair. *If only he were holding me in his arms, I could face all the rest of it.* It was just one more thing that couldn't be. She couldn't attend Aunt Alice. She couldn't nurse her or comfort her. She couldn't mend the rift between her and Smitty. She couldn't bring Amanda and Danny back together. She had helped create this chaos, but there was nothing she could do about it.

She went back into the house and arranged with Helen to be served dinner on a tray in her room, then she went upstairs and took a bath. She tried to nap, but it was fruitless. She put on a thin cotton robe and went out onto the balcony and stood for a long time, looking down at the garden. The sky was darkening earlier than usual, and the horizontal line of blue-gray seemed to be widoning. The sea was a murky gray, still frothed with white. The scene fit her mood.

At eight Helen carried in her tray. She put it on the low table in front of the settee.

"I have brought you cold chicken and salad—and soup," Helen said.

"With herbs?" Kaye asked teasingly.

Helen smiled and answered, "Soup—with no herbs."

"Thank you, Helen. How is my aunt?"

"She has eaten—only a little, but enough. She will sleep now. I know you would like to see her, but it is better to wait."

"I know you're right, but I'm so worried about her."

"Tomorrow we will see. I will be watchful tonight."

"What would I do without you?"

"You will be all right. Good night."

Kaye ate only a little of her dinner. When she had finished, she switched on the portable radio. She did not have to wait for what she wanted to hear. There was nothing on the station but news of the storm.

"...constantly. Weather instruments have now clocked the hurricane's gusts at one hundred eighty-five miles per hour, making it the most dangerous Caribbean storm of the century. Its speed has accelerated to twenty miles per hour, and it is expected to be in our area a few hours after dawn on Friday. For a short time its direction changed erratically to the southwest, but it has now veered north again. It is expected that its first contact with land will be over the southwest coast of Cuba, but due to the unpredictability of the storm, the weather service has posted hurricane warnings for the entire island of Jamaica. Evacuation from the island is strongly recommended. Where that is not possible, coastal residents are urged to move to high-ground inland sites. Stay tuned for further instructions.''

At nine-thirty the telephone rang. Kaye picked up the extension in her room after the first ring, hoping to prevent Aunt Alice's being disturbed. It was George Montague.

''Kaye? How are you?''

''I'm all right, George.''

''Have you had an opportunity to see Creighton?''

''Yes. I'm afraid it accomplished nothing. He's going ahead with his plans to leave.''

''I'm sorry. It was a long shot, but I thought it was worth it.''

''I did try, George. You can't know how hard I tried. But he is absolutely adamant.''

''He's a stubborn man.''

''It's more than that.''

''I know. It must be. Have you and Lady Alice made arrangements to leave?''

''To leave Montego?''

''Yes, to leave Jamaica. The odds are against the hurricane's hitting us directly, but if it does, the results could be disastrous.''

''I'm afraid my aunt wouldn't be able to leave in any case. I'm afraid she's too ill to make any kind of move.''

''Have you had a doctor in?''

''No, Helen seems to be in control of the situation. If Aunt Alice isn't better in the morning, we're going to call Dr. Burgoyne.''

"I would suggest you call him tonight. Or better yet, let me call him. He's an old schoolmate of mine and a close friend. By tomorrow he's going to be completely caught up in preparations for the storm, whether it hits us or not, and it would be better to have him there and not need him than to need him and not be able to get him. With your permission I'll make arrangements for him to be at Traymore at nine tomorrow."

"Oh, George, thank you. I'm sure that would be very wise."

"Are you really all right?"

"I don't think I know. The whole world seems to be falling apart."

"You mustn't feel abandoned."

"But I do. If only Creighton—"

"I know. In any case, I'm back in Montego for now. I'll be moving around a good deal, and it will be difficult for you to reach me. I'll telephone when I can."

"Thank you, George. I feel terribly alone here with Aunt Alice."

"You won't be. People will be banding together soon. They will all be struck by hurricane fever, and they will take comfort from the fact that there's safety in numbers. In the meantime, Henry will know what precautions should be taken."

"You've been very kind to me, and I'm grateful."

"I consider you a friend. You must try to get some sleep. Tomorrow is likely to be a very busy day for us all."

"I will. Thank you again for all your help. Good night."

Kaye tried to sleep then—without much success. She dozed off for short periods of time but always awoke suddenly, either from a dream or from the furious rushing noise of the wind. The last time she awoke it was to the sounds of hammering on the floor below. It was daylight.

She dressed hurriedly and went downstairs to find Henry and Helen and the rest of the staff nailing sheets of plywood to all the windows. While Henry was explaining that this was the first precautionary step against the storm, Dr. Burgoyne arrived. He was a short stocky man with a cheerful professional manner that did not hide a certain anxiety about the demands being made on his time. Kaye took him upstairs to Aunt Alice's room immediately and, after saying good-morning, left her alone with the doctor.

Dr. Burgoyne came downstairs again after half an hour. He found Kaye doing what she could to help with the precautions and took her aside. He was necessarily quite direct.

"Miss Belliston, there is no cause for alarm. I have been attending your aunt for some years now, and she is remarkably healthy for a woman of her age. She is obviously under some kind of stress, about which I did not have time to question her; perhaps you already know its source. She seems quite exhausted. This is a bad time for me to tell you that she should rest and be kept quiet, but I'm afraid that is my prescription. I've given her some mild tranquilizers. The dosage is on the vial I left with her. If the behavior of the storm makes it necessary to move her to some presumably safer place, it is perfectly all right, as long as she is moved with a minimum of discomfort. If I know Lady Alice, and I do, she will want to take part in the preparations for the storm. You must prevent that. If you do, she should be well again in a few days. I'm sorry I can't be more specific, but she is not physically sick. There's no cause for you to worry."

"Thank you, doctor. I'll do everything I can to keep her calm and quiet."

"Then there should be no further problems. I'll check with you as soon as I can, but I can't guarantee when that will be. I must get back to town now."

"I can't tell you how much I appreciate your coming."

"Your aunt is a very special patient. Goodbye for now."

Kaye was on her way upstairs when the telephone rang. She answered it in the drawing room.

"Hello."

"Kaye, it's Creighton. There's no time to talk about us. I've been in touch with the weather service, and the latest information is that the hurricane has changed course twice and is now headed straight for Jamaica. It could change again, of course, but we now have to assume that we are going to get the brunt of the storm. A large number of people protecting one place is far superior to individual families trying to hold their own in their own homes. Penrose is nine hundred and fifty feet above the bay—the highest of all the substantial houses. It's also the only one made completely of stone. It will be safest. There's no telling how long there will be telephone communication, so it's important that we begin now to get in touch with as many people as possible. I've made a list of those for you to contact. Have you pencil and paper?"

"Yes, right here by the phone."

"I want you to call the Marlowes."

"Yes, the Marlowes."

"And the Zimmermans and the Duckworths. Emphasize to the Zimmermans that at Round Hill they are particularly vulnerable to erosion. The Duckworths will be obstinate. She's going to want to protect her bloody dogs. Tell her the safest place for them is locked in the house—which is true. Tell them all they have until five

P.M. to board up their house and take whatever other precautions they can, then they must get to Penrose. If for any reason they can't do that, tell them to stay put, and we'll come and get them. And this is important: you must tell them that they are to open their houses as refuge to all the natives in the immediate area. Their tin-roofed shanties will be blown away like balsa wood. Those invited cannot bring any of their staff or their Jamaican neighbors to Penrose. I already have a hundred persons scheduled to be billeted here, and I'm trying to arrange to shuttle as many more people as possible from the low-lying areas. Have you got all that?''

"Yes, I'll start immediately."

"Good. Make the calls, and before you do anything else, bring Alice here to Penrose. Don't brook any argument from her. If she insists on taking Henry and/or Helen, it's all right."

"I think they'll want to stay at Traymore."

"Probably, but get Alice here as soon as possible. And come with her. There's work for you to do."

"I will."

"To hell with the work. I want you here—with me."

"And I want to be there—with you."

"If I'm not in when you arrive, make Alice comfortable and stay here until I come back or call you. Promise me that."

"I promise."

"I love you."

"I love you, too."

Suddenly the emptiness that had been assailing her for the past two days was gone. She had a compelling sense of purpose. She was needed, and all her strength came flooding back to her. She realized instantly it was not only her own strength—Creighton's strength seemed to be flowing into her.

She looked up the Marlowes' number and dialed it. Netty answered.

"Hello?" she said, and the nervousness was apparent, even in that one word.

"Netty, it's Kaye Belliston."

"Oh, Kaye. Are you all right?"

"Of course I'm all right."

"We're having a dreadful time. The storm—"

"I want you to listen to me, Netty. The safest thing for all of us is to be in one place. Now—"

"Harlan was saying that very thing just—"

"We're all going to Creighton's to ride out the hurricane. You must board up your house and do whatever else you can. Then by five you and Harlan must get to Penrose. Bring no one with you, but make it clear to all your people and all your neighbors that your house is theirs as a haven against the storm."

"Yes, of course. We would have done that—"

"Do you understand, Netty?"

"Yes, completely. We're to be at Creighton's before five."

"Good. I'll see you there."

She hung up and dialed the Zimmermans. Herman answered, and she explained the plan to him. She finished with, "Creighton said something about probable erosion at Round Hill. I don't know what that means, but I assume you do."

"I sure do. Thank God somebody's behaving sensibly. We're all boarded up. We can leave anytime."

"I think the sooner, the better. He strongly suggested that we turn our houses over to the servants and—"

"It's already done. We've had a steady stream of people moving in since eight."

"You're wonderful. I'll see you at Penrose as soon as I can get Aunt Alice ready to leave. Goodbye."

She called the Duckworths with far less confidence.

"Maude, this is Kaye Belliston."

"Oh, Kaye how are you?" she said as calmly as if Kaye were calling about a dinner party.

"I'm all right. We're all going to go to Creighton's to ride out the storm. Can you and Phillip get there?"

"Well, of course we could get there, my dear, but it's quite out of the question. First of all, there may not even be a storm, and second, if there is, I couldn't possibly leave my babies. Lady Priscilla is particularly afraid of storms. She always—"

"Maude, is Phillip there?"

He had already snatched the telephone out of his wife's hand.

"Hello. Who's this?"

"It's Kaye Belliston, Phillip. Creighton wants us all to go to Penrose to get through the storm."

"Damned sensible idea. Strongest house in Montego. Highest, too. We're almost finished battening down here." His voice became more distant as he turned away from the phone. "The bloody dogs will be fine, Maude." Then he was back. "When are we to go to Penrose?"

"As soon as you're ready. I'll see you there."

"Good show. Thank God for Creighton. Would have organized it myself twenty years earlier."

"I'm sure you would have. You're going to be a great help."

"I'm certainly going to try. Thank you for calling."

Kaye went upstairs to Aunt Alice's room. She knocked gently and opened the door. Aunt Alice was propped up against the pillows, looking somewhat less frail.

"How are you, darling?"

"I'm perfectly all right. I can't think why anyone sent for Dr. Burgoyne. I am not ill."

"I know you're not, and I'm glad you're not, because we're all going to Creighton's to weather the storm."

"I knew it would come to that. Perfectly sensible, of course, but I can't go there."

"Why not?"

"How can I accept the hospitality of a man I've banished from my own house?"

"I don't think that matters now."

"It matters to me."

"If everyone were coming here, would you exclude Creighton?"

"Of course not."

"It's the same thing. We've all got to pull together in this. Besides, if you don't go, I'm sure Creighton will come and get you."

Aunt Alice chuckled. "Yes, he would do that. I suppose you're right. Help me get my things together. Of course, it could be such a fuss over nothing."

"I think you know better than that."

"It's whistling in the dark, my dear. I was hoping you didn't know how bad it might be. If a hurricane with 185-mile-an-hour winds comes within fifty miles of here, we're in for it. If it hits directly, well...."

Aunt Alice threw back the covers and almost sprang out of bed. It was clear to Kaye that adversity was a companion to her aunt. It was medicine to her spirit— perhaps the only medicine there was.

Half an hour later Kaye was unnecessarily helping Aunt Alice into the Rolls.

"Now, Henry," Aunt Alice was saying, "you can stay with us at Penrose, or you can come back here, whichever you choose. It's entirely up to you."

"I'll come back here, Lady Alice. This is home."

"I knew you'd say that. You've told your family and friends to come to Traymore?"

"They're on the way, Lady Alice."

"Good. Well—" she looked out at the house "—goodbye, old girl. Alex's ghost will protect you and all within. Aren't you coming, Kaye?"

"I'm going to follow in the Morgan. I have a feeling we may need all the transportation we can get."

"Good thinking, girl! Drive on, Henry."

When they arrived at Penrose, Creighton was standing in the driveway, wearing jodhpurs and riding boots and a shirt darkened in patches by sweat. He also had on his Australian cavalry hat, and he carried a clipboard. He was directing the comings and going of a motley array of vehicles: Jeeps, Land Rovers, trucks, jalopies and elegant private automobiles. They carried what seemed to be tons of supplies: tinned food, flashlights, batteries, radios, plywood, sandbags, tools, blankets and water in every conceivable kind of container. Kaye pulled up in the Morgan as Aunt Alice was getting out of the Rolls. Creighton saw them immediately and reluctantly took a break from his frantic activities.

"Alice," he said. "I'm so relieved you're here."

"So am I, dear boy." With a twinkle in her eyes she added, "When I told you you were not welcome at Traymore, you will remember that I said nothing about my being welcome at Penrose."

"Is it any port in a storm, Alice?"

"Something like that. What can I do?"

"You can go inside and find yourself a comfortable bedroom, where you will stay until—"

"Creighton, don't make me feel useless."

"All right, then. Go upstairs and get yourself settled, then come down again and start organizing a first-aid station—the sitting room nearest the kitchen, I think. It's close to hot water and linens. Have someone make a sign so that anyone arriving with medical supplies will know where to take them. Commandeer people to help you. Raid the medicine chests in all the bathrooms for whatever they might yield. Enough to start with?''

"Oh, yes. How I love a fight!''

"You may not love this one if the enemy becomes as bad as they say it might.''

"Creighton, I am not taking this lightly. It's just that it's good to feel needed again.''

"You're always needed, Alice. Get to it.''

Alice hurried off toward the house, and Creighton turned to see Kaye standing by his side. He stared into her eyes for a brief moment, then took her by the shoulders and pulled her close to him. He kissed her almost fiercely.

"There isn't going to be time to talk or be together— not for a while, at least. I love you very much. Do you think you can drive the Rover?''

"Yes.''

"Go inside and help Alice get started on the first-aid station, then come back here to me. There are going to be endless trips down to the bay to pick up supplies and transport people inland and up into the hills. And for God's sake, bring water anytime you can find it. It may be days after the storm before there's an unpolluted water supply. We're stashing it in the shed next to the stables. There's to be no unnecessary use of even a drop of it. No cooling off, no bathing, not even drinking until you're parched. Did you get hold of the people I asked you to call?''

"Yes, all of them. They're on the way here.''

"Including the Duckworths?''

"Yes. Maude was as we expected her to be, but Phillip took her in hand. Creighton, what about Smitty?''

He frowned. "She won't come. She said something cryptic about not needing the help of those who had already abandoned her. I haven't a bloody notion what she was talking about, but there wasn't time to argue. Anyway, her house should be fairly secure. Let's hope there are people there to see to what has to be done. Are you all right?''

''Yes, perfectly. I guess I'm a chip off the block of my aunt. I love a fight. . .and I love you.''

A spark almost of passion fired Creighton's amber eyes. He touched her hair and said, ''It will be all over soon.''

''And then?''

''Let's just get through this.''

The day went so quickly that it was dark before Kaye expected it to be. Penrose looked as if it were under siege. Everything that might be damaged by the storm was either tied down or surrounded by sandbags. There was no time to count, but Kaye estimated that there were more than two hundred people on the estate. The Zimmermans and the Marlowes arrived and immediately went to work, as did the houseguests they brought with them. The Duckworths were the last to come. Maude muttered constantly about her Great Danes until Phillip assigned her to helping Alice in the first-aid station. She quickly forgot her dogs and her house and everything else as she rolled bandages and neatly shelved the meager supply of medicines. Everyone seemed to have a job. Creighton barked assignments to every new arrival, and those he missed found useful employment for themselves. Kaye made at least ten trips into town in the Rover. The chaos in Montego stood in her mind in stark comparison to the order at Penrose. There was no Creighton in town, and the people there, panicked by the wind and the churning gray sea and darkened sky, scurried about finding protection for themselves without regard for the general good. Yet there were pockets

of order brought about by the police and men like
George Montague, who seemed to be everywhere at
once. She saw him directing traffic in a cobblestone
square, helping to board up the post office, herding a
family into shelter.

It was there in town that the full sense of danger came
upon Kaye. The once serene jewel-blue bay was now
nature's weapon. Nine-foot waves lashed the coast,
tossing moored boats about like toys and crashing
against buildings that clearly could not long endure. The
air was filled with unlikely debris—garbage cans, chairs,
mattresses, chains, planks, posters, shards of glass,
clothing—all lifted and carried by the relentless wind.
Tall stately palm trees were bent almost to the ground
and seemed to be screaming in pain. On her last trip,
during a dusk indistinguishable from the rest of the gray
day, the storm surge, a gigantic wall of ocean water that
the hurricane pushed ahead of it, hit the coast. Trees
were uprooted and buildings were washed away. The
water rose to the level of the windows of abandoned
automobiles and flooded all the low-lying buildings that
had not been destroyed by the surge.

On her way back to Penrose, driving the winding
roads up the mountain, Kaye was afraid—and not without reason—that the Land Rover would be blown off
the road. She was fighting not only the coming darkness
and the tortuous path, but the wind, which was like a
great, pounding, incessant wave. When she pulled into
the driveway, she knew she could not go down the
mountain again until the storm had passed.

The sky, which for hours had been the color of charcoal, began to blacken. Kaye barely noticed the subtle
change from day into night. Penrose was an armed
camp—not armed against a human enemy but against
nature itself. Thanks mainly to Creighton, it was now

an oasis of calm. Every inch of floor space was occupied by the storm's refugees. The stable and all the other out-buildings had become home for countless families dispossessed by the storm. Cauldrons of soup steamed in the kitchen, and the hungry came by in neat files with no visible sense of urgency.

It was an hour before Kaye was able to unwind and feel in touch with the gentle harmony of Penrose. All at once she realized she had forgotten about Aunt Alice and Smitty and Amanda and Danny, and all at once she was aware of the absence of the one person she had not forgotten through all the hours of the hectic day. Where was Creighton? She was standing in the downstairs hall, surrounded by people who were coming and going with a sense of purpose. She seemed suddenly to have no pur-pose of her own beyond the waiting. Then she felt an arm around her shoulder, and she knew Creighton was with her.

"You must be exhausted," he said.

"No. I suppose I should be, but I'm not."

"Have you eaten?"

"No, I don't think I want to."

"All right, come with me."

He took her hand and led her outside toward the pool. They walked around the pool to the far side, where there was a view of the bay. She had been looking at Creighton constantly and hadn't noticed the transfor-mation that had taken place. When they were standing by the bougainvillea-covered wrought-iron fence be-tween them and the precipitous fall of land that dropped steeply toward the bay, she became aware of the eerie stillness. Not a leaf fluttered. There was not the faintest breeze. Overhead the sky was dark blue and dotted with myriad stars. There were still some lights on the crescent-shaped harbor, and they spread their glow on the placid sea. The world seemed to be caught in a great calm.

"Creighton, it's so beautiful. Has the storm passed us?"

"No. This calm is the surest indication that the hurricane is near. It will strike sometime after daylight. It will be terrible."

"I'm afraid."

"You'd be a fool if you weren't. All we can do, all of us, is keep our heads and try to help one another."

"Will you stay near me?"

"I'll try to. There'll be a great deal to be done. It's strange how the magnitude of a natural disaster reduces everything else to trivia. It makes truth seem necessary. It makes truth essential, because there may not be another chance for it. I'm going to tell you the truth now, without regard for the consequences. The first, the basic truth is that I love you."

"And I love you with all my heart."

"I know I've seemed cruel and brutal, and I've hated myself for it. Now I want you to understand. In our childhood there was a vicious rivalry between Adrian and me. I didn't create it. In fact, I tried desperately to destroy it, but I couldn't. I was everything our father wanted in a son, and Adrian was everything he hated. As he reached out to me, to the exclusion of Adrian, our mother went almost irrationally in the other direction. She embraced Adrian, completely blind to his weakness and treachery. While he was in college, he nurtured his appetites to the wildest excesses. He needed money desperately. With the help of a dishonest speculator in London, he forged ownership papers and began to sell off hundreds of acres of our father's land in Australia. It wasn't long before I found out what he was doing. I went to him and offered to help him make restitution if he would stop. He refused. I know now he wanted to be discovered; it was all part of his plan. I had no choice but to go to father and tell him what was happening. I did not know that all the ownership papers and other documents in the illegal transactions bore my signature, expertly forged by Adrian's accomplice. He had a dozen witnesses, all bribed, to testify that it was I who had sold the land. Our father believed my version of the story, but our mother clung to her illusions of Adrian's virtue. I still don't know if my father's fatal heart attack was attributable to Adrian's disloyalty, but before he died, he wrote Adrian out of his will. My father left a trust for mother sufficient to support her comfortably for the rest of her life. Everything else went to me—all the land, all the investments, millions of dollars.

"Adrian, of course, had gone to mother with all the forged documents and convinced her that it was I who had committed the crime. From that day, she has refused to see me or even speak to me. My letters during the next two years were returned unopened. That's why I came to Montego and started a new life. I'm sure you've been told I have no family. I've preferred it that way. Even Alice doesn't know my mother is still alive. And that is the supreme irony. You see, if I don't give money to Adrian when he demands it, if I don't do exactly as he tells me to do, he will go to mother and tell her the truth. He will tell her that through all these years of hating and ostracizing me, she has been punishing the wrong son. He'll tell her it's been he who has cheated her and lied to her and deceived her. And that truth will kill her. There is simply no doubt about that. I'm sure you find it unthinkable, but Adrian is quite capable of it, and he has told me he will do just that if I try to make any kind of life with you. I offered him everything I own to get out of my life, but if he accepted and I married you, he could extort money from you through his threat to me. You see, there is no way out. So I'm leaving Montego; I'm leaving you."

The silence of the night held them for a long time as they stood hand in hand. In the cool clarity of the dark, Kaye saw the truth for the first time. There were no answers to what Creighton had said. There was no forbidding him what he had to do. There seemed to Kaye to be nothing but emptiness.

"Why didn't you tell me earlier?"

"Because I was sure Adrian would find out I'd told you and go straight to mother. I couldn't take that chance. Do you understand that?"

"Yes, of course. Yet it would have been easier if I'd known."

"I know it would have, but there was nothing I could do about it. Adrian has reduced me to helplessness, and it's tortured me. That, too, is what Adrian wanted—to torture me out of his insane hatred of me. And how he's succeeded—never so much as in these past few weeks."

"And have you told me now because you think the hurricane might kill us all?"

"No. I've told you now because I trust you and love you; I've told you because I couldn't bear the burden alone any longer and because I believe your knowing will make it less painful for you. With just a little luck and a lot of hard work we'll survive the hurricane."

"And then?"

"I'll have the same options I have now. I'll still have to leave."

"And we'll never see each other again."

"No, we won't. Find somebody to love, Kaye. You're so worth loving."

"I don't think I can. It's you, only you, forever."

"It's such a waste—for both of us."

"Can we have tonight?"

"Yes. It's little enough to ask."

They went back into the house then and found it as still and quiet as the night. They walked to the bottom of the stairs, where Creighton took Kaye in his arms and held her close to him.

"Go upstairs, darling. I have one last call to make before the lines come down. I'll be there in a few minutes."

Kaye did as he asked without question. She was his now, for however brief a time, and there was no need for questions. As she reached the top of the stairs, she saw Adrian coming in the opposite direction. She was struck dumb at the sight of him. They stood motionless for a moment, Adrian looking down at her.

"The whiskey is downstairs, my dear," he said. "One can hardly get through a night like this without it. Will you join me?"

She started past him without speaking. He reached out and took her by the arm, stopping her. His eyes were clear and strangely sparkling.

"Ah, something has upset you," he said.

"Leave me alone. Please just leave me alone."

"Could it be that Creighton has been talking to you? I suppose it was inevitable that he would have to justify himself, but you mustn't believe the words of a man who is desperate."

There was still the need to protect Creighton. His having told her the truth about Adrian didn't give her license to express her own contempt of him.

"Adrian, I'm very tired, and tomorrow is going to be a very difficult day. I need to get some sleep."

He let go of her arm, and she went on up the stairs and down the hall. She had been in bed only a few minutes when Creighton came into the room.

"I've just talked to Smitty. I begged her to bring her guests over here, but she refused. She asked if you and Alice were here, and when I told her you were, she said she'd rather weather the storm among friends. What's happened between you?"

"You saw Amanda and Danny together in Kingston. You must have figured out that they're in love."

"Yes."

"I'm afraid Aunt Alice and I encouraged them... without telling Smitty any of it. Now she's found out, and she considers us traitors."

"Smitty is a very good friend and a very bad enemy. I'm sorry."

"I'm sorry for Aunt Alice, and I feel very guilty."

"You mustn't. There's hardly time in life for the guilt we deserve. There's no time at all for the made-up kind."

He lay down beside her, and she was soon asleep in his arms. With all that had happened between them and the storm that was about to happen, there was no opportunity, no time, for the intimacy they both longed for. There was time only for the renewal that sleep could bring. There was time at that moment only for survival. After that there could be a future... or there could be nothing.

He was gone when she awoke. She had no idea what time it was. The color and the texture of the day were unlike any she'd known previously. There was a yellow gray light at the windows, and the whole house seemed to be trembling. The wind no longer came in gusts. It was a steady relentless gale that sounded like a roaring locomotive. She hurried downstairs to find hundreds of people engaged in furious activity. She managed to find Christian, who told her that Creighton was in the library. Like every other room in the house, the library was swarming with people. Just as Kaye fought her way through the crowd and into the room, the wind shattered the glass of one of the French doors. The shards of glass were hurled through the room like hundreds of tiny knives to embed themselves in the flesh of those in their path. The sight of the flowing blood threatened panic, but those who were not wounded immediately began to minister to those who were. Above the din Kaye heard Creighton's voice.

"Damn it, I told you to board up those windows! Get more plywood and nail it on from the inside! Push the furniture against them. We've got to keep the bloody storm out there!"

Through the flapping glassless door Kaye saw the devastated garden. The flowers and plants had been torn from the earth. The lawn was littered with fallen trees and wooden debris. Suddenly she saw Wellington, terror-stricken, rearing on his hind legs and neighing at the ferocious wind. Then his whole massive body was blown backward, and he was somersaulted to the ground. He scrambled to his feet and galloped off out of her sight, his mane feathered wildly by the gale. What had been the crystal air was now a mass of water, not rain falling in drops but in a solid sheet, like an airborne river. Survival outside the protection of a building seemed an impossibility.

She heard Creighton calling her name. "Kaye! Kaye!"

She managed to force her way through the swirling sea of people to reach him. He took her by the shoulders roughly. "Are you all right?"

"Yes. What can I do?"

"Go back toward the kitchen and help Alice tend the people who are hurt. It's even worse than we thought it would be. There are twelve-foot waves in the harbor,

and most of the town is under water. George managed
to get here late last night. There was nothing left to do
down there. God knows how many people have died.
Don't for any reason go out of the house. Damn Smitty!
Her stupid pride kept her from coming here, and now
it's too late. A car would be blown off the road. I talked
to her about dawn, just as the storm hit. We were cut
off in the middle of our conversation. The lines blew
down, I expect. I have no idea what kind of preparations they've made there. Well, there's nothing to do
about it now. Go and help Alice.''

"Is that where I'll be of most use?"

"Yes."

"Don't worry about me, Creighton. I can do anything that's needed."

"I know you can, and while you're doing it, it might
be a good idea if you prayed a lot—not only for Smitty,
but for us. I've never seen anything like this.''

Smitty now had less need of prayers than Creighton
imagined. She had had need of them when he had talked
to her at the first light of day, for her mind had been
addled by her loss of Alice, and she had not been very
efficient at coping with the storm. Indeed, her house-
hold might have been wiped out, had it not been for the
help of an unwelcome savior.

But at six-thirty A.M. Danny Riordan had arrived at
Lady Smith-Croydon's house with eight other lifeguards from Doctor's Cave. He walked into a chaos
almost as terrifying as the chaos he had left at the beach.
Smitty was the first person he encountered as he burst
through the front door.

To Danny's amazement, Smitty had the presence of
mind to put her monocle to her eye before she spoke to
him. He was not accustomed to such aplomb in the presence of disaster.

"You are not welcome here, Mr. Riordan," she said. "There is other shelter nearby. We will manage without you."

"I don't need an invitation from you, Smitty. Amanda is here, and whether you like it or not, I'm going to be with her. You can stop me from marrying her, but you can't stop me from saving her life. I'll even save yours if I have to." He turned to the phalanx of young men behind him. "Don't pay any attention to Lady Smith-Croydon. Just secure the house."

The house, like Penrose, was swarming with refugees. Smitty had done that much at least. But they were disorganized and panicked. Danny pushed his way through them and saw Amanda coming out of the drawing room. He went to her and held her in his arms for a moment.

"I want you to find yourself a safe place and just stay there," he said.

"I want to help."

"All right. Try to get these people together and board up all the windows that haven't been done yet. We brought what we could, but I'm afraid it isn't very much. The whole Cave is wiped out. The dormitory blew away right around our ears. If your grandmother isn't going to help, stash her away somewhere."

"I am going to help, young man," Smitty said from behind him. "I am at least as good at this sort of thing as you are. London would never have survived the blitz if I hadn't been there. There are tools and all kinds of equipment in the storeroom behind the kitchen. Go and get them."

Danny took one minute to smile at her. "I really came here because I knew I'd be safer with you than I would anyplace else in Montego. You wouldn't let a little thing like a hurricane upset your routine."

"Just remember, young man, that if a hurricane can't do it, neither can you."

"I'll remember."

Within the next hour Danny and his cohorts had made Smitty's house more secure than she could have imagined. It was not impregnable—no house could be against the terrible force nature had brought to bear on the island—but within that same hour and in the midst of the disruption they were able to share the pots of tea and trays of sandwiches Smitty and the servants had somehow whipped together. There was no truce with the storm, but there was a subtle armistice within the newly assembled family in Smitty's home.

That house was nestled in a tiny valley, sheltered somewhat from the battering of the hurricane. Penrose, perched as it was on the crest of a hill, knew no such protection. The storm was merciless. It tore away the roof of the eastern side of the house, and the entire wing was flooded. The runoff crept through the halls and through the doorways, until most of the rooms were carpeted with murky water. And the rain continued to fall, and the wind blew against hastily erected barriers, which frequently gave way under the buffeting.

Just as there had been a general calm before the storm, there was an interior calm at Penrose. The work that could be done was done. The fury of the storm prevented any further effort. People squatted on the floors, huddled together for what meager comfort they could gain, and watched the world outside being torn apart. There was time now for private thoughts and what private pursuits the isolation would allow. Aunt Alice and Maude Duckworth sat together on a sofa, drinking sherry. George Montague stood at one of the boarded-up French doors, looking out through a crack in the planking at the torrent that, it seemed, would never abate. Phillip Duckworth stood tall as a pine behind his wife, as if he might be able to snatch her out of harm's way should the need arise. Christian stood in attendance in a corner of the room, as if it were teatime and his services might be required. Netty and Harlan, both tattered by their battle against the storm, stood by the bookcases hand in hand. Sylvia and Herman Zimmerman sat on another sofa, dazed by the memory of seeing their lovely house buried by the tons of mud that had slid down the mountain as they drove away in helpless flight. Kaye leaned against the edge of the desk, where Creighton sat with his head in his hands, crushed by the magnitude of the disaster that had beset them all. Ellis hung by Kaye, as though he were guarding her. Adrian, who had been astonishingly capable throughout the emergency, loitered, glass in hand, by the table that held the liquor. He was quite drunk now and made the only sound that could be heard above the howling of the wind.

"Why are you all so glum?" he asked, his speech thickened by alcohol. "You've all done yeoman's work, and we're all safe...at least if the bloody house isn't blown out from under us before it's all over. Oh, I admit it's a bit damp. But it will dry out before long. Which is more than I can say for myself. But then aridity is not a quality especially to be desired, is it? Is it, Creighton? No answer? Well, no matter. I've always found myself the only conversationalist worthy of my own talents. I can talk to myself for days on end and not need another bloody soul for company. It's a handy asset in my business. Which is no business at all." He was like an actor delivering a soliloquy. It was of no consequence whether the audience was listening to him. The sound of his own voice in his own ears was quite enough for him. He continued his oration as he walked uncertainly across the room to a front window from which the storm had torn away part of the protective planking. He picked up a coil of rope on his way. He fingered the rope caressingly as he stood at the window with the rain pelting in on him, soaking his hair and clothes.

"The rain is really quite refreshing. I fear, however, that it's diluting my drink. How has this rope managed to go unused during this great tragedy? Surely it was an oversight on your part, Creighton. There must have been something you could have tied down, or up, with it. I suppose I could hang myself with it so that it doesn't go completely to waste. Would that please you, Creighton? I certainly don't want to give you any trouble...." Suddenly Adrian's face changed. The alcoholic flush drained from his cheeks, and he was as pale as ashes. "Oh, my God! Oh, my God, Creighton! There's a child out there!"

Creighton was by his side in seconds. He saw what Adrian saw. It was not, as he'd suspected it might be, an alcoholic hallucination. There on the far side of the pool, pinned against the bottom of the denuded wrought-iron fence, was a tiny Jamaican boy who could not have been more than ten years old. Most of his clothes had been torn away by the wind. His bleeding arms were locked around the vertical bars of the fence, and only that precarious hold kept him from being blown away. His mouth was open, and he was obviously screaming in terror, though his screams were silent in the rush of the wind.

Before Creighton could move, Adrian had bolted from the room. He ran through the hall and was out the front door by the time Creighton had pulled himself away from the window. From the front doorway Creighton saw Adrian, staggered by the wind and the

downpour, making his way around the pool toward the
helpless boy. Creighton was blown off his feet as soon
as he reached the unsheltered driveway. He could still
see Adrian, bent against the wind, struggling toward the
fence. He did not know if it was the strength of heroism
or mere drunkenness that kept Adrian upright, but he
was there, his dark figure obscured by the wall of rain.
Creighton tried to get up but was blown back against the
house with a painful blow to his back. Dimly he saw
Adrian almost lose his footing but recover into a crouch
as he reached the boy. He tore the child away from the
fence and picked him up. The wind was too much, even
against their combined weight, and Adrian was blown
to the ground against the fence, the boy's sprawling
body sliding along beside him. He grabbed the boy's leg
and managed somehow to wrap two lengths of the rope
around the frail body. Still flat on the ground, he tied
the rope to the fence, which remained set in its cement
moorings because the wind blew through its spaced up-
rights. As Creighton tried again to get to his feet, he saw
his brother in the rain-blurred distance, struggling to
stand. When Adrian was almost erect, there was a sudden furious burst of wind, and his body was lifted into
the air like a flimsy scarecrow. It hung in the air above
the fence for a moment, then disappeared into the gray-
ness beyond the fence and the precipice.

Creighton tried to stand again, but again he was
blown off his feet. The boy was still there—a dim dark
shape tied to the swaying fence. He realized there was
only one way to reach him. Lying on his stomach and
digging his hands into the rough concrete surface, he
crawled around the pool. His hands were torn and
bleeding by the time he reached the boy. He untied the
rope and found the strength to scream.

"Get on my back! On my back!"

With the boy hugging him around the neck and nearly choking him, he managed to crawl back to the front of the house. Harlan and Herman had come out of the house and met him before he reached it. They had both been blown to the ground trying to get to him, but now they managed to stay on their feet. Herman threw the boy over his shoulder like a sack of flour, and Harlan grabbed Creighton by the waist and lugged him into the house.

The last thing Creighton remembered was falling out of Harlan's sturdy grasp and collapsing onto the floor of the entrance hall. When he awoke again, stretched out on a sofa in the drawing room of Penrose, he was aware first of the relative silence. For a moment he was not even sure what it was he didn't hear. Then he knew. The wind had stopped. He heard the pelting of the rain, but now it sounded like rain and not the torrential wave of water it had been. There was gray light where the boards had been blown from the windows. Next he missed the people, who had so recently reminded him of the crowds at Victoria Station in London. Dimly at the end of the sofa he saw Dr. Burgoyne's face, and then, just above, he saw Kaye's face very close to him. He saw her smile, and whatever was wrong in the world ceased to matter.

Gradually he noticed that Alice and the Duckworths and George and Christian were there... and Harlan and Netty and Ellis and Herman and Sylvia. And for no reason he could divine immediately, the world made sense again. Then, in the vague distance, he saw the little boy he had carried to safety on his back. He didn't know why he felt himself smiling or why it was the first thing he said, but he knew it was happening.

"You were a hell of a lot of trouble, young man. You've got to learn to come in out of the rain by yourself."

Then he got up. He felt Kaye's hand supporting him, and he accepted her help, but he soon found himself with his arm around her shoulder, leaning on her rather more dependently than he would have wished.

Without the slightest regard for the assembled company he kissed her, briefly and gently.

"I guess we made it," he said.

"Yes, we made it," Kaye answered.

"I'm pretty lucky to wake up in a room filled with friends."

"We're all pretty lucky to wake up at all," Alice commented. "And we are friends, aren't we?"

"Forever, Alice, forever and a day. I think I'd like to go outside and see how bad it is."

"Oh, it's not as bad as you may think," Herman said. "At least you still have a house. Ours is a big ant-hill. No condolences, please. I couldn't telephone, but I've already started a letter to my architect in New York. We're going to dig it out and build the same house on a stronger foundation. And Sylvia is already considering fabrics. In six months you'll never know it happened."

They all went out then onto what was left of the veranda, their spirits heightened by the optimism that inevitably accompanies survival.

The rain was still falling, and through it Creighton could see the rolling gray clouds above them. Kaye felt his body tighten as he looked out over the pool, where he had last seen Adrian. There was nothing either of them could say. They held each other closer, and that was all they could do.

"My God, I think the sun's trying to break through," Creighton said.

"Yes," Kaye agreed. "And not only the sun."

A car was pulling into the driveway. When it stopped, a uniformed chauffeur got out and opened an umbrella, then the car door. Smitty stepped out. Dressed in an immaculate garden dress, she was escorted to the veranda under the shelter of the umbrella. Her monocle was firmly in place, and her stride was slow and steady. Amanda and Danny were right behind her.

"The only thing to be done on the heels of a natural disaster is to resume social intercourse as quickly as possible. I have come for drinks." She paused and looked around until she found Alice. "My dear friend, will you forgive a crochety old woman? Oh, yes, I have come for drinks, but I have also come to present my granddaughter and her fine young man. Oh, Alice, let me plead a woman's prerogative in all this madness."

"Your plea is accepted if you will give your approval to the marriage of my niece to Creighton Jarvis. Not that your approval is needed."

"Well, of course it is. No marriage can take place in Montego without it."

"I'm afraid, if it's necessary, this one will," Creighton said.

"Well, better with it than without it. Now, Alice, we have to plan carefully, and—"

"Smitty," Creighton said, "I'm going to put this house back together, and Kaye and I are going to be married here." He looked down at Kaye and asked, "All right?"

"Anything you say, my darling."

"I guess we couldn't have a. . . ." Danny stammered through that much of the sentence.

"You guess you couldn't have what, Riordan?" Smitty barked.

"A double wedding."

"Have you lost your mind, young man?"

"I don't know, but if so, I lost it while I was saving your house."

"Saving my house hardly entitles you to my grand-daughter's hand."

"What does entitle me to your granddaughter's hand? Isn't it enough that I love her?"

"Creighton, would you speak sharply to this—this adolescent?"

"Of course I will, Smitty. Why don't you elope, Danny? Get a plane to Miami and get married."

"Creighton!" Smitty cried.

"For God's sake, Smitty, they've done every reasonable thing you could expect of them. At least let them get engaged with your grandiose approval."

She stared at Creighton with narrowed eyes, then she looked at Amanda and Danny. "I admit to being grand, but I have never been grandiose. All right, you may become engaged. But there is to be no wedding without my consent."

"But there is going to be ours," Kaye said.

"Yes, we have all the credentials we need, Smitty. We're in love."

"Yes, I can see that. It *is* all right with you, Alice?"

"Yes, it is. But I don't think it matters very much whether it's all right with me. Smitty, don't you remember being in love?"

"It isn't a matter of being or not being in—"

"Do you or don't you remember?"

She stared at Alice for a long moment, then very quietly she replied, "Yes, I remember."

"What else is there?" Alice asked her.

"Nothing, I suppose. Let's go into the house, Alice, and have a brandy together. I guess it's time to leave the young people to their own mistakes."

"And to their own wisdom, Smitty."

"Oh, if they only had ours! How much better off they'd be."

"I wonder. Come on, now. I think it's very old Courvoisier we're going to. It may drop dead before we get to it."

"So may we."

"Nonsense. We have to stay around for all these weddings and engagements." They linked arms and went into the house together.

"We can't let them drink alone," Herman said. Then he led the procession into the battered hulk of Penrose.

Only Amanda and Danny and Kaye and Creighton remained on the veranda. Kaye was snuggled against Creighton, and she looked up at him musingly.

"Creighton, how long will it take to make the house presentable?"

"I don't know. I haven't really checked the extent of the damage. Why?"

"I don't want to have to wait too long to become Mrs. Jarvis."

"We could take the advice I gave Danny and elope to Miami."

"I want a wedding, darling, not a funeral. Smitty and Aunt Alice would murder us if we cheated them out of the formalities."

"All right, we'll give them the biggest and best wedding they've ever seen. We'll invite everybody in Montego."

"And will we roast an ox for Smitty?"

"Oxen if necessary."

"Can't you get married right away?" Danny asked. "If you wait too long, I'll be back in Iowa."

"Oh, no, you won't," Creighton said. "You're going to be my best man if I have to burn down your college."

"And you will be my maid of honor, won't you, Amanda? If you can't have your own wedding, you can be part of ours."

"It's not quite the same thing," Danny said sorrowfully.

"It's close enough for now," Amanda put in, hugging him.

"And before you know it," Creighton began, "you will be having your own wedding, and Mr. and Mrs. Jarvis will be right there beside you."

"Promise?" Amanda asked.

"Promise," Kaye replied. "Mr. and Mrs. Jarvis are going to be Mr. and Mrs. Jarvis forever."

Creighton smiled down at her and said, "Forever... and ever and ever."